"Cade," she said urgently. "Can you hear me? Can you understand what I tell you?" There was no command in her voice now; it was low-pitched and melodious. It teased his memory, tugged at him till he stiffened with the remembrance. Only once had a woman called him his Armsman's given name. That was the day he entered the Order, before he took his vows. His mother had kissed him, he remembered now, kissed him, and whispered the new name softly, as this girl was saying it. Since that day, his eleventh birthday, no woman had dared tempt him to peril with a familiar address.

He lay still, thrusting aside the memory, refusing to reply.

"Cade," she said again. "There's not much time. They'll be coming soon. Can you understand me?"

The hands on the table moved, put down the needle and the swab, and floated toward him. She placed her palms on his cheeks, and turned his face up toward hers. Cade could not remember, even from childhood, the touch of hands like these. They were silken, but smooth—soft, resilient, unbelievably good to feel. They felt, he thought—and blushed as he thought—like the billowing stuff of the Emperor's ceremonial robe, when it brushed his face as he knelt at devotions on Audience Day.

This was no Audience Day. The hands of a commoner were on him, and contact with any female was forbidden to a Gunner.

GUNNER CADE

BY CYRIL JUDD
(C.M. KORNBLUTH & JUDITH MERRIL)
PLUS: TAKEOFF, BY C.M. KORNBLUTH

Postscript by

Frederik Pohl

A
JIM BÆN
PRESENTATION

TOR

A TOM DOHERTY ASSOCIATES BOOK

GUNNER CADE is copyright©1952 by C.M. Kornbluth and Judith Merril

TAKEOFF is copyright©1952 by C.M. Kornbluth

A TOR Book

Published by Tom Doherty Associates, Inc., 8-10 West 36th Street, New York, New York 10018

First TOR printing, April 1983

ISBN: 48-570-0

Cover art by Tom Kidd

Postscript copyright©1983 by Frederik Pohl.

Printed in the United States of America

Distributed by:
Pinnacle Books
1430 Broadway
New York, New York 10018

Gunner Cade

1

FAR BELOW the sleeping loft, in ancient cellars of re-inforced concrete, a relay closed in perfect silent auto-maton adjustment; up through the Chapter House, the tiny noises multipled and increased. The soft whir of machinery in the walls; the gurgle of condensing fluid in conditioners; the thumping of cookers where giant ladles stirred the breakfast mash; the beat of pistons pumping water to the top.

Gunner Cade, consecrate Brother in the Order of Armsmen, compliant student of the Klin Philosophy, and loyal citizen of the Realm of Man, stirred in his sleepbag on the scrubbed plastic floor. He half-heard the rising sounds of the machinery of the House, and recognized the almost imperceptible change in the rhythm of the air blowers. Not quite awake, he listened for the final sound of morning, the scraping noise of the bars at windows and gates, as they drew back reluctantly into the stone walls.

It is fitting that the Emperor rules.

It is fitting that the Armsmen serve the Emperor through the Power Master and our particular Stars.

While this is so all will be well, to the end of time.

The words came to his mind without effort, before he opened his eyes. He had not fumbled for them since his sixth year when, between his parents and himself, it had been somehow settled that he would become a Brother of the Order. For at least the six-thousandth time, his day began with the conscious affirmation of Klin.

The bars grated in their grooves, and at the instant, the first light struck through the slits of windows overhead. Cade shivered inside the scanty insulation of his bag and came fully awake, at once aware of the meaning of the chill. This was a Battle Morn.

The air blew steadily stronger and colder from the conditioners, tingling against his skin as Cade slipped from his sleepbag and folded it, deflated, into the precise small package that would fit the pocket of his cloak. Timing each action by the habits of thirteen years, he unbuckled his gunbelt, removed the gun, and closed away the belt and sleepbag in the locker that held his neatly folded uniform. It was by now reflexive action to open the gun and check the charge, then close the waterproof seal.

Battle Morn! With mounting elation, Cade performed each meticulous detail of the morning routine, his body operating like the smooth machine it was, while his mind woke gradually to the new day. He thought vaguely of commoners lolling late in bed, mumbling a morning thought of the Emperor and breaking their fast at a grossly laden table. He thought vaguely of Klin teachers waking with subtle and elaborate propositions that proved what any Gunner feels in his bones. He thought vaguely of his own Star of France, doubtless haggard this morning after a night vigil of meditation on the fitting course.

He thought, too, of the Emperor—the Given Healer; the Given Teacher; the Given Ruler—but, like a gun's blast came the thought: *this is not fitting.*

Guiltily he brought his attention back to the bare room, and saw with dismay that Gunner Harrow still lay in his bag, yawning and stretching.

The indecent gaping was infectious; Cade's mouth opened first with amazement, then to say sharply: "Battle Morn, Brother!"

"How does it find you?" Harrow replied, courteously, unashamed.

"Awake," Cade answered coolly, "and ready for a good death if that is fitting—or a *decorous* life if I am spared today."

The Marsman seemed to miss the reprimand entirely, but he climbed out of his bag, and began to deflate it. What kind of Chapter House did they have on Mars?

"How long till shower?" he asked, unconcerned.

"Seconds," was Cade's contemptuous answer. "Perhaps twenty or thirty."

The Marsman sprang to life with a speed that would

6

have done him credit under other circumstances. Cade watched with disgust as the other Gunner rushed for the wall cabinet and stuffed away his sleepbag, still unfolded not yet fully drained of last night's air. The gunbelt was thrown in on top, and the cabinet door slammed shut, with only an instant left to seal the water-closures of the gun. Then the ceiling vents opened, and the needle spray showered down and around the room. A cool invigorating stream of water splattered against the naked bodies of the men, cascaded down the three walls of the room, and drained out through the floor vent, leaving just enough dampness for the scouring by novices when the Gunners had left the room.

Cade took his eyes from the Marsman, and tried to tear away his thoughts as well. He watched devoutly while the swirling waters struck each wall in turn, touching his gun to his lips, *For the Teacher*, at the first impact; to his chest, *For the Healer*, at the next; and at the last, the long wall, to his brow, with awe, *For the Ruler, the Emperor.*

He tried not to think of Harrow in the room beside him, saluting the cleansing waters with an unchecked charge in his gun. It was true then, what they said about conditions on Mars. Laxity at any time was bad enough, but to let the peril of sloth pass from the previous day through the purifying waters of a Battle Morn was more than Cade could understand. A novice might meet the shower unprepared; an armiger might fail to check his charge beforehand; but how did Harrow ever rise to the rank of Gunner? And why was such a one sent to Cade on the eve of battle? Even now, his own Battle Morn meditations were disturbed.

Anger is a peril at all times. And anger is acutely unfitting on Battle Morn before the Klin teacher's lesson. Cade refused to think of it further. The water vents closed and he dressed without regard for the Marsman.

Each garment had its thought, soothing and enfolding: they brought peace.

UNDERSUIT: *like this the Order embraces the Realm.*

SHIRT: *the Order protects the Power Master, slave of the brain, loyal heart of the Realm.*

HOSE: *Armsmen are sturdy pillars; without them the*

Realm cannot stand, but without the Realm the Order cannot live.

BOOTS: *Gunners march where the Emperor wills; that is their glory.*

HELMET: *the Order protects the Emperor—the Given Teacher, the Given Healer, the Given Ruler—the brain and life of the Realm.*

CLOAK: *like this the Order wraps the Realm and shields it.*

Again he touched his gun to his lips: *for the Teacher;* to his chest: *for the Healer;* to his brow, with awe: *for the Ruler, the Emperor.*

Briskly, he released the waterclosures, and dropped the gun into the belt on his hip. A gong sounded in the wall, and Cade went to a cabinet for two steaming bowls of concentrate, freshly prepared in the giant mash cookers far below.

"Brother?" Harrow called across the open door.

Silence at this time was customary but not mandatory, Cade reminded himself—and Harrow was new to this Chapter.

"Yes, Brother," he said.

"Are there other Marsmen among us?"

"I know no others," Cade said, and congratulated himself on that fact. "How would it concern you?"

"It would please me," Harrow said formally. "A man likes to be among his own people in time of battle."

Cade could not answer him at first. What sort of talk was this? One didn't call himself a man in the Order. There were novices, armigers, Gunners, the Gunners Superior, and Arle himself, the Gunner Supreme. They were your brothers, elder or younger.

"You are among your own people," he said gently, refusing to allow himself to be tempted into the peril of anger. "We are your brothers all."

"But I am new among you," the other said. "My brothers here are strangers to me."

That was more reasonable. Cade could still remember his first battle for the Star of France, after he left the Denver Chapter where he spent his youth. "Your brothers will soon be beside you in battle," he reminded the newcomer. "An Armsman who has fought by your side is no stranger."

8

"That will be tomorrow," Harrow smiled. "And if I live through today, I shall not be here long after."

"Where, then?"

"Back to Mars!"

"How can that be?" Cade demanded. "Mars-born Gunners fight for Earthly Stars. Earth-born Gunners fight for the Star of Mars. That's fitting."

"Perhaps so, Brother; perhaps so. But a letter from my father at home says our Star has petitioned the Emperor to allow him all Mars-born Armsmen, and I would be one of them."

"Your Star is the Star of France," said Cade sharply. He himself had received Harrow's assignment yesterday, sealed by the Power Master, and counter-sealed by the Gunner Supreme. He was silent a moment, then could contain himself no longer. "By all that's fitting," he asked. "What sort of talk is this? Why does an Armsman speak of himself as a *man*? And how can you think of your 'own people,' other than your brothers in arms?"

The Mars-born Gunner hesitated. "It's newer on Mars. Six hundred years isn't a long time. We have a proverb —'Earth is changeless but Mars is young.' Families—I am descended from Erik Hogness and Mary Lara who mapped the northern hemisphere long ago. I know my cousins because of that. We all are descended from Erik Hogness and Mary Lara who mapped the northern hemisphere. I don't suppose you know anything about your eight-times great-grandfather or what he may have done?"

"I presume," said Cade stiffly, "that he did what was fitting to his station as I will do what is fitting to mine."

"Exactly," said Harrow, and fell silent—disconcertingly resembling a man who had wrung an admission from an opponent and won an argument by it.

Cade went stiffly to the door and opened it, leaving the empty bowls for Harrow to return. The line of Armsmen came in sight down the corridor, and they waited at attention to take their place among the Gunners, marching in silence and with downcast eyes along the route of procession to the lectory.

Seated on the front row of benches, with twenty rows apiece of armigers and novices behind, Cade was grateful that the Klin Teacher had not yet arrived. It left time

9

for him to dispel the perilous mood of irritation and suspicion. By the time the man did appear, Cade's troubled spirits had resolved into the proper quiet glow of appreciation.

It was fitting to be a Gunner; it was fitting to be a Klin Teacher; they were almost brothers in their dedication. The glow nearly vanished when the man began to speak.

Cade had heard many teachers who'd been worse; it made not a particle of difference in the Klin Philosophy whether it was expounded by a subtle, able teacher or a half-trained younger son of a Star, as this fellow appeared to be; what was fitting was fitting and would be until the end of time. But on a Battle Morn, Cade thought, a senior teacher might have been a reasonable tribute. *The peril of pride*, came a thought like a gun's blast, and he recoiled. In contrition he listened carefully, marking the youngster's words.

"Since the creation of the worlds ten thousand years ago the Order of Armsmen has existed and served the Emperor through the Power Master and the Stars. Klin says of armed men: 'They must be poor, because riches make men fear to lose them and fear is unfitting in an Armsman. They must be chaste because love of woman makes men love their rulers—the word *rulers* here means, as always, with Klin, the Emperor—less. They must be obedient because the consequence of disobedience is to make men refuse even the most gloriously profitable death.' These are the words of Klin, set down ten thousand years ago at the creation of the worlds."

It was wonderful, thought Cade, wonderful how it had all occurred together: the creation of the worlds, the Emperor to rule them, the Order to serve him and the Klin Philosophy to teach them how to serve. The fitness and beautiful economy of it never failed to awe him. He wondered if this creation was somehow THE Fitness, the original of which all others were reflections.

The Teacher leaned forward, speaking directly to those in the front row. "You Gunners are envied, but you do not envy. Klin says of you Gunners: 'They must be always occupied with fiddling details'—I should perhaps explain that a *fiddle* was a musical instrument; *fiddling* hence means *harmonious*, or proper. Another possibility is that *fiddling* is an error for *fitting*, but our earliest copies fail to bear this out—'with fiddling details so they will have no time to think. Let armed men think and the fat's in the fire.' "

Good old Klin! thought Cade affectionately. He liked the occasional earthy metaphors met with in the *Reflections on Government*. Stars and their courts sometimes diverted themselves for a day or two by playing at commoners' life; the same playfulness appeared in Klin when he took an image from the kitchen or the factory. The Teacher was explaining the way Klin's usage of *think* as applied to anybody below the rank of a Star was equated with the peril of pride, and how the homely kitchen-metaphor meant nothing less than universal ruin. "For Klin, as usual, softens the blow."

Irresistibly Cade's thoughts wandered to a subject he loved. As the young Teacher earnestly expounded, the Gunner thought of the grandeur of the Klin Philosophy: how copies of the *Reflections* were cherished in all the Chapter Houses of the Order, in all the cities of all the Stars of Earth, on sparsely settled Venus, the cold moons of the monster outer planets, on three man-made planetoids, and on Mars. What could be wrong with Harrow? How *could* he have gone awry with the Klin Philosophy to guide him? Was it possible that the Teachers on Mars failed to explain Klin adequately? Even commoners on Earth heard Teachers expound the suitable portion of the Philosophy. But Cade was warmly aware that the Armsmen's study of Klin was more profound and pure than the commoners'.

"—so I come to a subject which causes me some pain." Cade brought his mind back sharply to the words of the Teacher. This was the crucial part, the thing he had been waiting to hear. "It is not easy to contemplate willful wickedness, but I must tell you that unfit deeds fill the heart of the Star of Muscovy. Through certain sources our Star of France has learned that pride and greed possess his brother to the North. With sorrow he discovered that the Star of Muscovy intends to occupy Alsace-Lorraine with his Gunners. With sorrow he ordered your Superior to make ready for whatever countermeasures may be fit, and it has been done. As you know, this is Battle Morn."

Cade's heart thumped with rage at the proud and

greedy Star of Muscovy.

"Klin says of such as the Star of Muscovy: 'The wicked you have always with you. Make them your governors.' *Governors* is used metaphorically, in the obsolete sense of a device to regulate the speed of a heat engine—hence, the passage means that when a wicked person is bent on unfit deeds, you should increase your efforts towards fit and glorious deeds to counter him. There are many interesting images in the *Reflections* drawn from the world of pre-electronic—but that is by the way. I was saying that this is Battle Morn, and that before the sun has set many of you may have died. So I say to all of you, not knowing which will have the fortune: go on your fitting and glorious task without the peril of pride, and remember that there is nobody in the Realm of Man who would not eagerly change places with you."

He stepped down and Cade bowed his head for the thought: *The Klin Philosophy in a Gunner is like the charge in his gun.* It was a favorite of his, saying so much in so little if you had only a moment, but if you had more time it went on and on, drawing beautifully precise parallels for every circuit and element of the gun. But there was no time for that; the Superior, the Gunner Superior to the Star of France, had appeared. He cast a worried little glance at a window, through which the sun could be seen, and began at once:

"Brothers, our intelligence is that one hundred gunners, more or less, are now flying from an unknown Muscovite base to occupy the Forbach-Sarralbe triangle on the border of our Star's realm. Time of arrival—I can only say 'this afternoon or evening' and hope I am correct. The importance of the area is incalculable. It was a top secret until the information evidently got to Muscovy. *There is iron ore in the district.*"

A murmur swept the lectory, and Cade murmured with the rest in astonishment. Iron ore on Earth! Power metal still to be found on the ten-thousand-year-old planet after ten thousand years of mining for the stuff that drove engines and charged guns! All reserves were supposed to have been exhausted four hundred years ago; that was why rust-red Mars had been colonized, and from rust-red Mars for four hundred years had come Earth's iron.

"Enough, Brothers! Enough! Our plan will be roughly the same as that employed in our raid last month on Aachen—two divisions to the front, one in reserve. The first company under me will be based at Dieuze, about forty kilometers south of the triangle. The second company under Gunner Cade will be based at Metz, fifty kilometers west of the triangle. The third company will be in reserve, based at Nancy, seventy kilometers south-west of the triangle. The companies will proceed to their bases in two-man fliers immediately after this briefing.

"After arrival and the establishment of communications, my company and Gunner Cade's will send out air scouts to reconnoiter the triangle. If no enemy action is discovered from the air, scouts will parachute for recon on foot. The orders I will issue from that point on will depend on their reports. Man your fliers and take off at once, Brothers. May your deeds today be fitting and glorious."

2

CADE, icily calm, ran from the Chapter House two hundred meters to the flying field. He was not panting when he swung himself easily into his little craft. His fingers flew over the unlabeled switches and dials of the control panel. It had been many years since he'd relied on mnemonic jingles to recall the order and setting of the more than two hundred controls. As the red electronic warmup fog misted from the tail of the flier, his passenger, Armiger Kemble, vaulted in and was immediately slammed back against his uncushioned seat by a 3.25-G take-off.

Paris was a blur beneath them, the Paris that Cade, Denver-born, had seen only from the air and the windows of the Chapter House. Minutes later Reims flashed past to their left. The braking and landing in the square at Metz were as cruel as the take-off. Cade had never spared himself or anybody else on service, though he did not know that he was famous for it.

"Brother," he said to the battered Armiger, "line up the command set on Dieuze and Nancy." To his disgust Kemble juggled with the map, the compass and the verniers of the aiming circle for two minutes until he had laid beams on the fields at the reserve base and the other front-line command post. *The peril of pride*, he guiltily thought, choking down his annoyance. The twelve other ships of his company had landed by then.

"Brother Cade," said the voice of the Superior. "Scouts out!"

"Scouts out, Brother," he said, and waved two flyers aloft. From them a monotonous drone of "No enemy action" began over the command set.

The tune changed after five minutes: "Rendezvous with first company scouts over Forbach. No enemy action."

"Brother Cade," said the Superior, "order your scouts to jump. My fliers will provide cover."

Cade ordered: "Second company scouts—Gunner Arris, take over Gunner Meynall's flier on slave circuit. Brother Meynall, parachute into Forbach for recon on foot. Armiger Raymond, recon Sarreguemines. Armiger Bonfils, recon Sarralbe."

Brothers Meynall, Raymond and Bonfils reported successful landings. The Gunner in Forbach said; "No commoners about at all. As usual. I'm in the village square headed for the 'phone exchange. No en—" There was the sound of a gun and no further report.

Cade opened the Raymond-Bonfils circuit to the Superior and reserve company and snapped: "Take cover. Forbach is occupied. Gunner Arris return to base with fliers immediately."

The Superior's voice said: "First company fliers return to base immediately. Brothers Raymond and Bonfils, report!"

Armiger Raymond's voice said: "Sarreguemines is empty of commoners. I've taken over in the basement of a bakery whose windows command the square. I see movement at the windows of a building across the square—the town hall, 'phone exchange, water department and I don't know what else. It's just a village."

14

"Brother Bonfils, report!"

There was no answer.

"Brother Raymond, stand fast. We shall mount an attack. Hold your fire until the enemy is engaged and then select targets of opportunity. You will regard yourself as expendable."

"Yes, Brother."

"Third Company at Nancy, you are alerted. Second Company and Third Company, rendezvous with First Company in ten minutes, at 1036 hours, two kilometers south of the Sarralbe town square. Align your fliers for unloading to fight on foot; we shall conduct a frontal assault on Sarralbe and clear it of the enemy. The third company will be on the left wing, the second company will be our center, and the first company will be in the right wing. Gunner Cade, you will detail one flier to amuse the enemy with a parachute attack on the town hall as our skirmishers reach the square. Into action, Brothers."

"Load!" yelled Cade to his company and they tumbled into their craft. On the slave circuit he took the fliers up in dress-parade style, hurled them to the rendezvous and released the ships for individual landings. The first company was aligned straight as a string to his right, and moments later the third company touched down.

His Armiger Kemble had done a most unsatisfactory job lining up the communications, Cade reflected, but it was not fitting in a Gunner to hold a grievance. "Brother," he said, "I've chosen you to conduct the diversion our Superior ordered."

The youngster straightened proudly. "Yes, Brother," he said, repressing a pleased grin.

Cade spoke into his command set: "Gunner Orris. You will remain here in your flier during the attack, with Armiger Kemble as a passenger. On my signal you will take off and fly over the Sarralbe Town Hall, dropping Brother Kemble by parachute to create a diversion. After dropping him, return your flier to its present position and dismount to join the attack on foot."

The Armiger climbed out of Cade's flier to head for Orris' craft, but hesitated on the ground and turned to brag: "I'll bet I get a dozen of them before they get me."

"Well, perhaps, Brother," said Cade, and this time the

15

grin did break out as the Armiger marched down the line. Cade hadn't wanted to discourage him but the only Muscovite gunman he had a chance of killing before he was picked off in mid-air was their roof spotter. But how could he be expected to understand? Thirty seconds of confusion among the enemy could be vastly more important than killing thirty of their best Gunners.

The clock said 1036; men boiled out of the fliers and formed a skirmish line carefully ragged. The raised right arm of the Superior, far on the right of the line, went down and the brothers began to trudge forward, all with the same solid, deliberate stride . . .

Cade's eyes were on anywhere but his boots; they were scanning bushes for untoward movements, the ground for new dirt cast up in the digging of a foxhole, trees for unnatural man-sized clumps of foliage among the branches. But somehow he felt his feet in his boots, not painfully but happily. *Gunners march where the Emperor wills; that is their glory.*

Off to the right a gun blasted. The Superior's voice said in his helmet: "Enemy observation post, one novice. We got him but now they're alerted in town."

He told the men flanking him: "Enemy O.P. spotted us. Pass the word, brothers." It murmured down the line. Brothers who had absently let themselves drift into a dress-parade rank noticed it and lagged or hell-and-toed until the line was properly irregular again.

It was done none too soon. Some thirty meters to the left of Cade the excellently-camouflaged lid of a firing pit flipped up as the line passed. The Muscovite blasted two Armigers with a single shot before he was killed. Defilading fire into a straight rank would have netted him twenty. The wood grew thicker and direct flank contact was lost. "Scouts out," said the Superior's voice, and Cade waved two Gunners forward.

Their eloquent arms were the eyes of the company. One upraised and the company saw possible danger; it halted. The upraised arm down and forward and the company saw safety; it trudged on. Both arms moved forward in a gesture like clasping a great bundle of straw and the company was alarmed by something inexplainable; it inched forward with guns drawn, faces tingling. Both arms beating down like vultures' wings

16

and the company was face-to-face with grinning death; it hurled its fifty bodies to the ground to dodge the whistling scythe.

Grinding himself into the ground while his eyes methodically scanned before him for the well-concealed Muscovite combat patrol that had been harassing them, Cade thought: *It is fitting that we Gunmen serve.* He saw the unnatural movement of a bush and incinerated it. In the heart of the blaze was a black thing that capered and gibbered like a large ape: one more of the enemy charred to nonexistence. His blast had given away his position; automatically he snap-rolled two meters and saw flame blaze from a tree's lower branches to the spot he'd fired from. Before the blast from the tree expired he had answered it.

He thought: *While this is so, all will be well to the end of time.*

The surviving scout's arm went up with an air of finality. The company halted and the scout trotted back to Cade. "Ten meters of scrub and underbrush and then the town. Three rows of four-story stone houses and then the square, as I recall. The underbrush is clear. But those windows looking down on it—!"

"Plunging fire," Cade muttered, and he heard a sharp intake of breath from beside him. He turned to look sternly on the young armiger with the stricken face, but before he could reprove the lad, he heard Harrow, the Marsman, intervene.

"I hate it too," the Gunner said, and the unexpected note of sympathy broke the youngster completely.

"I can't stand it," he babbled, hysterically. "That feeling you get when it's coming at you from above and all the ground cover in the world won't help—all you can do is run! I can't stand it!"

"Quiet him," Cade said with disgust, and someone led the armiger away, but not before Cade noted his name. He would deal with it later.

"Brother," Harrow spoke in his ear, earnestly.

"What is it?" Cade snapped.

"Brother, I have an idea." He hesitated, but as Cade turned impatiently away, he rushed on: "Brother, let's give them plunging fire. No one would have to know."

"What are you talking about?" Cade asked blankly.

"There aren't any trees high enough or near enough."

The Marsman said wildly: "Cade, don't pretend to me. I can't be the only Gunner who ever thought of it! Who's going to know the difference? I mean—" His throat sealed; he couldn't get the words out.

"I'm glad to see you have some shame left," Cade said disgustedly. "I *know* what you mean." He turned aside and called out: "Bring back the coward armiger! Now," he went on as soon as the youngster was with them, "I want you to learn for yourself the consequences of submitting to the peril of fear. Your outburst made Gunner Harrow propose that we—we fire on the houses from our *fliers*."

The armiger looked down at his feet for a long moment and then faced his commander. He said hoarsely, "I didn't know there were people like that, sir. Sir, I should like to request the honor of being permitted to draw fire for our men."

"You have earned no honors," Cade snapped. "Nor does your rank entitle you to privileged requests." He looked meaningfully at the Mars-born Gunner.

Harrow wiped sweat from his face. "I would have got back to Mars," he said bitterly, "back with my own people, if I'd lived through this one."

"You deserve less than this, *Gunner* Harrow," Cade pronounced sternly into a sudden listening silence. The firing was momentarily stilled; the enemy was awaiting their action. All the armsmen of France within hearing distance of the episode had edged closer to be in on the final outcome. Cade seized the moment to impress an unforgettable lesson on his men. He said loudly:

"Klin wrote: 'Always assume mankind is essentially merciful; nothing else explains why crooks are regularly returned to office.' If you know as little of the Philosophy as you do of decency, Brother, I should explain that a *crook* is an implement formerly used by good shepherds and in this case stands, by a figure of speech, for the good shepherd himself. I shall obey Klin's precept of mercy. We need a Gunner to draw fire from the house windows so we can spot those which are—are you listening to me?"

The Mars-born Gunner was mumbling to himself; he looked up and said clearly, "Yes, Brother, I'm listening." But his lips kept moving as Cade went on: "We have to draw fire from the house windows so we can see which are manned, blast them with a volley and take the house in a rush."

"Yes, Brother, I'll draw their fire," said Harrow.

Cade wheeled suddenly, and confronted the rest of his company. "Are you armsmen," he demanded fiercely, "or commoner kitchen gossips? Back to your posts before the enemy discovers your weakness! And may the fighting scourge your minds of this memory. Such things are better forgotten."

He called the first and third companies on his helmet 'phone and filled them in—saying nothing of the disgraceful episode.

"Well done," the superior told him. "Rush the first row of houses immediately; we have your coordinates and will follow behind after you have secured a house or two."

Harrow's muttering had started again and become loud enough during the conversation to be a nuisance. He was repeating to himself:

"*It is fitting that the Emperor rules.*

"*It is fitting that the Power Master serves him.*

"*It is fitting that we Gunmen serve the Emperor through the Power Master and our particular Stars.*

"*While this is so, all will be well until the end of time.*"

Cade could not very well rebuke him.

Harrow distinguished himself in drawing fire from the house windows. In such an operation there is the risk that—well, call him the "target"—that the target will walk out in a state of exaltation, thinking more of the supreme service he is rendering than the actual job of rendering it. Cade was pleased and surprised at the desperate speed with which Harrow broke from the end of the wood and sped through the brush, his cloak flaring out behind him, displaying the two wide Gunner's bands at the hem: a new brown one above for France; and old red one below for Mars.

A bolt from one window missed him.

"Mark," snapped the first in a row of picked shots.

A bolt from another window blasted Harrow's left arm, and he kept running and even began to dodge.

"Mark," said the second of the sharp-shooters.

A third window spat fire at the dodging Gunner and hit the same burned arm.

"Mark."

Another bolt from another window smashed his legs from under him.

"Mark."

There was a little surge forward in the line of waiting stormers. Cade threw his arm up, hard and fast. "He's crawling," he said. "They'll finish him off."

From a small and innocent-looking stairwell window fire jetted.

"Mark."

"He's done," said Cade. "*While this is so all will be well* . . . Marksmen ready; stormers ready. Marksmen, fire. Stormers, charge." He led the way, crashing through the brush, with a torrent of flame gushing over his head: his marksmen, with the initiative of fire, pinning down the Muscovites at their windows—almost all of them. From two unsuspected windows fire blazed, chopping down two of the storming party. They were met with immediate counterfire from waiting marksmen in the wood. And by then there were ten Gunners in the dead ground against the house wall. With Cade in the lead, the armsmen of France swarmed down a narrow alley that separated house from house and blasted down a side door.

Like coursing hounds they flowed through the house, burning down five Muscovite armsmen already wounded by the neutralizing fire from the woods, finding two others dead at their windows. They lost one armiger of France, to the desperate dying fire of a wounded Muscovite. The house was theirs.

The rest of the company, except for a pair of guards, trudged across the brush and entered.

Cade stationed men at the vital upper windows and sat, panting, on the floor of a bare second-story room. All the rooms were more or less bare. It was probably so through all three villages. He had seen commoners migrating.

Clots of them, oozing slowly along the roads. Their chief people in ground cars, cursing at the foot-sloggers who wouldn't get aside. The carts, piled high with household goods. The sniveling, shrieking children. And yet—

and yet—there was a puzzle in it. Not always, but almost always, they knew in advance. The Muscovites, in possession of the great secret of the iron ore, had arrived to find that at least part of the secret was known to the lowliest commoner—enough at least to send him out on the road.

They were into the afternoon now, with nothing to do but wait for the first and third companies. This would last a week, easily: three villages to clear. Perhaps the feint at the city hall—if it came off today—would crumple the Muscovites. And when they got to Sarreguemines there would be Brother Raymond in the cellar—

He sat up with a guilty start. Nobody had checked the cellar in this very house, if it had one, probably because cellars didn't have windows. He got wearily to his feet and limped downstairs to the first floor. There seemed to be no further steps down—and then he saw a gap between the wall and an immense cherry-wood cabinet bare of its dishes and mementos. It creaked open when he tried it and there were his cellar steps with a guttering light at the bottom.

An old, old face, brown and wrinkled and ugly, was peering at him by the flickering light.

"Come up, commoner," he said. "I wish to look at you."

"No, sir," the wrinkled face squeaked in the voice of a woman. "No, sir, I cannot sir, to my shame. My daughter, the lazy slut, put me and my dear brother down here when the armed men were about to come, for she said she and her great fat husband couldn't be bothered with us. I cannot come up, sir, because my legs won't go, to my shame."

"Then send up your brother, commoner."

"No, sir," the hag squeaked. "My dear brother cannot come up, to my shame. My lazy slut of a daughter and her great fat husband did not leave the right food for him—he suffers from the wasting sickness and he must have the livers of animals every day—and so he died. Are you an armed man, sir?"

"I am a Gunner of the Order of Armsmen, commoner. Did you say you had food down there?" Cade suddenly realized he was ravenous.

"I did, sir, but not the right kind for my dear brother. I

have the bottled foods and the foods in boxes and sweet cakes; will you come down, armed man, sir?"

Cade prudently swung the great cherry-wood chest wide open and descended the stairs. The woman lighted his way to a corner with the candle; he expected to find a table or larder, but the light to his disgust flickered on the wasted body of a tall man propped against the cellar wall.

"That's no concern of mine, commoner," he said. "Where is the food? I'll take it and eat it upstairs."

"Armed man, sir, I must unlock three locks on this chest—" she gestured with the candle—"to get you that and my hands are old and slow, sir. Let me pour you a bit for your thirst first, sir. You are truly an armed man, sir?"

He ignored her babble as she poured him cider from a jug. "So that on your hip is a gun, sir? Is it true, sir, that you only have to point it at a person and he is shriveled and black at once?"

Cade nodded, suppressing his irritation with effort. She was old and foolish—but she was feeding him.

"And is it true, sir," she asked eagerly, "that a shriveled and black commoner cannot be told from a shriveled and black armed man?"

That it was impossible to let pass. He struck her mouth, wishing furiously that she would get the food and be done with it. And truly enough she did begin to fumble with the clanking old locks in the dark, but kept up her muttering: "I see it is true. I see it is true. That is what happens when something is true. I call my daughter a lazy slut and she strikes me on the mouth. I call her husband a greedy hog and he strikes me on the mouth. That is what happens—"

Rage is a peril, he told himself furiously. Rage is a peril. He gulped down the cider and repressed an impulse to throw the mug at the old fool's head or smash it on the old fool's floor while she fumbled endlessly with the clanking locks. He bent over to put it precisely on the floor, and toppled like a felled oak.

At once he knew what had happened and was appalled by the stupidity of it. He, a Gunner, was dying, poisoned by a babbling idiot of a commoner. Cade dragged feebly at his gun, and found the squeaking old woman had taken it first. Better to die that way, he thought in agony, though still a shameful horror. He hoped desperately as he felt consciousness slipping away that it would never become known. Some things were better forgotten.

The old woman was standing in front of him, making a sign, a detestable sign he half-remembered, like a parody of something you were dedicated to. And she skipped nimbly up and down the stairs with shrill, bat-like laughter. "I tricked you!" she squealed. "I tricked them all! I tricked my slut of a daughter and her greedy fat husband. I didn't want to go with them!" She stopped at last, grunting with animal effort as she tugged the body of her brother, an inch or less at a time, to the foot of the stairs. Cade's gun was in the waistband of her skirt.

As the last light glimmered out, he thought he saw the deep-etched leather lines of her face close to his. "I wanted an armed man, sir, that's what I wanted. And I have one!"

3

Peril ... Peril ... rage is a peril, and vanity, and love of ease ... This death was fraught with perils. Cade groaned in the endless dark, and the still-living flesh shrank with revulsion as the evil vision persisted and his limbs were logs of stone.

To come to this end, this useless end! He who had lived decorously, who had served fittingly, he, a sturdy pillar of the Emperor, Gunner Cade! *This end is not fitting!* He would have cried out bitterly, but his lips were icy barriers, frozen shut. He could not breathe a word of protest or command.

And still his heart beat pitilessly, pumping gall and fury through his veins.

Rage is peril. Cade turned his anger inward, seeking to bludgeon his spirit into a fit frame of mind before death came. *Armsmen march where the Emperor wills. Peril flees in the face of fitting service.*

Two visions filled his inner eye. He turned from the ancient ugly face of evil to the fair countenance of service and found at last the fitness that he sought. This death was proper. If She appeared, then all was well and would be till the end of time, for She came only at the last to the Armsman who marched where the Emperor willed and died in the service of his Star.

Then this was a fitting end, and the perils of rage and vanity had been only a trial. He looked again upon the ugly grinning face and found it had lost all power over him. The pure features of The Lady floated above and behind it and exaltation coursed through him as his heart beat on.

The heart beat on, and it was fitting, but it was not the end. The serene countenance of The Lady bent over him, and yet he lived. All Armsmen knew She came only at the last, and only to those who were fitted, yet . . .

He lived. He was not dead. The frozen lips moved as he muttered, "Vanity is a peril." He was alive, and the lined old leather face was only a hag he had seen before; the lady was a flower-faced commoner girl, beautiful to look on, but soullessly mortal.

"Very well," the crimson lips said clearly, not to him, but across his recumbent body to the hag. "Leave us now. They will be waiting for you in the chamber."

"The armed man lives," the old voice rasped in reply. "I served the armed man well and he still lives. My slut of a daughter would never believe I could do it. She left me behind for dead, she and her greedy . . ."

"Leave us now!" The younger woman was dressed in the gaudy rough cloth of a commoner, but her voice betrayed her habit of command. "Go to the chamber, and go quickly, or they may forget to wait."

Cade shuddered as the pincer fingers of the hag creased the flesh of his forearm. "He lives," she said again, and chuckled. "The armed man lives and his skin is warm." Her touch was a horror. Not as the touch of woman, for there was nothing womanish about her; she was past the age of peril. But his skin crawled as with vermin at the unclean fingering. He lashed out to strike her arm away, and discovered his hands were bound. The old woman shuffled slowly away toward a door, and while the young one watched her go, he pulled against the bonds, testing his strength.

Then the hag was gone, and he was alone with the young female commoner, who looked most unfittingly like a vision of glory, and spoke most presumptuously like a man of power.

The bonds were not too tight. He stopped pulling before she could discover that he might free himself.

She was watching him, and perversely he refused to look at her. His eyes took in every detail of the feature-less room: the unbroken elliptical curve of the ceiling and walls; the curved door, fitting into the shape of the wall, and almost indistinguishable from it; the bed on which he lay; a table beside him where the girl's long clean fingers played with a vial of colored fluid.

He watched, while she idly turned the cork in the vial to expose the needle end. He watched while she plucked a swab of cotton from a bowl, and doused it in colorless fluid from the only other object in the room, a small bottle on the table. He kept watching, even when the girl began to speak, his gaze obstinately fastened on her hands, away from the perilous beauty of her face.

"Cade," she said urgently. "Can you hear me? Can you understand what I tell you?" There was no command in her voice now; it was low-pitched and melodious. It teased his memory, tugged at him till he stiffened with the remembrance. Only once before had a woman called him his Armsman's given name. That was the day he entered the Order, before he took his vows. His mother had kissed him, he remembered now, kissed him, and whispered the new name softly, as this girl was saying it. Since that day, his eleventh birthday, no woman had dared to tempt him to peril with a familiar address.

He lay still, thrusting aside the memory, refusing to reply.

"Cade," she said again. "There's not much time. They'll be coming soon. Can you understand me?"

The hands on the table moved, put down the needle and the swab, and floated toward him. She placed her palms on his cheeks, and turned his face up toward hers. Cade could not remember, even from childhood, the touch of hands like these. They were silken, but smooth —soft, resilient, unbelievably good to feel. They felt, he thought—and blushed as he thought—like the billowing stuff of the Emperor's ceremonial robe, when it brushed his face as he knelt at devotions on Audience Day.

This was no Audience Day. The hands of a commoner were on him and contact with any female was forbidden. The blood receded from his face, and he shook his head violently, releasing himself from the perilous touch.

"I'm sorry," she said, "I'm sorry, Armsman, sir." Then, incredibly, she laughed. "I'm sorry I failed to address you properly, Sir, and profaned your chastity with my touch. Has it occurred to you that you are in trouble? What do you place first? The ritual of your Order, or your loyalty to the Emperor?"

"Armsmen march where the Emperor wills," he intoned. "That is their glory. Armsmen are sturdy pillars; without them the Realm cannot stand, but without the Realm the Order cannot . . ."

Boots, he thought. *Hose*. They were gone. He lifted his head a little, and pain stabbed at the back of his neck as he did so, but before he dropped back, he saw it all: garish crimson-patterned pyjamas of a commoner; soft-sole sandals of a city-worker. *No boots, no hose, no cloak, no gun!*

"What unfit place is this?" he exploded. "In the name of the Order of which I am a member, I demand that I be released and my gun returned before . . ."

"Quiet, you fool!" There was something in the command that stopped him. "You'll have them all here if you shout. Now listen quickly, if there's still time. You are the captive of a group that plots against the Emperor. I cannot tell you more now, but I am instructed to inject you with a substance which will . . ."

She stopped suddenly, and he too heard the steady footsteps coming nearer from—where? A corridor outside?

Something pressed against his lips, something smooth and slippery.

"Open your mouth, you idiot! Swallow it, quick! It will . . ."

The door opened smoothly from the wall, and the footsteps never lost a beat. They advanced to the center of the room, and stopped precisely, while their maker stared about him with an odd bemusement.

"I seek my cousin," he announced, to no one in particular.

"Your cousin is not here," the girl answered smoothly. "I am the helper of your cousin, and I will take you to him." Three steps took her to the rigidly erect figure, and she touched him lightly on the nape of the neck. "Follow me," she commanded.

With no change of expression on his pale face, the man turned and went after her, his uncannily steady footsteps marking time toward the door. But before they got there, it opened again, and a sharp-featured, worried face peered in. The newcomer was small and wiry, dressed in the grey uniform of the Klin Service, tunic belted properly over the creased trousers; domed hat set squarely on his head, boot-wraps neatly wound around his calves; he was breathing hard, and he closed the door hastily behind him, leaning against it till he regained composure.

"Here is your cousin," the girl said coldly. "He will take you in charge now."

Lying still on the bed, Cade instinctively stopped struggling with the bonds on his wrists, and let his eyelids drop closed, just as the man in grey looked toward him and asked:

"How is he? Any trouble?"

"He's no trouble," the girl's tone was contemptuous. "He's just coming to."

"Good." Cade heard the sharp intake of breath, and then the nervous edginess went out of the man's voice. "I am your cousin," he said evenly. "You will come with me."

"You are my cousin," answered the toneless voice of the sleepwalker. "I am to report that my mission is accomplished. I have succeeded in killing . . ."

"Come with me now. You will make your report in . . ."

" . . . killing the Deskman In Charge of . . ."

" . . . in another room. You will report to me priv . . ."

" . . . of the third district of Klin Serv . . ."

" . . . privately. In another room."

Cade let his eyelids flicker open enough to observe the agitation of the man in grey as the droning report went on, unmindful of the efforts at control.

27

" . . . Service. Am I to destroy myself now? The mission is successfully accomplished." It stopped at last.

And not a moment too soon. Cade's hands, now free, were safely at rest again when the man in grey turned back to look at him.

"Seems to be all right still," Cousin said stiffly, surveying him. Deliberately, Cade let his eyelids flutter. "He's coming out of it though. I better get this fellow out of the way."

"Perhaps you'd better." The girl's voice now expressed infinite disgust. "Is he one of yours?"

"No, I'm just taking his report. Larter put him under."

"Larter's new," she admitted, and fell silent.

"Well . . ." There was a moment's embarrassed silence, and Cade let his eyes open all the way, to find Cousin standing, hesitant, in the doorway. "Maybe I better stay around. He's a Gunman, you know. He might . . ."

"I said I can handle him," she replied. "Suppose you take care of your man before he gets . . . *watch out!*"

The sleepwalker's eyes were large and brilliant, fascinated by the needle on the table. He saw Cade, stretched out on the bed, and sudden animation flooded his face.

"Don't let them do it to you!" he screamed. "Don't let them touch you! They'll make you like me."

While the other man stood ashen-faced and horrified, the girl acted so swiftly that Cade might almost have admired her, if it were possible to use the word in connection with a female commoner. She was across the small room, and back again with the needle in her hand even as the man screamed his warning to Cade. Before the commoner could lift his arm to brush it aside, she drove the needle home, and the plunger after it.

"S-s-s-s-s-t!"

The man in grey was ready when she hissed at him.

"You will come with me," he intoned. "You will come with me now. You will come with me."

Cade had seen hypnotists at work before, but never with the aid of a drug so swift as this. He felt the capsule the girl had given him getting warm and moist between his lips. Horror seized him, but he waited as he knew he must till the door was closed behind those inhumanly even footsteps.

He knew exactly how fast the girl could move. *Gunners are sturdy pillars. It is fitting that we serve.* His timing was perfection itself as he spat the dangerous pill from his mouth and leaped from the bed. She had hardly time to turn from the door before his fist caught her a round blow on the side of the head, and she crumpled silently to the floor.

4

HE HAD to get out of here.

He had to get back to the Chapter House. He looked at the girl, sprawled on her face on the floor, and was uncomfortably aware of the feel of the rough commoner clothes against his own skin, and then acutely conscious of a blank feeling on his right hip, where his gun should be.

The Klin Philosophy in a Gunner is like the charge in his gun.

He remembered, and shuddered as he remembered, the awful calmness with which she had admitted plotting against the Emperor. *It is fitting that the Emperor rules. While this is so, all will be well till the end of time.*

Cade took his eyes from the crumpled figure of the girl, and examined the strangely featureless room once more. There was nothing new to be seen. He approached the inconspicuous door. Beyond it, there was a way out. This place of horrors, whatever and wherever it was, would have to be burned from the face of the earth, and the sooner he escaped the sooner it would happen. Without pride but with solid thankfulness he was glad that he, a full Gunner, was here instead of a novice of an Armiger.

Beyond the door was an empty corridor whose only purpose seemed to be the connection of the featureless room with other rooms fifty meters away. He was suddenly sure that he was underground. There were six doors at the end of the fifty-meter corridor, and he heard voices when he listened at five of them. Calmly he opened the sixth and walked into an empty room about ten by twenty meters, well-lit, equipped with simple benches and a little elevated platform at one end. Along one wall were three curtained booths whose purpose he could not fathom. But he dived into one with desperate speed at the sound of approaching voices.

The booth was in two sections separated by a thin curtain. In the rear section, against the wall, you could look out and not be looked in on. It was an arrangement apparently as insane as the grey, egg-shaped room, but it was a perfect observation post. Through the gauze-like inside curtain and the half-drawn, heavier outside curtain, he saw half a dozen commoners enter the place, chatting in low voices. Their clothes were of the usual cut, but a uniform drab brown instead of the ordinary gaudy particolor.

The drab-clad commoners fell silent and seated themselves on a front bench as others in more customary clothing began to straggle in. There were about fifty of them. One of the front-benchers rose and, standing in front of the little stage, did something that Cade recognized; he made the same detestable sign with which the old poisoner had mocked him. Watching carefully, the Gunner saw that it was an X overlaid with a P. The right hand touched the left shoulder, right hipbone, right shoulder, left hipbone, and then traced a line up from the navel to end in a curlicue over the face. It was manifestly a mockery of the Gunner's ten-thousand-year-old ritual when donning his gun. Cade coldly thought: *they'll pay for that.*

All the seated commoners repeated the sign, and the standing man began to speak, in a resonant, well-trained voice: "The first of the first of the good Cairo." He began making intricate signs involving much arm-waving. It went on for minutes, and Cade quickly lost interest, though the seated commoners were, as far as he could make out, following raptly. At last the commoner said: "That is how you shall be known. The first of the first."

Idiotically, twenty commoners from the back benches got up and filed out. Cade was astonished to see that some of them were silently weeping.

The speaker said when they had left: "The first of the first of the good Cairo in the second degree," and the lights went out, except for a blue spot on the platform. The speaker, standing a little to one side, went through the same signs as before, but much more slowly. The signs were coordinated with a playlet enacted on the stage by the other drab-clad commoners. It started with the speaker spreading his palms on his chest and an "actor" standing along in the center of the platform. Both speaker and actor then made a sweeping gesture with the right hand waist-high and palm down, and a second actor crawled onto the platform . . . and so on until the first actor, who had never moved, laid his hand successively on the heads of six persons, two of them women, who seemed pleased by the gesture.

About midway through the rigmarole Cade suddenly realized where he was and what it was all about. He was in a Place of Mystery! He knew little about the Mystery Cults. There were, he recalled, four or five of them, all making ridiculous pretensions to antiquity. Above all, they were ridiculous when you thought of them: commoners' institutions where fools paid to learn the "esoteric meaning" of gibberish phrases, mystic gestures and symbolic dramas. Presumably a few clever souls had made a good thing of it. They were always raiding each other for converts, and often with success. Frequenters of Mysteries were failures, stupid even for commoners, simply unable to grasp the propositions of the Klin Philosophy.

There were—let's see—the Joosh Mystery, which had invented a whole language called something like Hibber; the Scientific Mystery, which despised science and sometimes made a little trouble at the opening of new hospitals; and there were others, but he couldn't recall anything called the Cairo Mystery.

But it was frightening. If they could swallow the Mysteries, these weak-minded commoners could accept *any-thing* else—even a plot against the Realm of Man.

The lights were on again and the ridiculous proceedings outside apparently were drawing to a close when two more commoners entered. One of them was the man in grey—"Cousin."

He murmured something to the drab-clad speaker—

Cade could guess what. The Gunner burst from the booth toward the door at a dead run.

"Stop him!"

"Sacrilege!"

"A spy!"

"Get him! Get him!"

But of course they didn't. They just milled and babbled while Cade plowed through them, made the door—and found it locked.

"Cousin" announced loudly as Cade turned his back to the wall, "Seize him, beloved. It is a spy trying to steal our most secret rituals."

"He's lying," yelled Cade. "I am Gunner Cade of the Order of Armsmen. My Star is the Star of France. Commoners, I command you to open the door and make way for me."

"A ridiculous pose, spy," said Cousin smoothly. "If you are a Gunner, where is your gun? If you are of the Star of France *what are you doing here in Baltimore?*"

The commoners were impressed. Cade was confused. *In Baltimore?*

"Bear him down, my beloved!" shouted Cousin. "Bear down the spy and bring him to me!" The commoners muttered and surged and Cade was buried beneath their numbers. He saw the keen face of "Cousin" close to him, felt the stab of a needle in his arm. For the first time, he wondered how long he had been drugged. *Baltimore!* Of course, the Mysteries were world-wide. He could as easily had been in Zanzibar by now, or his native Denver, instead of France . . . or Baltimore.

There was no doubt about it; the Mysteries would have to be suppressed. Up to now they had been tolerated, for every Mystery solemnly claimed it was merely a minor auxiliary of the Klin Philosophy and that all adherents were primarily followers of Klin. Nobody had ever been fooled—until now.

"He'll be all right now," said Cousin. "Two of you pick him up and carry him. He won't struggle any more."

Gunners march where the Emperor wills; that is their glory. Cade struck out violently with arms and legs at once, as the commoners attempted to lift him from the floor. Nothing happened—nothing except that they lifted him easily and carried him out of the big room.

Vanity as a peril. An emotion flooded Cade, an unfamiliar feeling that identified itself with nothing since earliest childhood. He was frog-marched down the corridor, ignominiously helpless in the hands of two commoners, and understood that what he felt was shame.

They carried him into the featureless room again, and strapped him to the bed on which he had awakened—how long?—before. He heard Cousin say: "Thank you my beloved, in the name of good Cairo," and the door closed. Rage drove out shame and vanity both as a woman's voice said clearly: "You bloody fool!"

"He is, my dear," said "Cousin" unctuously. "But quite clever enough for us. Or he will be shortly, when he understands how to use the limited intelligence his Order has left him." Gleeful satisfaction trickled through the man's voice. "He is quite clever enough—he knows how to kill. And he is strong—strong enough to kill. Let me see the bruise he gave you. . . ."

"Take your busy little hands off me, Cousin. I'm all right. Where will you start him from?"

"He can come to in any park; it doesn't matter."

"If he fell off a bench he might be arrested. Some place with a table for him to lean on—?"

"You're right. We could dump him at Mistress Cannon's! How's that? A chaste Gunner at Mistress Cannon's!"

The girl's laughter was silvery. "I must go now," she said.

"Very well. Thank you, my beloved, in the name of the good Cairo." The door closed.

Cade felt his shoulders being adjusted on the table where he lay. He looked at grey nothingness. There was a click and he was looking at a black spot.

"Cousin's" voice said: "You notice that this room has little to distract the attention. It has no proper corners, no angles, nothing in the range of your sight for your eye to wander to. Either you look at that black dot or you close your eyes. It doesn't matter which to me. As you look at the black dot you will notice after a while that it seems to swing toward you and away from you, toward you and away from you. This is no mechanical trickery; it is simply your eye-muscles at work making the dot seem to swing toward you and away, first toward you and then away. You may close your eyes, but you will find it difficult to visualize anything but the dot swinging toward you and away, first toward you and then away. You can see nothing but the dot swinging toward you and away. . . ."

It was true; it was true. Whether Cade's eyes were open or closed, the black dot swung and melted at the edges, and seemed to grow and swallow the greyness and then melt again. He tried to cling to what was fitting—*like this the Order wraps the Realm and shields it*—but the diabolical hypnotist seemed to be reading his thoughts.

"Why fight me, master Cade? You have no boots. You have no hose. You have no shirt. You have no cloak. You have no gun. Only the dot swinging toward you and away; why fight me; why fight the dot swinging toward you and away? Why fight me? I'm your friend. I'll tell you what to do. You have no boots. You have no hose. You have no cloak. You have no gun. Why fight your friend? You only have the dot swinging toward you and away. Why fight me? I'll tell you what to do. Watch the dot swinging towards you and away. . . ."

He had no boots. He had no hose. He had no cloak. He had no gun. Why fight his friend? That girl, that evil girl had brought him to this. He hated her for making him, a Gunner—but he was not a gunner, he had no gun, he had nothing, he had nothing.

"You don't know. You don't know. You don't know. You don't know. You don't know. You don't know. You don't know. You don't know."

The self-awareness of Cade was no longer a burning fire that filled him from his scalp to his toes. It was fading at his extremities, the lights going out in his toes and fingers and skin, retreating, retreating.

"You will go to the palace and kill the Power Master with your hands. You will go to the palace and kill the Power Master with your hands."

He would go . . . his self-awareness, a dim light in his mind watched it happen and cried out too feebly. He would go to the palace and kill the Power Master with his hands. Who was he? He didn't know. He would go to the palace and kill the Power Master with his hands. Why would he? He didn't know. He would go to the palace and kill the Power Master with his hands. He didn't know. The spark of ego left to him watched it happen and was powerless to prevent it.

5

BLACKNESS and a bumping . . . rest and a sensation of acceleration . . . a passage of time and the emergence of sounds . . . a motor, and wind noise, and voices.

Laughter.

"Will he make it, do you think?"

"Who knows?"

"He's a Gunner. They can break your neck back in a second."

"I don't believe that stuff."

"Well, look at him! Muscles like iron."

"They pick 'em that way."

"Naw, it's the training they get. A Gunner can do it if anybody can."

"I don't know."

"Well, if he doesn't, the next one will. Or the next. Now we know we can do it. We'll take as many as we need."

"It's risky. It's too dangerous."

"Not the way we did it. The old lady came along with him."

A jolt.

"You've got to walk him to Cannon's."

"Two blocks! And he must weigh—"

"I know, but you've got to. I'm in my greys. What would a Klin Service officer be doing in Cannon's?"

"But—oh, all *right*. I wonder if he'll make it?"

Lurching progress down a dark street, kept from falling by a panting, cursing blur. A dim place with clinking noises and bright-colored blurs moving in it.

"E-e-easy, boy. Steady there—here's a nice corner table. You like this one? All righty, into the chair. Fold, curse you. *Fold.*" A dull blow in the stomach. "Tha-a-at's better. Two whiskies, dear."

"What's the matter witcha friend?"

"A little drunkie. I'm gonna leave him here after I have my shot. He always straightens up after a little nap."

"Yeah?"

"Yeah. I don't wanta see any change out of this, dear."

"Thass different."

"Back so quick, dear?"

"Here's ya whiskey."

"Righto. Mud in your eye and dribbling down your left cheek, dear. You hear me, fella? I'm going bye-bye now. I'll see you on the front page. Haw! I'll see you on the front page!" The talking blur went away and another, brighter-colored one came.

"Buy me a drink? You're pretty stiff, ain't you? Mind if I have yours? You look like you got enough. I'm Arlene. I'm from the south. You like girls from the south? What's the matter with you, anyway? If you're asleep why don't you close your eyes, big fella? Is this some kind of funny, funny joke? Oh, fall down dead. Comic!"

Another bright-colored blur: "Hello; you want company? I noticed you chased away Arlene and for that I don't blame you. All she knows is 'buy-me-a-drink'; I ain't like that. I like a nice, quiet talk myself once in a while. What do you do for fun, big fella—follow the horses? Play cards? Follow the wars? I'm a fighting fan myself. I go for Zanzibar. That Gunner Golos—man! This year already he's got seventeen raids and nine kills. That what you call a Gunner. Hey, big fella, wanna buy me a drink while we talk? Hey, what's the matter with you anyway? Oh, cripe. Out with his eyes open."

The blur went away. Vitality began to steal through sodden limbs, and urgent clarity flashed through the mind. *Go to the Palace and kill the Power Master.* The hands on the table stirred faintly and the mind inside whirred into motion, tabulating knowledge with easy familiarity.

You killed people with your hands by smashing them on the side of the neck with the side of the hand below the little finger—sudden but not positive. If you had time to work for thirty seconds without interruption you took them by the throat and smashed the tracheal cartilage with your thumbs.

Go to the Palace and kill the Power Master with your hands.

One hand crawled around the emptied whiskey glass and crushed it to fragments and powder. If you come up from behind you can break a back by locking one foot around the instep, putting your knee in the right place, and falling forward as you grasp the shoulders.

A gaudily dressed girl stood across the table. "I'm going to buy you a little drink, big fella. I won't take no for an answer. I got it right here."

His throat made a noise which was not yet speech, and his hands lifted off the table as she stood beside him with a small bottle. His arms would not lift more than an inch from the table. The drink in his mouth burned like fire.

"Listen to me, Cade," said the girl into his ear. "No scenes. No noise. No trouble. As you come to just sit still and listen to me."

Like waking up. Automatically the morning thought began to go through his mind. *It is fitting that the Emperor rules. It is fitting that the Power Master—*

"The Power Master!" he said hoarsely.

"It's all right," said the girl. "I gave you an antidote. You're not going to—do anything you don't want to."

Cade tried to stand but couldn't.

"You'll be all right in a couple of minutes," she said.

He saw her more clearly now. She was heavily made up, and the thick waves of her hair reflected the bright purple of her gossamer-sheer pyjamas. That didn't make sense. Only the starborne wore sheer; commoners' clothes were of heavy stuffs. But only commoner females wore pyjamas; starborne ladies dressed in gowns and robes. He shook his head, trying to clear it, and tore his eyes from the perfection of her body, clearly visible through the bizarre clothing.

Following his eyes, she flushed a little. "That's part of the act," she said. "I'm not."

Cade didn't try to understand what she was talking about. Her face was incredibly beautiful. "You're the same one," he said. "You're the commoner from that place."

"Lower your voice," she said coolly. "And this time, listen to me."

"You were with them before," he accused her. His speech was almost clear. His arms worked all right now.

"Not really. Don't you understand? If you'd swallowed the capsule I gave you in the hypnosis room, you'd never have gone under. But you had to bash me and make it on your own. See how far you got?"

She was right about that. He hadn't succeeded in getting out of the place.

"All right," she went on, when he didn't reply. "Maybe you're going to be reasonable after all. You're feeling better, aren't you? The—compulsion is gone? Try to remember that I came after you to give you the release drug."

Cade found he could move his legs. "Thank you for your assistance," he said stiffly. "I'm all right now. I have to get to—to the nearest Chapter House, I suppose, and make my report. I . . ." It went against all training and was perhaps even disobedient, but she had helped him. "I will neglect to include your description in my report."

"Still spouting high-and-mighty?" she said wearily. "Cade, you still don't understand it all. There are things you don't know. You can't . . ."

"Give me any further information you may have," he interrupted. "After that may it please the Ruler we two shall never meet again."

The words surprised him, even as he spoke them. Why should he be willing to protect this—creature—from her just punishment? Very well, she had helped him; that was only her duty as a common citizen of the Realm. He was a sworn Armsman. There was no reason to sit here listening to her insolence; the City Watch would deal with her.

"Cade . . ." She was giggling. That was intolerable. "Cade, have you ever had a drink before?"

"A drink? Certainly I have quenched my thirst many times." She was unfitting, upsetting, and insolent as well.

"No, I mean a drink—a strong alcoholic beverage."

"It is forbidden. . . ." He stopped, appalled. *For-*

bidden! . . . for love of woman makes men love their rulers less. . . .

"See here, commoner!" he began in a rage.

"Oh, *Cade!* Now you've done it. We've got to get out of here." Her voice changed to a nasal wheedle. "Let's get out of this place, honey, and come on home with me. I'll show you a real good time—"

She was cut off by the arrival of a massive woman. "I'm Mistress Cannon," said the newcomer. "What're you doing here, girlie? You ain't one of mine."

"We were just leaving, honest—wasn't we, big fella?"

"*I was,*" said Cade; he swayed as he rose to his feet. The girl followed, sticking close to him.

Mistress Cannon saw them grimly to the door. "If you come back, girlie," she said, "I may wrap a bar stool around your neck."

Outside, Cade peered curiously down the narrow darkness of the city street. How did commoners get places? There was no way even to orient himself. How had they expected him to get to the Palace?

He turned abruptly to the girl. "What city is this?" he demanded.

"Aberdeen."

That made sense. The ancient Proving Grounds where he himself and all the Armsmen for ten thousands of years had won their guns in trial and combat. The city of the Palace, the awesome Capitol of the Emperor himself. And in the Palace the High Office of the Power Master, the grim executive.

"There is a Chapter House," he remembered. "How do I get there?"

"Gunner, understand me. You aren't going to any Chapter House. That's the best and quickest way to get yourself killed."

A typical commoner's reaction, he thought, and found himself saddened to have had it from her. She had, after all, incurred some risk in defying the plotters.

"I assure you," he said kindly, "that the prospect of my eventual death in battle does not frighten me. You commoners don't understand it, but it is so. All I want to do is get this information into the proper hands and resume my fitting task as Gunner."

She made a puzzling, strangled noise and said after a long pause: "That's not what I meant. I'll speak more plainly. You had an alcoholic drink tonight—two of them, in fact. You're not accustomed to them. You are what is known, among us commoners—" She paused again, swallowing what seemed inexplicably like laughter. "—among us commoners as blasted, birdy, polluted, or drunk. I'll be merciful and assume that your being blasted, birdy, polluted or drunk accounts for your pompous stupidity. But you are not going anywhere by yourself. You're going to come with me, because that's the only safe place for you. Now please stop being foolish." Her face was turned up to his, pleading, and in the wandering rays of light from a distant streetlamp, even under the thick coating of cosmetics she seemed more than ever the perfect likeness of The Lady, the perfection of womanhood that could never be achieved by mortal females. Her hand slipped easily around his arm, and she clung to him, tugging at him, urging him to follow her.

Cade didn't strike her. He had every reason to, and yet, for some reason he could not bring himself to shake her off as he should have done, to throw her to the ground, and leave her and be rid of her peril forever. Instead he stood there, and the flesh of his arm crawled at the soft touch of her hand through the commoner's cloth he wore.

"If you have nothing more to tell me," he said coldly, "I'll leave you now." They were at a corner; he turned up the side street and noticed that there were brighter lights and taller buildings ahead.

The girl didn't let go. She ran along at his side, holding on, and talking in a furious undertone. "I'm trying to save your life, you bloody idiot. *Will* you stop this nonsense? You don't know what you're getting into!"

There was a watchman standing across the street, on the opposite corner, a symbol of familiar security in immaculate Service grey. Cade hesitated only an instant, remembering where he had last seen that uniform desecrated. But surely, surely, that was not cause enough to lose all faith.

He turned to the girl at his side. The touch of her hand was like fire against his arm. "Leave me now," he told her, "or I cannot promise you your safety."

"Cade, you *mustn't*!"

That was intolerable. *Love of woman*, he thought again, and shook off her arm as he would have brushed away an insect.

He strode out into the street. "Watchman!"

The man in Greys lolled idly on his corner.

"Watchman!" Cade called again. "I desire to be directed to the Chapter House of the Order of Armsmen."

"Your desires are no concern of mine, citizen."

Cade remembered his commoner's clothing, and swallowed his ire. "Can you direct me . . . sir?"

"If I see fit. And if your purpose is more fitting than your manner. What business have you there?"

"That is no concern . . ." He stopped himself. "I cannot tell you . . . sir. It is an affair of utmost privacy."

"Very well, then, citizen," the Serviceman laughed tolerantly. "Find your own way . . . privately." He was looking past Cade, over the Gunner's shoulder. "*She* with you?" he asked with alerted interest.

Cade turned to find the girl right behind him again.

"No," he said sharply.

"OK, girlie," the watchman demanded. "What're you doing out of the district?"

"The district . . ." For the first time, Cade saw the girl fumble and falter. "What do you . . .?"

"You know what I mean. You're not wearing that garter for jewelry, are you, girlie. You know you can't solicit outside the district. If you was with this citizen, now . . ." He looked meaningfully at Cade.

"She is *not* with me," the Gunner said firmly. "She followed me here, but . . ."

"That's a dirty lie," the girl whined, suddenly voluble. "This fella picks me up in a bar, we was in Cannon's place, you can ask anybody there, and he kicks up such a rumpus, they tossed us out, and then he says we're goin' to his place, and then we get out here to the corner and all of a sudden he remembers something else he wants to do, and leaves me flat. These guys that come in and get loaded and then don't know *what* they want . . . !" She wound up with a note of disgust.

"How about it, citizen? Was she with you?"

"She was not," Cade said emphatically. He was

41

staring at the garter the Serviceman seemed so concerned about. It was a slender chain of silver links fastened high on the girl's thigh, pulling the thin folds of her pyjamas tight against her flesh.

"Sorry, girlie," the Watchman said, firmly but not unkindly. "You know the rules. We're going to the Watch House."

"There, you see?" She turned on Cade in a fury. "See what you did? Now they'll cage me for soliciting, and I can't pay, so it means sitting it out in a cell, all on account of you don't know what you want. Come on, now, admit it how you made me come with you. Just tell him, that's all I ask."

Cade shook her off with disgust. "You were following me," he said. "I told you I'd keep you out of trouble if I could, but if you're going to insist on . . ."

"All right now," the Serviceman said, suddenly decisive. "That'll be enough out of both of you. You both come along and you can get it straightened out in the Watch House."

"I see no reason . . ." Cade began, and stopped even before the Watchman began to reach for the light club in his belt. He did see a reason, a good one: at a Watch House, he would be able to get transportation to the Chapter House. "Very well," he said coldly. "I shall be glad to come along."

"You *bloody* idiot," said the girl.

6

"Well, which one of you is making the complaint?" The bored officer behind the desk looked from the girl to Cade and back again.

Neither replied.

"She was out of her district," the other Watchman explained, "and they couldn't get together on whether she was with him or not, so I took 'em both along in case you wanted to hear it all."

"Official infringement on the girl, huh?" the Deskman muttered. "If she don't want to make a complaint we got nothing against the man. All right. Matron!" A stout clean-looking woman in grey got off a bench along the wall and approached the desk. "Take her along and get her name and registration. Fine is ten greens . . ."

"Ten greens!" the girl broke in miserably. "I haven't even got a blue on me. He was the first one tonight . . ."

"Ten greens," he said implacably, "or five days detention. Tell your troubles to the matron. Take her away. Now . . ." He turned to Cade as the stout woman led the girl away. "We'll take your name and address for the record and you can go. Those girls are getting out of hand. They'd be all over town if we let 'em get away with it."

It was too much to attempt to unravel now. Cade dismissed the puzzle from his mind, and said, in a low voice: "May I speak to you alone?"

"You out of your head, man? Speak up, what do you want?"

The Gunner looked around. No one was too close. He kept his voice low. "It would be well if you speak more respectfully, Watchman. I am *not* a commoner."

Comprehension came over the man's face. He stood up promptly, and led the Gunner into a small side room. "I'm sorry, Sir," he said hastily. "I had no idea. The gentlemen usually identify to the Watchman on street duty when such incidents occur. You're a young gentleman, Sir, and perhaps this is your first . . . little visit to the other half? You understand, Sir, you needn't have been bothered by coming here at all. Next time, Sir, if you'll just identify to . . ."

"I don't believe you quite understand," Cade stopped the meaningless flow. "I desired to come here. There is a service you can do for me and for the Realm."

"Yes, Sir. I know my duty, Sir, and I'll be glad to assist you in any way you deem fitting. If you'll just identify first, Sir, you understand I have to ask it, we can't chance ordinary citizens passing themselves off as . . ."

"Identify? How do I do that?"

"Your badge of rank, Sir." He hesitated, and saw confusion still on Cade's face. "Surely, Sir, you didn't come out without it?"

The Gunner understood at last. "You misunderstood, Watchman," he said indignantly. "And you presume too much. I have heard of the degenerates among our nobility who indulge in the—kind of escapade you seem to have in mind. I am not one of them. I am a Gunner in the Order of Armsmen, and I require your immediate assistance to reach the nearest Chapter House."

"You have no badge of rank?" the Watchman said grimly.

"Armsmen carry no prideful badges."

"Armsmen carry guns."

Cade kept his temper. "All you have to do is get in touch with the Chapter House. They can check my fingerprints, or there might be a Gunner there who can identify me personally."

The Deskman made no answer; he walked to the door and pushed it open.

"Hey, Bruge!" The Watchman of the street got to his feet, and came toward them. "You want to put a drunk-and-disorderly on this fella? He's either cockeyed drunk, or out of his head. Was he acting up outside?"

"The *girl* said he was drinking," the other man remembered.

"Well, you're the one'll have to register the complaint. I'm not letting him out of here tonight. He's been telling me in deepest confidence that he's really a Gunner in the Order...."

"Say, that's how the whole thing started," Bruge remembered. "He came up to me asking where was the Chapter House. I figured he was just a little crocked, and I wouldn't of pulled him in at all except for the argument with the girl. You think he's off his rocker?"

"I don't know." The Deskman was silent for a moment, then made up his mind. "I'll tell you what, you sign a d-and-d, and we'll see how he talks in the morning."

Cade could endure no more of it. He strode angrily between the two men. "I tell you," he announced loudly, "that I am Gunner Cade of the Order of Armsmen, and my Star is the Star of France. If you do not do what is necessary to identify me immediately, you will pay dearly for it later."

"Say, now . . ." Another Watchman, who had listened idly from the bench, stood up and joined them. "I'm a fighting fan myself. It's a real privilege to meet up with a real Gunner, first-hand." He was short and stout, and there was an idiotic smile on his beaming moon-face, but at least he seemed more alert than the others. "I hate to bother you, Sir, at a time like this, but I was having a little argument just yesterday with Bruge here and you could settle it for us. Could you tell me, sir, for instance, how many times you've been in action this year? Or, say, your five-year total?"

"I really don't remember," said Cade impatiently. "This is hardly a fitting time for talk of past actions. I must report immediately to the nearest Chapter House. If your superior sees fit to do his duty now and call the House for identification, I shall endeavor to forget the inconvenience I have suffered so far."

"How about it, Chief?" the moon-faced one appealed to the Deskman, turning his face away from Cade. "Why don't you let Bruge here make a call for the Gunner? It's only sporting, isn't it?"

There was an unexpected smile on the Deskman's face when he replied. "OK—go on, Bruge, you go call up." He winked in a friendly fashion.

"All right," said Bruge, disappointedly, and left the room.

"I wonder, Gunner Cade," Moon-face said easily, "how many men you've killed since you became armiger? Say in offensive actions compared with defensive actions?"

"Eh? Oh, I've never kept count, Watchman. No Gunner would." This fellow at least was civil. There was no harm in answering the man's questions while he waited. "Numbers killed don't mean everything in war. I've been in engagements where we'd have given half of our men to get control of a swell in the ground so unnoticeable that you probably wouldn't see it if you were looking at it."

"Think of that!" marvelled one of the watchmen. "Did you hear that? Just for a little swell in the ground that slobs like us wouldn't even notice. Hello, Jardin . . ." He hailed another man in grey who had just entered. "Here's the man you want," he told Moon-face, "Jardin can give you facts and figures on the Gunner."

"You mean Cade?" the new man said unhappily. "Yeah, I sure can. It's only eight kills for the second quarter. He would have hit twelve, sure, only . . ."

"Yeah, it's a shame all right," Moon-face broke in. "Jardin, I've got a real treat for you. A France fan like you and Gunner Cade is your favorite too. Well, here's the thrill of a lifetime, man. Gunner Cade, himself, in person. Jardin, meet the Gunner. Gunner Cade, Sir, this is a long-standing fan of yours."

Two more men had come in, and another was at the door. They were all standing around listening. Cade regretted his earlier impulse to answer the man's question. A distasteful familiarity was developing in Moon-face's attitude.

"Quit your kidding," Jardin was saying, almost angrily. "I don't see what's so funny when a good Gunner dies."

"I tell you the man says he's Gunner Cade. Isn't that true?" Moon-face appealed to the Gunner.

"I am Gunner Cade," he replied, with what dignity he could muster.

"Why, you . . . !"

The outburst from Jardin was stopped abruptly by the Deskman.

"All right, that's enough now," he said sharply. "This farce is no longer fitting to our honored dead. Jardin is right. Fellow," he said to Cade, "you picked the wrong Gunner and the wrong Watchman. Gunner Cade is dead. I know because Jardin here lost twenty greens to me on him. He was silly enough to bet on Cade for a better second-quarter total of kills than Golos of Zanzibar. Golos topped him with—but never mind that. Who are you, and what do you think you're doing impersonating a Gunner?"

"But I *am* Gunner Cade," he said, stupefied.

"Gunner Cade," said the officer patiently, "was killed last week in the kitchen of a house in some French town his company was attacking. They found his body. Now, fellow, who are you? Impersonating a Gunner is a serious offense."

For the first time, Cade realized that Bruge had left, not to call the Chapter House, but to collect the crowd of Watchmen who had assembled while they talked. There

46

were eleven of them in the room now—too many to over-power. He remained silent; insisting on the truth seemed hopeless.

"That's no d-and-d," the Deskman said in the silence. "We'll hold him for psych."

"Want me to sign the complaint?" It was Bruge, grinning like an ape.

"Yeah. Put him in a cage until morning and then to the psych."

"Watchman," said Cade steadily. "Will I be able to convince the psych, or is he just another commoner like you?"

"Hold him," somebody said. Two of them expertly caught Cade's arms. The questioner flicked a rubber truncheon across Cade's face. "Maybe you're crazy," he said, "but you'll show respect to officers of the Klin Service."

Cade stood there, the side of his jaw growing numb. He knew he could break loose from the Watchman holding him, or disable the man with the truncheon by one well-placed kick. But what would be the good of it. There were too many of them there. *It is fitting that we Gunmen serve*—but the thought trailed off into apathy.

"All right," said the man with the truncheon. "Put him in with Fledwick."

The Gunner let himself be led to a cell and locked in. He ignored his cellmate until the man said nervously: "Hello. What are you in for?"

"Never mind."

"Oh. Oh. I'm in here by mistake. My name is Fledwick Zisz. I'm a Klin Teacher . . . attached to the lectory at the Glory of the Realm ground car works. There was some mix-up in the collections, and in the confusion they concluded I was responsible. I should be out of here in a day or two."

Cade glanced uninterestedly at the man. "Thief!" was written all over him. So Klin Teachers could be thieves.

"What does a silver garter on a girl mean?" he suddenly demanded.

"Oh," said Fledwick. "I wouldn't know personally, of course." He told him.

Curse her, thought Cade. He wondered what had happened to her. She'd said she couldn't pay the fine. Probably she was locked up with a real prostitute. Curse them, you'd think they could tell the difference!

"My real vocation, of course, was military," said Fledwick.

"*What?*" said Cade.

Fledwick hastily changed his story. "I should have said, 'the military teachership.' I was never really happy at the Glory shop. I'd rather serve humbly as a Teacher in an obscure Chapter House of the Order." He raptly misquoted: "It is fitting for the Emperor to rule. It is fitting for the Power Master to serve the Emperor."

"Interested in the Order, eh? Do you know Gunner Cade?"

"Oh, *everybody* knows Gunner Cade. There wasn't a smile in the Glory shop the day we heard the news. The factory pool drew Cade in the 'stakes and it's play or pay. Not that I know much about gambling, but I—uh—happened to have organized the pool. It was so good for the employee morale. When I get out of here, though, I think I'll stick to dog bets. You get nice odds in a play-or-pay deal, but there's a perfectly human tendency to think you've been swindled when your Gunner is—so to speak—scratched and you don't get your money back. I've always thought—"

"Shut up," said Cade. You'd think the fools could tell the difference between her and—oh, *curse* her. He had worries of his own. For one thing, he seemed to be dead. He grinned without mirth. He had to get to the Chapter House and report on the Cairo Mystery, but he was in effect a commoner without even a name. A Gunner had no wife or family; no one to notify, no one to identify him except his Brothers in the Order—and the watchmen were not going to bother the Order. They *knew* Cade was dead.

He wondered if this were happening for the first time in the ten thousand years since creation.

Everything was all wrong; he couldn't think straight. He stretched out on the jail cot and longed for his harder, narrower sleepbag. *It is fitting that the Emperor rules*—He hoped she wouldn't antagonize them with her disrespectful way of talking. Curse her! Why hadn't she stayed in her own district? But that went to prove that she didn't really know anything about the trade, didn't it?

"You!" he growled at Fledwick. "Did you ever hear of a prostitute wandering out of her district by mistake?"

"Oh. Oh, no. Certainly not. Everybody knows where to go when he wants one. Or so I'm told."

A crazy thought came to Cade that if he were dead, he was released from his vows. That was nonsense. He wished he could talk to a real Klin Teacher, not this snivelling thief. A good Klin Teacher could always explain your perplexities, or find you one who could. He wanted to know how it happened that he had done all the right things and everything had turned out all wrong.

"You," he said. "What's the penalty for impersonating a Gunner?"

Fledwick scratched his nose and mused: "You picked a bad one, sir. It's twenty years!" He was jolted out of his apathy. "I'm sorry to be the one to tell you, but—"

"Shut up. I've got to think."

He thought—and realized with twisted amusement that one week ago he would have been equally horrified, but for another reason. He would have thought the penalty all too light.

Fledwick turned his face to the wall and sighed comfortably. Going to sleep, was he?

"You," said Cade. "Do you know who I am?"

"You didn't say, sir," yawned the Klin Teacher.

"I'm Gunner Cade, of the Order of Gunmen; my Star is the Star of France."

"But—" The teacher sat upon the bed and looked worriedly into Cade's angry face, "Oh. Of course," he said. "Of course you are, sir. I'm sorry I didn't recognize you." Thereafter he sat on the edge of his bed, stealing an occasional nervous glance at his cellmate. It made Cade feel a little better, but not much.

It is fitting that the Emperor rules—he hoped that leaving the "district" was not too serious an offense.

7

CADE OPENED his eyes.

Dingy walls, locked door, and the little Klin Teacher still sitting on the side of his bunk across the cage, fast asleep. At the thought of the man's futile determination to hold an all-night vigil over the maniac who had claimed to be a dead Gunner, Cade grinned—and realized abruptly that a grin was no way a Gunner of the Order to start his day. He hastily began his Morning Thoughts of the Order, but somewhere, far down inside him, there was a small wish that the Thoughts were not quite so long. He had a plan.

Seconds after completing the familiar meditation he was leaning over the other bunk, shaking the Klin Teacher's shoulder. Fledwick almost toppled to the floor and then sprang to his feet in a terrified awakening. He was about to shriek when the Gunner's big hand sealed his mouth.

"No noise," Cade told him. "Listen to me." He sat on Fledwick's bunk and urged the little crook down beside him. "I'm going to get out of here and I'll need your help to do it. Are you going to make trouble?"

"Oh, no sir," the Teacher answered too promptly and too heartily. "I'll be glad to help, sir."

"Good." Cade glanced at the lock on the cage door—an ordinary two-way guarded radionic. "I'll set the lock to open fifteen seconds after it is next opened from the outside. You'll have to raise some sort of noise to get a Watchman in here."

"You can set the lock?" Fledwick broke in. "Where did you learn—?"

"I told you. I am a Gunner of the Order. I expect your full cooperation because of that. I have a message of great importance which must be delivered to the Chapter House at once. Your service to me, by the way, should win you a pardon."

Cade read on the little man's face the collapse of a brief hope. Fledwick said brightly: "The pardon is immaterial. Whatever I can do to serve the Realm, I will do."

"Very well, you don't believe me. Then I will expect your full cooperation on the grounds that I must be a dangerous maniac who might tear you limb from limb for disobedience. Is *that* clear—and believable?"

"Yes," said Fledwick miserably.

"Excellent. Now listen: you will attract a guard's attention. Say you're ill or that I'm trying to murder you—anything to get him inside. He will come in, close the door and look at you. I will overpower him, the door will open and I will leave."

"May I ask what I am to do then? The City Watch has been known to mistreat prisoners who aided in escapes."

"Save your wit and call me sir! You may come along if you like. You would be useful because I know nothing of the city, of course."

He got up and went over to the lock.

Fledwick was next to him, peering over his shoulder. "You mean you're *really* going to try it? Sir?" There was awe in his voice.

"Of course, fool. That's what I've been saying." Under the Teacher's dubious stare he got to work on the lock. The cage-side half of its casing was off in less than a minute. It took no longer for his trained eye to analyze the circuits inside. Fledwick nervously sucked in his breath as the Gunner's sure fingers probed at tubes, relays and printed "wires." But it was child's play to avoid the temper-triggers that would have set alarms ringing, and the more sinister contacts designed to send lethal charges of electricity through meddlers—child's play for anybody who could re-wire a flier's control panel in a drizzly dawn.

Cade snapped the cover back on and told Fledwick: Begin!"

The little man was near tears. "Sir, couldn't we wait until after breakfast?"

"What would they give us?"

"Bread and fried sausage today," said the Teacher hopefully.

Cade pretended to consider, and decided: "No. I don't eat meat until nightfall. Did you forget that I am a

Gunner of the Realm?"

The little man pulled himself together and said evenly: "I *am* beginning to wonder. I had been thinking of warning the Watchman when he came."

"Don't! I can silence both of you, if I must."

"Yes, of course. But you needn't worry about me. Your work with the lock—If *we* get out I know of a clothing warehouse and a certain person who's interested in its contents—and to be frank, perhaps I was overoptimistic when I said the misunderstanding that brought me here was a minor one. There are certain complications."

"Such as being guilty?" suggested Cade. "Never mind. You should have a pardon from the Gunner Supreme for this morning's work. Meanwhile, think me burglar, lunatic or what you please, but start howling. It will be daylight soon."

Fledwick practiced with a couple of embarrassed groans and then cut loose with a ten-decibel shriek for help on the grounds that he was dying in agony.

Two watchmen appeared, looking just-waked-up and annoyed. To Fledwick, writhing on his bunk, one demanded: "What's wrong with you now?"

"Cramps!" yelled Fledwick. "Unendurable pain! My belly is on fire; my limbs are breaking!"

"Yes, yes," said the Watchman. He addressed Cade with exquisite politeness. "Oh starborne one, go sit on your bunk and put your hands on your knees. My mate's going to be watching you. One move and sleep-gas fills the block. We'll all have a little nap, but when you wake up the desk chief will pound you like a Gunner never was pounded before, oh starborne one."

He nodded to the other Watchman, who took his stand by a handle that obviously controlled the gas. Cade rejoiced behind an impressive face; the outside Watchman was a slow-moving, doltish-looking fellow.

Fingers played a clicking code on the lock's outside buttons and the door sprang open in a satisfactorily lively manner. The Watchman bent over Fledwick, now moaning faintly, as Cade counted seconds. As the door sprang open again, Cade was on his feet; before it had completed its arc the Gunner's fist was tingling and the inside Watchman lay crumpled half on Fledwick and half on the floor. Cade was through the open door and on the too-solid fellow outside after the man realized there was something badly wrong, but before he could do anything about it.

Fledwick was in the corridor by then. "Follow me," Cade ordered. It was odd, he fleetingly thought, to have somebody under your command who couldn't half-read your mind through endless training, somebody whose skills were a guess and whose fighting heart was a gamble. They passed empty cells on their way to the guard room. Its door was stout, equipped with a peep-hole and firmly locked in case of just such an emergency as this.

Through the peep-hole Cade saw three drowsy Watchmen. The liveliest was at a facsimile machine reading the early-morning edition of a newssheet as it oozed out.

"Boyer," called the newshound. "Grey Dasher won the last at Baltimore. That's one green you owe—where's Boyer?"

"Cell-block. Fledwick was yelling again."

"How long ago?"

"Keep calm. Just a second before you came in. He went with Marshal; they haven't been more than a minute."

Cade ducked as the newshound strode to the door and put his own eye to the peep-hole. "A minute's too long," he heard him say. "Marshal's the biggest fool in the Klin Service and that big maniac's in there with Fledwick . . . Put on your gas guns."

There were groans of protest. "Ah, can't we flood the block?"

"If we did, *I'd* have to fill out fifty pages of reports. Move, curse you!"

"Can you fire a gas gun?" whispered Cade. The Klin Teacher, trembling, shook his head.

"Then stay out of the way," Cade ordered. He was excited himself, by the novelty and his unarmed state. They say we don't know fear, he thought, but they're wrong. *Arle, Gunner Supreme, safely dwelling in a fearful place, I pledge that you'll have no shame for me in this action.* Tuned to battle pitch he thought of the good old man, the Gunner of Gunners, who would accept even the coming scuffle as another fit deed by another of his fit sons in the Order.

The stout door unlocked and the newshound came through first. Like a machine that couldn't help itself Cade smashed him paralyzingly with his right arm where the ribs and sternum meet and a great ganglion is unguarded. Cade's left hand took the Watchman's gun and fired two gas pellets through the half-opened door. One of the Watchmen outside had time to shoot before he went down, but his pellet burst harmlessly against a wall.

Fledwick muttered something despairing about "up to our necks," but Cade waved him along into the guard room. The Gunner reconnoitered the street, found it empty and returned for the Teacher.

"Come along," he said, pitching the gas gun onto the chest of a prostrate Watchman.

Fledwick promptly picked it up. "What did you do that for?" he demanded. Cade glared at him and he hastily added: "Sir."

"Put it back," said Cade. "It's no fit weapon for a Gunner. I used it only because I had to."

There was a look on Fledwick's face that the Gunner had seen before. It was partly puzzled resignation, partly kindliness and affection and—something else that was suspiciously like condescension. Cade had seen it from the starbornes of the Courts, and especially the ladies. He had seen it often and was puzzled as always.

"Don't you think, sir," said the Klin Teacher carefully, "that we might take the gas gun along in case another emergency arises? I can carry it for you if you find it too distasteful."

"Suit yourself," said Cade shortly, "but hurry." Fledwick dropped the weapon inside his blouse, securing it underneath the waistband.

"Sir," said the Klin Teacher again, "don't you think we should do something about these Watchmen? Roll them behind a door and lock it?"

Cade shrugged irritably. "Nonsense," he said. "We'll be at the Chapter House with everything well again before they're discovered." Fledwick sighed and followed him down the steps and along the empty streets. There was a light mist and a hint of dawn in the sky; the two green lights of the Watch House cast the shadows of the

Gunner and the Klin Teacher before them on the pavement, long and thin.

"How far is the Charter House?"

"Past the outskirts of Aberdeen, to the north. Five kilometers, say, on the Realm Highway—wide street two blocks west of here."

"I'll need a ground car."

"Car theft too!"

"Requisition in the service of the Realm," said Cade austerely. "You need have no part in it." Theft—requisition. Requisition—theft. How odd things were outside the Order! And sometimes how oddly interesting! He felt a little shame at the thought, and hastily reminded himself: *Gunners march where the Emperor wills—that is their glory.* Yes; march in soft-soled commoners' shoes, in a requisitioned ground car.

It would be easy—a pang went through him. How easy had it been for the girl? He would investigate with the greatest care. She might suffer from her association with him now that he had broken out. The Klin Servicemen would undoubtedly mistreat her unless they were made aware that his eye was on them. He had seen last night that they were not above petty personal vengeance. Not Teachers, they were nevertheless supposed to be the Arm of Klin; as the Teachers kept order in men's minds, the Watchmen kept order in the body politic. But what, after all, could you expect from commoners? He would have to let them know that his eye was on them in the matter of the girl.

"Here's a good one," said Fledwick. "From my own shop." Cade surveyed a Glory of the Realm ground car, parked and empty. Fledwick was peering through the window and announced with satisfaction: "Gauge says full-charged. It will get us there."

"Locked?" asked Cade. "I'll take care of—"

Fledwick waved him back calmly. "I happen to be able to handle this myself, because of my, well, familiarity with the model." The little man took off his belt, a regulation Klin uniform belt, to all appearances, until, surprisingly, it turned out to be very thin leather, folded triple. From within the folds he took a flat metal object and applied it to the Glory car's lock. There were clicks and the door swung open.

Cade stared at the Klin Teacher as he carefully replaced the object in his belt. Fledwick cleared his throat and explained: "I was planning to get one of the Glories out of savings from my meager stipend. There's a clever fellow in the lock shop who makes these, uh, door openers and I thought how convenient it would be to have one if I should ever mislay my combination."

"For the car you hadn't bought yet," said Cade.

"Oh. Oh, yes. Prudence, eh, sir? Prudence."

"That may be. I shall leave you now; there is no need for you to accompany me further and you know, I suppose, that Gunners may consort with those outside the Order only if it is unavoidable. I thank you for your services. You may find pleasure in the knowledge that you have been of service to the Realm." Cade prepared to enter the car.

"Sir," said Fledwick urgently, "I'd find more pleasure in accompanying you. That pardon you mentioned . . ."

"It will be sent to you."

"Sir, I ask you to think that it might be a little difficult to find me. All I desire is to see my humble lectory again, to serve fittingly in expounding the truth of Klin to the simple, honest workingfolk of the Glory shop, but until I get the pardon I'll be—perforce inaccessible."

"Get in," said Cade. "No, I'll drive. You might absent-mindedly pocket the steering panel." He started the car and gunned it down the street toward the Realm Highway.

"Hold it at fifteen per," Fledwick warned. "The radar meters kick up a barrier ahead if you speed."

Cade kept the car at fifteen with his eyes peeled for trouble—and open as well to a host of curious sights. The broad highway was lined with merchandising shops. Shops and shops selling foodstuffs in small quantities to individuals. Shops and shops selling commoners' garb, each only slightly different from the next. Shops and shops selling furniture for homes. It seemed such folly!

Fledwick turned on the ground car's radio; through the corner of his eye Cade saw him tuning carefully to a particular frequency not automatically served by the tap plates.

Why, Cade wondered, couldn't they all be sensible like

the Order? A single garb—not, he hastily told himself, resembling in any way the uniform of the Armsmen. Why not refectories where a thousand of them at a time could eat simple, standardized foods? His mental stereotype of a commoner returned to him: lax, flabby, gorging himself morning, noon and night.

How good it would be to get into the Chapter House in time for a plain breakfast, and to let the beloved routine flow over him. He knew it would quench the disturbing thoughts he had suffered during the last days. It was all a wonderful proof that the Rule of the Order was wise. *Nor shall any Brother be exposed to the perils of what lies without his Chapter House or the Field of Battle. Let Brothers be transported, by ground if need be, by air if possible, swiftly from Chapter House to Chapter House and swiftly from Chapter House to the Field of Battle.*

How right and fitting it was! The perils were many. Uncounted times he had let his mind be swayed from the Order and his duty in it. When he woke today he had almost willfully chafed at the morning meditation. He could feel the warmth of the Order that would soon enfold him—

"Cade!" shrilled Fledwick. "Listen!"

The radio was saying on what must be the official band: "—claiming to be the late Gunner Cade of France and the unbooked Klin Teacher Fledwick Zisz. Use medium-range gas guns. The Cade-impostor is known to be armed with a gas gun, and has the strength of a maniac. Zisz is unarmed and not dangerous. Repeat, all-Watch alert: bring in two men escaped this morning from Seventh District Watch House. They are an unidentified man claiming to be the late Gunner Cade of France—" It droned through a repeat and fell silent.

"They haven't missed the car yet," said Cade.

"They will," Fledwick assured him mournfully. "Or they have missed it and haven't connected it with us yet." He was gloomily silent for three blocks and then muttered angrily: "Unarmed and not dangerous!" He fingered the gas gun through his blouse. "Unarmed indeed! Sir, a little way more and we're out of the city. If they haven't got the noose tight yet—"

"Noose?"

"Blocking of exits from the city by Watchers. They'll

have every gate covered soon enough, but if they don't know about the car they'll cover the public transports first. We do have a chance." It was the first faint note of hope Fledwick had permitted himself.

Cade drove on at a steady fifteen per. The sun was up and traffic moving in the opposite direction, towards the city, grew heavier by the minute. Once they passed a city-bound car trapped by speed bars that had risen, cage-like, from the paving to hold the speeder for the Watch.

"They stop at the city gates," said Fledwick. "After that, you can speed up. The Watchers have nothing faster than this."

The noose was not yet tight. They rolled easily past a sleepy Watchman at the gate. Either he hadn't received the alert, or he assumed District Seven was no worry of his. Gunner's instinct kept Cade from taking Fledwick's advice and speeding. He rolled the car on at an inconspicuous twenty per, and the decision was sound. A green-topped Watch car from the city passed them and Fledwick shriveled where he sat. But it kept going on its way, never noticing the fugitives.

The highway was now dotted with cars. Just ahead, and off to the left, was a grey crag. "Chapter House," said Fledwick, pointing, and Cade sighed. The whole insanely unfitting episode at last was drawing to a close.

The radio spoke again: "To all Armsmen and Watchmen." The voice was vibrant and commanding. "To all Watchmen *and* Armsmen," said the voice again, slowly. "This command supersedes the previous all-Watch alert concerning the Cade-impostor and the unbooked Klin Teacher Fledwick Zisz. Both these men are heavily armed and both are dangerous. They are to be shot on sight. Armsmen: shoot to kill. Watchmen: use long-range gas guns. New orders for Watchmen and Armsmen both are: *shoot on sight*! These men are both dangerous. There is to be no parleying; no calls to surrender; no offer or granting of quarter. Your orders are to shoot on sight. No explanation of any Armsman or Watchman who fails to shoot on sight will be accepted.

"Description and records follow . . ."

Cade, in frozen shock, had slowed the car to a crawl, not daring to make a conspicuous stop. He listened to fair physical descriptions of both of them. His "record" was criminal insanity, homicidal mania. Fledwick's was an interminable list of petty and not-so-petty offenses of the something-for-nothing kind. He too was described as a homicidal maniac.

"You're armed and are dangerous now," Cade said stupidly.

His answer was a volley of wild curses. "You got me into this!" raved the little man. "What a fool I was! I could have done my five years standing on one foot! I had friends who could have raised my fine. And you had to bully me into making a break!"

Cade shook his head dazedly. Fledwick's flood of rage poured over him and drained away, powerless to effect him after the impact of the radio announcement.

"But I *am* Gunner Cade," he said quietly, aloud, as much to himself as to the unbooked Teacher.

8

"IT'S A MISTAKE—that's all," Cade said numbly.

"Very well." The little man's voice was acid. "Before we are killed because of this curious mistake will you decide on a course of action? We're still approaching your Brothers' House, and I want none of their hospitality."

"You're right," said Cade. "The Brothers," he said, feeling an unwarranted note of apology creeping into his voice, "the Brothers would obey the official-frequency command. It's their duty. I would myself, though the command was most—unusual. I don't think I've ever heard its like, not even for the worst criminal."

Fledwick was past his first fury. He studied Cade's bewilderment and said slowly: "Back in the cage, when I saw you fix the lock, I thought you were either a Gunner or a master burglar—the greatest master I ever heard of. And when you laid out five Watchers without working up a sweat I thought you were either a Gunner or a master burglar *and* the greatest strongarm bucko I ever saw. But when you tossed away that gas gun because it wasn't fitting, I *knew* you were a Gunner. Cade or not, you're a Gunner. So it's a mistake, but what can we do and where can we go?"

Cade suddenly laughed. The Order was perfect after all; the answer was so easy. He sent the car swinging in a bumpy U-turn over the parkway strips. "To the Gunner Supreme!" he said.

"The Gunner Supreme," echoed Fledwick blankly. "The chief of all the Gunners. Wouldn't he shoot us twice as fast as an ordinary Gunner? I don't understand."

"No, you don't," said Cade. He tried to think of some way to make the wonderful presence clear, knowing he would fail. Of all things in the Order, the meaning and being of the Gunner Supreme had most of all to be *felt*. "We in the Order are Brothers," he carefully began. "He is the father. The Power Master disposes of us to the several Stars, but the assignment is without force until it has been sealed with the seal that is in the gun-hilt of the Gunner Supreme.

"He touches his gun to ours before we first put them on as Armigers. If he didn't touch them we wouldn't be actual members of the Order. The memory of him touching our guns steadies our hands and makes our eyes keen and our wits quick in battle."

And there was more he could never tell to anybody. Those in the Order knew it without telling; those outside would never know. There were the times you didn't like to remember, times when your knees trembled and you sweated advancing into fire. Then you thought of *him*, watching you with concern clouding his brow, and you stopped trembling and sweating. You felt warm and sure advancing into fire to play your fitting part.

"This paragon of Gunners—" began Fledwick ironically.

"Silence, thief! I will not tolerate disrespect."

"I'm sorry . . . may I speak?"

"With decorum."

"You were right to rebuke me." His voice didn't sound quite sincere, but he had, Cade reflected, been through a

60

lot. And, being what he was, he didn't realize that the problem was *solved*—that the Gunner Supreme would understand and everything would be all right again. "Where," Fledwick asked, "does the Gunner Supreme live?"

From beloved ritual Cade quoted the answer: *"Nearby to the Caves of Washington, across the River Potomac to the south, in a mighty Cave that is not a Cave; it is called Alexandria."*

"The Caves of Washington!" squalled Fledwick. "I'll take my chances with the Watchers. Let me out! Stop the car and let me out!"

"Be still!" Cade yelled at him. "You ought to be ashamed. And educated man like you mouthing the follies of ignorant commoners. You *were* a Teacher of Klin, weren't you?"

Fledwick shuddered and subsided for a moment. Then he muttered: "I'm not such a fool. You know yourself it's dangerous. And don't forget, I was born 'an ignorant commoner.' You sprang it at me before I had time to think, that's all. I felt as if I were a child again, with my mother telling me: 'You be good or I'll take you to the Caves.' I can remember her very words." He shuddered. "How could I forget them?"

" 'I'll take you the Caves.

" 'And the Beetu-Nine will come and tear your fingers and toes off with white-hot knives of metal.

" 'And the Beetu-Five will come and pepper you with white-hot balls of metal.

" 'And the Beefai-voh will come and grate your arms and legs with white-hot metal graters.

" 'And last, if you are not a good boy, the Beethrie-Six will come in the dark and will hunt you out though you run from Cave to Cave in the darkness, screaming. The Beethrie-Six, which lumbers and grumbles, will breathe on you with its poison breath and that is the most horrible of all for your bones will turn to water *and you will burn forever.*' "

Fledwick shuddered and said feebly: "The old bitch. I should have kicked her in the belly." He was sweating greasily from his forehead. "I'm not a fool," he said belligerently, "but you don't deny there's *something* about the Caves, do you?"

Cade said shortly: "I wouldn't care to spend a night there, but we're not going to." Fledwick' reminiscence of his mother's threat had shocked him. No wonder, he thought, commoners were what they were. There was nothing in the Caves—he supposed. One simply, as a matter of course, calmly and rationally avoided the horrible things.

"Alert, all Armsmen and Watchmen!" said the radio. It wasn't the same vibrant, commanding voice that had issued the "Shoot on sight" order, but it was bad news—the bad news Cade had been expecting since then. "The Cade-imposter and the unbooked Klin Teacher Fledwick Zisz are now known to have stolen Glory of the Realm ground car AB-779. That is Glory of the Realm ground car AB-779. Watchmen are to shoot the occupants of this car on sight with long-range gas guns. When the occupants are paralyzed Watchmen are to take them with all possible speed to the nearest Chapter House of the Order for immediate execution by Armsmen. Armsmen's orders are unchanged. Shoot to kill; destroy the ground car on sight; kill the occupants if seen outside the car. That is Glory of the Realm ground car AB-779."

The broadcast cut off and the only sound in Glory of the Realm ground car AB-779 was the soft whimpering of Fledwick.

"Keep your nerve, man," Cade urged. "We'll be out of here in a moment." He stopped the car and rummaged through its map case for the Washington Area sheet. Then he stepped out of the car and yanked Fledwick out bodily, after him. Finally, Cade set the car's panel on self-steering at twenty per and opaqued the windows before he started it cityward on the highway.

Standing in the roadside scrub, the little thief followed the vanishing car with his eyes. "Now what are we going to do?" he asked lymphatically.

"Walk," said Cade grimly. "That way we may live to reach the Supreme. And stop snivelling. There's a good chance that an Armsman will spot the car and burn it without knowing it's empty. And then they won't have any easy time deciding that we got away."

The little man wouldn't stop sobbing.

"See here," said Cade. "If you're going to be like this

all the way, it'll be better for both of us if you dig in somewhere and take care of yourself for a few days while I make it alone:"

The unbooked teacher gave a last tremendous sniff and declared shakily: "No cursed chance of that, Gunner. Lead the way."

Cade led the way across a stubbly field for a starter.

For the Gunner the five days of overland march were refreshing and reassuring. Here at last was something familiar, something his years of training had fitted him for, something he understood completely. And to his surprise, Fledwick was no burden.

On the first day, for instance, they crawled on their bellies up to the chicken yard of a food factory through its great outlying vegetable fields. Cade was suddenly chagrined to discover that he didn't know what to do next. In action, if there was food you demanded it or took it; if there was none you went without. Here there was food—and it would be self-destruction to seize it in his usual fashion. But Fledwick's unusual belt gave up another instrument that sheared easily through the aluminum wire. Fledwick's pockets gave up peas he had picked and shelled along the way, and he scattered a few through the gap in the wire. A few repetitions and there were clucking chickens on their side of the barrier. The little man pounced silently four times and they crawled back through the vegetable field with a brace of fowl each at their belts.

After that Cade left the commissary to Fledwick, only reminding him that he did not eat meat before sundown and warning him that he wouldn't look kindly on Fledwick devouring a chicken while he chewed carrots.

Once they thought they were in danger of discovery. At an isolated paper mill on the second day they saw Watchmen, a dozen of them, drive up and fan out to beat a field—the wrong one. If they had picked the right one, Cade could have slipped through them with laughable ease, and so perhaps could Fledwick. Cade guessed he would be expert enough at slipping across an unfamiliar room in the dark without betraying himself by squeaks and bumps. From that to a polished job of scouting and patrolling was not as far a cry as he would have thought a few days earlier.

After the incident at the paper mill Cade surrendered to the ex-Teacher's pleading that he be taught the use of the gas gun. Disdainfully, for he still disliked handling the weapon, Cade stripped it a few times, showed Fledwick the correct sight-picture and told him that the rest was practice—necessarily dry-runs, since the number of pellets was limited. Fledwick practiced faithfully for a day, which was enough for the ignoble weapon in Cade's eyes. He went to some pains to explain to the ex-Teacher that gas gun and Gun were two entirely different things—that there was a complex symbolism and ceremony about the Gun of the Order which the gas gun, weapon of commoners, could not claim.

Cade learned as well as taught. In five days, it seemed to him, the cheerful conversation of the little man told him more about the world outside the Order than he had learned in the past thirteen years. He knew it was none of his affair to listen as Fledwick told of the life in shops and factories or the uses of restaurants, theaters, entertainment, radio, and dives. He consoled himself with occasional self-reminders that he didn't ask—he just listened. And there was a good half that he didn't understand because of linguistic difficulty. Fledwick had a twinned vocabulary. Half of it was respectable and the other half was a lively argot, richly anatomical, whose roots were in a shady world Cade had never known. Here and there a word was inescapably clear because of context.

Less articulate himself, Cade still tried to interpret to the ex-Teacher the meaning that the Order and its life had for him, a Gunner. But he found that although Fledwick sincerely admired the Order, he did so for all the wrong reasons. He seemed incapable of understanding the interior life—the rich complexity of ritual, the appropriateness of each formal thought, the way each Armsman moulded his life to Klin. Cade sadly suspected that the ex-Teacher saw the Gunner Supreme as a sort of glorified Klin Service Deskman. He could not seem to realize that, merely by *being himself*, the Gunner Supreme made the interior life of the Order tangible, that he was the personification of fitness and decorum. But Cade decided he could forgive Fledwick a lot after he had snared a plump turkey without a single gobble an hour before sundown.

The third afternoon Cade spent a full hour over his maps trying to avoid an inevitable decision. That night he insisted on a march of five kilometers by starlight alone. They woke at dawn, and Fledwick gasped at what he saw to the south.

"Is it—?" he asked hoarsely.

"It's the Caves of Washington. Skirting them fairly closely—three kilometers or so—is the only way we can avoid a huge detour around thickly-populated areas. I was afraid you'd balk if you saw them first by daylight." Cade did not add that he had feared he would have balked himself. He cheerily asked: "Did you ever think you'd spend a night this close to the Caves?"

"No," Fledwick shuddered.

They breakfasted on stolen—or requisitioned—fruit while Cade, less calm than he appeared, studied the battered skyline to the south. It was a horrible thing: a rambling mound of grey stone, with black gapings in its like eyes and mouths. Toward the peak there was a thing like the vertebrae of a man's backbone outlined against the morning sky. It was as though some great, square shaft had toppled and shattered where it struck. It was a horrible thing, and Arle, the Gunner Supreme, lived in a mighty Cave that was not a Cave. In the shadow of Washington, not even the negative was reassuring. Washington was a horror. It made him think of obscenities like firing from a flier. Or the women at Mistress Cannon's.

Cade found himself unable to swallow the fruit pulp. "Let's march," he growled at Fledwick, and the little man scrambled to his feet fast. They skirted the Caves with a generous margin and Fledwick kept up a running stream of nervous chatter—about places like Mistress Cannon's, it happened.

For once, in his nervousness, Cade asked a direct question. Had Fledwick ever heard of a woman wearing the garter who spoke unlike a commoner and had such-and-such eyes, hair and manner? The ex-Teacher badly misunderstood. He assured Cade that after this mess was cleared up, any time the Gunner was in Aberdeen he he could fix him up with the nicest piece who ever wore the garter and he would personally guarantee that Cade would never notice if she spoke like a commoner or a starborne—

Cade thundered at him and there was total silence until they reached the shining Potomac.

Fledwick couldn't swim. Cade made him water wings by tying his trouser cuffs, whipping them through the air until they ballooned and drawing the belt tight. He had to push the half-naked little thief into the river and toss the wings to him before he'd believe that the elementary field expedient, trusted by Armsmen for ten thousand years, would work. Cade towed him across and they dried out on the south bank as the Gunner oriented his map.

"That's it," he said, pointing to the East. And he felt covered with dirt for having given a thought to the commoner girl while he was this close to the Gunner Supreme.

Fledwick only grunted doubtfully. But when ten minutes of brisk walking brought them to a clearer view of the pile he stopped and said flatly: "It's more Caves."

"Oh, you fool!" snapped Cade. "*A mighty Cave that is no Cave* are the words. And you used to be a Klin Teacher! It obviously means that it looks like a Cave but isn't to be feared like one."

"Obvious to you, perhaps," Fledwick retorted. "But then so many things are perfectly clear to you."

"This is not one of them," the Gunner answered stiffly. "I intend to walk around it at a reasonable distance. Are you coming or aren't you?" Fledwick sat down obstinately and Cade started off to circumnavigate the gloomy, dome-shaped mound that should be the residence of Arle. It looked like Caves, right enough . . . he heard Fledwick pattering after him and declined to notice the little man when he caught up.

They marched around the crumbling dome, about three hundred meters from its rim—and it began to assume a shape on its western front that exactly justified the traditional description. The Cave that was no Cave was a gigantic building from one side and a mouldering ruin from the other.

"Fives," murmured Cade abstractedly studying it.

"Eh?" asked Fledwick, and the Gunner forgave him

for the sake of someone to tell his puzzling discovery to.

"Fives—five floors, five sides, a regular pentagon if it were not half cave, and I think five rings of construction of which we see only the outermost."

"Drop!" snapped Fledwick, and Cade dropped.

"Guards," muttered the ex-Teacher. "Armsmen? Watchmen?"

Cade studied the insignificantly small figures against the huge facade.

"Armsmen," he said, heavy-hearted. "We must assume they have received the order to kill us. We will have to wait until night to slip in and bring this before the Gunner Supreme himself. I would trust no one below him."

9

THEY SETTLED THEMSELVES in good cover on a grassy mound half a kilometer from the Building of Fives. Fledwick turned face-down and dozed off. The five days had taken a lot out of the city-bred man, Cade thought, but he'd been a good companion through it all: clever and quick, though no Armsman, useless only when his sharp mind raced ahead of his courage and petrified him with expected terrors.

For Cade there was no sleep. With his eyes trained steadily on the Building of Fives one part of his mind accumulated and stored the information he needed—the pattern of patrol, the number of guards, time between meetings at sentry posts, the structure of the building and the flesh and bones of the terrain around it. And all the while he pondered the deeper problem he had to solve.

Their chances of getting in were good. Without pride—*pride is a peril*—Cade knew he was among the best of the Emperor's Armsmen, but the necessary feat savored of the impossible. It was too much to expect that he, practically alone, could outwit or overcome a company of sentries. If he failed to pass them and so did not come into the presence of Arle, the Supreme, there had to be a way of getting him the word, whether Cade lived or died.

He ripped off a square of his ragged shirt for writing paper—and there was a flexible little knife Fledwick had casually extracted from his belt and lent him to eat with. A tiny puncture in the middle of each fingertip of his left hand. Then carefully, painfully, one finger at a time, he squeezed the drops of blood out until the friction pads were smeared with red. He pressed each finger to a once-white diamond in the patterned fabric of the shirt.

With a few more drops on the knife point he could write, one letter to a diamond:

CADE DID
NOT DIE
AT
SARRALBE
CAIRO
MYSTERY
BALTIMORE

That was enough. They could identify the prints, and perhaps even the blood. They could go to the house of the hag who had poisoned him, raid the Mystery with its underground corridors, check on the Watch House's "impostor," piece together the story—a thing he might not live to do.

Cade wiped the blade and his fingers to leave no signs that would puzzle or frighten Fledwick. The ragged cloth from his shirt he knotted about a small stone and dropped in his pocket.

With the last light of the sun the guard was changed at the House of Fives. Cade breathed easier when he saw that the night guard was no heavier than the day. It was a guard of honor, nothing more. All around the side that was not ruins paced single sentries on lonely fifty-meter posts, meeting under arc lights, turning to march through the dark until they met at the light marking the other end of the patrol. It was understandable. The staring cave mouths were fearsome enough to need little guarding.

Cade nudged his partner awake with his bare toes, broken through the ruins of commoners' sandals.

"Is it time?" Fledwick asked.

The Gunner nodded and explained. In two more hours the first alertness of the guards would have worn off and the lassitude of a ceremonial guard mount would be creeping on . . . not yet strong enough for them to fight against it. Every commander knew that time of night, the time to take green or lazy troops by surprise and teach them a lesson in alertness those who lived would never forget.

They would use their two hours until then to make the approach to the building. Fledwick chewed on a stolen turnip and finally asked: "And then? When we're there?"

Cade pointed to one particular arc light. Behind it, to the right, gaped the black emptiness of a cave mouth, barely distinguishable from shadows the arc lights cast of jagged rock on smoother rock. As they watched, two Gunners came in view, approaching with metrical precision from opposite sides to meet exactly under the light, saluted—gun to brow—and wheeled and marched off like synchronized puppets.

"Watch *him*," Cade pointed. "The one with the red stripe." Together they watched while the Gunner disappeared again into the blackness and waited until he emerged again, thirty meters beyond, in the brightness of the next sentry post. Here the arc lights showed not gaping ruins but the smooth surface of the building proper. Somewhere in between, invisible, was the junction of ruins and buildings.

"He's our man," said Cade simply.

"A friend of yours, sir?" asked Fledwick, over-politely.

"He's a Marsman," said Cade, ignoring the flippancy. "The Marsman has not been born who can meet an Earth Gunner in combat and win. Their training is lax and their devotion is lacking. We will take him in the dark, halfway between posts, silently. If we work swiftly and all goes well I will have time to take his cloak, boots and helmet and make his next round to the sentry post. If there is no time for that, I am afraid we will have to use the—gas gun—to stun the approaching sentry. Then," he concluded with a shrug, "we have the full pacing time to make our entrance."

Fledwick spat out a fibrous bit of turnip and stared

across the field at the sputtering lights. At last he looked up at the Gunner.

"The *full* pacing time? Almost a *whole* minute?"

"Fifty-three seconds. Even you can move that fast," Cade said scornfully.

"You noticed there were bars on the gates—sir?"

Cade was losing his temper. "I noticed," he growled. "I'm not a fool of a commoner."

"No, sir. I'm very much aware of that. Would you tell a fool of a commoner how we'll get through the barred gates in fifty-three seconds?"

"Serve you right if I didn't. But I can't expect you to show the courage of a Brother. We won't enter the barred gates at all. We'll go through the unbarred cave. It's got to lead into the Building." Cade's impassive face betrayed nothing—not that he was sure he lied; not that he knew death was minutes away for both of them. "We're starting now." He began to work his way down the hillock, ignoring frantic whispers from behind. At last rustling grass and heavy breathing told him that Fledwick was following. He smiled. The noise, he suspected, was to worry him and make him angry. But he knew that when silent sneaking was needed, Fledwick would deliver.

Ten meters down he paused. "You may stay behind if you like," he whispered. "I shall not think ill of you."

He waited in the dark and grinned at a sound between a curse and a sob, followed by more of the rustling and heavy breathing.

"Quiet!" he whispered sternly, and they began the passage.

A full two hours later they crept up to the very edge of the patrol posts and separated. Cade, crouching, thrilled to the awareness of all his muscles tensing for the spring. It was almost disappointingly easy when the split-second came and the Marsman fell silently, perhaps forever, on the concrete path. The neck blow was never certain—either way. Cade had tried not to hit too hard. To kill a Brother in combat was fit and glorious, but never had he heard of any precedent for what he did.

He stripped the silent figure with desperate haste and threw the garments onto himself. Cloak and *the Order wraps the Realm*; Helmet and *protects the Emperor*; Boots and *march where the Emperor wills*.

But the cursed boots wouldn't fit. He looked up and saw in the distance the opposite sentry approaching, almost in the circle of light. With infinite relief he heard the small hiss of the gas gun and saw the sentry drop, with only one arm in the pool of light beneath the arc. Now Cade no longer needed boots. He buckled on the Marsmans' gunbelt and felt sudden wild optimism come with the familiar weight on his hip. He flipped the message-wrapped stone from the pocket of his commoner's shirt under the cloak and dropped it by the felled Marsman. From somewhere Fledwick crept up beside him and together they raced for the yawning black hole in the ragged, moldering wall.

Cade leaped clear of the cave-mouth's jagged edge and found sure footing on the rubble inside. Fledwick couldn't make it. Cade hauled him in, shaking violently and gasping for breath. But Fledwick picked himself up and stumbled after Cade into the deepening darkness of the interior.

They heard voices and tramping boots, and a clear shout: "In here—loose rock—they went *inside*!"

There was anger in the voice, but something else too: awe.

Cade had not let himself think until now of the enormity of this campaign. He had attacked a Brother off the Field of Battle, and perhaps killed him. He had assisted a commoner, and worse, an unbooked Teacher, into classified ground. If successful, he would invade without request or warning the private dwelling of the Supreme. But somehow overshadowing all this was the realization: *you are in a cave, and you are none the worse for it*.

A blast of hot air rolled through the cave, followed by pungent ozone. "They're shooting into the—the cave," he told Fledwick. "Stay down and nothing will happen."

For minutes afterwards the air crackled above them and Cade lay motionless, waiting and hoping to be spared to complete his mission. He thought again of the terrible roster of his crimes, but they had been the only possible answer to crimes worse than he knew could exist. That men should plot against the Emperor . . .

71

The firing stopped. The two or three bends they had rounded were ample protection from the direct effects of the fire, it appeared. Voices echoed down the cave again, and Cade had a mind's eye picture of Gunners peering in cautiously, but never considering pursuit.

"—wasting fire. Get torches—"

"—we'll smoke them out—gone inside—"

Cade groped along the floor with one hand and then pulled himself cautiously over to Fledwick. "Get up," he whispered. "We can't stay here."

"I can't move," a broken voice whimpered too noisily. "You go ahead."

Wounded, Cade realized—or hurt when they hit the ground. He scooped up the little man and tossed him over his shoulder. He did not groan, Cade noted with surprise and respect. The Gunner started forward.

First, get away from the light. They had food in their pockets, a full-charged gun, a dozen gas-gun pellets and a knife apiece. If they could find a spring for water, a place to put their backs against, they could hold out for a long time; and a flood of new energy came with the mounting excitement of the thought that they might yet come out of this alive!

They turned a corner of some sort that cut off the last light from the entrance. Cade's eyes adjusted to the gloom; he could make out a little of the shape and structure of the cave. And his eyes confirmed what his feet and groping hands had told him . . . what he had known before, and told to Fledwick, but had not dared believe: the cave was artificial, a disused corridor in a decayed old building.

Cave and Building were one!

What was Washington?

He wished he could tell Fledwick, and examine the idea in the light of his quick, acquisitive intelligence. But the little thief was taking his injury nobly; this was no time for explanations.

The cave—he couldn't think of it as anything else yet—seemed endless; doors were on either side. Any one of the dust-choked rooms might do for a stand, but there was no need to choose one until the sounds of pursuit were heard.

On his shoulder the limp bundle wriggled and came alive.

"You can put me down now."

"Can you walk?"

"I think so."

Cade lowered the man to the ground and waited while Fledwick found his footing.

"You mean," the Gunner demanded with as much outrage as he could pack into a whisper, "you're not hurt?"

"I don't *think* so." Fledwick was unashamed. "No, not a scratch."

Cade kept a contemptuous silence.

"Where do we go?" asked Fledwick.

"I think," he said slowly, "if we keep on going we'll find our way to the other part of the Building."

"The *other* part? You really mean it?" The little man darted from one side of the corridor to the other, feeling the regularity of the walls, clutching the door jamb. "It is part of the Building! But it was a Cave?"

"I told you—*a Cave that is not a Cave*. But you chose to believe in your beasts and horrors and other commoner's tales. Keep moving." His brusqueness covered a churning confusion in his mind. If the Cave was simply a disused part of a building, why weren't they being followed by the sentries?

They rounded an angle in the corridor—an angle of Fives—and saw at the end of the new corridor, far ahead, a dim, luminous rectangle, like the light around the edges of a closed door.

10

FLEDWICK redeemed himself.

There was no radionic lock in existence, Cade was certain, that he could not open. But this door was locked in a manner the Gunner had never seen before, with an ancient mechanical device no longer in use anywhere—except among commoners.

The ex-Teacher seemed perfectly familiar with it. He removed from inside his surprising belt a bit of metal that he twisted in an opening in the lock.

Cade stepped up first, as was his due. The door opened easily an inch or two, and then, before the Gunner could adjust his eyes to the light, there was a voice.

"Who is it? Who's there?"

Cade almost laughed aloud. He had been ready for a challenge, the blast of a gun, conquest or defeat or even emptiness. He had been ready for almost anything except a startled question in a feminine voice. He pushed the door open and Fledwick followed him into the room.

Only two things were certain about her: she was starborne, a Lady of the Court; and she was just as surprised as he.

She stood erect beside a couch on which, he guessed, she had been resting when the door opened. Her eyes were wide with surprise, fast turning to anger, and their brilliance was intensified by the color of her hair, expertly tinted to a subtly matching blue-green shade. Only the starborne would or could wear that elaborate coif: soft coils of hair piled high on the crown of her head and scattered with seemingly random drifts of golden dust. As her anger grew, her eyes, too, seemed to flash with cold metallic glints.

The headdress marked her rank and her clothes confirmed it. She wore the privileged sheer of the nobility, not fashioned into obscene pyjamas as he had seen it once before, but a fluid draping of cobweb-stuff whose color echoed just a trace of hair and eyes . . . as seafoam carries the faintest vestige of the ocean hue. The same golden specks that dusted her hair were looped in fairy patterns through the fabric of the gown, and here and there, where the designer's scheme planned to attract the eye, the flowing robe was caught and held by artful incrustations of the dust.

Cade stood speechless. He had seen Ladies of the Court in such attire before, though not so close or so informally. But the vision itself was responsible for only part of his consternation. It was her presence here, in the private dwelling of the Gunner Supreme, that took his breath away.

The woman raised a delicately fashioned tube of gold to her lips and sucked on it. In a small bowl at the other end a coal seemed to glow and when she dropped her hand again a cloud of pale blue smoke came from her lips and drifted lazily across the room to where Cade stood. Its heavy fragrance dizzied him.

"*Well?*" demanded the woman.

The Gunner formally began: "We come in Klin's service—" and could think of nothing more to say. Something was terribly wrong. Was it possible that he had mistaken the ritual description of the place? Had the slow afternoon of planning and the violence of the night gone for nothing? It seemed, from the furnishings and the woman, to be the palace of a foreign Star. And what could he tell the lady of such a one?

Fledwick leaped into the breach. Words began to pour from him with practiced ease: "Oh, starborne Lady, if you have mercy to match even the smallest part of your beauty, hear me before you condemn us out of hand! We are your lowly servants! We throw ourselves at your feet—"

"Silence, fool!" the Gunner growled. "Lady! This commoner speaks only for himself. I am the servant of no woman but of my Emperor and my Star. Tell me who is the master of this house?"

She scanned him coldly, her eyes lingering on the discrepancies of his gear. "It is enough for you to know that I am its mistress," she said. "I see you wear stolen garments while you speak of loyalty."

There was no possibility at all that she would believe him, but Cade was suddenly and unspeakably weary of subterfuge. "I am no usurper," he said quietly. "I am Gunner Cade of the Order of Armsmen; my Star is the Star of France. They say I died in battle for my Star at Sarralbe, but I did not. I came here for audience with my father in the Order, Gunner Supreme Arle; if you are the mistress here I must have come wrongly. Whatever place this is, I demand assistance in the name of the Order. You will earn the thanks of the Supreme himself if—"

She was laughing a low, throaty chuckle of honest mirth. "So," she said at last, her voice catching to the tag ends of her laughter, "you are Gunner Cade. Then you—" She turned to the little thief. "You must be the unbooked Klin Teacher. And to think that you two sorry creatures are the . . . the *dangerous* homicidal maniacs the whole world is searching for! How did you find your way in here? And *where* did you get those uniforms?" She was a Lady with commoners; unthinkable that they would not obey if her voice had the proper whip-crack in it.

"The cloak and helmet that I wear are stolen," Cade told her flatly. "I got them less than an hour ago from a sentry at your gate. I also stole—"

"Starborne, have mercy!" shrieked Fledwick suddenly. "I am frightened. I am only a poor thief, but they are right about him. Call your master! Quickly! Give us in his power, starborne Lady, before he—oh, Lady, *he has a gun!*"

"Stupid!" she chided him, still smiling. "If he has, he can't use it. Do you suppose that an Armsman's gun is such a simple affair that any madman can fire it?" She took a step backward.

"I don't know," Fledwick shrieked with fear. "I don't *know!* But I beg you, Starborne, call your Lord! Call him now, before *he* kills us both!"

Cade listened to it all, incredulous and immobile: that this miserable, snivelling little creature, whose life he had saved more than once, should turn against him now . . . betray him *after* the danger was over! It was unbelievable.

The woman was watching him, he realized, out of the corner of her eye. She stepped back once more. Well, let her call her Lord, then, Cade thought angrily. That would serve his purpose; that was what he wanted . . .

The Lady took another backward step, as Fledwick went on pouring out his gibberish fright, and at last Cade understood what the little man was really up to.

He reached beneath his stolen cloak, and drew the Marsman's gun. He did not aim it at the woman, but pointed it instead at Fledwick's quivering head. "Traitor!" he shouted. "For this you die!"

The woman's nerve broke at last. She hurled herself across the room to a silk-hung wall and stabbed frantically at a rosette.

"Don't shoot!" wailed Fledwick, finally permitting

himself a broad wink. "Please don't shoot! I'm only a poor thief—"

While he babbled, Cade made a menacing grimace or two and wondered who would turn up. Any Star at all would do. He'd have his gun on him, Fledwick could barricade the place and a message would be sent at last to the Gunner Supreme, with the life of the Star, or whoever was this Lady's master, as hostage for its delivery.

The woman took a hand. "Stop this brawling!" she screamed. Fledwick stopped. Her face was white but proud. "Hear me," she said. "I've summoned—help. If there is bloodshed in my chambers your death is certain. It will not be a pleasant one. But I have a powerful protector." Good; good; thought Cade. The more powerful the better. We'll soon get this farce over with.

"If you surrender now," the woman went on, fighting for calm, "you will get justice, whatever that may be in your case." She stood composedly, waiting for a gunblast or a plea for mercy.

There was no need to continue play-acting. Cade holstered the gun; confident that he could out-draw whatever retainers the master of the place might appear with. Out of admiration for her he swallowed a smile of triumph before he said: "Thank you, Lady. And thank you, Fledwick. You know strategies that I have never been forced to practice."

Mopping his brow, the little thief said from the soul: "I suppose you think I wasn't afraid of that gun?"

"What nonsense is this—?" the woman began indignantly, but she went no further. The door opened and someone strode into the room.

"Moia!" the man called, seeing only the woman against the silk-hung wall. "What is it? You called—"

He followed her eyes to the two strangers, and they stared back, Fledwick with curiosity and apprehension and Cade with astonishment and veneration. He had automatically drawn the gun. Just as automatically, when he saw the proud, straight head, the gold band on the swirling cloak, the gun with a great seal on its hilt, he performed the Grand Salute of the Order, which is rendered only to the Gunner Supreme.

77

Abased on the floor, Cade heard the sonorous voice ask with concern: "You are unharmed?"

"Up to now." The Lady's shaky reassurance ended with a forced laugh.

"Good. You may rise, Gunner. Show me your face."

"He's no Gunner!" the woman cried. "He's the commoner posing as Cade! And he has a gun!"

Calmly, the Supreme said: "Do not fear. He is a Gunner, though the cloak he wears is not his own. Speak, Brother. What brings you here in this unseemly manner?"

Cade rose and holstered the gun he had proffered in the salute. With downcast eyes he said: "Sir, I am Gunner Cade of France. I come with an urgent message—"

"I have already received it. A most dramatic message, most effectively delivered. I was studying it when the Lady Moia's signal reached me. It was your work?"

"Yes, sir. I was not sure I could reach your person alive. Sir, I must warn you that there is a conspiracy, perhaps a dangerously powerful one, against—"

"You will tell me of it shortly. Your—the cloak you wear. It seems familiar. Or have you become a Marsman?"

"It was the property of a Brother in your service, sir. I hope I did not kill him. I knew no other way to come to you."

"He is dead. I owe you thanks for that. He guarded an important post and guarded it badly. I shall see to it that a better man replaces him, before others less friendly than you find their way to this room." He turned from Cade and addressed the Lady Moia: "We shall leave you now to rest and recover from this upsetting incident. I promise you the guards will be taught an unforgettable lesson. I will be back when I have heard this Brother's story." Their eyes met and Cade saw them smile as no Armsman should smile at a woman, and no woman should smile at an Armsman.

"Your story will be better told in my own quarters," Arle spoke, without self-consciousness, to Cade. "The Lady Moia's apartment is no place for gory tales." He looked absently about the room until his eyes fell on the open corridor door. "Yes," he muttered. "We must change that lock. You." For the first time he seemed to notice Fledwick. "Close the door and bolt it. There will be a new lock tomorrow, my dear," he added to the Lady Moia. "Meanwhile the bolt will serve. Will you be all right by yourself for a while?" His fingers dipped into a carved gold box on the table and took out a golden smoking pipe, like the one she herself held, and placed it absently between his lips.

"I'm all right now," she assured him with sudden nervousness. "You needn't worry, and the lock may be replaced whenver it's convenient. The pipe, sir!" The Gunner Supreme started. "It's a new plaything of mine," she said, with self-deprecating humor. "I doubt that you would care for it."

Arle took the tube from his lips and studied it as though he had never seen it before. "A strange plaything," he said disapprovingly. "Come along, Gunner. And you too, I suppose." That was for Fledwick.

The room he took them to was the first reassuring thing Cade had seen in the place. It was a lesson room like those you could find in any Chapter House. The walls were bare, with standard storage space, there was a table in the center and Order benches all around. Cade sat down on Arle's permissive signal; Fledwick remained standing.

"Now," said the Supreme, "let me hear your story."

Cade started. The mad business had gone through his mind so often that it was like a verbatim recitation: dopping and capture by a hag in Sarralbe; resurrection in Baltimore; the Cairo Mystery. He had waited so long to tell it and gone through so much for the opportunity that somehow now the whole business was a disappointment. And there was one final lunatic touch: the Gunner Supreme appeared little more interested in hearing the tale than Cade was in telling it. From time to time Arle asked a question or made a comment: "How many were there? Did they seem to be local people or from overseas? A wicked business, Brother! No recognizable Armsmen, of course?" But his eyes were glazed with boredom.

Could he lie to the incarnate Order? He stumbled in his story; the question burned in his mind, and then the fire went out. He was lying to Arle by omission. He was leaving out the girl of the Cairo Mystery, who had twice tried, the second time with success, to save him from hypnosis. He let the Gunner Supreme understand that he had automatically come to his senses on the street and then gone on to his arrest—"with some wearer of the garter who was following me"—for impersonating an Armsman. The rest was straightforward, including the attack on the guard and the long trip through the corridor. He told how Fledwick had forced the lock, and the Supreme examined the ex-Teacher's curious key with more interest than he had shown up to that point.

"Very well," he said finally, tossing the key to the table. "And then?"

"Then we entered the—the Lady Moia's apartment." Cade choked on the words.

The Lady Moia's apartment. I am its mistress. The Lady Moia rang—and the Gunner Supreme, the incarnation of the Order of Armsmen, answered the call. And quickly! Cade raised his eyes to the fine, proud old face.

"You're troubled, Brother," said the Supreme. "If it will ease your mind, I should tell you that the Lady Moia is one of the graces of this place. Visiting Stars and their Courts are not exposed to the rigors of an Armsman's life in Chapter House. It is the Lady Moia's task to prepare fitting apartments for them and to treat them with the ceremony that I, of course, cannot extend."

To be sure. It was so sensible. But the smile he had seen was unexplained, and it was unexplained why the Lady Moia, hostess and social aide, could summon the personification of the Order by a push on a concealed button.

His mind a dazed whirl, Cade said hoarsely: "I thank you, sir. There is no more to tell. You know the rest." Then, at a nervous cough from Fledwick, he hastened to emphasize his virtual promise to the little man of a pardon on grounds of service to the Realm.

"Quite right," said the Supreme, and Fledwick relaxed with a sigh.

Three Gunners entered on a summons from Arle. He told them: "This is the former Klin Teacher, Fledwick Zisz. You recall that there is an order out to kill him on sight as a homicidal maniac. I find that order was a gross error. He is a worthy member of the Realm who appears to have committed some trifling indiscretions.

Bring me materials for writing him a pardon on grounds of Service."

Cade stole a look at the unbooked Teacher and felt inexplicable shame as Fledwick avoided his eyes. He could not forget Lady Moia's apartment himself; how could Fledwick? He wished he could take the little man aside to tell him earnestly that it was still all right, that the Supreme's outward forms didn't count; that his inner life must be in complete harmony with Klin, that the relationship between the Supreme and the Lady Moia wasn't—what it obviously was.

Cade sat silently as the Supreme wrote the pardon and signed it in the flowing script that had been on all his own assignments. One of the Gunners dripped a blob of clear thermoplastic on the signature and Arle rapped it smartly with the hilt of his gun. The Seal.

The same seal Cade had sometimes, in secret excess of sentimental zeal, pressed ritually to his chest, mouth and brow because it had been touched by the Gun of the Supreme. He felt himself flushing scarlet, and turned his eyes away. Abruptly he rose, without a permissive sign, and went to Fledwick. "You're out of it," he said. "I've kept my promise. You weren't a bad companion."

The little man managed to look directly at him. "It's good of you to say so. And it's been worth it. How I wish I could have a picture of your face when I got us those chickens!" It was insolence, but Cade didn't mind. And Fledwick said gently, with that puzzling look Cade had got used to, but could never understand: "I'm sorry."

That was all. The Supreme handed him the pardon and waited impatiently through the little man's lavish protestations of gratitude. "My Gunners here," he said, "will take you in a ground car to Aberdeen. I think you'll have no trouble with them for an escort. There you should present your pardon to the Watch House and that absurd order will be withdrawn. Doubtless you wish to leave at once.

"And you, Gunner," Arle continued, "it's long since you've been in a sleeping loft." He summoned a novice and ordered: "Take this Brother to the night guard's sleeping loft. He will need a complete uniform in the morning."

Cade performed the abject Grand Salute before he

left; the Gunner Supreme acknowledged it with an absent-minded nod.

11

THE EMPTY SLEEPING LOFT at least was real and fitting. Cade took a sleepbag from the wall, undressed, belted on his gun and infalted the bag. For weeks he had been thinking that this was the night he would sleep well. Now he knew it would not be so. What had he said to Fledwick? "You're out of it." A puzzling thing for him to say. Cade paced to the window. Five floors below was a courtyard formed by the outer ring of the Building of Fives, the next ring and two connecting spokes. All the many windows on the court were dark, but a thin sliver of new moon showed white concrete down below. It seemed to be an isolated wing. Cade stared down into the moonlit courtyard as though he could hypnotize himself into numbness.

All right, he told himself angrily. Think about it. Think about the look they exchanged. The bare pretense of interest on the Supreme's face. The absent-minded, habitual air with which he picked up the smoking tube. What do you know about it? What do you know except that you're a Gunner, and how to be one?

Maybe *that's* the way a Gunner Supreme is supposed to be. Maybe they tell you the things they do for your own good, because you're too much of a fool to understand that it's got to be this way because—because of good reasons. Maybe there's a time when they do tell you in secret and show you how it all fits in the Klin Philosophy, like everything else. Maybe the whole thing, from the poisoned cider on down to this sleeping loft, was a great secret test of your conduct. What do you know about it?

It was too frightening. He recoiled from the brink of such thoughts. They had no business in his head, curse

82

them! He was a Gunner and he knew how to be a Gunner. He tried to think shop-talk, the best kind of talk there is. What kind of duty you had here, how long a tour they gave you, whether there was ever a chance of action or whether it was all ceremony and errands.

Think about the Cave that is not a Cave—a curious place. It made you nervous to think that you had been in a Cave and that it had just been a corridor, without lumbering, grumbling beasts prowling its dark lights. This Building of Fives—had it been created ten thousand years ago like the Caves of Washington, building-half and all? Or had there first been the Caves and then the building constructed against it? A filthy thought crept into his mind. Half-formed, it said to him that if there was such a building and you were up in a flier and—*no!* What was wrong with him? He'd have to go to a corrective Teacher if this went on! Was this churning confusion what lunacy was like?

He crawled into his sleepbag. That at least was good. Some six thousand daily repetitions had formed a powerful habit-pattern. Gratefully he let some of the brief meditations drift soothingly into his mind and across it, ironing out the perplexities. And tomorrow he'd have a proper uniform again. Undersuit, shirt, hose, boots—*where the Emperor wills*—cape, helmet . . . Cade was asleep in the empty loft.

He dreamed of the Gunner Supreme threatening the Lady Moia with a gun, and the Lady Moia turned into the girl of the Cairo Mystery. He tried to explain respectfully to the Supreme that it wasn't the Lady Moia any more and that he had no business shooting her. "Cade!" the girl called faintly. "Cade! Cade!"

The Gunner sat up abruptly. That call was no dream. He ripped open the quick release of his sleepbag and peered through the window into the courtyard. Four figures were dark against the concrete, one of them smaller than the others.

There was some sort of flurry down there and he saw the smaller figure in full, no longer foreshortened. Somebody had fallen or been knocked down. Now he got up, expostulating and waving something white, and was knocked down again. He struggled to his feet and held out the white thing with a desperate, pleading gesture, not only in the arm but in every curve of his small, expressive body.

Fledwick!

Cade needed no more interpretation of the scene below. It was all there in the little thief's offer of the paper. Cade knew the white scrap was the pardon, written and sealed by the Gunner Supreme. And he saw one of the three other men snatch it impatiently from Fledwick and tear it across.

As if he were remembering the scene instead of seeing it enacted, Cade stood helplessly at his window, waiting. He saw Fledwick shoved against the blank wall and saw the other three draw guns. He saw the partner of his five-day march burned down by three guns of the Order, fired simultaneously at low aperture. And last he saw the three remaining figures separate, two to a door in the inner ring, one through a door directly below, into the building where he himself stood watching.

He was sick, then and there, and after the spasm passed he realized that he had seen murder: murder with guns of the Order, wielded by Armsmen at the command of the Gunner Supreme, after Arle himself had lyingly granted and sealed a pardon.

This was no secret into which he would someday be initiated; this was no test of courage or belief. This was no less than lies, treachery and murder at the command of the Order, incarnate, the Gunner Supreme!

The door to the loft opened silently and a figure slipped without noise across the floor to Cade's inflated sleepbag.

"Were you looking for me, Brother?"

The assassin spun to face the harsh whisper, gun in hand. He was burned down before he fully realized that his intended victim was not helplessly asleep.

Cade's thoughts were crystal-clear and cold. His burned body had been found once before in Sarralbe; it would now be found again, to buy him precious time until the assassin-Armsman was found missing. He rolled the charred body into the sleepbag he had occupied and slowly burned the flimsy fabric to a cinder with a noiseless discharge at minimum aperture. Presumably anybody within earshot had been alerted to the crash of one lethal blast, but not two.

Cade donned his medley of commoner's garb and ill-fitting uniform and slipped out along the way he had been led, through empty corridors, down empty ramps. He knew only one way out. The wing seemed to be deserted, and he wondered if it was because it held the apartment of the Lady Moia or because it was where murder was done.

The lock on the inner door to the Lady's apartment was radionic. Cade solved it quickly and slipped through to the cushioned outer chamber. The room was dimly night-lit, still fragrant with the smoke of the golden pipes and the subtler scent that the Lady wore herself. He saw the glitter of golden trinkets on the table—boxes, pipes, things whose use he couldn't guess at—and realized that he had not yet plumbed the depths of the impossible. He was about to become a thief.

He did not know where he was going or how he would get there, but clearly the Houses of the Order were barred to him. For the first time in his life he would need money. Gold, he remembered from childhood, could be exchanged for money, or directly for goods. He reached for the glittering display and filled all the big pockets of the commoner's cloak. The sum of trifling metal objects made a surprising weight.

There was a third door to the room, and it stood ajar. He tiptoed across the floor and peered through to the Lady Moia's bedroom. She was asleep, alone, and Cade felt somehow relieved. The beautiful dark head stirred on the white pillow, and he drew back. Unskillfully, he worked the mechanical latch of the door to the Cave, nervous at each scratching clicking sound it made. But in the room beyond the Lady slept on, and at last the door swung open.

When he had come in with Fledwick, fleeing through dark corridors at midnight, his terrain-wise eyes had automatically measured and his brain recorded every turn and distance. He was able to retrace his steps and find the Cave opening in a matter of minutes.

The ceremonies patrol was not yet changed. He saw, casing the Cave-mouth at intervals, a new man instead of the Mars-born gunner whose cloak was now on Cade's back, but Arle's promise to the frightened Lady had otherwise not been acted on. Clearly, the Gunner

Supreme had every confidence in his assassins. Cade stood within the shadow of the Cave-mouth and watched the Gunners on their sentry-go, silhouetted by starlight and arc light as they met and marched and met again.

The fools! he thought, and then remembered what a prince of fools he was himself, and had been since the day of his decision in his sixth year—until less than an hour ago.

Leaving the Cave-mouth was infinitely easier than entering. This time he knew what waited on the other side: nothing but acres of high grass in which a man could hide forever. A *man*. The thought had come that way, unbidden: *a man*. Not a *Gunner*.

Cade was only one more shadow between the sputtering lights, a streak of darkness that the routine-fuddled minds of the sentries never saw. Safe in the tall grass, he lay still for long minutes, until he was certain there had been no alarm. Then, cautiously, he began to inch along. At last, over a fair-sized rise of ground, he rose and walked, heading for the river.

Soon, very soon, he would have to decide where he was going and what he would do. For now, he knew that Aberdeen and Baltimore were to the north. He was at the Potomac river again in a matter of minutes, but he could not cross by swimming, or even with the aid of water-wings like the pair he had made for Fledwick only yesterday. The gold would have weighed him down, and he was stubbornly determined not to abandon it.

He trudged on along the southern bank of the river looking for a log big enough to float him and small enough to steer, or for an unguarded bridge. The first dawn light was creeping into the sky when he heard angry voices over the brow of a knoll. Cade dropped and crawled through the rank grass to listen.

"Easy with it, curse you!"

"You can do better? Do it and shut your mouth!"

"You shut your own mouth. Yell like that and we'll both wind up in the crock on a sump tap."

"I can do a sump tap standing on one foot."

"I hope you have to some day, curse you, if I'm not in on it. I got better things to do with my time than standing on one foot in the crock for two years."

"Just go easy on the smokers is all I asked—"

Phrases were familiar. "Standing on one foot through a tap in a crock" meant "serving a short prison term with ease." That much he had learned from Fledwick. The talkers were criminals—like him. Cade stood up and saw two commoners in the hollow below, loading a small raft with flat boxes.

It was a moment before they realized that they were not alone. They saw him on the knoll and stood paralyzed, while he strode down on them.

"What're you up to?" he demanded.

"Sir, we're—we're—" stammered one. The other had sharper eyes. "Hey!" he said coldly, after studying Cade for a moment. "What is this—the shake? You're no Armsman."

"It's not a shake," Cade said. Another phrase from Fledwick.

"Well, what is it? A man doesn't take a chance on twenty years for nothing. You're in half a uniform and even that doesn't fit. And the gun's a fake if ever I saw one," the commoner pronounced proudly.

The other was disgusted. "Me falling for a phony uniform and a fake gun! On your way, big fellow. I don't want to know you before you get crocked for twenty."

"I want a ride on your raft. I can pay." Cade took a gold smoking-pipe box from a pocket. He was about to ask: "Is that enough?" but he saw from their faces that it was, and more. "I also want some commoner's clothes," he added, and then cursed himself silently for the betraying "commoner's"—but they didn't notice.

"Sure," said the man who couldn't be taken in by a fake gun. "We can take you across. But I don't know about clothes."

"I can fix that," the other man said hastily. "You're about my size. I'll be glad to sell what I'm wearing. Of course I ought to get something extra for selling you the blouse off my back—?"

Cade hefted the box. There seemed to be a lot of gold in it, but how much gold was a suit of clothes?

The man took his silence as refusal. "All right," he said. "I tried," and stripped down to his undersuit. He wasn't nearly as big as Cade, but his clothes were baggy enough to cover him. As Cade methodically transferred his plunger from one set of garments to the other, their eyes bulged.

"You'd better bury your toy," one of them warned. "A fake gun's the same as impersonating."

"I'll keep it," said Cade, dropping the skirt of his tunic over the gun. "Now get me across."

Watching the last gold ornament disappear, the un-bluffable commoner said tentatively: "We have some more transportation."

"Hey," said the other.

"Oh, shut your mouth. Can't you tell when a gaff's on the scramble?"

So, Cade reflected, he was a gaff on the scramble, who needed transportation. "What have you got?" he asked.

"Well, my rog, we're on the distribution end for a smoker works. To a gaff that won't sound like much, but a sump tap is a tap same as for gaffing. We get them from—from the manufacturer and put them across the river. A ground car picks them up there. The driver could—"

"For two gawdies like that last one," his partner interrupted determinedly, "we'll take you to the driver, vouch for you and tell him to drop you off anywhere along his route."

"One gawdy," Cade offered cautiously, wondering what a smoker was.

"Done," the friendlier one said promptly. Cade fished for and handed over a box about like the last one. The commoner caressed it and said: "Let's have a smoker on the bargain. They'll never miss 'em." Without waiting for an answer he opened one of the flat boxes on the raft and took three pellets from it. The two commoners dropped theirs into aluminum tubes, lit up and puffed, and Cade realized at last that "smokers" went into smoking pipes like those fancied by the Lady Moia.

"Thanks," he said, dropping his pellet into a pocket. "I'll save mine." They gave him a disgusted look and didn't answer. He realized he had made a more-or-less serious blunder. There were fit and unfit things among commoners too, and he didn't know how many more unfit things he could get away with.

The pellets lasted only a minute or so, leaving the men relaxed and gently talkative while Cade strained his ears and wits for usable information.

"I smoker too much," one of the men said regretfully. "I suppose it's the temptation from handling the stuff."

"It doesn't do you any harm."

"I don't feel right about it. Shoving the stuff's a living, but if the Emperor says we shouldn't, we shouldn't."

"What's the Emperor got to do with it?"

"Well, the first Emperor must have made the sump tables about what you can do and what you can't do."

"Oh, no. The first Emperor and the sump tables were made at the same time. Ask any Teacher."

"You better ask a Teacher yourself . . . but even if the first Emperor and the sump tables did get made at the same time, I wouldn't feel right about it."

"That's what I told my girl. With her it's buy me this and buy me that, and now she wants a sheer dress from a sump shop and I told her even if she got it she couldn't wear it where anybody would see her and even if she wore it in private she wouldn't feel right about it."

"Women," said the other one, shaking his head. "The sump tables are a fine thing for them. Otherwise they'd all be going around like starbornes and you wouldn't have a green in your nick—there's the car. Let's get across."

Cade had seen the blink of lights across the bank. The raft shoved off with Cade sitting on the cases, one man poling and the other, in his underwear, hanging onto the edge. The car, on a highway that paralleled the river bank for a kilometer, was a large passenger car of non-descript color and perculiarly dirty identification numbers.

"Who's that?" demanded the driver, joining them. He was a big man run to fat, and had a section of three-centimeter bronze pipe in his fist.

"Gaff on the scramble. A real rog. We said you might drop him along the route."

"*Would, not might*," Cade said.

"Got troubles enough," said the driver. "Scramble on, duff." Duff was obviously a ripe insult. The driver hefted his bronze pipe hopefully. Cade sighed and flattened him with a medium-hard left into his belly. To the others he said: "Look, you—you duffs. Give me back one of those boxes. And if you make any trouble I'll take them both back."

They conferred by glances and handed one of the boxes over. Cade showed it to the driver, who was sitting up and shaking his head dazedly. "This is for you if you drop me off where I want."

"Sure, rog," the driver said agreeably. "But I can't go off my route, you understand. I can't lose my job for a little extra clink."

"I'm going to Aberdeen," said Cade, with abrupt decision.

"Sure thing. Now if you'll wait while we load—"

The flat boxes of smokers went into a surprising variety of places in the car—under the seats, inside the cushions, behind removable panels.

Cade watched, and wondered why he had chosen Aberdeen. After a minute he stopped trying. He had to begin somewhere, and it might as well be with the girl. She knew something—more than he did anyhow. And with Fledwick murdered, she remained the only person who had not betrayed him at any time since he plunged into the month-long nightmare of conspiracy and disillusion. Besides, he assured himself, it was sound doctrine. The last place they would expect him to go would be the one place he'd been caught before.

Still musing, he sat beside the driver. "Where in Aberdeen?" the man asked when they were on the road.

"You know, Mistress Cannon's?"

"Yuh. I deliver there," said the driver, obviously disapproving.

Cade risked asking: "What's the matter with the place?" It might be a nest of spies.

"Nothing. The old woman's all right. I don't care what kind of a dive you go to. I said I'd take you and I will."

Thirteen years of conditioning do not vanish overnight. Cade was guilty and defensive: "I'm looking for somebody. A girl."

"What else? You don't have to tell me about it. I'll take you there, I said. Myself, I'm a family man. I don't go to lectory every day like some people, but I know what's fitting and what isn't."

"You're running smokers," Cade said indignantly.

"I don't have to feel good about it and maybe I don't. I don't smoker myself. It's not my fault if a lot of ignorant duffs that got born common can't rest without smoker-ing like a Star and his court. Say 'The Emperor wouldn't like it' and they pull a long face and say 'Oh, it can't matter much and I'll give twice as much to the lectory and the Emperor'll like that, won',t he?' Fools!"

Cade feebly agreed and the conversation died. As the moralistic evader of the sumptuary laws covered his route, Cade let himself doze off. He knew a man who would keep a bargain once it was made.

12

AT EACH START and stop Cade half-opened an eye and went back to sleep again. But finally the driver shook his shoulder.

Cade woke with a start. Through the window, across three feet of sun-splashed, dirty paving he could see stone steps leading down to a heavy door. Ahead, another set of steps apparently led up to another door that remained out of his vision.

They were in a narrow alley, barely wide enough for the slightly oversized car. On either side, continuous walls of soot-dusted cement rose to a height of three or four stories above the ground. There were no windows, no clearly marked building lines, nothing to mark the one spot from another but dirt and scars on the aging concrete, and the indentations of steps at regular intervals along both sides.

The driver took three neatly packaged bundles from inside the arm-rest of the front seat, closed it and held them expectantly.

"Well?" he demanded. "Sitting there all day? Open it."

Cade stiffened, and then made himself relax. He was among commoners now and would be treated as one himself. It was a lesson he would have to learn as thoroughly as any back in Novice School. His life depended on these lessons too. "Sorry," he mumbled. "Cannon's?"

91

"Don't you know it?"

Cade opened the door and muttered: "Looks different by daylight." He followed the driver down the stone steps. The man knocked rhythmically, and the door opened a little. Cade knew the beefy face at once.

Elaborately ignoring the driver, Mistress Cannon said hoarsely: "The drinking room doesn't open until nightfall, stranger. Glad to see you then."

The driver said, with interest: "I thought he was a friend of yours. Gaff on the scramble. Some people I know said he's a rog."

Her faded blue eyes swung slowly from Cade's face down his multi-striped clothes to the ragged scandals he still wore, and returned as slowly to his face.

"Might have seen him before," she admitted at last, grudgingly.

"Me, and my—clinks, too," Cade said quickly. The rest was inspired: "Last time I was here one of your girls took everything you left."

The woman placed him at last. "She was no girl of mine," she insisted defensively.

The driver had had enough. "That'll do," he said. "Fix it up any way you want to between you. I'm behind time now."

The door creaked farther open.

"You wait here," the woman told Cade, and led the driver out of the room. It was the kitchen of the establishment. Cade wandered about, touching nothing, but examining with intense curiosity the unfamiliar miscellany of supplies and equipment.

The big food rooms of Chapter Houses where Cade had spent hundreds of hours as a Novice were no more like this place than—than an Armsman's sleepbag was like the Lady Moia's couch. The single thing he could identify was a giant infrabroiler in one wall; it was identical with those used in the preparation of the evening meat meal in the Houses. But there the similarity ended. Through the transparent doors of the cooler he saw not an orderly procession of joints and roasts but a wild assortment of poultry, fish, meat, and sea food, jammed in helter-skelter. Along the opposite wall were more fruits and vegetables than he had known existed—pulpy luxuries, he thought, for degenerate tastes.

There was to be recognized, at last, a cooker designed to mix and warm in one operation the nutritious basic mash on which Armsmen mainly subsisted. But here, instead of being a gleaming, giant structure it was a battered old machine perched on a high shelf almost out of reach. For some reason, Cade concluded, mash wasn't popular at Cannon's.

On other shelves around the room there were hundreds of bright-faced packages, containing unknown ingredients for use in a dozen or more specialized mixers and heaters whose equal Cade had never seen before. Over it all was an air of cheerful disorder, jumbled but purposeful comfort that struck for Cade a haunting note of reminiscence.

So many things these last few days had stirred old memories: memories of a childhood he had dismissed forever when he took his vows. Already, he realized, he was unfitted for the Order. The ritual and routine that had been as much a part of life as breathing had proved itself dispensable. At times it had even seemed like folly. A corrective Teacher, he thought—and then wondered whether he wanted to be corrected. Of course he wanted to get back into the Order. But the Gunner Supreme. . . .

He coldly dismissed his personal tangle of loyalties. The first thing he needed was information, and that meant the girl.

"No girl of mine," Mistress Cannon had said. And long ago: "If you come back, girlie, I may wrap a bar stool around your neck." That didn't matter. He needed a starting point; one well down into the criminal half-world in which the girl had moved with such assurance. You went from one person to the next in that world: from the smugglers to the driver to Mistress Cannon's. A smile spread over his face. What would he have said not long ago if someone had told him he'd need the good will of a minor crook to gain admission to a—what did he call it—a dive? He, a Gunner among the best?

"Man," said the hoarse voice, "don't smile like that: I'm not as young as I used to be and my figure ain't all it once was, but I'm not so old either I don't get butterflies in the belly once in a while." Mistress Cannon stood in the doorway, eying him with an absurd mixture of good-fellowship and flirtatiousness. "And by the Power!" she chortled, "he can blush too! Big as a house, and built like an armed man, and a smile to give you goosebumps, and he can blush yet! Well, we got some girls that like 'em that way. Me, I like 'em loaded." There was an abrupt change in her manner. "Lazar says you're on the scramble. What're you carrying?"

He opened his mouth to answer, but didn't have a chance.

"Big fellow, there's plenty rogs before you who spent a day or a month upstairs and no questions asked or answered. No safer place in Eastcoast until—trouble—blows over. But I can't do it cheap. Lazar brought you in and I like your face myself or I wouldn't do it for all the clink in Aberdeen. Protection comes high any place. Here you get it with a nice room, three meals and all the—"

The woman liked to talk, Cade thought weakly, and let her go on. What was she was saying amounted to good luck. He could stay here—and the driver had assumed that this was just what he'd wanted.

The woman stopped for breath, wheezing a little, and Cade seized the chance: "You don't have to worry about money. I'm—I'm loaded. I can pay whatever you ask." In all the colorful flow of words, that much had been clear.

"What with?"

He pulled out the first thing his fingers touched in an outer pocket. It was a tiny, glittering piece of jeweled uselessness, five tiny bells hung on a thin wire loop. It tinkled distantly with almost inaudible music as he put it on the table. The woman's eyes were glued on the golden bauble.

"Practically valueless," she said composedly when she looked up. "Too hard to get rid of."

"I didn't know," Cade said apologetically, reaching for it. "Maybe something else—"

"All right!" she exploded, shaken again by heaves of flabby laughter. "Outbluffed on the first try. You have the other one, of course?" Cade, searching his pockets for a mate to the bauble, realized vaguely that he was supposed to have done something clever. He turned out on the table all he had and poked through it.

"I'm sorry," he said at last. "It doesn't seem to be here."

The woman looked up dazedly from the array. "You're sorry," she echoed. "It doesn't seem to be here." She looked at him again, searchingly and for a long minute. "What made you come here?" she asked quietly.

"First place I thought of," he said. Something was wrong. What commoner notion of fitness and unfitness had he violated now?

"Or the only place," she said, musingly. "And don't tell me it was liquor you were out on that other night. Maybe the tart you were with couldn't tell the difference, but I've been around for a lot of years. I know drunk when I see it and I know dope, too. A youngster like you . . . well, now I know you're good for your room. But wandering around loaded with gawdies you don't half know the value of—didn't anybody ever tell you not to jab up until the job was *through*? And that means selling it after the pick, too."

Cade could make nothing of it. "If you have a room for me," he said patiently, "you'll be well paid. That's all I'm asking of you."

For some reason, she was angry. "Then that's all you'll get! And when you start to yell for the stuff don't expect me to run it for you. Come on!" She jerked open a door and led the way up dark stairs. To herself she was grumbling: "You can't make a man talk if he doesn't want to, not even to somebody who wants to help. Think they'd have more sense!"

At the stair head she produced a ring of keys like the one Fledwick had used. She opened a door with one and handed it to Cade.

"That's the only one there is," she said. "You're safe up here. If you get hungry or if you get off your darby perch and want some fun, you can try the drinking room."

He closed the door on her and studied his quarters. The room was not light or clean. The shelves in the storage wall were stuck. It didn't matter; there was nothing to store. The bed was an ancient foldable such as he had seen only in commoners' houses entered during action.

It was hard to remember: he was in a commoner's house now, and living as one. He turned the key, locking himself in. Then he dumped his treasure trove on the cot, fingering the pieces thoughtfully. He hadn't made much of her talk, but her face had shown she was immensely excited over the—the gawdies. Or did that just mean boxes? *Why* had she been excited? They could be exchanged for money, or food. Money could be exchanged for clothes, food, shelter, entertainment. Fledwick, too, had been that way about money, if he had understood correctly. The little man had habitually run great risk of imprisonment and shame for its sake. And the men on the raft—they had tried to get extra gawdies from him. It all meant that he had something commoners wanted badly, and a lot of it.

He lay down on the bed and found its pulpy lumps unbearable. The floor was better than the mattress. To find the girl he would have to face the drinking room. Recalling the night he had been there, he remembered the noise, the smells, the drink he had been given, the close air, the foolish women. But the bar was his reason for being there. The girl of the Cairo Mystery had found him there before; there he might find her now. He thought about clothes—he would need some. And boots—slippers, rather. As a commonor he could not wear boots. And clean clothes. Even a commoner would not wear the same things all the time, he supposed.

Mistress Cannon had anticipated him. She was waiting in the drinking room below with news.

"Wish you'd come down a little sooner. I had old man Carlin hanging around, then he said he had to hit. But he'll be around first thing in the morning. I would've sent him up, only I figured you were sleeping the jab off."

Was he supposed to know who old man Carlin was? He asked.

"Carlin? He runs the sump shop around here: sells court clothes on the side. Why those tramps are willing to pay such crazy prices for it I never knew. To give the boy friends a thrill behind locked doors, I guess. Back when I had it I would've beat a man's ears off if he couldn't get a thrill out of me without fancy-pantsy court sheers on. *You aren't from the District, are you?*"

He hesitated, startled by the gunblast suddenness of the question.

"That's what I figured," she said soberly, lowering her voice. "Listen." She bent across the table toward him, and a too-musky, too-strong scent issued from the deep cleft between her breasts. "You want some good advice, I can give it to you. Even if you don't want it. You're on the scramble and you jab—a bad combination—and you don't want to get pumped, not by me or any other old bat. All right, that's smart enough, and you got sense enough not to try to lie when you're jabbed up. But you don't have to get up on the darby perch either, like you did with me. Listen—"

She stopped to wheeze, and went on earnestly: "I come into my kitchen this afternoon, and found you standing there grinning at yourself, and you could of had the whole house with a gold ribbon tied around it. Ten minutes later, you're giving me your high-and-mighty starborne act, and you come damn near not having any room here at all. A fella with a face like yours, and that build, he's a fool not to make some use of it. You don't want to talk, man . . . smile!" She straightened up and waved to the newcomer farther down the bar. "I got to tend to customers," she said. "You got a handle I can call you by, in case they ask?"

Cade smiled inwardly at the absurd advice—and at the question that came fast after it. For the first time since he'd met the Mistress, he looked her fully in the eye. She was hardly a perilous female, after all, in spite of her loose talk. He remained silent, but slowly and deliberately he let the inner smile spread on his face.

"That's it!" she crowed, delightedly. "You're no fool! Hey, Jana!"

A willowy brunette detached herself from the group of girls talking in a corner while they waited for the place to fill. She walked with studied languor toward them; the silvery garter on her thigh pulled the flimsy stuff of her trousers tight against her at each step.

"Jana, I want you to meet a friend of mine," Mistress Cannon said. "Nothing's too good for my friend, Smiley!" She winked at him, a lewd and terrifying wink as massive as a shrug, and bustled off.

"That's some send-off you got, Smiley," said the girl.

Her voice was husky and, quite automatically she assumed the same position Mistress Cannon had, leaning far forward and compressing her shoulders. Some commoner notion, he thought uneasily, as he observed that it exposed quite a lot of her to a table-mate.

"Yes," he said stiffly. "She's been very good to me."

"Say, I remember you!" Jana said abruptly. "You were in here last week. And were you troubled, brother! Were you troubled!"

Suddenly she frowned: "What's the matter, Smiley?"

He couldn't help it. The shock of being addressed as *brother* in this place by this woman showed on him.

"Nothing," he said.

"Nothing?" she asked wisely. "Listen, I see you're not drinking—" Cade followed her glance and noticed there was a small glass of vile-smelling stuff on the table. He pushed it away. "—and I've been arguing with Arlene about it ever since—you remember her? The little blonde over there in the corner?" Hope flared wildly, and vanished as he saw the girl she meant. "Anyhow, she says it wasn't liquor and I say I never saw a man your size and age out where he sat like you were. Not on liquor. You don't have to tell me if you don't want to, but—?"

She let it linger on a questioning note.

Cade, profiting by instruction, smiled directly at her, and held the smile until he felt foolish.

The results were unexpected and dramatic. She whistled, a long, low whistle that made half a dozen heads turn their way inquiringly. And she looked at him with such adoration as he had seen only a few times before, from new armigers on the Field of Battle.

"*Bro-ther!*" she sighed.

"Excuse me," said Cade in a strangled voice. He ran from the enemy, leaving her in complete and bewildered possession of the field.

13

CADE LEARNED FAST at Cannon's. He had to. His eyes and ears, trained for life-or-death differences in action, picked up words, glances and gestures; his battle-sharpened wits evaluated them. He survived.

And Cannon's learned about Cade, as much as was necessary. He was Smiley, and Cannon's etiquette permitted no further prying into his name or rank. He was talked about. Some said he was starborne, but no one asked. His full pockets and Jana's wagging tongue gave him the introduction and reputation he needed.

His build? He was obviously a strong-arm bucko. His rumored golden trinkets? He was obviously a master gaff—a burglar. His occasional lapses of memory and manners? He was obviously addicted to the most powerful narcotics. That too explained his otherwise inexplicable lack of interest in alcohol and women.

As a bucko and gaff he outranked most other habitués of the place: the ratty little pickpockets, the jumpy gamblers, the thoroughly detestable pimps. As a jabber of unknown drugs he even outranked the friendly, interesting, neatly dressed confidence men who occasionally passed through. Drugs were a romantic, desperate slap in the face of things as they were. Mistress Cannon disapproved—there had been a man of hers; she wouldn't talk about it. But to her hostesses it was the ultimate attraction.

Nightly Cade sat in the barroom at a corner table near the stairs with an untasted drink before him. Carlin, who dressed commoner girls and tramps secretly in court gowns, had taken his measure and provided him with blues and greens for as much of his plunder as he had chosen to display. The old man had dickered endlessly over each item, but with Mistress Cannon loudly supervising the transaction Cade emerged with two full sets of clothes made to order for him, two weeks of exorbitant "board" paid, and a surplus of clink. In his room, behind one of the storage shelves, he had found a hiding place for his remaining gawdies: one last golden box containing half a dozen smaller trifles.

With this much security—a place to live, new clothes, good food, clink in his pocket, an enviable reputation and a hidden reserve—he could turn his full attention to his quest for the girl of the Cairo Mystery. He asked few questions, but he listened always for a word that might lead to her. Every night he sat at his table, his chair turned to the door, watching every new arrival, buying drink for anyone who would talk—and that was everyone.

First there were Mistress Cannon and her girls. Then he could ask openly after he learned that it was not strange to seek renewal of acquaintance with a girl who had struck one's fancy. But none of them knew her, none remembered seeing her except that night when he had met her there.

It was a setback, but there was no other place to look except Baltimore—and they'd had no trouble handling him there once. If nothing at Cannon's led him to the girl he would act without her, and gradually an alternative plan formed. While it was growing, over the course of his two weeks' stay, he drank in everything he heard from the endless procession of people willing to talk while Smiley bought.

There was a Martian who had jumped ship, and taken to liquor and petty thievery. For two nights Cade listened to him curse the misstep: he babbled monotonously about the family and their little iron refinery; how there had been a girl back home and how he might have married and had children to grow up with the planet. The Marsman didn't come back the third night, or ever.

He wasted one night. This was on a quiet, well-spoken grey-haired man, himself a former gaff who had retired on his "earnings." He came for the first time on Smiley's fourth night in the bar and for almost a week he came again every night. He was a mine of information on criminal ways and means, nicknames, jargon. Watch corruption, organized prostitution, disposal of gaffed goods. On the last night, the wasted night, after chatting and drinking for an hour, he confided without warning that he was in possession of a secret truth unknown to

100

other men. Leaning across the table in excitement he whispered clearly: "Things have not always been as they are now!"

Cade remembered the rites of the Mystery and leaned forward himself to listen. But the hope was illusory; the gentle old man was a lunatic.

He'd found a book, he said, while gaffing years ago. It was called "Sixth Grade Reader." He thought it was incredibly old, and whispered, almost in Cade's ear: "More than ten thousand years!"

Cade leaned back in disgust while the madman rattled on. The book was full of stories, verses, anecdotes, many of them supposed to be based on fact and not fiction. But one thing they had in common: not one of them mentioned the Emperor, Klin, the Order, or the Realm of Man. "Don't you see what that means? Can't you see it for yourself? There was a time once when *There was no Emperor.*"

In the face of Smiley's bored disinterest he lost his caution and spoke loudly enough for Mistress Cannon, at the bar, to catch a few words. She stormed to the table in a loyal rage and threw him out. She later regretted it. Word got around and the incident brought on the only Watch raid during Smiley's stay at Cannon's.

The whole district was minutely sifted and Cade too had to submit to questioning. But the Watchers were looking for just one man, and Smiley's origins did not concern them. Later, word got to Cannon's that they had found the madman in the very act of airing his mania to jeering children on the street. He did not survive his first night in the Watch House. Those rubber truncheons, Cade remembered, and wondered whether it had been necessary to cope with the poor fool so drastically.

There were others who came to the table and talked. There was a pastel-clad young man who misunderstood Cade's lack of interest in the girls and immediately had the matter made crystal-clear to him. Mistress Cannon pitched him limply out with the usual hoarse injunction: "And don't you *ever* come back in here again!" But he probably didn't hear her.

One night there was a fat-faced, sententious fellow, a con man who had hit the skids because of liquor. Smiley bought many drinks for him because he had been in the

Cairo Mystery—and several others. He explained that the Mysteries were a good place to meet your johns, and was otherwise defensive. Cade dared to question him closely after the con man had poured down enough liquor to blur his brain and probably leave the incident a blank next morning. But he knew little enough. He'd never heard of hypnosis in connection with a Mystery. A featureless, egg-shaped room had nothing to do with the Cairo rites. Mysteries were strictly for the johns; the revenue from them was strictly for the blades, like him and Smiley. He proposed vaguely that they start a new Mystery with a new twist and take over all the other blades' johns. With his experience and Smiley's looks it'd be easy. Then he fell asleep across the table.

There were many others; but *she* never came and he never heard a word about her or anyone like her.

When the two weeks he allowed himself were past he knew vastly more than he had known before, but none of it led to the girl. It was time for the other plan.

Mistress Cannon protested hoarsely when he told her he was leaving. "I never saw a man go through a load like that so fast," she complained. "You didn't have to buy for everybody that said he was a rog. Listen—I made enough on that liquor to cover another week easy. You don't tell anybody about it and I'll let you stay. Two weeks won't do it in this town, but three weeks might. What about it?"

"It's not the money," he tried to explain. She was right about his blues and greens being gone, but she didn't know about the box of loot he still had in his room. "There's a job I've got to do. Something I promised before I came here."

"A promise doesn't count when you're hot!" she shouted. "What good will it do to try and keep your promise if you get picked up by the Watchers as soon as you step out of the door?"

He wasn't worried about that one. The Cannon grapevine was efficient and he knew the search for the "impostor" Cade had bogged down, at least locally. Two pedestrians had been incinerated by a young Armiger ten days ago. Though a strong order had been put out that identification of the two as the Cade-impostor and ex-Teacher Zisz was not confirmed as yet, the local

Watch had naturally slacked off its effort almost to zero. If Arle was making any search, it was undercover.

All Cade wanted was a place to leave everything he had except his gawdies and the better suit of commoners' garb. Reluctantly Mistress Cannon provided him with one of a pile of metal boxes in her kitchen: private vaults with self-set radionic locks, hidden under layers of foodstuffs.

Cade dressed in his room for the last time in the sober, dignified suit he had specified. Old Carlin had grumbled at the requirements: "Think you're going to Audience?" and Cade had smiled . . . but that, as a matter of fact, was exactly it: the alternative. The only one.

He could have tried to plunge into the Cairo Mystery and been hypnotized again for his troubles. He could have gone to a Chapter House and been burned down. But there was still, and always, the Emperor. This was the morning of the monthly Audience Day; he had timed it so.

Even here at Cannon's this much remained sure: the rogs and blades, the whores and hostesses were unfit people, but they were loyal to the Emperor, every one. There had been no trace of the conspiracy he sought. The insane burglar with his imaginary book had been an object of horror to them all.

The Realm is wide, thought Cade, *but not so wide that the Emperor will turn a deaf ear to any plea.*

His only fear was that he would not be believed when he told his complex and terrible story. The Emperor's benevolence would be sorely tried to comprehend a plot against him in an innocent Mystery; and to add to that the defection from fitness of the Gunner Supreme. Cade wondered what he himself would have thought of such a tale a few weeks ago.

But it would get to persons less full of loving-kindness than the Emperor. He had seen the iron-faced Power Master at ceremonies—a grim tower of a man; the gentle Emperor's mailed fist. Which was as it always had been, which was as it should be. It wasn't hard to visualize the Power Master believing enough of the story to investigate, and that was all that would be needed.

Cade had in his pockets as he left only half the remaining smaller gawdies and a handful of clink: three blues and a few greens. The gold box and the Gun of the Order were in the kitchen behind hardened bronze under a layer of meal. There was something like a tear in Mistress Cannon's bloodshot eye when she said: "Don't forget you're coming back. There's always a place for you here."

He promised to remember, and the promise was true. He hoped he would never have to see the place again; but he knew he wouldn't forget it to his dying day. Such—*irregularity*! No order in their lives or thoughts, no proportion, no object, no fitness. And yet there was a curious warmth, an unexpected sense of comradeship strangely like that he had felt for his Brothers in the Order, but somehow stronger. He wondered if all commoners had it or if it was the property of only the criminals and near-criminals.

When he closed the door behind him and started down the street he felt strangely alone. It was the same street down which he had walked in the lamplight with the elusive girl following behind. He rounded the corner, where another Watchman now stood, and trudged to the Palace in bitter solitude. What would happen would happen, he gloomily thought, and cursed himself for his gloom. He should have been full of honorable pride and exultation over the service he was about to render to the Emperor, but he was not. Instead he was worried about the commoner girl.

The girl, the girl, *the girl*! He had lied to the Gunner Supreme by not mentioning her—but only after he already had suspected that the Supreme was an unfit voluptuary, false to the Order. Hopefully he tried to persuade himself that she would come to no harm; realistically he knew that, harm or not, he could not lie to the Emperor and that she might well be caught and crushed in the wheels of justice he was about to set in motion.

14

As a RESPECTABLE-LOOKING COMMONER of the middle class, Cade was admitted without questioning through the Audience Gate, a towering arch in the great wall that enclosed the nerve-center of the Realm. The Palace proper, a graciously proportioned rose marble building, lay a hundred meters inside. A Klin Serviceman—the gold braid on his grey meant Palace Detail—led the newcomer to a crowd already waiting patiently in the plaza.

"Wait here," he said brusquely, and strode off.

Cade waited as further commoners arrived and the crowd began to fill the open square. He noticed, however, that from time to time one of the throng—usually well-dressed—would approach a loitering guard for a few words. Something would seem to change hands and the man or woman would be led off toward the Palace itself.

The Gunner managed to be nearby next time it happened; he smiled bitterly as his suspicions were confirmed. Even here in the Palace, under the very eyes of the Emperor, there was corruption almost in the open.

The next Serviceman to approach the crowd with a newcomer took him inside for the modest price of one green. And he gave Cade what the Gunner took to be complete instructions: "When you enter the Audience Hall, wait for the appearance of the Emperor. After he appears, face him at all times, standing. Keep silent until you're announced. Then, with your eyes lowered, not stepping over the white line, state your case in ten words or so."

"Ten words!"

"Have you no brief, commoner?" The guard was amazed.

A brief would be a written version of his case. Cade shook his head. "It doesn't matter," he said. "Ten words will be ample."

He turned down the Serviceman's friendly offer to locate a briefsman who would, of course, require something extra for a rush job. Ten words would be ample;

the ones he had in mind would create enough furor to give him all the time he'd need to state his case.

The guard left him finally outside the ornate door of the hall with a last stern order: "Stand right here until they let you in."

"And when is that supposed to be?" a fussily dressed man at Cade's elbow asked as the Serviceman walked away. "How long a wait *this* time?"

Before Cade could say he didn't know, a white-haired granny scolded: "It doesn't make any difference. It's a real treat, every minute of it. I've been promising myself this trip—I live in Northumberland, that's in England—for many years and it's a fine thing I finally got the greens for it saved, because I surely won't be here next year!"

"Perhaps not," said the man distantly. And then curiously: "What's your complaint for the Emperor?"

"Complaint? Complaint? Dear me, I have no complaint! I just want to see his kind face close up and say 'Greetings and love from a loyal old lady of Northumberland, England.' Don't you think he'll be pleased?"

Cade melted at her innocence. "I'm sure he will," he said warmly, and she beamed with pleasure.

"I dare say," said the fussily dressed man. "What *I* have to lay before the Emperor's justice and wisdom is a sound grievance—" He whipped out and began to unfold a manuscript of many pages. "—a sound grievance against my cursed neighbor Flyte, his slatternly wife and their four destructive brats. I've asked them politely, I've demanded firmly, I've—"

"Pardon." Cade shouldered past the man and seized the old lady from Northumberland by the arm. He had been watching again the ones who got beyond the Gate, and how they did it. To an expectant Serviceman he said: "Sir, my old mother here is worn from travel. We've been waiting since sun-up. When we can get into the Hall?"

"Why, it might be arranged very soon," the Serviceman said noncommittally.

Cade abandoned the effort; apparently there was nothing to do but pay. Bitterly he pulled another green from his pocket. He had just one more after that, and a few blues.

"It's only your old mother you want admitted?" the guard asked kindly. "You yourself wish to wait outside for her?"

Cade understood, wavered a moment and then handed him the last green he owned. It didn't matter. Once in the Hall, in the Emperor's own presence, there could be no more of this.

And he was in the Hall, with the puzzled, grateful old lady from Northumberland beside him, her arm tucked under his.

"Over there," the guard pointed. "And keep your voices low if you must speak."

There were two groups waiting, clearly distinguished from each other. One was composed of commoners, about fifty of them, nervously congregated behind a white-marble line in the oval hall's mosaic flooring. There were perhaps as many persons of rank chatting and strolling relaxedly at a little distance from the commoners. At the end of the hall was a raised dais where, he supposed, the Emperor would sit in state. By the dais was a thick pedestal a meter high. Klin guards stood stiffly here and there, with gas guns at their belts. The nearest of them gestured abruptly at Cade, and he hastily moved into the commoner's enclosure.

Granny was clutching his arm and pouring out twittery thanks. But Cade, already regretting the impulse, turned his back on her and worked his way through the other side of the group. He was joined a minute later by the overdressed fellow who had talked to him outside the Hall.

"I saw you couldn't persuade the guard," the man said, "so I paid without quibbling. I wonder how many more times the Greys will expect us to pay?"

"That had better be the last," Cade said grimly.

"Such a pity!" someone said from his other side.

"Eh?" Cade turned to see a sour-looking middle-aged woman, staring with pursed lips across the Hall at a space near the dais that had been empty only a few minutes ago. It was filling now with starbornes—Ladies, high dignitaries in the Klin Service and a few Brothers of the Order, their cloaks banded with Silver of Superiors below colored stripes that designated their Stars. Cade silently studied the stripes: Congo, Pacificisles, California, and of course Eastcoast. He had served under none of them; they would not be able to identify him on the spot. But at the same time they would not half-recognize him, assume he was the Cade-impostor and blast him where he stood.

"*Such* a trial to the Court!" the woman insisted, again pursing her lips and shaking her head with enjoyment.

"What?" asked Cade. She pointed and he realized he had asked the wrong question. "Who?" he amended it, and then he saw—

"*Who's that?*" he demanded, clutching the sleeve of the man next to him.

"What'd you say? Would you mind—this cloth crushes." He picked Cade's hand from his sleeve indignantly, but the Gunner never noticed. It was *she*: he was certain of it. Her back was turned to him and her hair was a brilliant, foolish shade of orange-red to match her gown, but somehow he was certain.

He turned to the woman beside him: "What about her? Who is she?"

"Don't you know?" She eyed him significantly. "The Lady *Jocelyn*," she whispered. "The peculiar one. You'd never think to look at her that she's a niece of the Emperor himself—"

The fussily dressed man interrupted with a snickering question to show that he was up on the latest Palace gossip: "The one that writes poems?"

"*Yes*. And I have a friend who works in the kitchens, not a cook but a dietician, of course, and she says the Lady Jocelyn reads them to *everybody*—whether they want to listen or not. Once she even began reciting to some commoners waiting just like us—"

But Cade was not listening. The Lady Jocelyn had turned to face them and her resemblance to the girl of the Mystery collapsed. The bright red hair, of course, was dyed. But even Cade, as little competent to judge women's clothes as any man alive, could see that it was a bad match to a wretchedly cut gown. She was round-shouldered and evidently near-sighted, for she stood with her head thrust forward like a crane. When she walked off a moment later after surveying the commoners indifferently, her gait was a foolish shamble. The only resemblance between this awkward misfit of the

Court and the vivid, commanding creature who had saved his life was in the nature of a caricature.

All around him there was a sighing and a straightening. The Emperor had entered, and was seating himself on the dais. Two Klin guards moved to the commoners' area and there was a subdued jockeying for position. Before Cade understood what was going on, one of the guards had relieved him of his last flew blues, examined the small sum with disgust and stationed him well to the end of the line. Curse it, how much more was he supposed to know that he didn't? He realized that the guard's instructions had not been instructions at all but a last-minute warning which hit only the things he *wasn't* supposed to do: not talk, not turn his back, not overstep the line, not be long-winded—a mere recapitulation of things he was supposed to know. What else was involved? The commoners he had known at Cannon's were loyal, but shied from the idea of an Audience. He saw plainly from the people he was with that it was a middle-class affair. What else was involved? He was glad he wasn't at the head of the line—and hastily fell into step as the line moved off to stop at the enigmatic pedestal before the dais. Cade saw the fussily dressed man at the head of the line; he dropped currency—*greens*!—on it and murmured to one of the guards.

Thank offering, love offering, something like that, he vaguely remembered now, much too late to do anything about it. He glowered at the white-haired granny halfway down the line and berated himself for the impulse that had made him pay her way in. She, canny, middle-class, had saved her money for the offering.

"Commoner Bolwen," the guard was saying, and the fussily dressed man said to the Emperor, with his eyes lowered: "I present a complaint against a rude and unfit person to my Emperor." He handed his bulky brief to the guard and backed away from the dais.

Not a blue on him, Cade thought, and the line was shortening with amazing efficiency. "Offering," they called it. Did that mean it was voluntary? Nobody was omitting it.

"I ask my Emperor to consider my brilliant son for the Klin Service."

"Loyal greetings to our Emperor from the city of

Buena Vista."

"I ask my Emperor's intercession in the bankruptcy case of my husband."

Cade looked up fleetingly at the Emperor's face for possible inspiration, and lost more time. The face was arrestingly different from what he had expected. It was not rapt and unworldly but thoughful, keen, penetrating—the face of a Senior Teacher, a scholar.

There was a guard at Cade's side, muttering: "Offering in your left hand."

Cade opened his mouth to speak, and the guard said: "Silence."

"But—" said Cade. Instantly the guard's gas gun was out, ready to fire. The guard jerked his head at the door. He was no moon-faced, sluggish, run-of-the-mill Watchman, Cade saw, but a picked member of the Service: no fighting man, but a most efficient guard who could drop him at the hint of a false move. And there were other guards looking their way . . . Cade silently stepped out of the line and backed to the great door, with the guard's eyes never leaving him.

Outside the Hall the guard delivered a short, withering lecture on commoners who didn't know their duties and would consume the Emperor's invaluable time as though it were the time of a shop-attendant. Cade gathered that the offering was another of the commoner's inviolable laws—even stronger than the one that made you use a smoker pellet when it was offered to you. Something as trivial as that, and it had barred him for a month from bringing his case to the Emperor!

The ridiculous injustice of it was suddenly more than he could take. Like an untested Brother suddenly thrust into battle, Cade choked on panic and despair. But for him, now, there was no faith in the Gunner Supreme to carry him through the moment of ordeal. There was no one, no reason for him to carry this burden at all. He who had dedicated his life and every deed in it to the Emperor was turned away because he didn't have greens to drop into a platter!

The guard was snarling that he had showed disgusting disrespect for the Emperor—

"Respect for the Emperor?" he burst out wildly. "What do you know about it, grey-suited fool? I'm risking my life to be here. There's a conspiracy against the Emperor! I was trying to warn—" His self-pity was cooled by a dash of cold fear. Next he'd be telling his name. Next the gas gun would go off in his face. And then there would be no awakening.

But the grey-clad guard had backed away, his weapon firmly trained on Cade's face and his finger white on the trigger. "Conspiracy, is it?" said the guard. "You're mad. Or . . . whatever you are, this is a matter for Armsmen. *Walk.*"

Cade trudged emptily down the corridor. He had said it and he would pay for it. There was an Auxiliary Chapter House in the Palace, and every Gunner worthy of his Gun would have a description of the Cade-impostor firmly planted in his memory.

"In there." It was an elevator that soared to the top of the Palace and it let them out at an anteroom where an Armiger stood guard.

"Sir," said the Serviceman, "please call the Gunner of the Day." The Armiger stared at Cade, and there was no recognition in the stare; he spoke into a wall panel, and the door opened. They marched through the Ready Room into the Charge Room, where the Gunner of the Day waited. Cade stared downward at the familiar plastic flooring of a Chapter House, as he approached the desk. He could brace himself against the inevitable tearing blast of flame; he could not bring himself to look his executioner in the eye.

There was no blast. Instead there came a voice—dry, precise, familiar, and astonished: "Why, we thought you were—!"

"Silence!" said Cade swiftly. The Gunner was Kendall of Denver, a companion for years before his assignment to France. After the first show of surprise, Kendall's long face was impassive. Cade knew his former Brother's mind: form a theory and act on it. By now he would have decided that Cade had been on one of the Order's infrequent secret assignments. And he would never mistake Cade for the hunted Cade-impostor.

"Guard, is there a charge?" Gunner Kendall asked.

"Sir, this cursed fellow failed to make the voluntary offering in Audience, he talked in the Emperor's presence, and when I pulled him out of line he yelled about

111

a conspiracy. I suppose he's mad, but if there's anything to it, I—"

"Quite right. I'll take charge. Return to your post."

When they were alone, Kendall grinned hugely. "We all thought you were dead, Brother. There's even an order out to kill someone impersonating you. You took a fine chance coming here. We have Brothers Rosso and Banker in the Palace detail besides me; they'll be glad to hear the news. How may I help you?"

Escort to the Emperor? No; now the Emperor need not be troubled with it. The Emperor's right arm would set this crazy muddle right. "Take me to the Power Master, Brother. At once."

Kendall led the way without question. Through corridors, down ramps, through antechambers, Cade saw doors open and salutes snap to the trim uniform of the Gunner.

They passed through a great apartment at last that was far from ornate. There was an antechamber where men and women sat and waited. There was a brightly lit, vast communications room in back, where hundreds of youngsters tended solid banks of sending and receiving signal units. There was a great room behind that, where men at long tables elaborated outgoing messages and brifed incoming ones. There were many, many smaller rooms further behind, where older men could be seen talking into dictating machines or writing, and consulting lists and folders as they worked. Endlessly, messengers went to and fro. Cade's first glimpse of the complex machinery of administration.

In a final anteroom, alone, they sat and waited. Cade felt the eerie sensation of being spy-rayed, but the orifice was too cunningly concealed for him to spot it.

"Gunner Kendall, come in and bring the commoner," said a voice at length—and Cade stiffened. It was the vibrant, commanding voice he could never forget; the voice that had broadcast the "kill-on-sight" command.

He followed Kendall from the anteroom into a place whose like he had never seen before. It had every comfort of the Lady Moia's bedchamber, but was sternly masculine in its simplicity. The whole room pointed to a table where the iron-visaged Power Master sat, and Cade rejoiced. This was the man who would crush the conspiracy and root out the decadent Gunner Supreme . . .

"Sir," said Kendall in his precise way, "this is Gunner Cade, mistakenly supposed dead. He asked me to bring him to you."

"My spy ray showed me that he is unarmed," said the Power Master. "See to it that he does not seize your weapon." He got up from the table as Kendall backed away from Cade, with confusion on his face. Cade saw that the Power Master wore a gun of the Order—a gun he deliberately unbuckled and flung on the table with a crash. Slowly he approached Cade.

The man was fully as tall as Cade, and heavier. His muscles were rock-hard knots where Cade's were sliding steel bands. Cade was a boxer, the Power Master—a strangler. With his face half a meter from Cade's, he said, in the voice that once had ordered his death: "Are you going to kill me, Gunner? This is your chance."

Cade told him steadily: "I am not here to kill you, sir. I'm here to give you information vital to the Realm."

The Power Master stared into his eyes for a long, silent minute, and then suddenly grinned. He returned to the table to buckle on his gun. "You're sure he's Cade?" he asked, with his back turned.

"No possible doubt, sir," said Kendall. "We were novices together."

"Cade, who else knows about this?"

"Nobody, sir. Only Brother Kendall."

"Good." The Power Master swung around with the gun in his hand. A stab of flame from it blasted the life out of Gunner Kendall. Cade saw the muzzle of the gun turn to train steadily on him as Kendall toppled to the floor.

15

"SIT DOWN," said the Power Master. He laid his gun on the polished table as Cade collapsed into a capacious chair. Numbly he thought: it wasn't murder like Fledwick; Kendall is—was—a Gunner under arms. He could have drawn . . . but *why?*

"I can use you," said the Power Master. "I can always use a first-rate Armsman who's had a look below the surface and kept his head. You could be especially useful to me because, as far as the world knows, you are dead—now that Kendall has been silenced. Also you seem to have an unusual, useful immunity to hypnosis."

"You know about it," said Cade stupidly.

The Power Master grinned and said, rolling the words: "The Great Conspiracy. Yes; I have my representatives in the Great Conspiracy. I was alarmed when they advised me that a most able Gunner had been turned loose with a compulsion to take my life—and even more alarmed when I found you had slipped through the fingers of the fools of the City Watch."

The girl—was she *his* spy in the Mystery?

"Now," said the Power Master briskly, "tell me about your recovery from their hypnosis."

'I was left in a drinking room to come to my senses," Cade said slowly, uncertain of what to tell. If she was his spy—but he risked it. He might be shot down like Kendall, but he would know. "I felt the compulsion mounting," he said evenly, "and then it went away for no apparent reason. It has not returned. I left the place looking for a Chapter House. One of the women followed me, and we were both arrested by the Watch."

The Power Master looked up sharply, and Cade was certain that there was surprise in the glance. "You don't know who the woman was?"

"No," said Cade. That much, at least, was true.

"You're sure?"

"I've been trying to find out," he admitted, shamelessly, and the Power Master did not bother to repress a cynical smile. Cade didn't care: the girl was no spy of the Power Master's. His claim that the hypnotic compulsion had vanished by itself stood unchallenged. In spite of his bullying show of omniscience, the man did not really know everything.

"Tell me the rest," said the Power Master. "What happened to your partner in criminal insanity—the unbooked Teacher?"

Cade told him of their cross-country journey, the shattering discoveries at the Building of Fives that climaxed in the treacherous murder of Fledwick. The Power Master smiled again at the involuntary pain in Cade's voice as he mentioned the presence of the Lady Moia. And he nodded approvingly as Cade told him of his two weeks at Cannon's—"waiting for the hue-and-cry to die down"—and of his failure to reach the Emperor.

"You've done well," he pronounced judiciously at last. "Now I want to know whether you've profited by it all.

"Since your novitiate, Cade, you've been filled full of brotherhood and misinformation. You've been doing all the right things, but for the wrong reasons. If you can learn the right reasons . . . Tell me first: why did you Gunners of France fight the Gunners of Muscovy?"

"Because they tried to seize an iron deposit belonging to our Star," Cade said simply. Where was the man leading?

"*There was no iron deposit.* One of my people faked a geological survey report for the Star of France and seeded a little Mars iron at the site. I held it in reserve as a bone of contention. When the French Star was making overtures to the Muscovite Star concerning a combination of forces, I let the news of the 'iron deposit' leak to Muscovy, with the results that you know. There will be no combination between France and Muscovy now, or for many years to come."

It was an elaborate joke, Cade decided, and in very bad taste.

"All your wars are like that," said the Power Master, grimly. "They are useful things to keep the Stars diverted and divided. That is the purpose of the Great Conspiracy as well—though the Stars who think they are behind it do not know this. It requires immense funds to keep a vast underground organization going; the half-dozen or so Stars now supporting the Cairo Mystery conspiracy will soon be bled white and drop off, while others take their place. My agents will keep anything serious from ever coming of the Cairo affair, of course. I confess it almost got out of hand, but that is a risk one must run."

This was no joke, Cade numbly realized. It was the end of his world. "What do the Stars who . . . think . . . they are behind the conspiracy want?" he asked, fighting for calm.

"They want to kill me, of course, and go their own wild way. They want more, and more, and more Armsmen. They want to fight bigger and bigger wars, and destroy more and more villages. . . . You've been taught that the Stars are loyal to the Realm, the way commoners are loyal to the Stars. The truth is that the Stars are the worst enemy the Realm has. Without a Power Master to keep them out of harm they'd have the Realm a wreck in one man's lifetime.

"And your precious Gunner Supreme. Cade, I suppose you think he's the first one like that in ten thousand years and will be the last one like that until the end of time?"

"That was my hope," Cade said wearily.

"Disabuse yourself. Most of them have been like that; most of them *will* be . . . must be, if you can understand. Arle is plotting, if you please, to supplant me, merging the two offices. It is only to be expected. A Gunner such as yourself may survive years of combat because he has brains. He becomes a Gunner Superior, in intimate contact with a Star. He figures in the Star's plottings. The women of the Court, fascinated by the novelty of a man they can't have, bend every effort to seducing him and usually succeed. His vows are broken, he misses the active life of battle, he intrigues for election to the office of the Supreme. By the time he wins it he is a very ordinary voluptuary with a taste for power, like our friend Arle.

"But Cade, this is the key; don't forget it: *there must be a Gunner Supreme.* As a fighting man you know that. Many a time the fact that the Supreme lived somewhere and embodied your notion of the Order has saved your life or saved the day for your command. The fact that the Supreme in the flesh is not what you think doesn't matter at all."

Cade leaned forward. The abominable thing he was about to say was a ball in his throat, choking him so he had to get rid of it: "The Emperor?" he asked. "The Emperor? Why does he allow it? Why?"

"The Emperor is another lie," the Power Master said calmly. "The Emperor can't stop it. He's just a man—an ordinary one. If he attempted to make suggestions about my task of running the Realm, I would very properly ignore them. Emperors who have offered too many such suggestions in the past, Cade, have died young. Their Power Masters killed them. It will happen again.

"And that's as it should be. As you know, the line of the Power Master descends by adoption and the line of the Emperor by male primogeniture. The Power Master chooses a tried man to succeed himself. The Emperor gets what chance sends him. Of course the line of the Power Master is stronger, so of course it must rule."

His voice rose almost to a roar. "*But there must be an Emperor*. The Power Master is unloved: he sends people to death; he collects taxes; he sets speed limits. The Emperor does none of this; he simply exists and is loved because everybody is told to love him. People do it—again, the right thing for the wrong person. If they didn't love him, what would happen to the Realm? Think of such a thing as all the commoners becoming criminals. What would we do when the Watch Houses were all filled? What would we do if they kept attacking the Watch Houses until all the gas-gun charges were used up? But they don't all become criminals. They love the Emperor and don't want to sadden him with unfit deeds."

The Power Master rose, holstering his gun, and began to pace the room restlessly. "I am asking you to think, Cade," he said with blazing intensity. "I don't want to throw away a fine tool like you. I am asking you to think. Things are not what they seem, not what you thought they were.

"For many years you did your best work because you didn't know the right reasons. Now it's different. There are other jobs for you, and you won't be able to do them if you're blinded by the lies you used to believe. Remember always that the Realm as it is *works*. It's been kept working for ten thousand years by things being as they are and not as they seem. It can be kept working to the end of time as long as there are resolute men to shove the structure back into balance when it shows signs of toppling."

Stopping for a moment at the feet of the slain Gunner Kendall, he said simply: "That was for the happiness of millions. They are happy, almost all of them. Gunners are contented, the Klin Service is contented, the Courts are contented, the commoners are contented. Let things change, let the structure crash and where would they be? Give each commoner the power I hold and what would he make of it? Would he be contented or would be run amuck?

"Cade, I don't want to . . . lose you. Think straight. Is there anything really unfit about the work I do, the work I want you to do for me? You made a trade of killing because the trade was called the Order of Armsmen. My trade is conserving the stability and contentment of every subject of the Realm of Man."

The passionately sincere voice pounded on, battering at Cade's will. The Power Master spoke of the vows Cade had taken, and he destroyed their logic completely. Cade had dedicated himself to the service of the Emperor—who was no more than the powerless, ceremonial excuse for the Power Master. With ruthless obscenity of detail he told Cade what he had given up in life in exchange for a sterile athleticism.

He spoke of food and drunkenness and drugs; of dancing and music and love: the whole sensual world Cade had thought well lost. He wooed the Gunner with two intermingling siren songs—the fitness of his new service under the Power Master and the indulgence of himself that was possible in it.

It would have been easy to tumble into the trap. Cade had been drained empty of the certainties of a lifetime. The Power Master said there was only one other set of certainties, and that if Cade would only let himself be filled with them there would be the most wonderful consquences any powerful man of normal appetites would want.

It was easy to listen, it would have been easy to accept, but . . . Cade knew there was even more than he'd been told. There was one thing that did not fit in the new world, and that was the girl. The girl who had not wanted the Power Master killed, or the Gunner either. The girl who had warned Cade—rightly—that he would be going to his death if he tried to reaffiliate with the Order.

There was no all-powerful, all-loving Emperor any more; there were no loyal Stars; there was only the Power Master—and the girl. So, thought Cade, treachery is the order of the day and has been for ten thousand years. He knew what answer he would give the Power Master, the answer he had to give to stay alive, but he was not ready to give it yet. A lifetime of training in strategy made him sharply aware that a quick surrender would be wrong.

"I must ask for time, sir," he said painfully. "You realize this is . . . very new to me. My vows have been part of me for many years, and it's less than a month since I . . . died . . . in battle. May I have leave to spend a day in meditation?"

The Power Master's lips quirked with inner amusement. "One day? You may have it, and welcome. And you may spend it in my own apartment. I have a room you should find comfortable."

16

THE ROOM was comfortable by any standards Cade had known; it was second in luxury only to the smothering softness of the Lady Moia's apartment. Compared to Mistress Cannon's mean quarters or the sleeping lofts of a Chapter House it offered every comfort a dog-tired man could ask. And it was also, unmistakably, a prison.

There were no bars to guard the windows and presumably the "shoot-on-sight" order had lost its force. Yet Cade was certain he could not leave the place alive without the express permission of its master. If there had been any doubt about the answer he must give tomorrow, this room would have resolved it.

And it went deeper. If he'd had any tendency to give that answer in good faith, or any hesitation at the thought of falsely declaring his allegiance, the room dispelled it. Given freedom, he might have found it hard to return and commit himself to treachery and deceit with a lying honesty to any one but himself. And perhaps to the girl—if he could find her.

The Gunner slept well that night. After breakfast had been brought him his host appeared.

Cade did not wait to be asked. Saluting, he said: "My decision is made; it was not a hard one. I am in your service. What is my first assignment?"

The Power Master smiled. "One that has been awaiting you. The Realm is threatened—has been threatened increasingly—by the unbounded egotism and short-sightedness of one Star against whom I cannot operate in the usual way. Until now . . . until now I have been searching for a man who could do what was necessary. You are the man."

He paused, and the silence in the room was explosive.

"You will go to Mars," he said finlly, "and arrange the death of the Star of Mars. You will return alive. The details are your own concern. I can supply you with a flier and with money—whether to buy men or machines I do not care."

Cade's mind accepted the job as a tactical problem, putting off for the time being the vital decision as to whether the commission would be fulfilled. For now, it would be necessary to act . . . even to think . . . in terms of fulfillment.

"I will need an identity."

"Choose it. I said the details were your own concern. I can offer, merely as a suggestion, that you would do well to adopt the identity of a lapsed Armiger—you have known such cases—who took to the district. You might as well put the time you spent in that brothel to some use. And I can assure you that under such an identity you'll find yourself in the Court of Mars. Yes," he said in answer to Cade's look of shocked inquiry, "things are that bad. Did you suppose I'd send you to kill a Star for anything less serious? Now, when you've decided on your course of action and prepared a list of your needs, call me—" He indicated a red button on the wall communicator. "Either I or a trusted servant will be there."

As he pointed, the set chimed. The Power Master depressed the button.

"Here."

"Message, sir. Shall I bring it?"

"To the outer room." And to Cade: "Call when you're ready."

The Gunner lost no time. He seated himself at a desk at one end of the room, and was already listing the funds, transport, and identification he would need when the door opened again.

"You are going to have a visitor," the Power Master said coldly. "I am very interested in knowing just how she discovered—"

"She? *Who*?" Cade was on his feet, the list forgotten.

"Whom do you suppose? How many Ladies of the Palace do you know?"

It was the Lady Moia, then. And the memory of her still hurt. It would take time to recover from the shocks of that night. "One, sir, as I told you," he said formally. "And I would prefer not to see her if that is possible."

"It is not possible. She knows you are here and I have no grounds for refusing her admission without revealing your identity. *How did she know you were here*?" the vibrant voice demanded.

"Sir, I don't know. I haven't seen her since the Building of Fives—"

"The Building of Fives? You spoke only of the Lady Moia there." He peered closely into Cade's puzzled face and suddenly burst into a wide, wolfish grin. "You *don't* know!" he exploded. "My virtuous Gunner, this is the girl for whom you waited two weeks at Cannon's—I had a report from there last night, an hour after you went to sleep—a mysterious girl, a girl whom you had met just once." He was dragging it out, enjoying himself hugely. "Oh, Cade, you were so *upright* yesterday; so true to your vows. How could you have . . . neglected . . . a little thing like telling your master about the girl?"

Cade felt the blood rush to his face, but it was not the reflex of shame. It was she; she had found him after his futile, stupid hunt for her. And she was no commoner or wearer of the garter, but a Lady of the Court!

"No," laughed the Power Master. "I won't spoil the joke. You'll learn who she is shortly from her own— shall I say, delicate?—lips." The facade of grimness relaxed; the Power Master sat comfortably on the couch, chuckling. "If it's any satisfaction to you, Cade, I will admit that my respect for you, my hopes for you, have risen. I can use a man who knows how to keep his mouth shut. So she Saw Life after all?" His intonation was heavily satirical, amused. "Proof again that the simplest answer may sometimes be right. The whole Palace has

121

been buzzing about it for three weeks, and I thought I knew better!"

Cade tried to concentrate on what he was hearing and make sense of it. "The whole Palace?" he asked uncertainly. "You mean you knew about her? The whole Palace knew?" Then why, he wondered, all the secrecy now? Why was he a prisoner here? None of it fitted with the Power Master's attitude of yesterday.

"Yes, of course. But *they* all thought it was the daring impostor-Cade she met . . . and only I knew it was the real Gunner, chaste and pure. Or so I thought. Now it seems I had the right information, but they have the right interpretation of it all. And to think of the horror on your face yesterday when I talked of these wicked matters! Cade, you impress me; you'll be a good man to have in my service." He broke out chuckling again. "I keep wondering . . . she must have made a peculiar-looking tart. What did she look like? She's so—*you* know."

"So beautiful?" asked Cade.

The Power Master stared at him wonderingly. "We'd better get you off to Mars," he said dryly, and glanced at a paper he held in his hand. "She says she recognized you yesterday in Court but didn't want to 'betray you.' Now that I've 'captured' you she wants to see you before you die."

Abruptly he ceased to be a man enjoying himself. "Cade," he said grimly, "I can understand and excuse your lie by omission of yesterday *if* it was prompted by mistaken loyalty to your little friend. You are, after all, unsophisticated. But if I find there's anything more to it, your little friend's visit will be quite literally the last you will enjoy before you die."

The door closed behind him and Cade sank into a chair, burying his face in his hands. Had he gone mad? Had everybody?

"Traitor, face me! They said you lied and I did not believe them, but I know now. Look me in the eye if you dare!"

Cade jumped up. He hadn't heard the door open; the first thing to reach his ears was the unpleasant whine of her voice, contrasting ludicrously with the melodramatic words. He looked at her, heartsick as he realized the monstrous joke somebody was perpetrating. It was the Lady Jocelyn. He had noticed the resemblance himself yesterday—*but who else could know about it*?

"Traitor," she said, "*look on my face* and see how you erred when you thought to victimize a foolish and ignorant commoner girl. *Look on my face.*"

He looked, and something impossible was happening. The Lady Jocelyn's squint-stooped head moved back to sit proudly on her slim throat. Her round-shouldered stance straightened for a moment and settled to a supple, erect figure. The near-sighted, peering eyes flashed with humor and arrogance. She still wore an ill-fitting robe of lurid orange and her stringy hair still missed matching the color of her robe, but none of these things mattered. It was she.

"Have you nothing to say for yourself in your shame?" she demanded, in a voice that was also a caricature.

"A thousand pardons, Lady," he said hoarsely, his heart thudding. "If I had known, if you had permitted some word of your rank to cross your lips I could not have lied to you." *If Fledwick could hear me now*! The girl winked and nodded "go on."

"Surely your warm heart will understand and forgive when I say that only your beauty drove me to my crime." The story seemed to be that the Lady Jocelyn, the Palace butt, had gone out on the town incognito and been arrested, to the hilarity of the Palace wits. She was pretending to assume that he was under death sentence for daring to insult her by taking her at her face value.

"Forgive?" she declaimed. "Forgive? Justice will be done; there is nothing to forgive. A life for an insult to the blood imperial. I have come to console you, fellow. Bring a chair for me. You may sit at my feet."

Cade did as he was told, by now far beyond any effort to take control of the situation. He knelt as she sat down and pulled a sheaf of manuscript from a sagging pocket in her voluminous robe.

"I shall console you for an hour by reading from my works." She launched into what he supposed was a poem:

> *"There is no whisper uttered in the Realm*
> *That goes unheard. By night, by day, no voice*
> *Is raised involuntarily or by choice*
> *Unheard by him who holds the Palace helm."*

She cleared her throat and Cade nodded, jerking his
head a little at the wall communicator. He understood.

> *"The doors are many in the Realm of Man;*
> *This door unguarded, that door triply sealed;*
> *Each loyal subject wearing like a shield*
> *The key: to live as fitly as he can."*

Her knee pressed sharply against Cade's shoulder
during the three words "this door unguarded." He
managed to concentrate on the message.

> *"Starborne or common, we must take and use*
> *The lives that we are handed for our lot.*
> *Great Klin can tell us what to do or not;*
> *Not now or ever is it ours to choose."*

The words were take and use—*now.*

She rattled her sheaf of manuscript, and from its
bulky folds a flat case slid; he caught it before it struck
the floor. *Take and use—now.* It was the smallest size of
'caster. He had it open in an instant and saw a half-hour
reel of recorded tape ready to roll. All dials were at zero.

> *"My voice is small; I do not know the way*
> *To reach all of the willing hands that serve,*
> *Setting at ease the flesh and bone and nerve.*
> *But if I spoke like thunder, I would say:*
> *Good people, follow Klin by night and day."*

My voice—I do not know—setting. Swiftly he mixed bass
and treble volumes to match her voice—and hoped the
spy-mike system was anything but high-fidelity. He
started the tape on a quick nod from the girl and was
relieved to find that he'd done well. In a very fair
approximation of her adenoidal whine the 'caster
immediately began to drone out:

"What beauty lies in loyalty! What joy!
Is there a heart that throbs with lesser thrill—"

He placed the box carefully on her chair as she rose and followed her silently from the room. The Power Master, on the other end of the mike, was welcome to his share of the Lady Jocelyn's verses.

17

SHE LED CADE through endless twisting dark passageways and stairs. Doors opened at a touch from her hand where no doors seemed to be, and never once did they encounter another person in their flight. There was more to the Palace than met the eye, Cade realized . . .

When they emerged at last it was into a narrow alley like those of the district where Cade had spent two weeks. A ground car whisked them away from the alley door. Cade never saw who was driving. He followed the girl into the back seat and turned to her promptly with the thanks and questions uppermost in his mind, but she put one finger to her crookedly painted mouth and shook her head.

Cade sat back, forcing his body to relax, but his mind was busy, fascinated by the puzzle of her constantly shifting personality. She had been a commoner at their first meeting, but one with an air of command, an important person in the Cairo Mystery. Then she had been a wearer of the garter, openly seductive—and vulgar. And now a Lady of the Court, a niece of the Emperor himself!

He knew now that the first time she had been a spy; he did not know for whom.

The second time she was in masquerade. The Palace thought it was on holiday—he knew it was not.

This time he could not doubt her true identity; but the awkward, graceless, shambling fool of the Audience

Hall was not the same Lady Jocelyn who sat beside him now, erect and confident.

All he had learned so far was what she was not—except two things; that she was still, and always, even under the make-up of her Palace role, exquisitely beautiful, and that she had rescued him again . . . for what?

The car came to a discreet stop at the edge of a field and the girl gestured him to open the door. She led him briskly across the field to an ancient, unpainted structure; Cade had no chance to look at the vanishing car.

"Open it," she said, at the door of the building, and her voice was the commanding voice of the egg-shaped room. Cade heaved a wooden bar out of double sockets and pushed the double door open.

There was a space flier inside—twelve meters of polished alloy.

"You can fly this, Gunner," she said. It was a statement, not a question.

"I've taken fliers to the Moon and back," he told her. She looked worried. "Not Mars?"

"I can take it to Mars," he said—and he or any Gunner could.

"I hope so. This flier is loaded and fueled, with food aboard." She pressed a folded paper into his hands. "These are the coordinates of your landing-point on Mars. There will be friends waiting there, or they will arrive shortly after your landing. If you take off immediately you will probably be out of radar range before they can pursue."

"They?" he demanded. "The Power Master's fliers?" As far as he knew, the Power Master disposed only of frighters and ferries, without a ram in his space fleet.

"Cade," she said steadily, "we have no time. I've helped you before, against your will. Now I ask you to take off immediately—without questions or argument. First you must strike me—knock me unconscious."

"*What*?"

"You've done it before," she said angrily. "I must have a cover story to delay them with while you get clear."

Cade looked down at her, at the brilliant eyes and lovely face beneath the grotesque make-up. It was strangely pleasant, this warmth he felt . . . strangely unlike the peril he had been taught to expect from such nearness to a woman. It felt much as the touch of the Gunner Supreme's seal to his lips had felt in another life. Even as the thought came his lips tingled.

"Cade!" she said furiously. "I tell you, there's no time to waste. The tape gave us a half-hour at the most, even if they didn't get suspicious before then. Do as I say!"

A Palace ground car roared down the highway across the field, braked screechingly and began to back up.

"They're here," she said bitterly.

With only a momentary hesitation Cade struck her as she had said he must—but he did not leave her lying there to cover his escape. He picked her up and raced into the building and up the ramp to the control compartment lock standing open and waiting. He buckled her limp body into an acceleration couch and clanged the lock shut as a shouted challenge to surrender echoed in the building.

He slipped into the pilot's seat and reflex took over. Straps, buckles, neck brace, grid one temperature and voltage, grid two temperature and voltage, first stage discharge buildup and fire.

His blackout lasted only a few seconds. He turned in his straps, craning his neck to see the couch. She was still unconscious. Indicators flashed on the panel and his hands worked efficiently, as if with a life of their own, even though he had not flown out of atmosphere for three years. For ten minutes he was necessarily a part of the ship, his nerve system joined with its circuits by his swift-moving fingers on the controls. Last of all he cut in the flier's radars and unbuckled himself.

He kicked himself over to the couch, frightened, to feel the girl's neck. She shouldn't be out that long, he worried. But she was and there was nothing he could do about it.

Distractedly he began to search the ship for medical equipment. He braced himself in toe-holds, spun open the air port of the control compartment and floated into a cargo room perhaps three meters deep. In there, except for the space filled by an oversized loading lock, the bulkheads were lined with locked cabinets. Floating free in the compartment were four sealed crates. It was cargo, not medicine, here.

Aft of the cargo compartment was a bunk-lined cabin with a tiny galley and a vapor cabinet—the living quarters. She would want water. He filled a valve bag from the tap and gummed it to his thigh with a scoop of paste from one of the ship's omnipresent pots. When he kicked his way back into the control compartment, he found that the girl had freed herself from the couch and was swaying against a bulkhead with an uncertain hold on a grabiron.

"You fool," she said in a deadly voice.

"You told me to take the ship to Mars," he said flatly. "That's what I'm doing."

"Give me that water," she said, and drank inexpertly from the valve. "Cade," she said at last, "I suppose you meant well but this means death for us both. Did you suppose they'd let you chase off into space with a member of the Emperor's family on board? They'll destroy us and I will be reported killed—'unfortunately' —in the action. If you'd listened to me, I could have given you time for a safe escape."

Cade pointed to the stern-chase radar. "Look," he said. "There's nothing in sight—one pip."

"*Where?*" She pushed off from the grabiron and landed, clutching, by the screen.

"See?" he showed her. "A meteorite, most likely. Or even another ship. But not after us. They couldn't get into the air in less than two hours. Not unless they have fliers fueled and ready to go. By then we'll—"

"Suppose they have?" she blazed. "Wasn't *this* ship ready to go? Have you learned nothing? Do you still think the Realm's what it seems to be? This ship has been waiting six years for a Gunner to fly it and now it's to be destroyed because of your folly!"

Cade floated before the screen, watching the green point on the grey ground. It was just becoming recognizable as three bunched points. Each second that passed made them more distinct. "Fliers," he said. "What are they—cargoes, ferries, recons, rams?"

"I don't know," she said venomously. "I'm no Gunner. Rams, most likely."

"With you on board?" Rams were designed for annihilative action. They matched velocities with their quarry and crushed it with their armored prows. It meant death to all aboard the victim.

"I see you're still living in your ethical dream-world," she said. "I'm just a good excuse for the attack, Cade. If only you'd listened to me. What are you going to do now?"

"Outrun them if I can." He floated into his seat again. "I can try an evasive course and accelerate all the ship will take." It wouldn't be enough, and he knew it. "If the other pilots are inferior—"

"They won't be!" she snapped. He wondered whether she knew that rams had relays of pilots, always fresh, always solving for the difference while the quarry took evasive action, always waiting for the moment when the victim's single pilot tired after hours of dodging and began to repeat his tactics.

He reset the stern radar for maximum magnification and got a silhouette of three ugly fliers, smaller than his own, with anvil-like beaks. They were rams.

"Cade, listen to me." Her voice compelled attention. It was more than a tone of command, more than the urgency of the words. It carried a desperate seriousness that made him pause.

"I'm listening."

"You'll have to fight them, Cade. There's no other way."

He looked at her unbelievingly.

"There are guns aboard," she said, not meeting his eye.

"*What are you talking about?*"

"You know what." She looked squarely at him, without shame. "Fire on them!" she said.

18

IT HAD BEEN A ROTTEN THING to hear from the lips of the lax and dissolute Mars-born gunner who had died in France. To hear *her* speak the unspeakable tore his heart.

"It's for our lives, Cade!" she pleaded, shamelessly.

"Our lives!" he was passionately scornful. "What kind of lives would they be with a memory like that?"

"For the Realm of Man, then! The mission we are on!"

"What mission?" He laughed bitterly. "For a lie, a farce, a bad joke on the lips of the Power Master? What is the Realm of Man to me? A weakling Emperor, a murderous Power Master, a lying lecher of a Gunner Supreme! I have nothing left, Lady, except determination not to soil myself."

"Jetters and bombles!" she exploded, pleading no longer. "That's the way you're thinking—precisely like a commoner's brat terrified of the Beetu-five and the Beefai-voh!"

"I have no fear of the Beefai-voh and I don't believe in bombles," he said coldly. "I believe there are things one knows are wrong, detestably wrong, and I refuse to do them. I wish—I wish you hadn't said it."

She was fighting for calm. "I see I'll have to tell you some things. I won't try to pledge you to secrecy; your promise would be meaningless. But I hope that if the time comes, you'll let them torture you to death without revealing what I say, or that it was I who said it."

He kept silence.

"You've never heard the word 'history,' Cade."

He looked up in surprise. He had—used by the mad little burglar who'd been beaten to death in the Watch House.

She went on, frowning with concentration: "History is the true story of changes in man's social organization over periods of time."

"But—" he began, with an incredulous laugh.

"Never mind! You'll say it's meaningless. That 'changes' and 'social organization' are words that just can't be used together—that 'changed social organization' is a senseless noise. But you're wrong.

"I cannot tell you my sources, but I assure you that there have been many forms of social organization—and that the world was *not* created ten thousand years ago."

Her burning conviction amazed him. Was she mad, too? As mad as the little burglar?

"Try to understand this: thousands of years ago there was a social organization without Emperor or Stars. It was destroyed *by people firing from fliers*. That was a terrible way to fight. It killed the innocent—mother and child, armed man and unarmed. It poisoned food so that people died in agony. It destroyed sewer and water systems so that homes became stinking places of corruption.

"The social organization was destroyed. Homes and cities were abandoned—yes these people had cities; ours still bear their names. They lived like talking, suffering animals who only knew that things had once been better. Every year they forgot more of what that something better had been like, but they never forgot the supreme horror of death from the skies. Every year the details of it grew more cloudy and the thing itself grew more terrible."

Cade nodded involuntarily. Like a night attack, he thought; the less you saw the worse it was.

"There were centers of recovery—but that's no part of my story. You said you didn't believe in jetters and bombles? Cade, the jetters and bombles were *real*. The Beefai-voh and the rest of them are the names of the fliers that brought the supreme horror to that social organization."

"The Caves!" said Cade. The place called Washington, the rumbled ruinous blocks of stone with staring black eyes in them, haunted by the bombles—

"Yes, the Caves! The Caves everybody is afraid of and nobody can explain." She paused, almost breathless, then went on, tensely: "Cade, you must fight. If you don't, you're throwing our lives away on folly."

Cade didn't believe it. The vague appeal to sketchy evidence—it was as if a patrol leader came back and reported: "Sir, I didn't see it but I think there's a two-company enemy group somewhere up there in some direction or other." He gripped a grabiron in his fist until his knuckles went white. Ten thousand years of Emperor, Klin, Power Master, the Order and the Stars and the commoners . . . *that* was the world.

"They're coming up fast," she said emotionlessly, staring at the screen.

"Where are the guns?" he said hoarsely, not meeting her eye. And he knew he was only pretending to believe her story, pretending it was true so he could save her and himself at any cost in self-loathing.

"In the chart locker. Ten, I believe."

"Ten guns. He would be able to fire at unheard-of-aperture until coils fused and toss one aside for another. Ten guns—like that. As though a gun were not an individual thing, one to an Armsman, touched by the Gunner Supreme. . . .

"We must get space suits on," he said. He opened the locker and began to select his own units. Even after three years, he remembered his sizes. He dogged a pair of Number Seven legs against the bulkhead and tugged himself into them, donned Number Five arm pieces and sealed a torso unit around his body and to the limb units. He selected units for the girl and helped her into them; she didn't know how.

"Helmets now?" she asked calmly.

"Better carry the—the guns to the cargo room first." They made two arm-loads. Cade wiped a palmful of paste against a cargo-room bulkhead and stuck his load to it in a near row. The girl ranged hers beside them.

"Helmets now," he said. "Then you go back to the control room. I'll airtight this section and open the cargo lock. You watch the screens—do you know the alarms?" She shook her head. "The proximity alarm is a loud buzzer. I won't hear it in vacuum; you call me on the suit intercom when it goes off. Just talk into the helmet. If I succeed in driving them off you'll have to bleed air out of the control room until pressure is low enough for me to open the door against it. You hold down the switch on the upper left of the control array that's labeled 'Space Cock.' Can you do that?"

She nodded; they clamped on the plastic domes and sealed them. "Testing intercom. Do you hear me?"

"I hear you," sounded tinnily inside his helmet. "Can you turn your volume down?"

He did. "Is that better?"

"Thank you." That was all. A casual thanks for lowering his volume and not a word about his decision. Didn't she realize what he was doing for her? Was she fool enough to think he believed her wild "history"?

He sealed the fore and aft doors and plucked one of the guns from the bulkhead. Full-charged. No number. What did a gun without a number mean? A gun without

132

an Armsman matching it was unthinkable—but here were ten of them. Cade set each gun for maximum aperture and tight band, bled the air out of the compartment by a manual valve and spun open the big cargo lock.

After that there was nothing to do. He floated and waited and tried not to think. But in that he failed.

He knew Armsmen were Armsmen: fighters, masters of the Gun's complexity, masters of fighting, the only masters of fighting there were. That was an essential datum. He knew they were in the service of the Emperor —but that datum had crumbled under the ruthless words of the Power Master. He had known the Gunner Supreme was the embodied perfections of the Order, and that datum was a lie. He had known that it was abomination to fire from a flier—and found himself about to commit the abomination. He had known that for Armsmen there was only one woman, and not a woman of flesh: She who came fleetingly to those who died in battle, and in her fleeting passage rewarded Armsmen for their lives of abstinence. But he knew that for him there was another woman now—sometime mystagogue, traitress, whore, weak-minded noblewoman, expounder of insane 'history.' What did he know and how did he know it? He knew that, false to the Order and to She who came, he wanted this woman and did not know her secret.

"Proximity alarm," said the voice in his helmet.

"Message received," he said automatically in Armsman style and smiled bitterly at himself.

Cade kicked his way to the array of guns. Two he gummed to his thighs and two he clasped in his gauntlets. It was a grotesque situation. One man, one gun, it was supposed to be. But why? he demanded. Why not one man, two guns; one man, four guns; one man, as many guns as he needs and can lay his hands on? He shoved off to a port and began a hand-over-hand, spiderlike crawl from one quartz disk to the next, peering into the star-powdered blackness. The sun was astern of the flier; it would throw the rams into glaring relief. They wouldn't be able to stalk the victim in its own shadow.

There was a triple wink of light that became a blaze ripping past the ports. The rams had overshot in their first try at becoming part of the same physical system as their prey. They would return. . . .

Cade wondered whether there could be peace in the Mysteries from the confusions that plagued him, and recoiled from the thought. He knew them, at least, for what they were: traps for the johns and clink for the blades. Peace? Perhaps there was peace at Mistress Cannon's, where a man could wallow deep until not one ray of sunlight found him. At Cannon's you could drink and drug and couple while you had the greens, and then it was a simple matter to haunt dark streets until you found your nervous, late-going commoner. And then you could drink and drug and couple again where no ray of sunlight could find you. If firing from a flier was right, could a life at Cannon's be wrong?

The rams appeared ahead again and the flier seemed to gain and overtake them. Cade knew it was an illusory triumph; he was being bracketed. They were far astern now.

What did he know and how did he know it? He knew the Order of the Klin Philosophy and the Realm of Man had been created ten thousand years ago. He knew it because he had been told it by everyone. How did they know it? Because they had been told it by everyone. Cade's mind floated, anchorless, like his body. He didn't believe in jetters and bombles. That was for children. But he did believe in not firing from fliers. That was for Armsmen. Children and Armsmen had been told all about it.

"*I'll take you to the Caves.*

"*And the Beau-nine will come to tear your fingers and toes off with white-hot knives of metal.*

"*And the Beetu-five will come to pepper you with white-hot balls of metal.*

"*And the Beefai-voh will come and grate your arms and legs with white-hot metal graters.*

"*And last, if you are not a good boy, the Beethrie-six will come in the dark and will hunt you out though you run from Cave to Cave, screaming in the darkness. The Beethrie-six, which lumbers and grumbles, will breathe on you with its poison breath and that is the most horrible of all, for your bones will turn to water and you will burn forever.*"

The three rams blazed past the open port again and

seemed to hang in space far ahead of the flier. Their next "short" might do it.

"*Clennie's filthy. He told me he made a nail-hole in the wall and peeks at his sister every morning when she gets dressed. Anybody who'd do that would fire from a flier.*"

"*—embarrassing but necessary questions have to be put by the entrance board. Candidate Cade, with love of the Emperor in your heart, can you truthfully say that at night you have only normal and healthy dreams, free from such degrading fantasies as demonstrations of affection for other boys and firing a gun while flying?*"

"*—but oh, my pupils, there is worse yet to tell. This unfortunate young man who began by neglecting his Klin lessons did not end merely as a coward and thief. On reconnaisance flight he lost altitude and came under the fire of ground troops. I need not name the Thing he did; you can guess. Smitten by remorse after his unspeakable deed he properly took his life, but conceive if you can the shame of his Brothers—*"

"*—heartbroken, but it had to be done. I never knew he had a rotten spot in him, but I saw the paper myself. He 'solved' Tactics VII, if you please, with a smoke screen —sending a flier over the enemy left flank and having the Gunner set fire to the trees with a low-aperture blast of his gun, uh... from the, uh, from the air. It just shows you can't be too careful—*"

"*I receive this gun to use in such a way that my Emperor, my Gunner Supreme and my Brothers in the Order will never have cause to sorrow—*"

"*They're bunched in the square; we'll have to blast them out with a frontal smash. Cade, take your flier over for an estimate of their strength. Leave your gun here; we know they're low on charges and it wouldn't do to have yours fall into their hands if you're shot down.*"

The flier seemed to shoot past the rams again. The next time, velocities would match . . .

No; it would never do for him to take his gun. He remembered soaring over the plaza, tacking and veering as flame squirted from the densely massed troops below, busy with his counting. He dropped an imaginary grid over them, counted the number of men in one imaginary square and multiplied by the total number of imaginary squares as he shot back to the command post

135

on the outskirts of the Rhineland village with his estimate and joined in the costly advance on foot.

He had been told and he believed. How much else, he thought—as though a harsh light had suddenly been turned on—had he been told and believed against all common sense and reason?

Bring on your rams!

This time it was neither a short nor an over. Suddenly the three rams stood, less than a kilometer off, as though frozen in space.

They were smaller than Cade's freighter and boasted a wealth of propulsion units, as against the freighter's central main thrust tube and concentric ring of smaller steering tubes. He rejoiced as he saw conning bubbles rise simultaneously on the three craft just behind their ugly, solid anvil-beaks.

A propulsion unit came into play on the outermost of the rams—the reserve. Red haze jetted from a midships tube precisely perpendicular to the main thrust and the ram drifted outward to double its distance from the flier. Its forward component remained unchanged; it neither fell behind nor drifted ahead.

Aboard the two rams in action there must be relief at the flier's failure to take evasive action; they would now be plotting the simplest of symmetrical double-collision courses. Presently one of the rams would jet "over" or "under" its quarry to stand out on the other side the same distance as its mate; simultaneously the rams would add equal and opposite lateral thrust in amount proportional to their distance from the flier, and the victim would be crushed between the two ugly anvil-beaks.

Cade didn't know what standard doctrine was for ramming distance, but he was content to improvise.

Both rams showed red exhaust-mist. One was standing in closer; the other was moving "up" to hem the quarry in. Cade anchored himself at the lip of the open cargo lock; the conning bubble of the oncoming ram was sun-bright in his sights.

The gun gushed energy for three seconds before it failed. Cade hurled it through the lock into space and snatched another from his right thigh. It was not needed. The conning blister was still there, but blackened and discolored. He couldn't tell whether it had been pierced, but the ram issued uncertain gushes of red mist from one tube and then another, tacking and veering, and then flashed off at full thrust in what seemed to be the start of a turnaround curve.

The other ram was still working itself painstakingly around the flier with conservative jets of exhaust. Cade, half-through the lock, emptied the full charge of the second gun and a third at his hull, and saw sun-lit diamond flashes spraying through space—debris from exploding ports! The ram didn't wait for more, and when Cade looked for the reserve craft it was gone.

A good engagement, thought Cade. Presumably they wore space suits aboard the rams in action, so he could claim no kills. The conning blister hadn't shattered like the ports—perhaps because it had been extruded into space-cold for only a few seconds and the gun hadn't tickled it hard enough to set up destruction strain. And the psychology of it was important, too. The terrifying novelty of a ship-to-ship firefight, of a gun being used from a flier—Cade laughed thunderously inside the helmet at himself, at Clennie, at the embarrassed entrance board examiner, at the Klin Teacher with his moral lesson, at Novice Lorca's smoke screen, at the Oath of the Gun, at the Gunner Superior of France and his frontal smash.

A small, tinny voice in his ears yelled: "Turn your volume down! Turn it down!"

"I'm sorry, Lady," he said chuckling. "Did you see how I routed them? Now if you can find the space-cock I'll be able to open the door."

She found it and bled control-compartment air into space until he could shove the door open, airtight it again and start the control-compartment pressure building.

19

HE HELPED her take her helmet off, and then she helped him. They stood looking at each other, waiting for adequate words. Her eyes dropped first, and Cade momentarily felt she was ashamed of the thing she had made him do, the faith she had shaken and then destroyed.

But it made no difference now; the faith was destroyed—and for what? Cade stared long and hard at the Lady Jocelyn and a fresh torrent of laughter burst from him, the sound echoing and re-echoing in the vaulted compartment.

It was so ludicrous. There she stood, feet hooked under a toe-hold, a squat and misshapen figure no more womanly than the radars or the hulking compression pump. On top of the bulky mass of padding and metal and fabric the flaming, orange-red hair of the Lady of the Court was tangled and matted. Her face paint, never designed for beauty, was smudged and rubbed until she seemed a mocking distortion of the woman to whose beauty he had awakened a month ago in an underground center of intrigue.

He did not answer the mute question in her eyes and she did not choose to put it into words. Instead she said quietly: "Help me with my suit, please."

Cade, suddenly sobered, showed her how to unseal the members and stow them in the locker. And then, though he had thought himself past being shocked by the woman, she took him by surprise again. As though she were a commoner domestic she said: "I'll fix us something to eat. Is pressure up in the cargo room?"

He checked the gauge and spun the door open for her. "Don't come in for a few minutes," she said. "I'll be changing my clothes and washing up."

How many was a *few*? Cade spent half an hour getting out of his own suit, minutely inspecting it and stowing it away, and performed as many other jobs as he could find. There were not many. At last, cautiously, he hauled himself through the cargo room to the third compartment aft, the living quarters. Its door stood open and he went in.

"Oh, there you are. I was going to call you." She was at the tiny cooker, and two valved bottles of mash were beginning to gush steam. "There's a table and benches," she said, and he clicked them out of the wall, staring.

She had washed up. The soiled Court mask was scrubbed away and the perfection of her face was a renewed surprise. Her hair was bound with a cloth as if it were still damp from washing—he hoped the hair-dye had washed out. And instead of her sagging orange robe she wore a fresh set of mechanic's coveralls. The sleeves and legs were rolled and the belt pulled tight to her waist. She looked trim . . . and tempting. How did a man—a man not in the Order—go about telling a woman that she was beautiful?

"You've time to wash," she said pointedly.

"Of course, thanks," he said, and kicked over to the vapor chamber and thrust his head and hands in to be scrubbed by the swirling, warm mist and dried by the air blast. Turning to the table he realized with sudden alarm that he was expected to sit across it from her.

"Excuse me," he said, found a coverall for himself, and fled to the control room to change and pull himself together. To sit across the table from her and look at her while he ate! He told himself it was a first step. The sooner he unlearned his role of Gunner the simpler life would be. The mash would help. There was no sundown in space, but his stomach knew the time—mid-afternoon—and he was sure it wouldn't accept meat food for two hours. The coveralls helped too. He was glad to rid himself at last of the commoner's-best-suit he had bought at Cannon's with stolen money. Coveralls were a far cry from boots and cloak, but he had worn them in his Novice years.

Eating was easier than he had expected. There were thigh-straps on the benches and the table had a gummy top. It was an illusion of gravity at a time when the digestive system could use such assistance. The girl didn't speak as they solemnly chewed their mash, sucked water from their bottles and fished carefully through the trap of the jar for chunks of fruit that had carefully dehydrated crusts but were juicy inside.

At last Cade said: "Tell me more."

"More about what?" she asked coolly. He knew she

understood what he meant.

"You know what. 'History,' for instance. Or, more to the point, what cargo we are carrying and to whom?" He had not forgotten, even while fighting off the rams, the locked cabinets and sealed crates.

"There's nothing more to tell."

"You said before take-off that the ship had been waiting six years."

"It was nothing. Forget about it."

"So you're a liar too?" he asked hotly. *Anger is a peril.* The thought came unsummoned and he pushed it away; the direful warnings of Armsmen's training no longer bound him. "What other accomplishments does the Emperor's niece have?" he demanded. "I've seen you as traitor, whore, and spy. Thief too? Is the flier yours? Or is it just something you decided to make use of—like me?"

"*Get out of here!*" Her face was white and tense with rage. "Get—out—of—here," she repeated through clenched teeth.

Cade unbuckled the thigh straps and rose slowly, holding the table. He had been used long enough, by Stars and the Order and by her, at the risk of his life. Things were going to go his way for a change. "Do you really think you can get out of answering like this?" he said coldly. Coldly he looked down at the girl's trembling shoulders and, thinking of Mistress Cannon who had taught him how, he forced a smile.

She was silent, lips compressed to choke back the words she might regret, eyes flashing the fury she was trying to control.

"It's not that easy," he said. "Even a Gunner can learn the facts of life, eventually. You've done everything you could to destroy the meaning of my vows. What makes you think you can still count on the behavior they imposed?" She was rigidly holding onto herself, but he knew she couldn't keep it up.

"Have you forgotten that I spent three weeks out in the world without you—learning things you never taught me? I saw another woman like you, too. You don't imagine you're the only one being used by an ambitious traitor? I don't know who your master is, but I know hers. The Lady Moia . . ."

"*Get out of here!*" she screamed. "*Get out! Now!*" Tears streamed down her face as she freed herself and stood but she was not sobbing.

"No." He pulled himself one "step" toward her around the small table. "Not until you answer me. You may be content to serve your own master, but I tell you that *I* am tired of being used. For thirteen years the Order used me as it pleased, and I was willing. Then I 'died,' and the Cairo people tried to use me as their murderer. Their chosen victim, your friend the Power Master, tried to use me the same way against the Star of Mars. By the Realm!, even a drunken con man at Cannon's thought he could use me for *his* ends. I've had enough! Do you understand that?"

He stopped, realizing that his tirade had given her a chance to gather her own control. "You saved me twice," he added more quietly, "when others tried to use me. Why? Why, to use me yourself, of course. To fly this ship. *What for? For whom?* This time I'm going to know!"

He let the last words ring a moment in the air, and then he snapped at her: "Whose cargo are we carrying? What's in it? *Whose woman are you?*"

"My own!"

He hadn't been watching for it; he had looked for collapse.

Her hand stung as it whipped across his cheek. He seized her arms as she floundered from the floor; they drifted together against a bulkhead. "Answer me!" he said sharply. She was crying now, sobbing in an agony of frustration and defeat. He felt her tense body relax, helpless and beaten.

She would fight no more. He knew he could release her and she would tell him what he wanted to know. He meant to release her; he started to. But in some way he did not understand, his hands refused to obey him. Her body was close to his and her face turned up, suddenly startled and questioning.

He had never done it before; he didn't know how to do it. But his face bent down and for a long time, a timeless moment, his lips were on hers.

She pulled away at last, and he held fast to a grabiron, oblivious to everything except the surging new sensations in him. This was how a man, an ordinary man, felt about a woman. This was what had been denied him all his life. This was what the Power Master had ruthlessly described in words. This was what brought the Gunner Supreme scurrying from planetary and Realm affairs to the side of the Lady Moia. This was what Jana had offered him at Cannon's. And none of them had quite understood that it was a thing without meaning to him—until now.

He looked up at her, standing across the room from him now, and made another discovery. She was quite helpless against him; he could take her when he liked. And that wasn't what he wanted.

He had kissed her, but that was not all. She had kissed him, and a whole new world had been in it.

"Jocelyn," he said quietly. He could taste the word in his mouth. It was a plea and a caress.

She said coldly; "I thought that this at least I would be spared from you. I will tell you as much as I can and then ask you to leave me alone."

"Jocelyn," he said again. She ignored it.

"I served as spy in the Cairo Mystery, yes. You should be glad I did. And you may believe me or not as you like, but I am neither whore nor thief. I serve the Realm of Man. As for the cargo, it does not concern you, and I would be a traitor for the first time if I told you more than that. Now will you go?"

"If you wish." There was nothing more to learn, and much that he had learned unsought needed thinking over.

He left the room without looking at her again, and did not try to speak to her again that day. She slept in the cabin aft and he tried to sleep on the acceleration couch in the control room, while thoughts tormented him.

Thinking was no help. He was bound to her, whatever she was, whosever game she played. But no matter how he turned and twisted each new fact, he saw nothing but a reasonless and chaotic conflict. She served the Realm of Man? So claimed the Power Master, off-hand killer and father of lies that he was. So doubtless claimed the weakling Emperor, the rebellious Stars, the treacherous Gunner Supreme.

He had no reason to suppose there was sense to it at

all. Always before things had had meaning: each ritual gesture, each emphasis of wording, each studied maneuver in battle had had a meaning and a place in the fitting world of Klin. But now it seemed instead that there was just a world of random forces, clashing because of this man's lust or that man's pride. How could he demand more of her than the world offered?

In the morning he was hungry and it was not unreasonable to go to the galley for food. She was distant and polite and for the better part of a week she remained so. Then he tried once more to question her.

He asked again about History. She bit her lip and told him she never should have spoken as she did and never would have told what she had except to save their lives. "You would do best to forget you ever heard the word."

"Can I forget that I have fired from a flier?" he asked gravely and she looked away.

About the cargo she would not speak at all, and his bitterness grew daily at the galling thought that he was expected to be a pawn in some game and be content with the role—he who had led companies and would surely have risen to the rank of Superior.

There were four days left to the voyage when he decided to force the cargo. He could have done it openly; she was powerless to prevent him. But he insured his privacy by noisily rattling the handle of the door to the cabin at midnight by the chronometer. She must have been sleeping lightly. In less time than it would have taken him to actually open the door he heard the dogs on the other side thud to. He rattled again, noisily, and then went off, grumbling as loudly as was reasonable. He smiled grimly, wondering when she would find the courage to come out—and more grimly still when he recalled that all the flier's food was on the other side of the dogged-down door. Well, he had fasted for three days before. And now he would find out who was playing with his life.

The metal sheathing on the free-floating crates yielded easily to the lowest aperture of a gun. The contents of the crate nearest the break-through point were also metallic, but were undamaged by the blast of the gun. It was guns that were in the crate—at least a thousand of them. Guns of the Order, or replicas, full-charged and without numbers. He was not really surprised.

Methodically Cade opened the three other crates—all the same. And the lockers? The locks were radionic and not simple, but he solved them, each quicker than the last, and sampled the contents.

At the end he went back to the control room making no effort to cover up his work.

Ten thousand guns of the Order, bound for Mars. He knew now for whom the Lady Jocelyn worked.

He slept, and in the morning tried the cabin door. It was still dogged down, and he called on the ship's interphone.

"What do you want?" she asked coldly.

"First, to apologize for disturbing your sleep."

"Very well."

"And something to eat."

"I can't see how to get it to you," she said indifferently.

"You can't afford to starve me. I still have to land the ship, you know."

"I have no intention of starving you." There was a hint of humor in her voice. "I was thinking it might be a good idea to weaken you a little."

"I've weakened already," he said. "I did some hard work last night, and I need food."

"What kind of work?"

"I'll show you when you come out." He didn't have to wait long. There was a scant ten minutes of silence, before she called back:

"If I bring you some food, will you give me your word not to make a fool of yourself?"

"Certainly," he said cheerfully, "if you feel there is any value in the word of a lapsed Armsman. By what shall I swear?"

Silence.

Then, almost timidly: "By yourself."

And it was thoughtfully he answered: "By myself, I swear that I will do nothing to distress you."

"All right. Five minutes," she said, and cut off.

Cade waited. He heard the dogs thud back and the door open. Silence then, and he made himself sit still and wait. Ludicrously, a valved bottle of mash floated through the open door from the cargo room. It must have drifted from her hand when she saw the ripped-open cargo. Cade watched the bottle bump to a gentle stop, and rebound from the bulkhead to drift within his reach. He was hungry; he wanted the food; but he let it go slowly past him. Jocelyn floated in a moment later, pale but self-possessed.

"All right," she said. "Now you know. Don't ask me to explain, because I won't. I can't. Not if you tried to get it out of me by torture. I have some loyalties I do not violate."

"I have not," he said briefly. "What was left of them you violated for me. And I'm not going to ask you to explain. You keep forgetting that I've talked to others besides you these last few weeks. The Power Master, for instance. And a miserable little Marsman who came to Cannon's to forget his loneliness. And—" He thought of the Mars-born Gunner, Harrow, who had died for a terrible sin, "—and others," he finished shortly.

Cade picked the bottle of mash from the air and tasted it.

"All right," she said and dropped all pretense of indifference. "Just what is it that you imagine you understand?" He let the bottle go; the mash was cold and he was no longer hungry.

"To start with, I know what loyalty you hold."

He waited, but she said nothing. "I won't pretend to understand why an Imperial Lady should serve as spy for the Star of Mars, but—" He paused with satisfaction. Her face was impassive, but one sharp indrawn breath had given her away. "Do you deny it?"

"No. No, I don't deny it."

"Then perhaps you will want to explain it?"

She was thoughtful and she spoke reluctantly: "No. I can't. What else do you know?"

"Why should I tell you?" He was beginning forthrightly now. "Why should I answer your questions?"

"Because I know more than you do. Because there are some things it's dangerous to know. Besides," she added, "I can't possibly tell you more until I find out just how much you *do* know."

"All right." He had nothing to lose . . . and he wanted to talk about it. "I'll tell you what I know and what

I think:

"First, I have known for some time that the Star of Mars is petitioning the Emperor for the assignment of Mars-born Armsmen to his Court. Till now, of course, they have always been dispersed among the Earth Stars. But a month or more ago, requests were being made for the return of seasoned Mars-born Gunners, and for the retention of native novices on Mars when they reached the rank of Armiger.

"Second, I know the Power Master is determined that this petition shall not be granted. I *think* I know why—"

She leaned forward just a little, eager for what he might say next.

He went on, deliberately shifting his ground.

"—why Mars wants its Armsmen at home, and why the Power Master will not allow it. The reason is so obvious it would never occur to anyone outside the little clique of schemers and tricksters and—History students in which you live! It's Mars iron, nothing more."

She sat back again and seemed almost bored; this was nothing new to her. Then he was on the right track.

"All of Earth's machinery needs Mars iron. If the Star of Mars had an Order of his own, composed entirely of Marsmen, with their peculiar devotion to their homes and families—I've talked with them, and I know how they feel—then he would hold more real power than the Emper . . . than the Power Master himself."

He laughed out loud, remembering the waking formula that had prepared him for the day each morning for six thousand days of his life.

"*It is fitting that Armsmen serve the Emperor through the Power Master and our particular Stars. While this is so, all will be well to the end of time,*" he quoted aloud. "I said that many times each day for many years," he told her.

"I think the Star of Mars knows his request will never be granted, and I think he is now preparing to train an outlaw Order of his own to serve the same purpose."

A fleeting smile crossed her lips; in spite of everything, Cade realized, she still thought of him as a Gunner, with a Gunner's attitudes. She could not possibly have realized how much she was revealing with that small smile of satisfaction.

He had half-guessed before, but he was certain now, that the training of outlaw Armsmen had already begun. It took three years of novitiate drill before a Brother was given a practice gun in the Order proper. How many of them were there? How many half-trained, whole-hearted Marsmen waiting right now for the guns he was bringing on this ship?

For the first time in ten thousand years, guns would be fired that had never been touched by the Gunner Supreme. Then he remembered: not in ten thousand years. In History . . . how long was that?

"What purpose?" she asked.

Cade snapped to attention.

"Oh, a private armed force of his own. A force powerful enough to make a stand against the Earth-born Armsmen. It wouldn't have to equal the combined strength of all Earth forces. Nothing near that. He must know the Power Master will never let Earth Stars combine to that extent. These guns, the guns you would have had me carry unawares if you could, will make him strong enough to become Power Master—or Emperor in your uncle's place."

He stopped talking and waited. She said nothing.

"Well," he asked impatiently. "Can you deny it? Any of it?"

"No," she said slowly. "None of it. Except one thing. I am—you *must* understand, Cade—I am no man's paid spy!" She said the words with such unmistakable contempt that for the moment Cade found them hard to disbelieve.

"Then, *why*?" he asked intently. "What are you working for?"

She smiled. "I told you once: for the Realm of Man." And her earnestness lost all meaning because once more she had refused an answer. But she went on: "Cade, you found me first in the Cairo Mystery. You didn't trust me then, and you discovered later that you *should* have trusted. Do you know what I was doing there?"

"The Great Conspiracy!" he sneered. "Every Star a Power Master! Add chaos and confusion to cruelty and unreason! Yes, I know what you were doing there!"

"If you'd think with your brain instead of your anger," she snapped, "you'd realize how wrong *that* is. No, *wait* a minute," she said quickly as he opened his mouth to protest, and went on, talking fast: "I wasn't working for the Conspiracy; you must know that by now. Why should I have tried to save you from the drug? I have no special fondness for the Power Master." She paused for breath; and Cade had to admit that that made sense. It was the single paradox that kept the rest of what he knew from forming a clear picture.

She resolved it. "Cade," she said steadily, "much of what you've said today is true—*most* of it. There are some facts you still don't know, facts I don't dare tell you. They're dangerous even for me to know; for you, they would be fatal. The lives of other people are involved, and of one more important than you or—that doesn't matter now. But you can surely see, with what you *do* know, why I was working in the Conspiracy?"

"Why yes, of course—because your master ordered it!"

Her hands balled into furious fists, shaking in impotent anger at his refusal to be swayed. "Because—I—needed—*you!*" She spaced the words evenly in a last effort at control. "You or any Armsman I could get; someone to fly this ship. I *told* you it's been waiting for six years. Waiting for a pilot, nothing more. And I got the pilot. Now do you see? I couldn't let you kill the Power Master. I couldn't let him kill you either. I needed you for this."

Well, he thought bitterly, now it fitted. It all hung together. She'd had a job to do, and she had done it, calmly betraying one group after another, to accomplish it. And he himself . . . he was a pilot for the Star of Mars. And nothing more.

She took stunned silence for surrender. "You *do* understand?" she asked more quietly. "Cade, later perhaps, I can tell you more, but now—"

"Now you've said enough. Unless, of course, you want to tell me—being *no man's paid spy*—just why you chose to act against the Great Conspiracy in favor of another one just like it? What makes you favor Mars' conspiracy?"

"Not conspiracy! Healing!" The dam broke at last; words and dreams held back too long began to flow out now in passionate floods. "Healing the life of man," she said proudly. "Saving it from the dead grip of the Power Master and the Klin Philosophy! How *can* I make you understand?" Her face passed from earnest pleading to the raptness of a visionary. "I've told you about History, but it's still just a word to you. You haven't studied—

"You don't know what 'science' means, do you? Of course not; the word is half forbidden and half forgotten because science means change and change means threat, to the Klin stasis and to the Power Master.

"Mankind is dying, Cade, because men are chained to their machines and forbidden to make new ones. Don't you see that one by one the machines will wear out and—"

"No," he said warily. "I don't see. The Brothers of the Order build new machines. When old ones are gone, new ones are always ready. Klin Teachers study and build machines."

"But no new ones," she said. "Science means *new* things, Cade; searching for the truth with no roads closed, no directions forbidden. Cade, there was a time—I know from History—when men powered their machines with the metal uranium. It's gone now. Thorium was used next, and now it's gone too. And now the iron. Earth's iron is gone. When the Mars iron is gone too, what next? There should be ten million men working day and night to find a new power source, but there are none.

"There are other ways to destroy civilization besides firing from fliers! They'll have to stop making fliers and ground cars. The cities will become great sewers when the pumps stop turning. Inlanders will get sick, with ugly lumps of wild tissue growing from their necks, because there won't be anybody to bring them fish and salt from the oceans. Babies will grow up crooked because there won't be power for the milking machines in the food factories, or for the boats that catch the cod and shark. Animals will overrun the growing food because there won't be wire fences or power to charge them. Diseases will rot mankind because there won't be power for the biodrug factories." She stopped, worn out with her own intensity, and watched him silently. "Does it mean anything to you?" she asked with a touch of bitterness.

"I don't know," he said bemused. He was thinking of

what the Power Master had said to him that day, with Kendall dead on the floor. It made this much sense at least: that here were two honestly opposing forces. The Power Master's view of the world made more sense, from what he had seen of it, than Jocelyn's, but . . . if he could believe her instead, a man could have something to fight for again.

"All that," she said quietly, "can be cured by science. And there are other things—'art' is one. Another word, Cade. It means exploring this universe and making new universes with language and sound and light. It makes you laugh and weep and wonder; no man alive today can understand the joy of making and giving art, or the joy of receiving it from the maker.

"You don't know what 'freedom' is. But perhaps you'll learn—soon. I hope—" She hesitated and looked up at him defiantly. "I hope when we reach Mars you will accept service under the Star of Mars. He is the man to follow at this time. But for now, *I cannot tell you more.*"

"Then I won't ask," he said. There was too much to think about already. And he knew all he really needed: he had learned the meaning of at least one new word, and that was "love."

20

THEY HAD three days of space: days in which Cade found it less and less difficult to remember that the Order was behind him. The old life was finished; the old certainties gone. There was just one certainty now—a woman. The only possible woman for Cade in the new life, just as the Lady of the Order had been the only possible woman for Cade the Armsman. Until they landed he could share a growing friendship and . . . something more. What might come later he did not know, except for one thing: if they lived through the landing on Mars he would find some way to stay at her side. The Star of Mars could be no worse a master than the Star of France. Surely he was a worthier one than the Power Master.

Knowing this much and no more, Cade used the time he had to win the liking and strenghten the confidence of the Lady Jocelyn. Never had he known himself capable of such fluent conversation or such avid listening.

Too quickly, Mars filled the heavens and Jocelyn's gentle friendliness disappeared behind a barrage of preparations and crisp instructions.

The coordinates she designed took them to a craggy basin in the southern hemisphere, less than a hundred kilometers from the capital city of Mars.

The spot had obviously been chosen to afford a combination of convenience and secrecy. From the air it was one of those blank patches that showed neither red nor green, but only featureless grey. No red meant no iron: none of the characteristic family-operated strip mine refinery complexes of Mars. No green meant no water: no farms and farm-families raising vegetables and goat meat for the miners and city-dwellers of the planet. Featureless grey meant unobserved isolation.

Cade braked the big flier to a stop on level ground as though it were a ground car. He unbuckled himself from the control seat and looked out of a port at a desolate valley surrounded by gnarled old hills as high as any on sandstorm-lashed Mars. Jocelyn at his side surveyed the emptiness impatiently. She was already swathed in bulky synthetic furs.

Cade found a suit for himself and donned it. He came back to find her pacing the small area of cabin floor.

"Can your lungs take Mars air?" she demanded.

He nodded. "I've fought in the Alps and the Taurus." With Brothers crumpling about him, he remembered—brave men, tireless men who happened to lack the body machinery for battle on half-rations of air. "How about you? There's a respirator in the locker."

"I've been here before." She stopped him with a nervous gesture at the air lock.

Cade set the mechanism in motion and there was an equalizing outrush of air. Momentarily his sight dimmed and he had to cling to an iron for support. The girl, lighter and with bigger lungs, recovered before he did and was through the lock before he could walk certainly. Her eyes swept the horizon anxiously. "Your butcher-work on the crates isn't going to make things easier," she said. "We'd better start unloading and have the—the cargo ready to go."

"To go to the Star of Mars?"

"Yes."

He followed her back into the ship and opened the cargo port amidships. While she emptied locker after locker, Cade moved the bulkier crates outside. Fifty meters from the flier the pile of guns grew tall. But at every trip the girl's impatient scanning of the horizon was repeated.

"I assume your friends are late?" he asked uneasily.

"The less you assume, the better," she said. And then she uttered a gasp of relief. There was a black dot topping a hill and then another—dozens, hundreds at last.

"The Armsmen of Mars?" He was torn between surprise at their unexpected numbers and contempt for their ragged approach.

"Far from Armsmen, Cade. The word is 'patriots.' You've heard it before." There was an unreadable quality in her voice. Cade could not tell whether she despised these people or admired them. "It means that they love their homeland. They are devoted more to Mars and its ruler than to the Emperor."

He couldn't help it; a shudder went through him at the thought—and a moment later he was smiling at the shudder.

"They're just porters then."

She started to shake her head and then said: "In effect, yes. Just porters."

The crowd was drawing nearer. Patriots or porters, whatever they were, Cade saw clearly that there were no Armsmen among them. They were farmers, miners, clerks from the city. They walked easily as you'd expect Mars-born people to, and clearly had no difficulty with Mars air. Their clothes were lighter than the furs he and Jocelyn wore against the chill. And they all carried uncouth sacks over their shoulders. Cade thought of the guns jostled and scraping together in the sacks and set his teeth obstinately: a gun now was just a killing-tool, the way a saw was just a cutting-tool.

There were boys in their teens and not a few women

among the mob; it numbered some nine hundred, to carry about fifty thousand guns.

How, he wondered, could this rabble keep a secret? And then he thought of Harrow, the dead Gunner: ". . . a man likes to be among his own people . . . it's newer on Mars . . . I don't suppose you know anything about your eight-times great-grandfather. . . ." If all these people shared that feeling!"

With the crowd came noise, the undisciplined chatter of nine hundred·excited people. A tall, lean-faced fellow in his middle years turned to the rest and yelled sharply through the thin air: "Just shut up, all of you! Shut up and stand where you are!" A few lieutenants repeated the crude command. After a minute the shipward drift of the crowd halted and there was silence.

The man said to Cade: "I'm Tucker. There wasn't anything said about a woman. Who's she?"

The Lady Jocelyn said dramatically: "A daughter of Mars." If there was the faintest tinge of mockery in her voice, only Cade thought he heard it.

The lean-faced man said, feelingly: "Mars blesses you, sister."

"Mars blesses us all, from the highest to the lowest." It seemed to be password and countersign.

Tucker said: "We're glad to have a high-born Lady among us, sister. I was told the flier of the ship wouldn't be a brother?"

"Not yet. He will be. He is an Earth-born Gunner who will train Marsmen for the day of liberty."

"It's growing," said Tucker rapturously. "Nothing can stop it!" It was beginning to sound more like the mystic nonsense of the Cairo gang than businesslike military identification procedure.

The mob was getting noisy again and military procedure took another body-blow. Tucker turned and bawled at them: "You all shut up now! Get into some kind of a line and get your sacks open. And don't take all day!" Cade watched them milling and groaned at the thought of turning such a mob into Armsmen. But he swallowed his disgust; what she wanted of him, he would do.

They did get whipped into line eventually by roaring non-coms. Cade couldn't make out whether these were merely temporary, self-appointed leaders, or whether there was any organization in this gang. But somehow a dozen Marsmen got busy sorting out sixty-gun piles from the heap and dumping them into waiting sacks. The guns couldn't have been carried under Earth gravity, but their weight on Mars constituted no more than a good working load. Cade was very glad that guns of the Order had two centimeters of six-kilogram trigger pull before you hit a five-gram pull and firing contact. There were no accidents.

Jocelyn told him busily: "We won't need the ship and I don't want to leave it here for a monument. Shoot it off to somewhere on automatic take-off."

It was sound doctrine. By the time the empty flier roared off, its ultimate destination an aimless orbit in space, the tail-end of the line of porters was snaking past a melting pile of guns. Tucker, the lean-faced "patriot" leader, was yelling again, trying to make himself heard over the combined noise of rockets and rabble, to get them to form a new line of march heading out of the valley.

As the noise of the vanishing flier was lost in the distant sky, the man's shouts were drowned out again by the terrifying crescendo of jets. Not one ship this time, but a fleet. An instant later a hundred or more space-recon fliers roared low over the hill-rimmed basin.

They fanned out beautifully to land beyond the crags in a perfectly executed envelopment on the largest scale Cade had ever seen. He wondered numbly whether the brilliant maneuver had been performed on individual piloting or slave-circuit control.

The Martian rabble broke its uneven ranks. Nine hundred of them milled pointlessly about asking each other frightened, stupid questions; the total effect was a thought-shattering roar. The Lady Jocelyn's hand gripped Cade's arm through the wadded sleeve of his furs. Her face was deathly pale. He must have radar stations on Deimos and Phobos, Cade thought, to pin-point us like that. . . .

Then there was a voice, the kind of voice nine-year-old Cade, Gunner-to-be, had thought the Emperor spoke with. It roared like thunder through the basin of rock, breaking against the rim and rebounding in echoes—the

154

voice of the Power Master, the voice Cade would never fail to know whether it spoke cynically across a room, commandingly over the radio, or majestically into the thin air of Mars.

"Marsmen, my Gunners are taking up positions surrounding you. You will drop your bags of weapons and walk to the foot of the hills to surrender. I want only the two persons who landed by flier. They must be held but the rest of you will be released after a search. You have fifteen minutes to do this. If you do not, my Gunners will advance, firing."

Silence from the hills and a growing mutter from the crowd.

"Who are they?"

"Who's the man from the flier?"

"They said he's no brother!"

"*Get rid of the guns!*"

"They'll burn us down where we stand."

"What will we do?"

"*What will we do?*"

Cade shook his head dazedly; Tucker was glaring at him.

"*He's lying!*" shrilled a clear voice—Jocelyn's. "He's lying! Do you think he'll let you go when you're helpless? He'll kill you all!"

Her warning was lost in the roar, except to Tucker and Cade. The lean-faced Marsman said to her slowly: "*When* we're helpless? We're helpless now. We've drilled some, but we don't know guns."

With the brutal mob-noise for a background, Jocelyn spoke again, softly and almost to herself. "Two hundred years," she said emotionlessly. "Two hundred years of planning, two hundred years of waiting, two hundred years of terror: waiting for a traitor or a fool to talk, but nobody did. One gun, two guns, a dozen guns a year at last, waiting—"

She was swaying as she stood; Cade braced her with his arm.

"What a dream it was . . . and we came so close. Mars in rebellion, the Klin Philosophy shaken, Armsmen split, the Power Master defied! Men on Mars—men everywhere—thinking for themselves, challenging the traditions that tied them down. Thinking and challenging!" A blaze that had kindled briefly in her eyes seemed to die.

"We underestimated," she said flatly. Now she was talking to Cade. "We didn't allow for the dead weight of things as they are. Two hundred years . . . I hope my uncle will not suffer when he dies."

Her uncle. Cade hung on to that and comprehension came at last. "The Emperor," he said slowly, "your uncle—the Emperor; he knows of this?"

"Yes, of course." There were tears behind her voice Cade marveled at his blindness, not to have understood before. It was so obvious; this way it all made sense.

"The Emperor—the last five Emperors, powerless in everything except knowledge. They and a few others in the family, a handful of men and women. Three generations ago the reigning Emperor saw that Mars was the key, that the rulers of Mars would rebel and the Mars populace would be with them. The Emperor-Mars pact was concluded fifty-five years ago. My uncle wrote the petition for Mars-born Armsmen. What a great dream it was! But what difference does it make now?"

I hope my uncle will not suffer when he dies. But he would; the Emperor would suffer and so would she. The Power Master would not let them die until he had wrung from them every bit of information that they held.

Abruptly the voice of thunder said: "Eight minutes!" and the Mars rabble flowed around them, scared, angry and confused, demanding to be told what to do and what it meant.

Tucker had been listening, dazed. "If we could fight," he said hoarsely, working his hands. "If we could only fight!"

"Thinking and challenging," echoed Cade. "Thinking and challenging." Five years to make a novice. Ten for an Armiger. Fifteen for a Gunner. To face Gunners with anything less than Gunners was like opposing guns of the Order with wooden clubs. Tucker knew that, and still dared to think: *if we could fight.*

They were patriots, Cade thought; now he new what it meant. They were frightened now, with reason, but still they held their sacks of guns. They weren't ready to give in.

Cade said the impossible: "*We can fight them.*"

"*Armsmen?*" said the girl.

But there was wild hope on Tucker's lean face.

"They're trained," he said foolishly. "They've had three years."

"There's no other way," Cade said to Jocelyn, ignoring the Marsman. "It's a cleaner death, and—*you* taught me to challenge the rules."

He fired his own gun straight up in a three-second burst at full aperture and a stunned silence fell on the crowd.

"I am Gunner Cade of the Order of Armsmen," he shouted into the thin air. "You have guns—more guns than the Armsmen in the hills. I will show you how to use them."

21

THOUGHTS BLAZED through his mind. The complex gun; the thing no commoner could master: First Study of the Primary Circuits of the Gun, Ceremonial of the Gun, Order of Recharging, After-charging Checklist, Malfunctions of the Booster Circuit, the Sighting Picture, The Gun's Inner Meaning in Klin, Aperture and Band Settings for Various Actions. In studied sequence they flashed across his mind, and one by one he threw them out.

"The way to use your gun," he shouted, "is to point it and pull the trigger. If it stops firing, throw it away and grab another." To Tucker he said swiftly: "Have you a dozen men the others will listen to?"

The lean-faced man nodded. "Get them here," Cade said. While the names were being shouted he turned to scan the encircling hills. Against the sky he could see the slender rods of radionic grinds faintly discernable—ten or so, spaced around the rim of hills. What contempt they must hold him in to expose command posts like that!

Where to attack with his rabble? Straight ahead there was a nice little pass in the hills. Standard doctrine was for the defenders to command such a pass by plunging fire. Standard doctrine in the attack was to draw fire from the defenders, pin down the defenders exposed by their fire and storm the pass. The Marsmen had no training to prepare themselves for such an encounter. But off to the right was an ugly little cliff—a cliff nobody in his right mind would bother to attack or defend. It would be covered by a Gunner or so, no matter how unlikely it was. But was it so unlikely to be scaled by Marsmen to whom the air and gravity were normal—?

"Here are the men." Cade looked over the dozen lieutenants Tucker had called up and proceeded to instruct them. A long line of teachers would have cringed at his instruction. He showed them only the triggers, the band and aperture sets, and the charge gauges. They didn't need to know how to recharge; there were guns to spare. They didn't need to know the care of guns, the circuits, the ritual, the inner meanings—all they needed was to know how to shoot. As he showed them, his wonder almost equaled theirs at the simplicity of it all.

"We will head for that cliff," he said, pointing. "Try to show your men what I showed you before we get there. Don't try to keep order on the march. The worse it looks, the better. That's all."

He gave them a minute and then stepped off for the rim of hills. He yelled a command which he dimly realized was more ancient than the Order itself and exactly as old as History:

"*Follow me!*"

"For Mars! For the Star of Mars!" someone shrieked insanely, and others took up the howl. Cade didn't look behind him. If he had them all, good. If he didn't, there was nothing to be done about it. Perhaps some would start with him and others hesitate and follow—so much the better. To the ring of steady-eyed Armsmen watching from the hills, this charge across the plain would seem a panic flight. Even if they had picked up the gist of his orders to the mob with a three-meter directional mike trained on him, or seen the scattered efforts of lieutenants to instruct their groups it would seem inconceivable to them that commoners would fight.

Not that they would; Cade knew it well enough. They'd balk at the first blast of well-aimed fire. They'd shriek and run like—commoners. Mars or Earth, a commoner's a commoner; sluggish, overstuffed, stupid, soft. *Point your guns and pull the trigger*. Fine words, he mocked himself, fine words! They were supposed to have had three years of "training"—form-fours on the village square, no doubt, an hour a week. Even that didn't show. None of them had *seen* a gun before.

Thinking and challenging, he mocked. Thinking indeed, that challenged the one bedrock truth he knew: that Armsmen were Armsmen, fighters, gun-handlers, the only fighters there were.

In was insanity; *that* truth he knew, and the other truth that made insanity his only course. If the fight was lost, he was already dead, and so was *she*.

She was running alongside, keeping pace with his strides. "Do you think—?" she asked wildly. "Cade, it's the *Power Master's Guard*! They can defeat any force of Armsmen in the Realm."

"We're not Armsmen," he growled. "We're a rabble of crazy *patriots*. We don't know how to fight, but we seem to have something to fight *for*. Now fall back. Get into the middle of this gang and leave yourself room to run when they stampede."

"I won't!"

"You—*will*!"

Meekly she fell back and Cade strode on. Admit it, fool! he raged. Admit it! You're playing a game, a child's farce—the way you used to play Superior and Novice back in Denver. They've forged a ring of fire around you and you're charging into death: solitary death, because that mob will break and run and well you know it.

A farce? Very well; play it out as best you can, he told himself, Gunner Cade, trained Armsman, master of fighting that you are—*fight*!

He swung on grimly and the worn, ancient cliffs loomed ahead, grotesque engravings of wind and sand and centuries on deathless stone. If the Armsmen opened fire now, he was lost with his half-trained rabble. They'd never know enough to spread; they'd bunch like sheep and die in a crushed mob. If they reached the dead area under the cliff there might be a momentary postponement of the butchery.

The Armsmen would have fired before now, if they expected trouble. They must be looking for a desperate attempt to push through the nice little pass and escape.

The attack of the Marsmen would have to be swift and deadly. They might take the hill! It was a thing that would rock the foundation of the Order.

"For the Star! For the Star of Mars!" he heard them howling behind him, and grinned coldly. *Patriots*! Perhaps patriots were what you needed for a murderous, suicidal assault.

His feet slipped once on rubble and the shadow of a crag was on his face. "Give me two of your guns, brother," he said to a boy with bulging eyes and a fixed grin on his face. "Up the cliff!" he shouted over his shoulder at the rabble. "*Follow me—charge!*" He broke into a run and noted coldly that the thin air roughly canceled the advantage of the lesser Mars gravity. The youth at his side, still breathing easily, pushed ahead —and fell a moment later with the fixed grin still on his face and both legs charred away by a long-range blast.

Automatically Cade blasted the crag from which the fire had come. The fire-fight had been joined.

Make it or break it now, he thought. Face your death, fire a counterblast or two to let them know you were there, to make them pause a bit and wonder a bit and perhaps fear a bit before your commoners broke and ran.

"*Follow me! Up!*"

The lean-faced Tucker raced past Cade screaming: "For the Star of Mars!" His sack of guns flapped and bobbed as he began to scrabble up the cliff. There were others—wild-eyed men, a panting youth, a leathery woman—who passed Cade.

Behind him there were yells and the blast of guns. He hoped he wouldn't be burned in the back by one of the Marsmen's ill-aimed guns after coming this far. . . .

The fire-fight grew severe as he pantingly climbed the cliff. From the hills it was rapid and deadly. From the Marsmen it was a torrent whose effect he couldn't guess at. The noise the guns made was a senseless blend of small-aperture buzz and wide-aperture roar. Cade scrambled grimly up and hoisted himself over the jagged cliff-edge into the racket of a first-class battle. A rudimentary squad of Marsmen was blasting Armsmen across a wind-row of fallen comrades. They had learned about aperture by now, Cade saw with bleak satisfaction, and they were learning how to rush from crag to crag, to take isolated Armsmen in pockets of the eroded rock by flanking fire. Incredibly, in spite of the numbers of their dead, they were gaining ground. Armsmen were falling.

They didn't need his gun. Cade turned from the shooting and stationed himself at the cliff head, splitting the steady stream of Marsmen as they gained the peak, sending half to the right and half into the fighting to the left.

"Tucker!" he yelled.

The lean-faced Marsman who had led the assault up the cliff was still alive. "Tucker, take this gang on the right and work them through the hills. Keep them moving, keep them firing, keep them yelling. I'll work the rest around the left. If you see any sign of the Armsmen's withdrawing to regroup, keep your men moving, but come and check with me. That's all."

"Yes, brother." Like old times, thought Cade—except that he was fighting now to overthrow all he had once fought for . . . and for Jocelyn.

He dared not think of that. He had not seen her once since the beginning. Now he had a job to do and was doing well. It had occurred to him at last that they might win.

The cliff-top fighters' insanely extravagant fire had done its work. This immediate arc of the hills was cleared of Armsmen. He saw that the Marsmen were sorted out into elementary squads and platoons—a lesson of battle, or fruit of their crude training? Whichever it was, it gave him leaders.

"*Follow me!*"

And they followed eagerly as he led them left, well down on the reverse slope of the hills. They worked the ragged terrain with style, arranging themselves into units of three—the useful skirmishers' triangle, from which any fighter can rush to take ground under the covering fire of the other two. Was this, Cade wondered wearily, what he had given his life to? This bag of tricks that a crowd of fanatical farmers discovered for themselves at the cost of a few lives? He dropped beneath the blast of an Armsman from a shadowing crag, and did no more philosophizing. When the crag had been undercut and toppled on the Brother, there was a new blast to face, and another, and still another.

Then they were back on the ridge of the hills and found they had taken a command post and its equipment. Some of the Marsmen paused to marvel at the radionic mast and mappers and communicator.

"Keep moving, blast you!" Cade raved at them. "Keep moving and keep firing!"

He lashed them on over the mound of dead Armsmen and into a blazing linked fire from a dozen wind-carved pockets in the rock. They had learned well. The Marsmen rushed from one eroded spire to the next . . . at the cost of a dozen lives they secured flanking positions and withering enfilade fire wiped out the defending Armsmen in seconds.

He cursed them forward, and the next fire they met was scattered, rear-guard stuff—three men trying to fire like thirty. It was the retreat he had, half-crazily, hoped for: not a flight but a consolidation of forces. The Armsmen would be grouped soon in one mass capable of putting out an interlaced ring of fire. In spite of his green troops' astonishing performance so far, Cade bitterly knew he could not pit them against any such formation.

The mast of another command post was in their newly won territory by the time they had mopped up the rear guard. He shouted a cease-fire and led his men straight over the rim of the hills instead of working along the reverse slope for cover. He wanted to waste no precious time while there were Armsmen to be killed. They shot down a communications man, still sending; otherwise the command post had been abandoned. Cade eagerly took his binoculars and studied the work of Tucker's men, to the right. They were strung out more than they ought to be, but one post had fallen to them and another was under attack. Signs of retreat were clear on Tucker's front also.

A sudden ferocious flurry of blasts ten meters from

him sent Cade sprawling to the ground.

"What kind of cursed scouts do you call your cursed selves?" he raved at his men. "When I said kill them, I meant kill them! Let's clean up this cursed ground!"

They grinned at him like wolves, and followed in a wild surge that broke through the thin rear-guard screen and clawed with fire into a regrouped main guard. "Feint at us, will they?" he yelled, only half-hearing himself in the roar of blasters at full aperture. Before the butchery was over his Marsmen had lost heavily and still another command post was in their hands. The Armsmen's retreat this time was no feint. . . .

He sent scouts forward to harry the Armsmen. From the captured post, he studied neatly ranked recon fliers, two hundred meters from the reverse slopes of the circling hills. And something incredible was happening. The ant-like figures of Armsmen were making for the fliers. They weren't going to stand and fight. They were racing for their fliers, doubling and swerving, boiling out in panic from behind the rocks.

"Fire on them!" yelled Cade. "Pass the word to fire!" There would be no hits except an occasional accident, but it would let the Armsmen know *he* was there. . . .

A few of the ant-like figures knelt and returned blasts, fearing a rush.

Tucker was there. "You told me," the lean-faced man panted, "you told me to report, but I couldn't get away—"

Cade didn't rebuke him, and Tucker ventured a note of triumph: "Gunner, we got their headquarters! That stopped them, didn't it?"

"It shouldn't," Cade said—and then realized the full extent of what had happened. Laughter burst from his lips. "Yes," he said, "that stopped them." Even with his words they heard the first of the fliers blast off at maximum. A moment later there was another.

Cade followed his second in command across the now-secure inner plain to inspect the headquarters post for himself. The roar of his snipers' guns, mingled with jets on take-off, was sweet to his ears.

Eagerly he examined the remains of the command post the Marsman had taken, and there was no mistake possible. It was a well-selected position, as good a headquarters as the terrain could offer. It commanded a good escape route down the reverse slope to the fliers and a good 360-degree field of fire and observation. But the fury of five hundred Marsmen had overwhelmed the strategic knowledge of ten thousand years. The place was a shambles of ruined equipment of command. And over the rubble were strewn the bodies of Armsmen.

Cade let out a long halloo: "*Hold your fire! Pass the word!*" The command rang victoriously along the hills.

He walked to the central control panel of the communicator set and looked down at the crooked corpse that lay over it, a corpse half-charred and without a cloak. He rolled the body over and stared into the granite countenance of the Power Master.

Dead! Dead because he would not give his power to a subordinate. Because he had to witness the victory himself. He hadn't expected battle; none of them had.

The cease-fire had been luckily timed. Earlier it might not have been obeyed. Later it might have occurred without an order. Even so there were irreconcilables who could not bear the helpless retreat of Armsmen by the hundreds to their fliers. Several continued to fire for a minute, and one woman ran shrieking down the rocks until she was picked off.

Cade watched the cloaked and helmeted figures swarming into the slender space ships, blasting off northward, lifting on slave-control the empty crafts whose complements would never fly again. They would take news of this day with them and spread it through the Realm of Man.

It was incredible that they should have won, thought Cade—but no more incredible than that commoners should have fought at all.

Patriotism?

Wearily, he studied the Marsmen sprawled on the ground nearby. One little knot was singing some song or other about Mars. Others were talking loudly, with exaggerated laughter. One man was sobbing hysterically; he seemed to be unwounded. Many sat in silence with furrowed brows, or in near-silence, exchanging halting words.

"Yes," Cade heard, "but what if more of them come back?"

"There will be more of us. I have five brothers—"

"Yes! My boys are big for their age—yes—"

"They killed Manley, I don't know what I'll say to his wife."

"They'll take care of us. Her too."

"They *better* take care of us—"

Cade walked restlessly along the ridge, looking for something he dared not think about, through the territory that had been held until minutes ago by Power Master and Order and all the other trappings of the past.

Patriotism! The Brothers would be more wary the next time they were sent to fight against it. It was easy to imagine the bored confidence with which the five-hundred-odd Armsmen had left their fliers and climbed the hills. They had thought themselves out on an elaborate policing job; they had found themselves well-placed observation posts with good fields of fire out of sheer habit. Then they had found their line broken by an impossible frontal assault and one command post destroyed in a matter of minutes. The loss of two or more posts had made it necessary to regroup, to *retreat from commoners*. And when the headquarters post was lost. . . .

Ordinarily it wouldn't matter. Next-in-command-takes-over, quite automatically, in less time than it takes to say. But to these stunned Armsmen, it must have been a last straw in a nightmarish overload of their capacity to adjust.

It was the very impossibility of the attack, the inability of trained men, tradition-steeped, to believe it could happen, that had done it. When the Marsmen had scaled that cliff, the Brothers of the Order had lost their initiative of fire, and that was fatal.

They had all lost their initiative of fire now—Stars, Klin Teachers, The Order, the next Power Master. They would never win it back as long as battle-worn Marsmen could sit on a hilltop saying: "I have five brothers . . . my boys are big for their age. . . ."

What had the Power Master said? "If they kept attacking the Watch Houses until all the gas guns were used up . . . We must have an Emperor for the commoners to love. . . ."

But there was no Power Master now, and the Emperor—The Emperor himself had made this battle possible. The Emperor and . . .

Until this moment he had not let himself think about her: not in the battle, for fear of doing less than his utmost; not afterwards, for fear of what he might learn. But now it was all right.

She came stumbling across the scarred rock, her face sober, her body drooping with fatigue but her head held regally high.

"Thank you, Gunner Cade, for my uncle and for me."

She spoke formally, but he understood. There were no words with which he could have voiced his own joy. She was alive, unharmed. His arms could have told her, and his lips, but not with words.

"You owe no thanks to me," he said, "but to yourself and to our brothers here."

Then their eyes met and even ceremonious language was impossible.

"Ho, Gunner!" It was Tucker, coming from below. "I'm getting them together down below. Should we leave a guard here?"

"What for—?" With difficulty, Cade brought himself back to the moment and its realities. "Can you men carry more? Some of the equipment is worth salvaging."

Tucker turned over some of the headquarters rubble with his toe. "Any of this?"

"I'll look it over," he said, and turned to Jocelyn. "May I see you first? A few words—"

"Of course." She took his arm and he helped her down eroded steps to a sheltered place.

"What now?" he asked simply.

"Now? To the Star of Mars, to the Court. Then—well, perhaps we could go back. The Power Master had no heir designated; it might be safe to return to Earth. There will be endless confusion there and probably safety. But the Star of Mars would surely give you command of all fighting."

The words hung in the air.

"And you?" Cade asked.

"I don't know. There will be things to do. I'm not used to being idle."

"I wouldn't like to be his Gunner Superior," Cade said

166

slowly. "I think I might like to marry someday."

"Oh, Cade!" There was laughter in her eyes. "This isn't Earth. It wouldn't be the Order again. Most of your Armsmen, if you call them that, would be married."

"That's true," he said. "I didn't think of that. The old habits—Jocelyn, I—" How could he say it? "You're the blood of the Emperor!" he cried out.

"The Emperor," she said softly, "is a man, too. A wise man. And married."

Now he knew there was no way to say it; words were not enough. As once before in anger, but now with tenderness, he seized her in his arms and pulled her to him. As once before in surprise, but now with full knowledge, she kissed him back.

For minutes they sat together, until a shadow began to lenghten across them. Cade stood and pulled her to her feet.

"There's work to do," he said.

"Work for both of us, my darling."

"My darling." He said the new word wonderingly, and then smiled. He had so much to learn.

TAKEOFF

1

Morning of a bureaucrat.

On the wall behind his desk Daniel Holland, general manager of the U.S. Atomic Energy Commission, had hung the following:

His diploma from Harvard Law, '39;

A photograph of himself shaking hands with his hero, the late David Lilienthal, first A.E.C. chairman;

His certificate of honorable active service in the Army of the United States as a first lieutenant, in the Judge Advocate General's Department, dated February 12, 1945;

A letter of commendation from the general counsel of the T.V.A., which included best wishes for his former assistant's success in the new and challenging field of public administration he was entering;

A diploma declaring in Latin that he was an honorary Doctor of Laws of the University of North Carolina as of June 15, 1956;

A blowup of *The New Republic's* vitriolic paragraph on his "Bureaucracy versus the People" (New York, 1956);

A blowup of *Time* magazine's vitriolic paragraph on his "Red Tape Empires" (New York, 1957);

Signed photographs of heroes (Lilienthal, the late Senator McMahon); industrialists (Henry Kaiser, the late Charles E. Wilson of General Motors, Wilson Stuart of Western Aircraft, the late John B. Watson of International Business Machines); scientists (James B. Conant, J. Robert Oppenheimer); and politicians (Chief Justice Palmer, Senator John Marshall Butler of Maryland, ex-President Truman, ex-President Warren, President Douglas);

An extract from the January 27, 1947, hearings of the Senate half of the joint Senate-House Committee on Atomic Energy—held in connection with confirmation of the President's appointees to the A.E.C., particularly that of Lilienthal—which ran as follows:

Senator McKellar (*to Mr. Lilienthal*): *Did it not seem to you to be remarkable that in connection with experiments that have been carried on since the days of Alexander the Great, when he had his Macedonian scientists trying to split the atom, the President of the United States would discharge General Groves, the discoverer of the greatest secret that the world has ever known, the greatest discovery, scientific discovery, that has ever been made, to turn the whole matter over to you; who never really knew, except from what you saw in the newspapers, that the Government was even thinking about atomic energy?*

The Chairman: *Let us have it quiet, please.*

Senator McKellar: *You are willing to admit, are you, that this secret, or the first history of it, dated from the time when Alexander the Great had his Macedonian scientists trying to make this discovery, and then Lucretius wrote a poem about it, about two thousand years ago? And everybody has been trying to discover it, or most scientists have been trying to discuss it, ever since. And do you not really think that General Groves, for having discovered it, is entitled to some little credit for it?*

"Read that," said Holland to his first caller of the morning. "Go on, read it."

James MacIlheny, Los Angeles insurance man and president of the American Society for Space Flight, gave him an inquiring look and slowly read the extract.

"I suppose," MacIlheny said at last, "your point is that you wouldn't be able to justify granting my request if Congress called you to account."

"Exactly. I'm a lawyer myself; I know how they think. Right-wrong, black-white, convicted-acquitted. Exactly why should A.E.C. 'co-operate and exchange information with' you people? If you're any good, we ought to hire you. If you aren't any good, we oughtn't to waste time on you."

"Are those your personal views, Mr. Holland?" asked MacIlheny, flushing.

Holland sighed. "My personal views are on the record in a couple of out-of-print books, a few magazine articles, and far too many congressional-hearing minutes. You didn't come here to discuss my personal views; you came for an answer to a question. The answer has got to be 'no.' "

"I came on your invitation——" MacIlheny began angrily, and then he pulled himself together. "I'm not going to waste time losing my temper. I just want you to consider some facts. American Government rocket research is scattered all over hell—Army, Navy, Air Force, Bureau of Standards, Coast and Geodetic Survey, and God-alone-knows-where-else. You gentlemen don't let much news out, but obviously we're getting nowhere. We would have had a manned rocket on the moon ten years ago if we were! I'm speaking for some people who know the problem, a lot of them trained, technical men. We've got the drawings. We've had some of them for fifteen years! All that's needed is money and fuel, atomic fuel——"

Holland looked at his watch, and MacIlheny stopped in mid-flight. "I see it's not getting through," he said bitterly. "When the Russian or Argentine lunar guided missiles begin to fall on America you'll have a lot to be proud of, Mr. Holland." He started for the door. Before he was out, Holland's secretary was in, summoned by a buzzer.

"Let's hit the mail, Charlie," Holland said, lighting a cigarette and emptying his overflowing "in" basket on his desk.

Ryan's bid on the Missoula construction job. "Tell him very firmly that I want him to get the contract because of his experience, but that his bid's ridiculously high. Scare him a little."

Damages claim from an ex-A.E.C. employee's lawyer, alleging loss of virility from radiation exposure. "Tell Morton to write this shyster absolutely nothing doing;

it's utterly ridiculous. Hint that we'll have him up before his state bar association if he pesters us any more. And follow through if he does!"

Dr. Mornay at Oak Ridge still wanted to publish his article arguing for employment of foreign-born scientific personnel in the A.E.C. "Write him a very nice letter. Say I've seriously considered his arguments but I still think publication would be a grave error on his part. See my previous letter for reasons and ask him just to consider what Senator Hoyt would make of his attitude."

The governor of Nevada wanted him to speak at a dam dedication. "Tell him no, I never speak, sorry."

Personnel report from Missoula Directed Ops. "Greenleaf's lost three more good men, damn it. Acknowledge his letter of transmittal—warm personal reguards. And tell Weiss to look over the table of organization for a spot we can switch him to where he'll stay in grade but won't be a boss-man."

Half-year fiscal estimate from Holloway at Chalk River Liaison Group in Canada. "Acknowledge it but don't say yes or no. Make copies for Budget and Comptroller. Tell Weiss to ride them for an opinion but not to give them any idea whether I think it's high, low, or perfect. I want to know what *they* think by tomorrow afternoon."

Messenger query from the A.P. on Hoyt's speech in the Senate. "Tell them I haven't seen the text yet and haven't had a chance to check A.E.C. medical records against the Senator's allegations. Add that in my personal experience I've never met an alcoholic scientist and until I do I'll continue to doubt that there is any such animal. Put some jokes in it."

The retiring Regional Security and Intelligence Office agent in charge at Los Angeles wanted to know Holland's views on who should succeed him. Records of three senior agents attached. "Tell him Anheier looks like the best bet."

The Iranian ambassador, with an air of injured innocence, wanted to know why his country's exchange students had been barred even from nonrestricted A.E.C. facilities. "Tell him it was a State Department decision. Put in some kind of a dig so he'll know I know they started it with our kids. Clear it with Senate before I see it."

A rambling petition from the Reverend Oliver Townsend Warner, Omaha spellbinder. "I can't make head or tail of this. Tell Weiss to answer it some way or other. I don't want to see any more stuff from Warner; he may have a following but the man's a crank."

Recruiting program report from Personnel Office. "Acknowledge this and tell them I'm not happy about it. Tell them I want on my desk next Monday morning some constructive ideas about roping better junior personnel in, and keeping them with us. Tell them it's perfectly plain that we're getting the third-rate graduates of the third-rate schools and it's got to stop."

Letter from Regional Security and Intelligence officer at Chicago; the F.B.I. had turned over derogatory information against Dr. Oslonski, mathematical physicist. "Hell. Write Oslonski a personal letter and tell him I'm sorry but he's going to be suspended from duty and barred from the grounds again. Tell him we'll get his clearance over with in the minimum possible time and I know it's a lot of foolishness but policy is policy and we've got to think of the papers and Congress. Ask him please to consider the letter a very private communication. And process the S. and I. advisory."

A North Dakota senator wanted a job for his daughter, who had just graduated from Bennington. "Tell Morton to write him that Organization and Personnel hires, not the general manager."

Dr. Redford at Los Angeles wanted to resign; he said he felt he was getting nowhere. "Ask him please, as a personal favor to me, to delay action on his resignation until I've been able to have a talk with him. Put in something about our acute shortage of first-line men. And teletype the director there to rush-reply a report on the trouble."

A red-bordered, courier-transmitted letter from the Secretary of the Department of the Interior, stamped *Secret*. He wanted to know when he would be able to figure on results from A.E.C.'s A.D.M.P.—Atomic Demolition Material Program—in connection with planning for Sierra Reclamation Project. "Tell Interior we haven't got a thing for him and haven't got a date. The feeling among the A.D.M.P. boys is that they've been off on a blind alley for the past years and ought to resurvey their approach to the problem. I'm giving them another month because Scientific Advisory claims the theory is sound. That's secret, by courier."

Hanford's quarterly omnibus report. "Acknowledge it and give it to Weiss to brief for me."

Messenger query from the Bennet newspapers; what about a rumor from Los Angeles that the A.E.C. had launched a great and costly program for a space-rocket atomic fuel. "Tell them A.E.C. did not, does not, and probably will not contemplate a space-rocket fuel program. Say I think I know where the rumor started and that it's absolutely without foundation, impossible to launch such a program without diverting needed weaponeering personnel, etcetera."

Field Investigations wanted to know whether they should tell the Attorney General about a trucking line they caught swindling the A.E.C. "Tell them I don't want prosecution except as a last resort. I do want restitution of the grafted dough, I want the Blue Streak board of directors to fire the president and his damn cousin in the dispatcher's office, and most of all I want Field Investigations to keep these things from happening instead of catching them *after* they happen."

And so on.

MacIlheny went disconsolately to his room at the Willard and packed. They wouldn't start charging him for another day until 3:00 P.M.: he opened his portable and began tapping out his overdue "President's Message" for *Starward*, monthly bulletin of the American Society for Space Flight. It flowed more easily than usual. MacIlheny was sore.

Fellow Members:
   I am writing this shortly after being given a verbal spanking by a high muckamuck of the A.E.C. I was told in effect to pick up my marbles and not bother the older boys; the Government isn't interested in us bumbling amateurs. I can't say I enjoyed this after my hopes had been raised by the ex-

change of several letters and an invitation to see Mr. Holland about it "the next time I was in Washington." I suppose I mistook routine for genuine interest. But I've learned something out of this disheartening experience.

It's this: we've been wasting a lot of time in the A.S.F.S.F. by romancing about how the Government would some day automatically take cognizance of our sincere and persistent work. My experience today duplicates what happened in 1946, when our campaign for the Government to release unnecessarily classified rocketry art was the flop of the year.

You all know where we stand. Twenty years of theoretical work and math have taken us as far as we can go alone. We now need somebody else's money and somebody else's fuel. A lot of people have money, but under existing circumstances only the A.E.C. can have or ever be likely to have atomic fuel.

The way I feel about it, our next step is fundraising—lots of it—hat-in-hand begging at the doors of industrial firms and scientific foundations. With that money we can go on from the drawing board to practical experimental work on bits and pieces of space ship, lab-testing our drawing-board gadgets until we know they work and can prove it to anybody—even an A.E.C. general manager.

When we have worked the bugs out of our jato firing circuits, our deadlight gaskets, our manhole seals, our acceleration couches, and the hundred-and-one accessories of space flight, we'll be in a new position. We will be able to go to the A.E.C. and tell them: "Here's a space ship. Give us fuel for it. If you don't, we'll hold you up to the scorn and anger of the country you are blindly refusing to defend."

James MacIlheny
President, A.S.F.S.F.

MacIlheny sat back, breathing hard and feeling more composed. There was no point to hating Holland, but it had been tragic to find him, a keyman, afraid of anything new and even afraid to admit it, hiding behind Congress.

He still had some time to kill. He took from his brief case a report by the A.S.F.S.F. Orbit Computation Committee (two brilliant youngsters from Cal Tech, a Laguna Beach matron to punch the calculating machine and a flow-analysis engineer from Hughes Aircraft) entitled "Refined Calculations of Grazing Ellipse Braking Trajectories for a Mars Landing After a Flight Near Apposition." Dutifully he tried to read, but at the bottom of its first mimeographed page the report ran into the calculus of variations. MacIlheny knew no mathematics; he was no scientist and he did not pretend to be one. He was a rocket crank, he knew it, and it was twisting his life.

He threw himself into a chair and thought bitterly of the United States moon base that should have been established ten years ago, that should be growing now with the arrival of every monthly rocket. He knew it by heart; the observatory where telescopes—of moderate size, but unhampered by Earth's dense and shimmering atmosphere—would solve new stellar mysteries every day; the electronics lab where space-suited engineers would combine and recombine vacuum-tube elements with all outdoors for their vacuum tube; the hydroponics tanks growing green stuff for air and food, fed exhaled carbon dioxide and animal waste, producing oxygen and animal food under the raw sunlight on the Moon.

And he could see a most important area dotted with launchers for small, unmanned rockets with fission-bomb war heads, ready to smash any nation that hit the United States first.

He could see it; why not they? The scattered, uncoordinated, conservative rocketry since World War II had produced what?

Army guided missiles, roaring across arcs of the Pacific every now and then on practice runs.

Air Force altitude jobs squirting up on liquid fuel from the deserts of the Southwest. There was a great, strange, powder-blue city of half a million souls at White Sands, New Mexico, where colonels spoke only to

176

generals and generals spoke only to God. They were "working on" the space-flight problem; they were "getting out the bugs."

The Coast and Geodetic Survey firing its mapping rockets up and over, up and over, eternally, coast to coast, taking strips and strips of pictures.

The Bureau of Standards shooting up its cosmic-ray research rockets; for ten years they "had been developing" a space suit for walking on the Moon. (There were space-suit drawings in the A.S.F.S.F. files—had been for fifteen years.)

The Navy had its rockets, too. You could fire them from submarines, destroyers, cruisers, and special rocket-launching battlewagons that cost maybe sixty-odd what a space ship would stand you.

MacIlheny glumly told himself: might as well get to the airport. No point hanging around here.

He checked out, carrying his light overnight bag and portable. An inconspicuous man followed him to the airport; he had been following MacIlheny for weeks. They both enjoyed the walk; it was a coldly sun-bright January day.

2

There was an immense documentation on Michael Novak, but it was no more extensive than the paper work on any other A.E.C. employee. For everyone—from scrubwoman to Nobel-prize physicist—the A.E.C. had one; so-and-so was eighty-seven years old and dribbled when he ate. Their backgrounds were checked to the times of their birth (it had once been suggested, in effect, that their backgrounds be checked to nine months before their birth—this by a congressman who thought illegitimacy should be sufficient reasion for denying an applicant employment by the A.E.C.).

The Security and Intelligence Office files could tell

you that Michael Novak had been born in New York City, but not that he had played squat tag under and around the pillars of the Canarsie Line elevated shortly before it was torn down. They could tell you that his mother and father had died when he was sixteen, but not that he had loved them. They could tell you that he had begun a brilliant record of scholarship-grabbing in high school, but not that he grabbed out of loneliness and fear.

Rensselaer Polytechnic Institute: aeronautical engineering (but he had been afraid to fly; heights were terrifying) and a junior-year switch to ceramic engineering, inexplicable to the A.E.C. years later.

A ten-month affair with a leggy, tough, young sophomore from the Troy Day College for Women. They interviewed her after ten years as a plump and proper Scarsdale matron; she told the Security men yes, their information was correct; and no, Michael had shown no signs of sexual abnormality.

Summer jobs at Corning Glass and Elpico Pottery, Steubenville, Ohio (but not endless tension: will they do what I tell them, or laugh in my face? Are they laughing at me now? Is that laughter I hear?). Ten years later they told the Security men sure I remember him, he was a good kid; no, he never talked radical or stuff like that; he worked like hell and he never said much (and maybe I better not tell this guy about the time the kid beat the ears off Wyrostek when he put the white lead in the kid's coverall pocket).

Scholarship graduate study at the University of Illinois, the Hopkins Prize Essay in Ceramic Engineering (with at first much envy of the scatterbrained kids who coasted four years to a B.A., later thin disgust, and last a half-hearted acceptance of things as they were).

The teaching fellowship. The doctoral dissertation on "Fabrication of Tubular Forms from Boron-Based High-Tensile Refractory Pastes by Extrusion." Publication of excerpts from this in the *Journal* of the Society of Ceramic Engineers brought him his bid from the A.E.C. They needed his specialty in N.E.P.A.—Nuclear Energy for the Propulsion of Aircraft.

He had taken it, his records showed, but they did not

show the dream world he had thought N.E.P.A. would be, or the dismaying reality it was.

N.E.P.A. turned out to be one hour in the lab and three hours at the desk; bending the knee to seniors and being looked at oddly if you didn't understand that juniors bend the knee to you. It was wangling the high-temperature furnace for your tests and then finding that you'd been bumped out of your alloted time by a section chief or a group director riding a hobby. It was ordering twenty pounds of chemically pure boron and getting fifty-three pounds of commerical grade. It was, too often, getting ahead on an intricate problem and then learning by accident that it had been solved last year by somebody else in some other division. It was trying to search the records before starting your next job and being told that you weren't eligible to see classified material higher than *Confidential*. It was stamping your own results *Restricted* or at most *Confidential* and being told that it was safer, all things considered, to stamp them *Secret* and stay out of trouble.

It was being treated like a spy.

It was, in spite of all this, a chance to work a little at new and exciting problems.

And then, his records showed, in August of his second year, he had been transferred to Argonne National Laboratory, Chicago, as N.E.P.A. Refractories Group Liaison with Neutron Path Prediction Division of the Mathematical Physics Section. The records did not say why a ceramic engineer specializing in high-tensile refractories and with a smattering of aircraft background had been assigned to work in an immensely abstruse field of pure nuclear theory for which he had not the slightest preparation or aptitude.

From August to mid-December, the records said, he bombarded the office of Dr. Hurlbut, director of Argonne Lab, with queries, petitions, and requests for a rectification of his absurd assignment, but the records showed no answers. Finally, the records showed that he resigned from A.E.C. without prior notice— forfeiting all salaries and allowances due or to become due—on a certain day toward the end of the year.

This is what happened on that day:

Novak stopped in the cafeteria downstairs for a second cup of coffee before beginning another baffling day at Neutron Path Prediction—a day he hoped would be his last if Hurlbut had looked into the situation.

"Hi, there," he said to a youngster from Reactor Design. The boy mumbled something and walked past Novak's table to one in the corner.

Oh, fine. Now he was a leper just because he was the victim of some administrative foolishness. It occurred to him that perhaps he had become a bore about his troubles and people didn't want to hear any more about them. Well, he was sick of the mess himself.

A girl computer walked past with coffee and a piece of fudge cake. "Hi, there," he said with less confidence. She had always been good for a big smile, but this time she really gave out.

"Oh, Dr. Novak," she gulped, "I think it's just *rotten.*"

What was this—a gag? "Well, I hope to get it fixed up soon, Grace."

She sat down. "You're filing a grievance? You certainly ought to. A man in your position——"

"*Grievance?* Why, no! I actually saw Hurlbut yesterday, and I just grabbed him in the corridor and told him my troubles. I said that evidently my memos weren't getting through to him. He was very pleasant about it and he said he'd take immediate action."

She looked at him with pity in her eyes and said: "Excuse me." She picked up her tray and fled.

The kid was kidding—or nuts. Hurlbut would straighten things out. He was a notorious scientist-on-the-make, always flying all over the map for speaking dates at small, important gatherings of big people. You saw him often on the front pages and seldom in the laboratory, but he got his paper work cleaned up each month.

Novak finished his coffee and climbed the stairs to the Mathematical Physics Section. He automatically checked the bulletin board in passing and was brought up short by his own name.

FROM THE OFFICE OF THE DIRECTOR

To: Dr. Michael Novack (NPPD) Re: Requested Transfer

Your request is denied. The Director wishes to call your attention to your poor record of production even on the routine tasks it was thought best you be assigned to.

The Director suggests that a more co-operative attitude, harder work, and less griping will get you farther than your recent attempts at office intrigue and buttonholing of busy senior officers.

"The man's crazy," somebody said at his shoulder. "You have a perfect grievance case to take to the——"

Novak ignored him. He ripped the memo from the board and walked unsteadily from the bare white corridors of the Mathematical Physics Section, through endless halls, and into the Administrative Division—carpets, beige walls, mahogany, business suits, pretty secretaries in pretty dresses walking briskly through these wonders.

He pushed open a mahogany door, and a receptionist stopped doing her nails to say: "Who shall I say is—hey! You can't go in there!"

In the carpeted office beyond, a secretary said: "What's this? What do you want?" He pushed on through the door that said: *Dr. Hurlbut's Secretary.*

Dr. Hurlbut's secretary wore a business suit that fitted like a bathing suit, and she said: "Oops! You weren't announced; you startled me. Wait a minute; Dr. Hurlbut is engaged——"

Novak walked right past her into the director's mahogany-furnished, oak-paneled office while she fluttered behind him. Hurlbut, looking like the official pictures of himself, was sitting behind half an acre of desk. A man with him gaped like a fish as Novak burst in.

Novak slapped the memo on the desk and asked: "*Did you write this?*"

The director, impeccably clothed, barbered, and manicured, rose looking faintly amused. He read the notice and said: "You're Novak, aren't you? Yes, I wrote it. And I had it posted instead of slipping it into your box because I thought it would have a favorable effect on morale in general. Some of the section chiefs have been getting sadly lax. No doubt you were wondering."

He had been warned by the "personality card" that ac-
companied Novak on his transfer to expect such piffling
outbursts. However, the man worked like the devil if
you just slapped him down and kept hectoring him. One
of those essentially guilt-ridden types, the director
thought complacently. So pitifully few of us are smooth-
running, well-oiled, efficient machines . . .

"Here's my resignation," said Novak. He gave his
resignation to Hurlbut on the point of the jaw. The
Director turned up the whites of his eyes before he hit
the gray broadloom carpeting in his office, and the man
with him gaped more fishily than ever. The secretary
shrieked, and Novak walked out, rubbing the split skin
on his knuckles. It was the first moment of pure satisfaction he had enjoyed since they took him off refractories at N.E.P.A.

Nobody pulled the alarm. It wasn't the kind of thing
Hurlbut would want on the front pages. Novak walked,
whistling and unmolested, across the lawn in front of
Administration to the main gate. He unpinned his badge
and gave it to a guard, saying cheerfully: "I won't be
back."

"Somebody leave ya a fortune?" the guard kidded.

"Uh, no," said Novak, and the mood of pure satisfaction suddenly evaporated. Nobody had left him a
fortune, and he had just put a large, indelible blot on his
career.

The first thing he did when he got back to his hotel
was phone a situation-wanted ad to *Ceramic Industries*.
Luckily he caught the magazine as it was closing its
forms on classifieds; subscribers would have his ad in
ten days.

3

They were ten bad days.

The local employment agencies had some openings for
him, but only one was any good and he was turned down
at the interview. It was a scientific supply house that

needed a man to take over the crucibles and refractories department; it involved research. The president regretfully explained that they were looking for somebody a little more mature, a little more experienced in handling men, somebody who could take orders——

Novak was sure the crack meant that he knew about his informal resignation from A.E.C. and disapproved heartily.

All the other offers were lousy little jobs; mixing and testing batches in run-down Ohio potteries, with pay to match and research opportunities zero.

Novak went to cheap movies and ate in cheap cafeterias until the answers to his ad started coming in. A spark-plug company in Newark made the best offer in the first batch; the rest were terrible. One desperate owner of a near-bankrupt East Liverpool pottery offered to take him on as full partner in lieu of salary. "I feel certain that with a technical man as well qualified as yourself virtually in charge of production and with me handling design and sales we would weather our present crisis and that the ultimate rewards will be rich. Trusting you will give this proposal your serious——"

Novak held off wiring the Newark outfit to see what the next day would bring. It brought more low-grade offers and a curious letter from Los Angeles.

The letterhead was just an office number and an address. The writer, J. Friml, very formally offered Dr. Novak interesting full-time work in refractories research and development connected with very high-altitude jet aircraft. Adequate laboratory facilities would be made available, as well as trained assistance if required. The salary specified in his advertisement was satisfactory. If the proposition aroused Dr. Novak's interest, would he please wire collect and a telegraphed money order sufficient to cover round-trip expenses to Los Angeles would be forthcoming.

One of the big, coast aircraft outfits? It couldn't be anything else, but why secrecy? The letter was an intriguing trap, with the promised money order for bait. Maybe they wouldn't want him after all, but there was nothing wrong with a free trip to Los Angeles to see what they were up to. That is, if they really sent the money.

He wired J. Friml, collect, at the address on the letter-head:

INTERESTED YOUR OFFER BUT APPRECIATE FURTHER DETAILS IF POSSIBLE.

The next morning a more-than-ample money order was slipped under his door, with the accompanying message:

FULL DETAILS FORTHCOMING AT INTERVIEW; PLEASE CALL ON US AT YOUR CONVENIENCE WIRING IN ADVANCE. OUR OFFICE OPEN DAILY EXCEPT SUNDAY NINE FIVE. J. FRIML, SECRETARY TREASURER.

Of *what*?

Novak laughed at the way he was being openly hooked by curiousity and a small cash bribe, and phoned for an airline reservation.

He left his bag at the Los Angeles airport and showered in a pay booth. He had wired that he would appear that morning. Novak gave the address to a cabby and asked: "What part of town's that?"

"Well," said the cabby. "I'll tell you. It's kind of an old-fashioned part of town. Nothing's *wrong* with it."

"Old-fashioned" turned out to be a euphemism for "run-down." They stopped at a very dirty eight-story corner office building with one elevator. The lobby was paved with cracked octagonal tile. The lobby directory of tenants was enormous. It listed upwards of two hundred tenant firms in the building, quadrupled and quintupled up in its fifty-odd offices. Under *f* Novak found J. Friml, Room 714."

"Seven," he bleakly told the unshaven elevator man. Whatever was upstairs, it wasn't a big, coast plane factory.

Room 712 stopped him dead in the corridor with the audacity of the lettering on its glass door. It claimed to house the Arlington National Cemetery Association, the Lakeside Realty Corporation, the Western Equitable Insurance Agency, the California Veterans League, Farm and Home Publications, and the Kut-Rite Metal Novelties Company in one small office.

But at Room 714 his heart sank like a stone. The lettering said modestly: *American Society for Space Flight.*

I might have known, he thought glumly. Southern California! He braced himself to enter. They would be crackpots, the lab would be somebody's garage, they would try to meet their pay roll by selling building lots on Jupiter . . . but they were paying for his time this morning. He went in.

"Dr. Novak?" said a young man. Nod. "I'm Friml. This is Mr. MacIlheny, president of our organization." MacIlheny was a rawboned, middle-aged man with a determined look. Friml was sharp-faced, eye-glassed, very neat and cold.

"I'm afraid you might think you were brought here under false pretenses, Doctor," said MacIlheny, as if daring him to admit it.

Friml said: "Sit down." And Novak did, and looked around. The place was clean and small with three good desks, a wall banked with good files—including big, shallow blue-print files—and no decorations.

"I asked for research and development work," Novak said cautiously. "You were within your rights replying to my ad if you've got some for me."

MacIlheny cracked his knuckles and said abruptly: "The anonymous offer was my idea. I was afraid you'd dismiss us as a joke. We don't get a very good press."

"Suppose you tell me what you're all about." It was their money he was here on.

"The A.S.F.S.F. is about twenty years old, if you count a predecessor society that was a little on the juvenile side. They 'experimented' with powder rockets and never got anywhere, of course. They just wanted to hear things go bang.

"An older element got in later—engineers from the aircraft plants, science students from Cal Tech and all the other schools—and reorganized the Society. We had a tremendous boom, of course, after the war—the V-2s and the atom bomb. Membership shot up to five thousand around the country. It dropped in a couple of years to fifteen hundred or so, and that's where we stand now."

Friml consulted a card: "One thousand, four hundred, and seventy-eight."

"Thanks. I've been president for ten years, even though I'm not a technical man, just an insurance agent. But they keep re-electing me so I guess everybody's happy.

"What we've been doing is research on paper. Haven't had the money for anything else until recently. Last January I went to Washington to see the A.E.C. about backing, but it was no dice. With the approval of the membership I went the rounds of the industrial firms looking for contributions. Some foresighted outfits came through very handsomely and we were able to go to work.

"There was a big debate about whether we should proceed on a 'bits-and-pieces' basis or whether we should shoot the works on a full-scale steel mock-up of a moon ship. The mock-up won, and we've made very satisfactory progress since. We've rented a few acres in the desert south of Barstow and put up shops and——" He couldn't keep the pride out of his voice. He opened his desk drawer and passed Novak an eight-by-ten glossy print. "Here."

He studied it carefully: a glamor photograph of a gleaming, massive, bomb-shaped thing standing on its tail in the desert with prefab huts in the background. It was six times taller than a man who stood beside it, leaning with a studied air against a delta-shaped fin. That was a lot of metal—*a lot* of metal, Novak thought with a rising excitement. If the picture wasn't fake, they had money and the thing made a little more sense.

"Very impressive," he said, returning the picture. "What would my job be?"

"Our engineer in charge, Mr. Clifton, is a remarkable man—you'll like him—but he doesn't know refractories. It seems to be all he doesn't know! And our plans include a ceramic exhaust throat liner and an internal steering vane. We have the shapes, theoretically calculated, but the material has to be developed and the pieces fabricated."

"Internal steering vane. Like the graphite vanes in the various German bombardment rockets?"

"Yes, with some refinements," MacIlheny said. "It's got to be that way, though I don't envy you the job of developing a material that will take the heat and

186

mechanical shock. Side-steering rockets would be much simpler, wouldn't they? But the practical complications you run into—each separate steering jet means a separate electrical system, a separate fuel pump, perforating structural members and losing strength, adding weight without a corresponding thrust gain."

"You said you weren't a technical man?" asked Novak.

MacIlheny said impatiently: "Far from it. But I've been in this thing heart and soul for a long time and I've picked up some stuff." He hesitated. "Dr. Novak, do you have a thick hide?"

"I suppose so."

"You'll need it if you go to work for us—crackpots."

Novak didn't say anything and MacIlheny handed him some press clippings:

LOCAL MEN SEE STARS;
BUILDING SPACE SHIP

and

BUCK ROGERS HEARTS BEAT
BENEATH BUSINESS SUITS.

There were others.

"We never claimed," said MacIlheny a little bitterly, "that the *Prototype's* going to take off for the Moon next week or ever. We down-pedal sensationalism; there are perfectly valid military and scientific reasons for space-ship research. We've tried to make it perfectly clear that she's a full-scale model for study purposes, but the damned papers don't care. I know it's scared some good men away from the society and I'd hate to tell you how much it's cut into my business, but my lawyer tells me I'd be a fool to sue." He looked at his watch. "I owed you that much information, Doctor. Now tell me frankly whether you're available."

Novak hesitated.

"Look," said MacIlheny. "Why don't you take a look at the field and the *Prototype*? I have to run, but Friml will be glad to drive you out. You've got to meet Clifton."

When MacIlheny had left, Friml said: "Let's eat first." They went to a businessman's restaurant. Friml had hardly a word to say for himself through the meal, and he kept silence through the drive west to Barstow as the irrigated, roadside land turned arid and then to desert.

"You aren't an enthusiast?" Novak finally asked.

"I'm secretary-treasurer," said Friml.

"Um. Was Mr. MacIlheny deliberately not mentioning the names of the firms that contribute to the A.S.F.S.F.? I thought I caught that."

"You were correct. Contributions are private, by request of the donors. You saw those newspaper clippings?"

His tone was vinegar. Friml was a man who didn't think the game was worth the kidding you took for playing it. Then why the devil was he the outfit's secretary-treasurer?

They were driving down a secondary black-top road when the *Prototype* came into view. It had the only vertical lines in the landscape for as far as the eye could see, and looked sky-piercing. A quadrangle of well-built prefabs surrounded it, and the area was wire-fenced. Signs at intervals forbade trespassing.

There was a youngster reading at a sort of sentry box in the fencing. He glanced at Friml and waved him through. Friml crawled his car to a parking area, where late models were outnumbered by jalopies, and brought it alongside of a monstrous, antique, maroon Rolls Royce. "Mr. Clifton's," he said, vinegar again. "He should be in here." He led Novak to the largest of the prefabs, a twelve-foot Quonset some thirty feet long and mounted on a concrete base.

It was a machine shop. Serious-eyed kids were squinting as they filed at bits of bronze. A girl was running a surface grinder that gushed a plume of small, dull red, hot-looking sparks. High-carbon steel, Novak thought automatically. Piece that size costs plenty.

Clifton, Friml's pointed finger said.

The man was in dungaree pants and a dirty undershirt—no, the top of an old-fashioned union suit with buttons. He was bending over a slow-turning engine lathe, boring out a cast-iron fitting. The boring bar chattered suddenly and he snarled at it: "A-a-ah, ya dirty dog ya!" and slapped off the power switch.

"Mr. Clifton," Friml hailed him, "this is Dr. Michael Novak, the ceramics man I told you about yesterday."

"Harya, Jay. Harya, Mike," he said, giving Novak an oily grip. He needed a shave and he needed some dentistry. He didn't look like any engineer in charge that Novak had ever seen before. He was a completely unimpressive Skid Row type, with a hoarse voice to match.

Clifton was staring at him appraisingly. "So ya wanna join the space hounds, hah? Where's ya Buck Rogers pistol?"

There was a pause.

"Conversation-stopper," said Friml with a meager smile. "He's got a million of them. Mr. Clifton, would you show Dr. Novak around if it doesn't interrupt anything important?"

Clifton said: "Nah. Bar dug into the finish bore on the flange. I gotta scrap it now; I was crazy to try cast iron. That'll learn me to try and save you guys money; next time I cut the fitting outta nice, expensive, mild steel bar stock. Come on, Mike. Mars or bust, hah?"

He led Novak out of the machine shop and wiped his oily hands on the union suit's top. "You any good?" he asked. "I told the kids I don't want no lid on my hands."

"What's a lid?" Novak demanded.

"Morse-man talk. Fighting word."

"You were a telegrapher?" asked Novak. It seemed to be the only thing to say.

"I been everything! Farmer, seaman, gigolo in B.A., glass blower, tool maker, aero-engineer—bet ya don't believe a goddam word I'm saying."

Disgustedly Novak said: "You win." The whole thing was out of the question—crack-pot enthusiasts backing this loudmouthed phony.

"Ask me anything, Mike! Go ahead, ask me anything!" Clifton grinned at him like a terrier.

Novak shrugged and said: "Integral of u to the n, log u, d-u."

Clifton fired back: "U to the n-plus-one, bracket, log u over n-plus-one, minus one over n-plus-one-square, unbracket—plus C. Ask me a hard one, Mike!"

It was the right answer. Novak happened to remember it as an examination problem that had stuck in his head. Normally you'd look it up in a table of integrals. "Where'd you go to school?" he asked, baffled.

"School? School? What the hell would I go to school

189

for?" Clifton grinned. "I'm a self-made man, Mike. Look at that rocket, space hound. Look at her."

They had wandered to the *Prototype's* base. Close up, the rocket was a structure of beautifully welded steel plates, with a sewer-pipe opening at the rear and no visible means of propulsion.

"The kids love her," Clifton said softly. "I love her. She's my best girl, the round-heeled old bat."

"What would you use for fuel?" Novak demanded.

He laughed. "How the hell should I know, pal? All I know is we need escape velocity, so I build her to take the mechanical shock of escape velocity. *You* worry about the fuel. The kids tell me it's gotta be atomic so you gotta give 'em a throat-liner material that can really take it from here to Mars and back. Oh, you got a job on your hands when you join the space hounds, Mike!"

"This is the craziest thing I ever heard of," said Novak.

Clifton was suddenly serious. "Maybe it ain't so crazy. We work out everything except fuel and then we go to the A.E.C. and say *give*. Do they hold out on us or do they start work on an atomic fuel? The kids got it all figured out. We do our part, A.E.C. does theirs. Why not?"

Novak laughed shortly, remembering the spy mania he had lived in for two years. "They'll do their part," he said. "They'll start by sending a hundred Security and Intelligence boys to kick you off the premises so they can run it themselves."

Clifton slapped him on the back. "*That's* the spirit!" he yelled. "You'll win your Galactic Cross of Merit yet, pal! You're hired!"

"Don't rush me," said Novak, half angrily. "Are they honestly going to deliver on a real lab for me if I sign up? Maybe they don't realize I'll need heavy stuff—rock crushers, ball mills, arc furnaces—maybe a solar furnace would be good out here on the desert. That kind of equipment costs real money."

"They'll deliver," Clifton said solemnly. "Don't low-rate the kids. I'm working from their blue prints and they're good. Sure, there's bugs—the kids are human. I just had to chuck out their whole system for jettisoning *Proto's* aerodynamic nose. Too gadgety. Now I'm testing a barometer to fire a powder charge that'll blow away the nose when she's out of atmosphere—whole rig's external, no holes in the hull, no gasket problem. And they design on the conservative side—inclined to underestimate strength of materials. But, by and large, a ver-ry, ver-ry realistic bunch."

Novak was still finding it impossible to decide whether Clifton was a fake, an ignoramus, or a genius. "Where've you worked?" he asked.

"My last job was project engineer with Western Air. They fired me all right, no fear of that. I wear their letter next to my heart." He hauled a bulging, greasy wallet from the left hip pocket of the dungarees, rummaged through it, and came up with a wad of paper. Unfolded, it said restrainedly that the personnel manager of Western Aircraft regretted that the Company had no option but to terminate Mr. Clifton's employment since Mr. Clifton had categorically declined to apologize to Dr. Holden.

An eighteen-year-old boy with a crew cut came up and demanded: "Cliff, on the nylon ropes the blue print says they have to test to one-fifty pounds apiece. Does that just mean parting strength of the ropes or the whole rig—ropes whipped to the D-rings and the D-rings anchored in the frame?"

"Be with ya in a minute, Sammy. Go and wait for me." The boy left and Clifton asked: "Think it's a forgery, Mike?"

"Of course not——" began Novak, and then he saw the engineer grinning. He handed back the letter and asked: "Have you been a forger too? Mr. Clifton——"

"Cliff!"

"——Cliff, how did you get hooked up with this? I'm damned if I know what to make of the setup."

"Neither do I. But I don't care. I got hooked up with them when Western canned me. I can't get another aircraft job because of the industrial black list, and I can't get a Government job because I'm a subversive agent or a spy or some goddamned thing like that." Suddenly he sounded bitter.

"How's that?"

"They don't tell you—*you* know that; your ad said you was with the A.E.C.—but I guess it's because I been around the world a couple of times. *Maybe*, they figure,

191

just *maybe*, old Cliff sold out when we wasn't watching him. Also my wife's a foreigner, so better be safe than sorry, says Uncle Sam."

"I know that game," Novak said. "Doesn't matter. You wouldn't have lasted five minutes with A.E.C. even if they did hire you."

"Well, well! So I didn't miss a thing! Look, Mike. I gotta go show my kids how to wipe their noses, so I'll let ya rassle with your conscience and I hope to see you around." He gave Novak the oily grip again and walked cockily from the base of the rocket to the Quonsets.

Friml was at Novak's side instantly, looking impatient.

Driving back to Los Angeles, Novak asked bluntly: "Are you people building a moon ship or aren't you?"

"If the A.S.F.S.F. is building a moon ship," said Friml, "I don't want to hear about it. I should tell you that, whatever is being built, they've got a well-kept set of books and a *strictly* controlled audit on the purchasing." He gave Novak a little sidelong look. "One man they tried before Clifton made a very common mistake. He thought that because he knew technical matters and I didn't, he could pad his purchases by arrangement with the vendors' salesmen and I'd be none the wiser. It took exactly eight days for me to see through his plan."

"I get the hint," said Novak wearily. "But I still don't know whether I want the job. Was Clifton really a project engineer with Western Air?"

"I really don't know. I have absolutely no responsibility for procurement of personnel. I can tell you that he has no local or F.B.I. criminal record. I consider it a part of my job to check that far on employees whose duties include recommending expenditures."

Friml left him at the Los Angeles Airport at his request. Novak said he'd get in touch with him in the morning and let him know one way or the other; then he picked up his bag and took a taxi to a downtown hotel. It was 4:30 when he checked in, and he placed a call at once to the personnel department of Western Aircraft.

"I'd like to inquire," he said, "about the employment record of a Mr. Clifton. He says in his, uh, application to us that he was employed as a project engineer at Western Air last year."

"Yes, sir. Mr. Clifton's first name, sir?"

"Ah, I can't make it out from his signature." If he had been told Clifton's first name, he couldn't remember it.

"One moment, sir . . . we have a Mr. August Clifton, project engineer, employed two years and five months, separated January seventeenth last year——"

"What's the reason for separation?"

"It says 'incompatibility with supervisory personnel.' "

"That's the one. Thanks very much, miss."

"But don't you want efficiency, health, and the rest of it, sir?"

"Thanks, no." He didn't need them. Anybody who hung on for two years and five months at Western as a projects man and only got fired after a fight *was* efficient and healthy and the rest of it; otherwise he wouldn't have lasted two hours and five minutes. It wasn't like the A.E.C.; at Western, you produced.

No, he thought, stretching out in his clothes on the bed; it wasn't like the A.E.C., and neither was the A.S.F.S.F. He felt a moment of panic at the thought, and knew why he felt it.

Spent enough time in Government and it unmanned you. Each pay check drawn on the Treasury took that much more of yourself away from yourself. Each one of the stiff, blue-green paper oblongs punched with I.B.M. code slots made you that much more willing to forget you might be running a pointless repeat of a research that had been done, and done, and done, with nobody the wiser, in scattered and classified labs across the country.

Each swig from the public teat had more and more poppy juice in it. Gradually you forgot you had been another kind of person, holding ideas, fighting for them, working until dawn on coffee, falling for women, getting drunk sometimes. You turned gray after enough of the poppy juice—nice gray.

You said: "Well, now, I wouldn't put it that way," and "There's something to be said on both sides, of course," and "It doesn't pay to go overboard; the big thing is to keep your objectivity."

The nice gray people married early and had a child or two right away to demonstrate that they were normal family men. They had hobbies and talked about them to demonstrate that they weren't one-sided cranks. They drank a little, to demonstrate that they weren't puritans, but not much, to demonstrate that they weren't drunks.

Novak wondered if they tasted bile, as he was tasting it now, thinking of what he had almost become.

4

In the morning he phoned the A.S.F.S.F. office that he wanted the job. Friml's cold voice said: "That's fine, Dr. Novak. Mr. MacIlheny will be here for the next half-hour, and I have a contract ready. If you can make it right over——"

The contract hog-tied Novak for one year with options to conduct refractory research and development under the direction of the Society. The salary was the one he had specified in his ad. Novak raised his eyebrows at one clause; it released the employer from liability claims arising out of radiation damage to the employee.

"You really think the Government's going to let you play with hot stuff?" he asked.

He shouldn't have said "play." MacIlheny was hurt and annoyed. "We expect," he said testily, "that the A.E.C. will co-operate with us as a serious research group when we enter the propulsion stage of the program. They'll be fools if they don't, and we intend to let the country know about it."

Novak shrugged and signed. So did the two Society officers, with the elevator man and the building porter as witnesses. MacIlheny shook Novak's hand ceremoniously after the witnesses were shooed out. "The first thing we want," he said, "is a list of what you'll need and a lab layout. Provisional, of course. There should be some changes after you study the problem in detail?"

"I think not," Novak told him. "A lab's a lab. It's what you do with it that counts. How high can I go?"

Friml looked alarmed. MacIlheny said: "I won't tell you that the sky's the limit. But get what you need, and if you see a chance to save us money without handicapping yourself, take it. Give us the maximum estimated cost and the people you think are the best suppliers for each item."

"*Reputable* firms," said Friml. "The kind of people who'd be prepared to send me a notarized invoice on each purchase."

Novak found the public library and had himself a big morning in the technical reading room, playing with catalogues and trade-magazine ads. After lunch he came back with quadrille paper and a three-cornered scale. The afternoon went like lightning; he spent it drawing up equipment and supplies lists and making dream layouts for a refractories lab. What he wound up with was an oblong floor plan with a straight-through flow: storage to grinding-and-grading to compounding to firing to cooling to testing. Drunk with power, he threw in a small private office for himself.

Construction costs he knew nothing about, but by combing the used-machinery classifieds he kept equipment and supplies down to thirty-two thousand dollars. He had dinner and returned to the library to read about solar furnaces until they put him out at the ten-o'clock closing.

The next day Friml was up to his neck in page proofs of the A.S.F.S.F. organ *Starward*. Looking mad enough to spit, the secretary-treasurer said: "There's a publications committee, but believe it or not all five of them say they're too rushed right now and will I please do their work for them. Some of the rank and file resent my drawing a salary. I hope you'll bear that in mind when you hear them ripping me up the back—as you surely will."

He shoved the proofs aside and began to tick his way down Novak's lists. "There's a Marchand calculator in Mr. Clifton's laboratory," he said. "Wouldn't that do for both of you, or must you have one of your own?"

"I can use his."

Friml crossed the Marchand off the list. "I see you want a—a continuous distilled-water outfit. Wouldn't it be cheaper and just as good to install a tank, and truck distilled water in from the city? After all, it's for sale."

"I'm afraid not. I have to have it pure—not the stuff you buy for storage batteries and steam irons. The minute you put distilled water into a glass jar it begins to dissolve impurities out of the glass. Mine has to be made fresh and stored in a tin-lined tank."

"I didn't know that," said Friml. He put a light check mark next to the still, and Novak knew this human ferret would investigate it. Maybe he suspected him of planning to bilk the A.S.F.S.F. by making corn liquor on the side.

"Um. This vacuum pump. Mr. Clifton's had a Cenco Hyvac idle since he completed port-gasket tests a month ago. You might check with him as to its present availability . . . otherwise I see no duplications. This will probably be approved by Mr. MacIlheny in a day or two and then we can let the contract for the construction of your lab. I suggest that you spend the day at the field with Mr. Clifton to clear a location for it and exchange views generally. You can take the bus to Barstow and any taxi from there. If you want to be reimbursed you should save the bus-ticket stub and get a receipt from the taxi driver for my files. And tonight there's the membership meeting. Mr. MacIlheny asked me to tell you that he'd appreciate a brief talk from you—about five minutes and not too technical."

Friml dove back into the page proofs of *Starward*, and Novak left, feeling a little deflated.

The Greyhound got him to Barstow in ninety minutes. A leather-faced man in a Ford with "Taxi" painted on it said sure he knew where the field was: a two-dollar drive. On the road he asked Novak cautiously: "You one of the scientists?"

"No," said Novak. He humbly thought of himself as an engineer.

"Rocket field's been real good for the town," the driver admitted. "But scientists——" He shook his head. "Wouldn't mind some advice from an older man, would you?"

"Why, no."

"Just—watch out. You can't trust them."

"Scientists?"

"Scientists. I don't say they're all like that, but there's drinkers among them and you know how a drinker is when he gets to talking. Fighting Bob proved it. Not just talk."

This was in reference to the Hoyt speech that claimed on a basis of some very wobbly statistics that the A.E.C. was full of alcoholics. "That so?" asked Novak spinelessly.

"Proved it with figures. And you never know what a scientist's up to."

Enough of this nonsense. "Well, out at the field they're up to building a dummy of a moon ship to find out if it can be done."

"You ain't heard?" The driver's surprise was genuine.

"Heard about what? I'm new here."

"Well, that explains it. It's no dummy moon ship. It's camouflage for an oil-drilling rig. They struck oil there. The scientists are experimenting with it to make cheap gasoline. I heard it from the lineman that tends their power line."

"Well, he's wrong," Novak said. "I've been on the grounds and they aren't doing anything but working on the ship."

The driver shook his head. "Nossir," he said positively. "The thing's a dummy all right, but not for a space ship. Space ships don't work. Nothing there for the rocket to push against. It stands to reason you can't fly where there's no air for it to push against. You could fire a cannon to the Moon if you made one big enough, but no man could stand the shock. I *read* about it."

"In the Bennet newspapers?" asked Novak nastily, exasperated at last.

"Sure," said the driver, not realizing that he was being insulted. "Real American papers. Back up Fighting Bob to the hilt." The driver went on to lavish praise of the Bennet-Hoyt line on foreign policy (go it alone, talk ferociously enough and you won't have to fight); economics (everybody should and must have everything he wants without taking it from anybody else); and military affairs (armed forces second to none and an end to the crushing tax burden for support of the armed forces).

Novak stopped listening quite early in the game and merely interjected an occasional automatic "uh-huh" at the pauses. After a while the *Prototype* appeared ahead and he stopped even that.

The rocket, standing alone in the desert like a monument, was still awe-inspiring. At the sentry box he introduced himself, and the boy on guard shook his hand warmly. "Glad to have you inboard, sir," he said. The word was unmistakably "inboard"—and when Novak had it figured out he had to bite his lip to keep from laughing. The kid was using rocket-ship slang before there were any rocket ships!

The boy never noticed his effort; he was too busy apologizing for stopping him. "You see, Doctor, people don't take our work seriously. Folks used to drive out here the first month and interrupt and even expect us to lend them our drinking water that we trucked out. As if we were here for their entertainment! Finally a gang of little devils broke into one of the Quonsets after dark and smashed everything they could reach. Four thousand dollars' worth of damage in twenty minutes! We were sick. What *makes* people like that? So we had to put up a real fence and mount guard, even if it doesn't look good. But of course we have nothing to hide."

"Of course——" began Novak. But the boy's face had suddenly changed. He was staring, open-mouthed. "What's the matter?" snapped Novak, beginning to inspect himself. "Have I got a scorpion on me?"

"No," said the boy, and looked away embarrassed. "I'm sorry," he said. "Only it suddenly hit me—maybe you'll be one of the people inboard when she—when she goes. But I shouldn't ask."

"The last I heard," Novak said, "*she* is a full-sized mockup and isn't going anywhere."

The boy winked one eye slowly.

"All right," Novak shrugged, amused. "Have it your way and I'll see you on Mars. Where's Mr. Clifton?"

"Back of the machine shop—a new testing rig."

Crossing the quadrangle, Novak passed the *Prototype* and stopped for another look. To the Moon? This colossal pile of steel? It was as easy to visualize the Eiffel Tower picking up its four legs and waddling across Paris. No wonder the taxi driver didn't believe in space flight—and no wonder the kid at the gate did. *Credo quia impossibilis*, or however it went. There were people like that.

He heard Clifton before he saw him. The engineer in charge was yelling: "Harder! *Harder*! Is that all the hard ya can bounce? *Harder*!" And a girl was laughing.

Back of the machine shop, in its shadow, Clifton was standing with a stop watch over a vaguely coffin-shaped block of molded rubber swung from a framework by rope. Most of the ropes were milky nylon. Six of them were manila and had big tension balances, like laundry scales, hooked into them. Towering over Clifton and the frame-work was a twelve-foot gas-pipe scaffold, and a pretty girl in shorts was climbing a ladder to the top of it.

As Novak watched, she hurled herself from the scaffold into the coffin. Clifton, blaspheming, snapped his stop watch and tried to read the jumping needles on the dials of all six balances at the same time.

"Hello," Novak said.

"Harya, Mike. Mike, this is Amy helping out. Like my rig?"

"I thought they worked all this out at the Wright-Patterson A.F.B. Space Medicine School. It *is* an acceleration couch, isn't it?"

"Kindly do not speak to me about Air Force Space Medicine," said Clifton distinctly. "It happens to be mostly bushwah. Ya know what happened? They had this ejector-seat problem, blowing a jet pilot out of a plane because he'd get cut in half if he tried to climb out at 600 m.p.h. So they had an acceleration problem and they licked it fine and dandy. So a publicity-crazy general says acceleration is acceleration, what's good enough for an ejector seat is good enough for a space ship and anyway nobody knows what the hell space flight is like so why worry?"

Clifton folded his arms, puffed out his chest, and assumed the Napoleonic stance, with one foot forward and the knee bent. His hoarse voice became an oily parody of the general's. "My gallant public relations officers! Let us enlighten the taxpaying public on what miracles us air force geniuses pass off daily before breakfast. Let us enlighten them via the metropolitan dailies and wire services with pictures. Let us tell them that we have solved all the medical problems of space flight and have established a school of space medicine to prove it. You may now kiss my hand and proceed to your typewriters at the gallop. To hell with the Navy!"

The girl laughed and said: "Cliff, it *can't* be that bad. And if you keep talking treason they'll lock you up and you'll pine away without your sweetheart there." She meant *Pronto*.

"A-a-ah, what do you know about it, ya dumb Vassar broad? What time's Iron Jaw pick you up? Time for any more bounces?"

"Barnard, not Vassar," she said, "and no time for more bounces, because he said he'd be here at noon and Grady is the world's best chauffeur." She took a wrap-around skirt from a lower horizontal of the gas-pipe scaffolding and tied it on. "Are you a new member, Mike?" she asked.

"I'm going to work on the reaction chamber and throat liner."

"Metal or ceramic?"

"Ceramic refractories is my field."

"Yes, but what about strength? I was thinking about tungsten metal as a throat-liner material. It's a little fantastic because it oxidizes in air at red heat, but I have an idea. You install a tungsten liner and then install a concentric liner to shield it. The ceramic liner takes the heat of the exhaust until the ship is out of atmosphere and then you jettison it, exposing the tungsten. In vacuum, tungsten holds up to better than three thousand centigrade——"

Clifton bulled into it. "Ya crazy as a bunny rabbit, Amy! What about atmosphere on Mars or Venus? What about the return trip to Earth? What about working the tungsten? That stuff crystallizes if ya look at it nasty. What about paying for it? Ya might as well use platinum for cost. And what about limited supply? Ya think America's going to do without tool bits and new light bulbs for a year so ya can have five tons of tungsten to play with? Didn't they teach economics at Miss Twitchell's or whatever it was?"

It was exactly noon by Novak's watch and a black Lincoln rolled through the gate and parked.

"See you at the meeting, Cliff? Glad to have met you, Mike." The girl smiled, and hurried to the car. Novak saw a white-haired man in the back open the door for her, and the car drove off.

"Who was *that*?" Novak asked.

"She's Miss Amelia Earhart Stuart to the society pages," Clifton grinned. "In case ya don't read the society pages, she's the daughter of Wilson Stuart—my old boss at Western. She got bit by the space bug and it drives him crazy. The old man's a roughneck like me but he's in a wheel chair now. Wrecked his heart years ago test-flying. He's been looking backwards ever since; he thinks we're dangerous crackpots. I hear ya got the job okay. Where do you want the lab?"

They left the test rig and walked around the machine-shop Quonset. Clifton stopped for a moment to measure the *Prototype* with his eye. It was habitual.

"How much of a crew does she—would she—hold?" Novak asked.

"Room for three," Clifton said, still looking at her.

"Navigator, engineer—and what?"

"Stowaway, of course!" Clifton roared. "Where ya been all ya life? A girl stowaway in a tin brasseer with maybe a cellophane space suit on. Buckle down, Mike! On the ball or I don't put ya in for the Galactic Cross of Merit!"

Novak wouldn't let himself be kidded. "The youngster at the gate might stow away," he said. "He thinks the *Prototype* is going to take off some day and we just aren't telling the public about it."

Clifton shook his head—regretfully. "Not without the A.E.C. develops a rocket fuel and gives it to us. The bottom two thirds of her is a hollow shell except for structural members. I wish the kid was right. It'd be quite a trip and they'd have quite a time keeping me off the passenger list. But I built the old bat, and I know."

Novak picked an area for his lab and Clifton okayed it. They had lunch from a refrigerator in the machine shop, with a dozen kids hanging on their words.

"Give ya an idea of what we're up against, Mike," Clifton said around a pressed-ham sandwich. "The man-hole for *Proto*. It's got to open and close, it's got to take direct sunlight in space, it's got to take space-cold when it's in shadow. What gasket material do you use? What sealing pressure do you use? Nobody can begin to guess.

Some conditions you can't duplicate in a lab. So what some smart cookie in the A.S.F.S.F. figured out ten years ago was a wring fit, like jo-blocks. Ya know what I mean?"

Novak did—super-smooth surfaces, the kind on hundred-dollar gauges. Put two of those surfaces together and they clung as if they were magnetized. The theory was that the molecules of the surfaces interpenetrate and the two pieces become—almost—the same piece. "Ingenious," he said.

"Ingenious," muttered Clifton. "I guess that's the word. Because nobody ever in the history of machine shops put a jo-block finish on pieces that size. I got a friend in South Bend, so I sent him the rough-machined manhole cover and seating. The Studebaker people happen to have a big superfinish boring mill left over from the war, sitting in a corner covered with cosmoline. Maybe my friend can con them into taking off the grease and machining a superfinish onto our parts. If not, I'll try to handscrape them. If I can't do it on circular pieces—and I probably can't—I'll scrap them and order square forgings. You think *you* got troubles with your throat liner?"

"Generally, what kind of shape is *Proto* in?"

"Generally, damn fine shape. I finish testing the acceleration couch today. If it passes I order two more pads from Akron and install them. Then we're all ready to go except for the manhole problem and a little matter of a fuel and propulsion system that oughtta be cleared up in eight-ten years. A detail."

Clifton picked his teeth and led Novak to a blueprint file. He yanked open one of the big, flat drawers and pulled out a 36-by-48 blueprint. "Here we are," he said. "The chamber, liner, and vane. You're gonna have to make it; you might as well look it over. I'm gonna appoint a volunteer and supervise some more crash dives."

Novak took the print to an empty corner of the shop and spread it out on a workbench. He looked first at the ruled box in the lower right-hand corner for specifications. He noted that the drawing had been made some three months ago by "J. MacI." and checked by him. Material: ceramic refractory; melting point higher than 3,000° C.; coefficient of expansion, less than .000,004; bulk modulus . . .

Novak laughed incredulously.

It was *all* there—stretch, twist, and bulk moduli, coefficient of elasticity, everything except how to make it. MacIlheny had laid down complete specifications for the not-yet-developed liner material. A childish performance! He suspected that the president of the A.S.F.S.F. was simply showing off his technical smattering and was mighty proud of himself. Novak wondered how to tell MacIlheny tactfully that under the circumstances it would be smarter to lay down specifications in the most general terms.

He studied them again and laughed again. Sure he could probably turn out something like that—one of the boron carbides. But it would be a hell of a note if A.E.C. came up with a 3,750-degree fuel and they had a 3,500-degree liner, or if the A.E.C. came up with a hydroxide fuel that would dissolve a liner which was only acidproof. What MacIlheny should have said was something simpler and humbler, like: "Give us the best compromise you can between strength and thermal-shock resistance. And, please, as much immunity to all forms of chemical attack as you can manage."

Well, he'd tell him nicely—somehow.

Novak looked from the specifications to the drawings themselves and thought at first that there had been some mistake—the right drawings on the wrong sheet, the wrong drawings on the right sheet—but after a puzzled moment he recognized them vaguely as a reaction chamber and throat liner.

They were all wrong; all, all wrong.

He knew quite well from N.E.P.A. what reaction chambers and throat liners for jet craft looked like. He knew standard design doctrine for flow, turbulence, Venturi effect, and the rest of it. There were tricks that had been declassified when newer, better tricks came along. This—this *thing*—blithely by-passed the published tricks and went in for odd notions of its own. The ratio of combustion volume to throat volume was unheard of. The taper was unheard of. The cross section was an ellipse of carefully defined eccentricity instead of the circle it should be. There was only one hole for fuel injection—only one hole! Ridiculous.

While the shop was filled with the noise of a youngster inexpertly hack-sawing sheet metal in a corner, Novak slowly realized that it was not ridiculous at all. It wasn't MacIlheny showing off; no, not at all. Anybody who could read a popular-science magazine knew enough not to design a chamber and throat like that.

But MacIlheny knew better.

He walked slowly out to the back of the shop where Clifton was clocking dives into the acceleration couch. "Cliff," he said, "can I see you for a minute?"

"Sure, Mike. As long as ya don't expect any help from me."

Together they looked down at the spread blue print, and Novak said: "The kid at the gate was right. They are going to take off some day and they just aren't telling the public about it."

"What ya talking?" demanded Clifton. "All I see there is lines on paper. Don't try to kid a kidder, Mike."

Novak said: "The specs are for me to develop a material to handle a certain particular fuel with known heat, thrust, and chemical properties. The drawings are the wrong shape. Very wrong. I know conventional jet theory and I have never seen anything like the shapes they want for the chamber and throat of. that—thing —out there."

"Maybe it's a mistake," Clifton said uncertainly.

Then he cursed himself. "Mistake! Mistake! Why don't I act my age? Mistakes like this them boys don't make. The acceleration couch. They designed it eight years ago on paper. It works better than them things the Air Force been designing and building and field-testing for fifteen years now."

Novak said: "People who can do that aren't going to get the throat and chamber so wrong they don't look like any throat and chamber ever used before. *They've got a fuel and they know its performance.*"

Clifton was looking at the data. "MacIlheny designed it—it says here. An insurance man three months ago sat down to design a chamber and throat, did it, checked it, and turned it over to you to develop the material and fabricate the pieces. I wonder where he got it, Mike. Russia? Argentina? China?"

"Twenty countries have atomic energy programs," Novak said. "And one year ago the A.S.F.S.F. suddenly got a lot of money—a hell of a lot of money. I ordered thirty-two thousand dollars' worth of gear and Friml didn't turn a hair."

Clifton muttered: "A couple of million bucks so far, I figure it. Gray-market steel. Rush construction—overtime never bothered them as long as the work got done. Stringing the power line, drilling the well. A couple million bucks and nobody tells ya where it came from." He turned to Novak and gripped his arm earnestly. "Nah, Mike," he said deftly. "It's *crazy*. Why should a country do research on foreign soil through stooges. It just ain't possible."

"Oh, God!" said Novak. His stomach turned over.

"What's the matter, kid?"

"I just thought of a swell reason," he said slowly. "What if a small country like the Netherlands, or a densely populated country like India, stumbled on a rocket fuel? And what if that fuel were terribly dangerous? Maybe it could go off by accident and take a couple of hundred miles of terrain with it. Maybe it's radiologically bad and poisons everybody for a hundred miles around if it escapes. Wouldn't they want the proving ground to be outside their own country in that case?"

There was a long pause.

Clifton said: "Yeah. I think they might. If it blows up on their own ground they lose all their space-ship talent and don't get a space ship. If it blows up on our ground they also don't get a space ship, but they do deprive Uncle Sam of a lot of space-ship talent. But how—*if* the fuel don't blow up California—do they take over the space ship?"

"I don't know, Cliff. Maybe MacIlheny flies it to Leningrad and the Red Army takes it from there. Maybe Friml flies it to Buenos Aires and the Guardia Peronista."

"Maybe," said Cliff. "Say, Mike, I understand in these cloak-and-dagger things they kill ya if ya find out too much."

"Yeah, I've heard of that, Cliff. Maybe we'll get the Galactic Cross of Merit posthumously. Cliff, *why* would anybody want to get to the Moon bad enough to do it in a crazy way like this?"

The engineer took a gnawed hunk of tobacco from his hip pocket and bit off a cud. "I can tell ya what MacIlheny told me. Our president, I used to think, was just a space hound and used the military-necessity argument to cover it up. Now, I don't know. Maybe the military argument was foremost in his mind all the time.

"MacIlheny says the first country to the Moon has got it *made*. First rocket ship establishes a feeble little pressure dome with one man left in it. If he's lucky he lives until the second trip, which brings him a buddy, more food and oxygen, and a stronger outer shell for his pressure dome. After about ten trips you got a corporal's squad on the Moon nicely dug in and you can start bringing them radar gear and launchers for bombardment rockets homing on earth points.

"Nobody can reach ya there, get it? *Nobody*. The first trip has always gotta bring enough stuff to keep one man alive—if he's lucky—until the next trip. It takes a lotta stuff when ya figure air and water. The first country to get there has the bulge because when country two lands their moon pioneer the corporal's squad men hike on over in their space suits and stick a pin in his pressure dome and—he dies. Second country can complain to the U.N., and what can they prove? The U.N. don't have observers on the Moon. And if the second country jumps the first country with an A-bomb attack, they're gonna *die*. Because they can't jump the retaliation base on the Moon."

He squirted tobacco juice between his teeth. "That's simplified for the kiddies," he said, "but that's about the way MacIlheny tells it."

"Sounds reasonable," Novak said. "Personally I am going right now to the nearest regional A.E.C. Security and Intelligence Office. You want to come along?" He hoped he had put the question casually. It had occurred to him that, for all his apparent surprise, Clifton was a logical candidate for Spy Number One.

"Sure," said Clifton. "I'll drive you. There's bound to be one in L.A."

5

There was, in the Federal Building.

Anheier, the agent in charge, was a tall, calm man. "Just one minute, gentlemen," he said, and spoke into his intercom. "The file on the American Society for Space Flight, Los Angeles," he said, and smiled at their surprise. "We're not a Gestapo," he said, "but we have a job to do. It's the investigation of possible threats to national security as they may involve atomic energy. Naturally the space-flight group would be of interest to us. If the people of this country only knew the patience and thoroughness—here we are."

The file was bulky. Anheier studied it in silence for minutes. "During the past fifteen years derogatory informations have been filed from time to time, first with the F.B.I. and later with us. The investigations that followed did not produce evidence of any law violations. Since that's the case, I can tell you that the most recent investigation followed a complaint from a certain rank-and-file member that Mr. Joel Friml, your secretary-treasurer, was a foreign agent. We found Mr. Friml's background spotless and broke down the complainant. It was a simple case of jealousy. There seems to be a certain amount of, say, spite work and politics in an organization as—as visionary as yours."

"Are you suggesting that we're cranks?" Novak demanded stiffly. "I'm a Doctor of Philosophy of the University of Illinois and I've held a responsible position with the A.E.C. And Mr. Clifton has been a project engineer with Western Aircraft."

"By no means, by no means!" Anheier said hastily. "I know your backgrounds, gentlemen." There was something on his face that was the next thing to a smile. Novak was suddenly, sickeningly sure that Anheier, with patience and thoroughness, had learned how he had socked his A.E.C. director in the jaw and how Clifton had been fired after a fight with his boss. A couple of congenital hotheads, Anheier would calmly decide; unemployables who can't get along with people; crank denouncers and accusers.

Anheier was saying, poker-faced: "Of course we want complete depositions from you on your, your information." He buzzed and a stenographer came in with a small, black, court machine. "And if investigation seems in order, of course we'll get going with no lost time. First give your name and personal data to the stenographer and then your facts, if you please." He leaned back calmly, and the stenographer zipped out the paper box of his machine and poised his fingers. He looked bored.

"My name is Michael Novak," Novak said, fighting to keep his voice calm and clear. The stenographer's fingers bumped the keys and the paper tape moved up an inch. "I live at the Revere Hotel in Los Angeles. I am a ceramic engineer with my B.Sc. from Rensselaer Polytechnic Institute and M.Sc. and Ph.D. from the University of Illionis. I was employed after getting my doctorate by the U.S. Atomic Energy Commission in various grades, the last and highest being A.E.C.18. I—I left the A.E.C. last month and took employment with an organization called the American Society for Space Flight at its Los Angeles headquarters.

"I had no previous knowledge of this organization. I was told by officers that it is now making a full-scale metal mock-up of a moon ship to study structural and engineering problems. Purportedly it has no space-ship fuel in mind and intends to ask the co-operation of the A.E.C. in solving this problem after it has solved all the other problems connected with the design of a space ship.

"I believe, however, that this is a cover story. I believe that about one year ago the organization was supplied with funds to build an actual space ship by a foreign power which has developed a space-ship fuel.

"My reasons for believing this are that the organization has liberal funds behind it which are supposed to be private contributions from industry, but there are no signs of outside interests in the project; further, I was ordered to execute an extremely unorthodox design for a reaction chamber and throat liner, which strongly suggests that the organization has an atomic space-ship fuel and knows its characteristics.

"I want to emphasize that the unorthodox design which aroused my suspicions was purportedly drawn and checked by James MacIlheny, president of the organization, an insurance man who disclaims any special technical training. In other, nonvital details of the space ship, designing was done mostly by technical men employed in the aircraft industry and by local college students and teachers following space flight as a hobby of a technical nature. It is my belief that the reaction chamber and throat liner were designed by a foreign power to fit their atomic fuel and were furnished to MacIlheny.

"I do not know why a foreign power should erect a space ship off its own territory. One possibility that occurs to me is that their fuel might be extremely dangerous from a radiological or explosive standpoint or both, and that the foreign power may be unwilling to risk a catastrophic explosion on its own ground or radiation sickness to large numbers of its own valued personnel."

He stopped and thought—but that was all there was to say.

Anheier said calmly: "Thank you, Dr. Novak. And now Mr. Clifton, please."

The engineer cleared his throat and said aggressively: "I'm August Clifton. I been a self-educated aero engineer for nine years. For Douglas I designed the B-108 air frame and I rode production line at their Omaha plant. Then I worked for Western Air, specializing in control systems for multijet aircraft. Last year I left Western and went to work for the A.S.F.S.F.

"My ideas about the A.S.F.S.F.'s backing and what they're up to are the same as Novak's. I been around the Society longer, so I can say more definitely than him that there is not one sign of any business or industry having any stake in what's going on out at the field. That's all."

"Thanks, Mr. Clifton. They'll be typed in a moment." The stenographer left. "I understand there's one prominent industrialist who shows some interest in the Society? Mr. Stuart?" There was a ponderously roguish note in Anheier's voice.

"Ya crazy, Anheier," Clifton said disgustedly. "He's just looking after his daughter. *You* think we're nuts? You should hear Iron Jaw take off on us!"

"I know," smiled Anheier hastily. "I was only joking."

"What about MacIlheny?" asked Novak. "Have you investigated him?"

Anheier leafed through the A.S.F.S.F. file. "Thoroughly," he said. "Mr. MacIlheny is a typical spy——"

"*What?*"

"——I mean to say, he's the kind of fellow who's in a good position to spy, but he isn't and doesn't. He has no foreign contacts and none of the known foreign agents in this country have gone anywhere near him——"

"What ya talking?" demanded Clifton. "You mean there's spies running around and you don't pick them up?"

"I said foreign agents—news-service men, exchange students, businessmen, duly registered propaganda people, diplomatic and consular personnel—there's no end to them. *They* don't break any laws, but they recruit people who do. God knows *how* they recruit them. Every American knows that since the Rosenberg cases the penalty for espionage by a citizen is, in effect, death. That's the way the country wanted it, and that's the way it is."

"Why do you say MacIlheny's typical?" asked Novak. He had a half-formed hope that this human iceberg might give them some practical words on technique, even if he refused to get excited about their news.

"Mata Hari's out," said Anheier comfortably. "You've seen spies in the papers, Dr. Novak." To be sure, he had—ordinary faces, bewildered, ashamed, cowering from the flash bulbs. "I came up via the accountancy route myself so I didn't see a great deal of the espionage side," Anheier confessed a bit wistfully. "But I can tell you that your modern spy in America is a part-timer earning a legitimate living at some legitimate line. Import-export used to be a favorite, but it was too obvious."

"Hell, I should think so," grinned Clifton.

Anheier went on: "Now they recruit whatever they can, and get technical people whenever possible. This is because your typical state secret nowadays is not a map or code or military agreement but an industrial process.

"The Manhattan District under General Groves and the British wartime atomic establishment were veritable sieves. The Russians learned free of charge that calutron separation of U-235 from U-238 was impractical and had to be abandoned. They learned, apparently, that gaseous diffusion is *the* way to get the fissionable isotope. They learned that implosion with shaped charges is a practical way to assemble a critical mass of fissionable material. They were saved millions of dead-ended man-hours by this information.

"Security's taken a nice little upswing since then, but we still have secrets and there still are spies, even though the penalty is death. Some do it for money, some are fanatics—some, I suppose, just don't realize the seriousness of it. Here are your depositions, gentlemen."

They read them and signed them.

Anheier shook their heads and said: "I want to thank you both for doing your patriotic duty as you saw it. I assure you that your information will be carefully studied and appropriate action will be taken. If you learn of anything else affecting national security in the atomic area in your opinion, I hope you won't hesitate to let us know about it." Clearly it was a speech he had made hundreds of times—or thousands. The brush-off.

"Mr. Anheier," Novak said, "what if we take this to the F.B.I.? They might regard it more seriously than you seem to."

The big, calm man put his palms out protestingly. "Please, Dr. Novak," he said. "I assure you that your information will be thoroughly processed. As to the F.B.I., you're perfectly free to go to them if you wish, but it would be wasted motion. Cases in the atomic area that come to the F.B.I. are automatically bucked to us—a basic policy decision, and a wise one in my opinion. Technical factors and classified information are so often involved——"

In the street Novak said disgustedly: "He didn't ask us any questions. He didn't ask us whether we were going to quit or not."

"Well—are we?"

"I guess I am—I don't know, Cliff. Maybe I'm wrong about the whole business. Maybe I'm as crazy as Anheier thinks I am."

"Let's go to my place," Clifton said. "We oughtta go to the A.S.F.S.F. membership meeting tonight after we eat."

"Cripes, I'm supposed to make a speech!"

"Just tell 'em hello."

They got into Clifton's car, the long, tall, 1930 Rolls with the lovingly maintained power plant, and roared through Los Angeles. Clifton drove like a maniac, glaring down from his height on underslung late models below and passing them with muttered fusillades of curses. "Me, I like a car with *character*," he growled, barreling the Rolls around a '56 Buick.

His home was in a pretty, wooded canyon dotted with houses. Gravel flew as he spun into the driveway.

"Come and meet Lilly," he said.

Outside, the Clifton house was an ordinary five-room bungalow. Inside it was the dope-dream of a hobbyist run amuck. Like geologic strata, tools and supplies overlaid the furniture. Novak recognized plasticene, clay, glazes, modeling tools and hooks, easels, sketch boxes, cameras, projectors, enlargers, gold-leaf burnishers, leather tools, jewelers' tools and the gear of carpenters, machinists, plumbers, electricians and radio hams. Lilly was placidly reading an astrology magazine in the middle of the debris. She was about thirty-five: a plump, gray-eyed blonde in halter and shorts. The sight of her seemed to pick Clifton up like a shot of brandy.

"Mama!" he yelled, kissing her loudly. "I'm sick of you. I brought you this here young man for you to run away with. Kindly leave without making no unnecessary disturbance. His name is Mike."

"Hallo," she said calmly. "Don't pay him no attention; he alvays yokes. Excuse how I talk; I am Danish. How many letters you got in your full complete name?"

"Uh—twelve."

"Good," she dimpled. "I am tvelve also. We will be friends, it means."

"I'm very glad," Novak said faintly.

"Mike, you been factored?"

"I don't think I understand——"

"It's biomat'ematics. You know? You go to a biomat'e-maticist and he finds the mat-ematical for-moola of you subconscious and he factors out the traumas. It's va-a-ary simple." Her face fell a little. "Only I got a Danish-speaking subconscious of course,

212

so vit' me it goes a liddle slow. Funny"—she shook her head—"same t'ing happened to me years ago vit' di'netics. Cliff, you gonna give Mike a drink or is he like the other young feller you had here last month? Feller that broke the big mirror and you nineteen-inch cat'ode-ray tube and my Svedish pitcher——"

"How the hell was I supposed to know?" he roared. In an aside: "That was Friml, Mike. He got pretty bad."

"Friml?" asked Novak incredulously. The ice-water kid?

"He should go to a biomat'ematicist," sighed Lilly. "If ever a boy needed factoring, it's him. Make me only a liddle one please; I don't eat yet today."

She had a little martini and Clifton and Novak had big ones.

"We all go to the meeting tonight I guess? First I want *biftek aux pommes de terre* someplace."

"What the hell, Mama!" Clifton objected. "This time yesterday you were a vegetarian for life."

"I changed my mind," she said. "Go get shaved up and dress you'self and we go someplace for *biftek*."

When Clifton appeared—shaved, dressed, and subdued—Lilly was still in the bedroom, putting on finishing touches. The two men had another martini apiece.

"What about the contracts?" Novak asked.

Clifton understood. "If they try to hold us to them we could just lie down on the job and let them pay us. Hate to work it like that, though. It'd be dull."

"It's still the craziest business I ever heard of."

Lilly appeared, looking sexy in a black dinner dress with a coronet of blond hair swept up from her creamy neck. Clifton let out a long, loud wolf-howl and said: "The hell with the beefsteaks and the meeting. Let's——"

"Later," said Lilly firmly.

As the maroon Rolls thundered down the canyon, Clifton said casually: "I may quit the space hounds, Mama."

"So what you gonna do for a yob?"

"Buy you a red dress and turn mack, I guess. Nah, ya too old and ugly. Maybe I'll open a radio shop or ship out again for an electrician; I guess I still got my card. I kinda hate to leave my best girl out there in the desert, but the whole thing's a joke. She's pretty, but she'll never amount to a damn."

Novak knew why he was lying about the reason. *I understand in these cloak-and-dagger things they kill ya if ya find out too much.*

6

They had a dinner at a downtown restaurant and were at the A.S.F.S.F. meeting hall by 8:30. Novak was alarmed when the building turned out to be the Los Angeles Slovak Sokol Hall, rented for the occasion.

"Foreigners!" he exclaimed. "Does the A.S.F.S.F. go around *looking* for jams to get into?"

"Relax, Mike," Clifton told him. "The Sokol's strictly American by now. They got a long anti-Communist record."

Still, fretted Novak, foreigners—Slavic foreigners. The building was in the same run-down area that housed the Society's business office. It was liberally hung with American flags and patriotic sentiments. Inconspicuous on the lobby walls were a few photographs of group calisthenics and marchers in Czech national costumes, from decades ago.

A well-worn placard on an easel said that the A.S.F.S.F. meeting was being held at 8:30 in the main hall, straight ahead and up the stairs.

About a score of people in the lobby were having final smokes and talking. Novak could divide them easily into two types: juvenile space hounds and employed hobbyists. The hobbyists were what you'd see at any engineers' convention: pipe-smokers, smiling men, neat, tanned. The space hounds were any collection of juvenile enthusiasts anywhere—more mature than an equal number of hot-rod addicts, perhaps, but still given to nervous laughter, horseplay, and catchwords.

Their entrance had been the signal for the younger element to surround Clifton and bombard him with questions.

"Cliff, how she coming?"

"Mr. Clifton, need a good carpenter at the field?"

"How's the acceleration couch coming, Cliff?"

"Could we get that boring mill at South Bend?"

"Shaddap!" said Clifton. "Leave a man breathe, will ya!" They loved him for it. "What's the movie tonight?"

"A stinker," one girl told him. "*Pirates of the Void*, with Marsha Denny and Lawrence Malone. Strictly for yocks."

"They show a space-flight movie," Clifton explained to Novak. "There ain't enough business to kill the time and send everybody home in the proper state of exhaustion." He towed his wife and Novak up the stairs, where a youngster at a card table challenged their membership. They were clamorously identified by a dozen youngsters and went in. The hall seated about four hundred and had a stage with a movie screen and more American flags.

"Better sit in the back——" began Clifton, and then: "For God's sake!" It was Anheier, smiling nervously.

"Hello," said the Security man. "I thought I'd combine business with pleasure. Marsha Denny's a great favorite of mine and I understand there's going to be a preview tonight."

"Well, enjoy yourself," Clifton said coldly. He took Lilly and Novak to the left rear corner of the auditorium and they sat down. He told his wife: "An A.E.C. guy we met. A creep."

MacIlheny climbed to the stage and called to stragglers in the back of the hall: "Okay, men. Let's go." They found seats.

Crack went the gavel. "The-meeting-is-called-to-order. The-chair-will-entertain-a-motion-to-adopt-the-standard-agenda-as-laid-down-in-the-organization's-bylaws."

"So move," said somebody, and there was a ragged chorus of seconds.

"All-in-favor-signify-by-raising-one-hand-any-opposed? The-motion-seems-to-be-and-is-carried. First-on-the-agenda-is-the-reading-of-previous-meetings-minutes."

Somebody stuck his hand up, was recognized, and moved that the minutes be accepted as read. The motion was seconded and carried without excitement. So were motions to accept and adopt reports of the membership, orbit computation, publications, finance, structural problems and control mechanisms committees.

"Making good time," Clifton commented.

Under "good and welfare" a belligerent-looking youngster got recognized and demanded the impeachment of the secretary-treasurer. There was a very mild, mixed demonstration: some applause and some yells of "Sit down!" and "Shuddup!" MacIlheny rapped for order.

"The motion is in order," he wearily announced. "Is there a second?" There was—another belligerent kid.

"In seconding this motion," he said loudly, "I just want to go over some ground that's probably familiar to us all. With due respect to the majority's decision, I still feel that there's no place for salaried employees in the A.S.F.S.F. But if there *has* to be a paid secretary-treasurer, I'm damned if I see why an outsider with no special interest in space flight——"

Friml was on his feet in the front row, clamoring for recognition on a point of personal privilege.

"Damn it, Friml, I wasn't insulting you——"

"That's for the chair to decide, Mr. Grady! I suggest you pipe down and let him."

"Who're you telling to——"

MacIlheny hammered for silence. "Chair recognizes Mr. Friml."

"I simply want a ruling on the propriety of Mr. Grady's language. Thank you."

"The chair rules that Mr. Grady's remarks were improper and cautions him to moderate his language."

Breathing hard, the youngster tried again. "In seconding this motion to impeach, I want to point out that there are members with *much* more seniority in the organization than Mr. Friml and with a long-demonstrated record of interest in space flight which he cannot match."

MacIlheny called for debate and recognized one of the engineer-types.

"It should be evident to all of us," the engineer said soothingly, "that the criterion for the secretary-treasurer's office ought to be *competence*. We're not playing with marbles any more—I'm happy to say. And I for one am very much relieved that we have the services of a man with a B.B.A., an M.B.A., and a C.P.A. after his name.

"Now, I may have more organizational experience than Mr. Grady, since I've been somewhat active in the A.S.M.E. and the aeronautical societies. I name no names—but in one of those groups we were unwise enough to elect a treasurer who, with all the good will in the world, simply didn't know how to handle the job. We were rooked blind before we knew what hit us, and it took a year to straighten the records out. I don't want that to happen to the A.S.F.S.F., and I seriously urge that the members here vote against the impeachment. Let's not monkey with a smooth-running machine. Which is what we've got now."

There was a lot of applause.

A thin, dark girl, rather plain, was recognized. Her voice was shrill with neurotic hatred. "I don't know what's become of the A.S.F.S.F. In one year I've seen a decent, democratic organization turned into a little despotism with half a dozen people—if that!—running the works while the plain members are left in the dark. Who is this Friml? How do we know he's so good if we don't know the amount and nature of the contributions he handles? And *Mr.* August Clifton, whom everybody is so proud of, I happen to know he was fired from Western Aircraft! The fact is, MacIlheny's got some cash donors in his hip pocket and we're all afraid to whisper because he might——"

MacIlheny pounded for silence. "The chair rules Miss Gingrich out of order," he said. "This is debate on a motion to impeach Mr. Friml and not to reconsider a policy of accepting contributions in confidence, which was approved by the membership as the minutes show. Miss Stuart, you're recognized."

Amy Stuart got up looking grim. "I want to make two statements. First, on a point of personal privilege, that Mr. Clifton was fired from Western because he was too high-spirited to get along in a rather conservative outfit and not for incompetence. More than once I've heard my father say that Mr. Clifton was—or almost was—the best man he had working for him.

"Second, I move to close debate."

"Second the motion," somebody called from the floor.

Miss Gingrich was on her feet shrilling: "Gag rule! Nobody can open his mouth around here except the Holy Three and their stooges! We were doing all right before MacIlheny——" The rest was lost in shouts of disapproval and the whacking of the gavel. The girl stood silently for a moment and then sat down, trembling.

"Motion to close debate has been made and seconded. This motion takes precedence and is unamendable. All in favor raise one hand." A forest of hands went up. "Any opposed?" Maybe twenty. "The motion is carried. we now have before us a motion to impeach Mr. Friml, our secretary-treasurer. All in favor?" The same twenty hands. "Opposed?" The forest of hands rose again, and a few kids cried: "No, no!"

"The motion is defeated. Unless there are further matters under good and welfare"—he was refusing to let his eye be caught, and half a dozen members were trying to catch it—"we will proceed to the introduction of a new A.S.F.S.F. full-time scientific worker. Dr. Michael Novak comes to us from two years with the United States Atomic Energy Commission. He has been working with high-tensile, refractory ceramic materials—a vital field in rocketry; I'm sure the application to our work is obvious to all. Dr. Novak."

He was on his feet and starting down the aisle to a polite burst of applause. They might be spies or they might not; he might be working for them tomorrow or he might not, but meanwhile there was a certain rigmarole you went through at these things, and he knew it well.

"Mr. President, members, and guests, thank you." Now the joke. "My field of work stems from very early times. It was a cave man who founded ceramic engineering when he accidentally let a mud-daubed wicker basket fall into his campfire and pulled it out, after the fire died down, the first earthenware pot. I presume he did not realize that he was also a very important pioneer of space flight." A satisfactory chuckle.

Now the erudition. "Basically, my problem is to develop a material which is strong, workable, and heat-resistant. For some years the way to tackle such a job has been to hunt the material among the so-called 'solid solutions.' An alloy is a familiar example of a solid solution—the kind in which both the solvent and the solute are metals.

"The substance tungsten carbide is well known to any of you who have machine-shop experience. It is a solid solution with one nonmetallic constituent, and its properties have revolutionized industrial production. Dies and tool bits of this fantastically hard stuff have probably increased the productivity of this country by several per cent with no other changes being put into effect. Idle time of machine tools has been reduced because tungsten-carbide bits go on, and on, and on without resharpening. Idle time on presses of all sorts has been reduced because tungsten-carbide dies go on, and on, and on without replacement.

"This is only one example of the way Mother Nature comes up with the answer to your particular problem if you ask her in the right way. She also offers among the solid solutions the chromium and cobalt carbides, which top tungsten carbide for refractory qualities, and the boron carbides with which I intend to work.

"In the solid solutions there is a situation that rules out dramatic, abrupt crystallizations of one's problem. An organic chemist trying to synthesize a particular molecule may leap up with a shriek of 'eureka—I've got it!' And so he may, for an organic molecule either is there or it isn't: a yes-or-no situation. But in working with solutions rather than compounds, there is continuous variation of solvent to solute. Theoretically, it would take an infinite amount of time to explore the properties of *every* boron carbide, even if their properties varied simply and continuously with the ratio of constituents alone. But it is more complicated than that.

"Actually the properties you seek in your carbides do not appear when you turn out a batch fresh from your crucible. There is the complicated business of aging, in which the carbide spends a certain time at a certain temperature. Two more variables. And in some cases the aging should be conducted in a special atmosphere—perhaps helium or argon. Another variable! And secondary properties must be considered. For example, the standard ceramic bond to metal is obtained by heating both parts to red heat and plunging them into liquid air. There are carbides that may have every other desirable property but which cannot take such a drastic thermal shock."

MacIlheny, in the front row, was looking at his watch. Time for the windup. "I hope I've given you an idea of what we're up against. But I hope I haven't given you an idea that the problem's uncrackable in a less-than-infinite amount of time, because it isn't. Experiments in some number must be made, but mathematics comes to the aid of the researcher to tell him when he's on the right track and when he's going astray. With the aid of the theory of least squares, plenty of sweat, and a little dumb luck I hope before long to be able to report to you that I've developed a material which can take the heat and thrust of any escape-velocity fuel which may some day come along."

The applause was generous.

Back in his seat, Clifton said: "It sounded swell, Mike. Did it mean anything?" And Lilly said: "Don' be so foolish, Cliff. Was a byoo-tiful speech."

"We have the privilege tonight," MacIlheny was saying, "of being the first audience in this area to see the new spaceflight film *Pirates of the Void*——" There were a few ironical cheers. "——through the kindness of Mr. Riefenstahl of United Productions' promotion staff. Audience comment cards will be available on the way out. I think it would be only fair and courteous if all of us made it a point to get one and fill it out, giving our—*serious*—opinion of the movie. And I'd like to add that Sokol Hall has made *two* projection machines available to us, so that this time there will be no interruption for changing between reels." The cheers at that were not ironical.

"I'm gonna the men's room," Clifton announced, and left.

"Cliff don't like movies much," Lilly announced proudly. "He'll be back."

The lights went out and *Pirates of the Void* went on with a fanfare and the United Productions monogram.

The movie, thought Novak as he watched, was another case of the public's faith that space flight is an impossibility. It was a fable in which the actors wore odd garments: the men, shiny coveralls; and the women, shiny · shorts and bras. The time was far in the future—far enough for there to be pirates of space and a Space Navy of the United World to battle them. Space flight tomorrow, but never space flight today. *But MacIlheny had a fuel and knew its performance.*

He leaned back, wishing he could smoke, and saw Marsha Denny's problem unfold. Marsha was a nurse in the Space Navy and she had a brother (but there was a plant indicating that he wasn't really her brother, though she didn't yet know that) in the Pirate Fleet, high up. She was in love with Lawrence Malone, who took the part of the muscular G-2 of the Space Navy and had assigned himself the mission of penetrating the Pirate Fleet in the guise of a deserter from the regulars.

Somehow fifteen minutes of it passed, and Lilly leaned across the seat between them. "Mike," she asked worriedly, "you mind doing somet'ing for me? You go and find Cliff? He's gone an awful long time."

"Why sure," he whispered. "Glad to get out of here."

He slipped from the dark auditorium and promptly lit a cigarette. *Men's Room*, said a sign with an arrow. He followed it to a big, empty washroom with six booths. One of the doors was closed.

"Cliff?" he called, embarrassed. There was no answer.

Cliff must be in the corridor somewhere. His eye was caught by the shine of gold on the corner of a washstand. A wedding band—Cliff's wedding band? Slipped it off before he washed his hands? There was no engraving in it and he didn't remember what Cliff's ring looked like; just that he wore one.

Maybe——

"Mister," he said to the closed door, "I found a gold ring on the washstand. You lose it?"

There was no answer. A thread of crimson blood snaked from under the closed door, slowly over the tiled floor, seeking a bright brass drain.

I understand in these cloak-and-dagger things they kill ya if ya find out too much.

Novak fell on his hands and knees to peer through the six-inch gap between the bottom of the door and the floor. He saw two shod feet, oddly lax, a dangling hand, a little pool of blood, and a small pistol.

He went to pieces and pounded on the door, shouting.

It was latched. Novak darted from the washroom to the main hall; Anheier was there, who didn't believe there was anything to their story. He blundered into the darkness where, on the screen, two silvery space ships of the impossible future were slashing at each other with many-colored rays that cracked and roared on the sound track.

"*Anheier!*" Novak yelled hysterically. "Where are you?" Dark heads turned to stare at him. Somebody stumbled his way across a row of knees and hurried to him.

"Dr. Novak!" asked the Security man. "What's the matter?" People shushed them loudly, and Anheier took Novak's arm, drawing him into the corridor.

Novak said: "There's somebody in a booth in the washroom. I saw blood. And a gun. I'm afraid it's Clifton."

Anheier hurried down the corridor without a word. In the washroom he went into an adjoining booth and climbed up on its bowl to peer over the partition.

"Bad," he said flatly, hopping down. He took a long nail file from his pocket, inserted it between the door edge and jamb and flipped up the latch. The door swung open outwards. "Don't touch anything," Anheier said.

Clifton was in the booth. His clothes were arranged. He was sprawled on the seat with his head down on his chest and his shoulders against the rear wall. There was a great hole in the back of his head, below the crown.

"Get to a phone," Anheier said. "Call the city police and report a homicide here."

Novak remembered a pay phone in the lobby downstairs and ran. Just like a magazine cartoon he crazily thought, when he found a woman talking in it on the other side of the folding glass door. He rapped on the glass imperatively and the woman turned. It was Amy Stuart. She smiled recognition, spoke another few words into the phone, and decisively hung up.

"I'm sorry to be such a gossip," she said, "but that bloody movie——"

"Thanks," he said hastily, and ducked into the phone booth. He saw Lilly coming down the stairs, looking more than a little worried.

The police switchboard took his call with glacial calm and said not to do anything, there would be a car there in less than five minutes.

Lilly and the Stuart girl were waiting outside. "Mike," Lilly burst out, "what's wrong? I sent you out to look for Cliff, you come back and holler for that A.E.C. feller, and you run to the phone. You talk straight vit' me please, Mike."

"Lilly," he said, "Cliff's dead. Shot to death. I'm— I'm sorry——"

She said something in a foreign language and fainted on his arm. Amy Stuart said sharply: "Here. Into this chair." He lugged her clumsily into a deep, leather club chair.

"Was what you said true?" she demanded angrily, doing things to Lilly's clothes.

"Quite true," he said. "There's an A.E.C. Security man there now. I was calling the police. Do you know Mrs. Clifton?"

"Fairly well. How horrible for her. They loved each other. What could have happened? *What could have happened?*" Her voice was shrill.

"Take it easy," he told her flatly. "I think you're getting hysterical and that won't do any good."

She swallowed. "Yes—I suppose I was." She fussed efficiently over Lilly for a moment or two. "That's all," she said. "Nothing else you can do for a faint. God, how horrible for her! God, how I hate killers and killing. That bloody movie. World of tomorrow. Death rays flash the life out of five hundred people aboard a ship—call them Space Pirates and it's all right. Call them Space Navy and it's all right, too, as long as you kill Space Pirates to match. They're sitting up there laughing at it. What'll they think when they come out and find somebody's really dead? Who could have done it, Dr. Novak? It's unbelievable."

"I believe it. Miss Stuart, what'll we do with Mrs. Clifton? She and Cliff live alone—lived alone. Could you get a nurse——"

"I'll take her to my place. Father has a resident doctor. I think perhaps I'd better start now. The police would want to question her. It'd be inhuman."

"I think you'd better wait, Miss Stuart. It's—homicide, after all."

"That's absurd. All they could do is badger her out of

her wits with questions, and what could she have to tell them about it?"

"Look—poor little rich girl," Novak snarled, angry, nasty, and scared. "Cliff was killed and I may be killed, too, if the cops don't figure this thing out. I'm not going to handicap them by letting witnesses disappear. You just stay put, will you?"

"Coward!" she flared.

The argument was broken up by the arrival of four policemen from a radio car.

Novak said to the one with stripes on his sleeve: "I'm Dr. Michael Novak. I found a man named August Clifton in the washroom, dead. An A.E.C. Security man I know was here, so I put it in his hands. He's upstairs with Clifton now. This is Clifton's wife."

"All right," said the sergeant. "Homicide cars'll be here any minute. Wykoff, you and Martinez keep people from leaving. Don't let 'em use that phone. Sam, come with me." He stumped up the stairs with a patrolman.

It must have been Martinez, small and flat-faced, who asked Novak: "What's going on here anyway, Doc? Ain't this the Cheskies' place? We never have any trouble with the Cheskies."

"It's rented for the night. By the American Society for Space Flight."

"Uh," said Martinez doubtfully. "Borderline cases. Did the guy kill himself?"

"He did not!"

"Aw-*right*, Doc! You don't have to get nasty just because I asked." And Martinez, offended, joined Wykoff at the door. Novak knew he had sounded nasty, and wondered how close he was to hysteria himself.

Anheier came down the stairs slowly, preoccupied. "What's this?" he asked.

"Clifton's wife. I told her. And Miss Stuart. Mr. Anheier from the A.E.C. Security and Intelligence Office."

"Los Angeles regional agent in charge," Anheier said automatically.

"Mr. Anheier," said the girl, "can't I take Mrs. Clifton out of this? Before the other police and the reporters get here?"

"I'm not in charge," he said mildly, "but if you ask me

224

it wouldn't be a good idea at all. Best to take our medicine and get it over with. What do you two think of Clifton's emotional stability?"

"He was brilliant, but——" Amy Stuart began, and then shut her mouth with a snap. "Are you suggesting that he took his own life?" she asked coldly. "That's quite incredible."

Anheier shrugged. "The sergeant thought so. It's for the coroner to say finally, of course."

"Look," said Novak, laboring to keep his voice reasonable. "You and I know damned well——"

"*Novak*," said Anheier. "Can I talk to you for a minute?"

Novak stared at him and they went to the foot of the stairs. The Security man said quietly: "I know what you think. You think Clifton was murdered in connection with the—stuff—you told me this afternoon."

"I think there's an espionage angle," Novak said. "and I know you had your mind made up that Clifton and I were cranks. Man, doesn't this change anything? He's *dead*!"

Anheier considered. "I'll meet you halfway," he said. "When you tell your story to the cops, keep it straight. Don't babble to reporters about your suspicions. Just leave out your opinion that Clifton was murdered. *If* there's an espionage angle, this is no time to give it to the papers."

"How does that add up to meeting me halfway?" Novak asked bitterly.

"I want to see you after tonight's fuss is over. I'll find you in on the big picture. Meanwhile, don't prejudice our position with loose talk. Here's Homicide now. Watch yourself."

Homicide was three sedans full of photographers, detectives, and uniformed police. Reporters and press photographers were at their heels. A Lieutenant Kahn was the big wheel. Novak watched Anheier brief Kahn calmly and competently and felt a charge of resentment. The big picture—what was it? Perhaps smoothly meshing crews of agents were preparing tonight to seize members of a conspiracy ramified far beyond his small glimpse——

The lieutenant was firing orders. "Nobody, but nobody, leaves the building until I say so. You, yank that press guy out of the phone booth; that line's for us. Sergeant, make an announcement to the movie audience upstairs. Doc, bring Mrs. Clifton to and let her cry it out. I'll want to talk to her later. No reporters past the stairs for now. Where's this Novak? Come on, let's view the remains."

Now there were two white-faced A.S.F.S.F. kids in the washroom as well as the radio-car sergeant and patrolman. The sergeant saluted and said: "They came in a minute ago, lieutenant. I hold them. Didn't want a stampede."

"Good. Take them down to the lobby with a bull to watch them. Start taking your pictures, Ivy. Let's *go*, you f.p. men! Where's Kelly? Dr. Novak, you found the body, didn't you? Tell us just what happened while it's still fresh in your mind." A uniformed policeman stood at Novak's elbow with an open stenographic pad.

Don't prejudice our position. Fine words; did they mean anything? Fumblingly, Novak went over it all, from Lilly's first worried request to the end. Halfway through he remembered about the ring, went through his pockets, and produced it. Through it all, Anheier's calm eyes were on him. In deference to the big picture and the unprejudiced position he said nothing about foreign powers, space-ship fuel, or espionage—and wondered if he was a fool.

The scene blended into a slow nightmare that dragged on until 1:00 A.M. Parts of the nightmare were: glaring lights from the Homicide photographers' power packs, Lilly conscious again and hysterical, Amy Stuart yelling at the police to leave her alone, Friml clutching him to ask shakily whether he thought Clifton had been embezzling, sly-eyed reporters hinting about him and Lilly, MacIlheny groaning that this would set back the A.S.F.S.F. ten years and telling his story to the police again and again and again.

Finally there was quiet. The names of A.S.F.S.F. members present had been taken and they had been sent home, kids and engineers. Amy had taken Lilly home. The police had folded their tripods, packed their fingerprint gear and gone. Last of all an ambulance whined away from the door with a canvas bag in its belly.

Left in the lobby of Slovak Sokol Hall were Novak, Anheier, and a stooped janitor grumbling to himself and turning out the building lights.

"You said you wanted to talk to me," Novak said wearily.

Anheier hesitated. "Let's have a drink. I know a bar up the street." Novak, wrung out like a dishrag, followed him from the hall. The waiting janitor pointedly clicked off the last light.

The bar was dim and quiet. Half a dozen moody beer-sippers were ranged on its stools. Anheier glanced at them and said: "Table okay? I have a reason."

"Sure." The Security man picked one well to the rear. "Watch the bartender," he said softly.

"Eh?" Novak asked, startled, and got no answer. He watched. The bartender, old and fat, deliberately mopped at his bar. At last he trudged to the end of the bar, lifted the flap, plodded to their table, and said: "Yuh?"

"You got double-shot glasses?" Anheier asked.

The bartender glared at him. "Yuh."

"I want a double scotch. You got Poland Water?"

The bartender compressed his mouth and shook his head.

"I want soda with it then. Novak?"

"Same for me," Novak said.

The bartender turned and plodded back to the bar, limping a little. Novak watched him as he slowly went through the ritual of pouring. "What's all this about?" he asked.

"Watch him," Anheier said, and laughed. The bartender's head immediately swiveled up at their table. His glare was frightening. It was murderous.

He brought them their drinks and Novak noticed that his limp had grown more marked. His fingers trembled when he set the tray down and picked up Anheier's bill.

"Keep the change," Anheier said easily, and the bartender's hand tremor grew worse. Wordlessly the man trudged from the table, rang up the sale, and resumed mopping.

"Would you mind telling me——" Novak began, picking up his double-shot glass.

"Don't drink that," Anheier said. "It may be poison."

227

Novak's heart bounded. This, by God, was it! Poison, spies, the papers, and Anheier was admitting he'd been right all along!

"Let's get out of here," the Security man said. He got up, leaving his own glass untouched, and they left. Novak's back crawled as he walked out behind Anheier. A thrown stiletto—a bullet——

They made it to the street, alive, and Novak waited to be filled in on the big picture while they walked: he apprehensively and Anheier with icy calm.

"I noticed that old boy come on duty while I was having a beer before the meeting," the Security man said. "He made me think of you. Paranoia. A beautifully developed persecution complex; one of these days he's going to kill somebody."

Novak stopped walking. "He's not a spy?" he asked stupidly.

"No," Anheier said with surprise. "He's a clinical exhibit, and a hell of a man to hire for a bartender. While I was finishing my beer, somebody complained about the weather and he took it as a personal insult. Two lushes were lying about how much money they made. He told them to cut out the roundabout remarks; how much money he made was his business and no cheap jerks could horn in on it. You noticed the limp? We were picking on him by making him walk to the table. I laughed and he *knew* I was laughing at him. Knew I was one of his enemies plotting against him right under his nose."

"You're telling me that I have a persecution complex, Anheier? That I'm crazy?" Novak asked hoarsely.

The Security man said: "Don't put words in my mouth. I am saying you've got a fixed idea about espionage which makes no sense at all to me—and I'm a pro about espionage; you're a grass-green amateur.

"What have you *got*? A drawing that doesn't look right to you. Why the devil should it? Mysterious financial backing of the rocket club. All corporate financing is mysterious. The big boys divulge exactly as much as the law forces them to—and a lot of them try to get away with less. Every S.E.C. order issued means somebody tried just that. And Clifton got shot through the head; that's supposed to be the clincher that should convince even me. Do you think suicides don't occur?"

Automatically they were walking again and the Security man's reasonable, logical voice went on. "I didn't go to that meeting tonight to investigate your allegations; I went for laughs and to see the movie. Novak, it's always tragic to see a person acquiring a fixed idea. They never realize what's happening to them. If you try to set them right, you only succeed in giving them more 'evidence.' You know the job I have. Lord, the people I have to see! A week doesn't go by without some poor old duffer turning up and asking me to make the A.E.C. stop sending death rays through him. If they get violent we call the city police . . ."

"That sounds like a threat, Anheier."

"It wasn't meant to. But I'm not surprised that you thought it did. Frankly, Novak, have you considered what your record for the past year is like? I looked you up."

Novak considered, in a cold fury. A transfer—an idiotic transfer. Unsuitable work. Hurlbut's vicious memorandum. The blowup. Affiliating with a bunch of space hounds. Superficially Anheier might look right. Inside himself he knew better.

"It won't wash," he said evenly. "You're not talking me out of anything. There's going to be an inquest on Clifton and I'm going to speak my piece."

"*Better not. And this time it is a threat.*"

It was exhilarating. "So it's out in the open now. Good. You'll do what?"

"I want very badly to talk you out of your mistaken notion," Anheier said broodingly. "But if I can't, I've got to warn you that you're monkeying with the buzz saw. If the opposition papers get hold of your allegations, there will be hell to pay in the A.E.C. We'll have a spy scare. Security and Intelligence will look bad. Research and Development will look bad because the headlines say another country has beaten us to the punch on rocket fuel. We'll be judged by millions not on the strength of what we do for the nation's security but on what the headlines say we don't do. And all because one Dr. Michael Novak spoke his piece. Novak, do you think we won't counter-punch?"

Novak snorted. "What could you do? I happen to

be right."

The Security man gave him a pitying look and muttered: "If you smear us, we'll smear you."

Novak suddenly no longer felt exhilarated. It was a frightening word. "That's blackmail," he said angrily, but his knees had gone weak.

"Please don't put it that way." The Security man sounded genuinely pained. "You think you're right and I think you're wrong. If you want to talk to me and give me your side, okay. I'll talk to you and give you my side.

"But if you speak up at the inquest or go to the papers in any other way—we'll have to fight you in the papers. It's your choice of weapons. You can damage A.E.C. terribly with an unfounded spy scare. Naturally we'll hit back. And what can we do except try and impeach your credibility by spreading unfavorable facts about you on the record?"

In a low, embarrassed voice he went on: "Everybody's done things he's ashamed of. I know I have. I know you have. Boyhood indiscretions—adventures. Girls, traffic summonses. Friends of friends of friends who were Communists. And there were imaginative or inaccurate people who knew you slightly, maybe disliked you, and told our interviewers anything they pleased. We have a deposition in your file from a fellow you beat out on a scholarship exam. He says he saw you cheating in the examination room. Our evaluators disregard it, but will the headline-readers? What about your inefficiency at Argonne? Your fight with Dr. Hurlbut?"

Novak was feeling ill. "If you people libel me," he said, "I can sue. And I will."

Anheier slowly shook his head. "What with?" he asked. "Who would hire the man whom the headlines called a lunatic, a pervert, a cheat, a drunkard, a radical, and heaven-knows-what-else? None of it *proved*, but—'where there's smoke there's fire,' and the 'Indefinable Something behind the Mysterious All This.'" Anheier's voice became strangely compassionate. "I mean it about the buzz saw," he said. "Surely you know of people who fought a smear and wound up in jail for perjury . . ."

He did.

"All right, Anheier," Novak said softly and bitterly. "You've made up my mind for me. I was going to speak my piece at the inquest and get out of town. Now it seems I've got to do your work for you.

"A foreign power's operating under your nose and they've just murdered an American as a minor detail of a plan to bring America to its knees. So I'll keep my mouth shut and stick with the A.S.F.S.F. If I live, I'll blow this thing open. And then God help you, Anheier; I'm going to throw you to the wolves."

He walked unsteadily down a side street away from the Security man. Anheier stared after him, poker-faced.

7

Afternoon of a bureaucrat.

Daniel Holland wished he were in the privacy of his office where he could swallow some soda and burp. He was lunching with the commissioners, four trenchermen, and had taken aboard too much duck with wild rice. And the commissioners were giving him hell, in a nice, extroverted way, for the slow—in fact, almost negligible—progress of A.D.M.P., the Atomic Demolition Material Program. A.D.M.P. was scheduled to provide very shortly atomic explosives that would move mountains in the American Southwest, sculpture watersheds into improved irrigation patterns, and demonstrate to a politically shaky area which elected six senators that the current Administration was the dry-farmer's guide, philosopher, and friend. In actual fact, A.D.M.P. had provided only a vast amount of dubious paper work, and some experimental results which only an insanely optimistic evaluator would describe with even so cautious a word as "promising."

The chairman of the Commission, a paunchy, battered veteran of thirty years in county, state, and national politics, told Holland gently: "Interior's pushing us hard, Dan—very hard. You know he's got the Chief's ear, of course. And it's our opinion that he's not being unreasonable. All he wants is a definite date—give or take a month—that they can start whether the date's a month from now or a year from now, but he needs it for planning and publicity. Of course the work's got to get going before the nominating conventions, but that's absolutely the only restriction on the program. Now, what are we going to tell him?"

"I don't just know offhand, Bill," Holland grumbled. "No doubt about it, A.D.M.P.'s bogged down. I have some suggestions about getting it out of the mud, but they involve basic policy."

The first commissioner was a handsome, muscular man who had gracefully lived down the tag of "wonder boy" pinned on him when he became a university president at the age of thirty-six. He was currently on leave from the executive directorship of a great foundaton dedicated to the proposition that visual education is on the beam and all else is dross. He roared jovially at the general manager: "Well, spill your guts, Dan. That's our little old job, you know. Let's canvass your suggestions informally right now. If they click we can program them for an on-the-record session."

"You asked for it, Cap," Holland said. "First, we need —I mean *need*—about a dozen good men who happen to be teaching or working in industry around the country right now. One's a Yugoslav refugee with relations left in the old country. Another was a Young Communist League member, fairly active, in 1937 and '38. Another was once tried and acquitted on a morals charge—some little girl got mad at him and told lies. Another—well, I won't bother listing them all. You get the idea."

The second commissioner was a spare, white-headed ex newspaperman: Pulitzer Prize, *Times* Washington Bureau chief, author, diplomatic correspondent, journalism-school dean, intimate of the great, recipient of very many honorary degrees. He shook his head more—to use a cliché that never would have appeared in his copy—in sorrow than in anger. "Now Dan," he said, "this is no time to tinker with the machinery. If there's one thing about A.E.C. that's smooth-running now, it's clearance. Congress is mostly happy—except for Hoyt's gang; the papers are happy—except for the opposition rags; and the public's got confidence in the personnel of their A.E.C. We simply can't start *that* fight all over again. What else did you have in mind?"

"Second," Holland said impassively, "we're being

232

slowed down by declassification and down-classification. I've drummed into the boys that most material should be merely *Restricted, Confidential* covers most of what's left, and the *Secret* classification should be sparingly used. But they're scared, or conservative, or only human, or taking the safest way or whatever you want to blame it on. Every time I give them hell there's a little flurry of *Confidential* and *Restricted* and then the *Secret* begins to mount up again and we're back in the same old rut: boys in Los Alamos doing work that's been done in Hanford and not knowing about it. Maybe because of the limited distribution of *Secret* material. Maybe because the Los Alamos boys aren't in high enough grade for access to it. Gentlemen, I think something basic is required to correct this condition."

The third commissioner was a New York investment banker who had doubled his family fortune in ten legendary years on Wall Street and served his country for the next ten as a diplomatic trouble shooter in the Near East. He was still a formidable welterweight boxer and—to the dismay of the first commissioner—could speak Arabic, Turkish, and Court Persian. Alone on the current Commission, he had thought it his duty to master what he could of nuclear physics and its mathematical tools. Diffidently he said: "That's a tough one, Dan. But I don't see what choice we had or have. Our policy, arrived at in the best interests of the national security, is to 'classify' all A.E.C. data to the extent required to prevent it from being of use to potential enemies of the United States.' It's broad, I grant you. But the demands of national security won't be satisfied with anything narrower."

"Neither will Congress," said the second commissioner.

"Neither will the voters," grunted the chairman. "Dan, we'll just have to leave that one in your lap for you to lick as an administrative problem—*within the limits of our policy*. Just a suggestion: what about setting up a special classifications-review unit charged with checking the point-of-origin classifications on new data under a directive to declassify or down-classify whenever possible? You'd be able to keep a single unit here in Washington under your thumb easier than the assorted managers and directors out in the field. About how much would an outfit like that cost?"

Embarrassing moment. How to tell them that Weiss had worked such a plan for three months and found it impracticable? "Well, Bill, it would stand us maybe two million a year in salaries and overhead. But I see a lot of complications. The personnel in the new unit would have to be scientists or they wouldn't know what they were doing. God knows where we'd get enough of them to keep up with all the data A.E.C. grinds out—you know the scientific man-power picture. And you'd have a hell of a turnover because scientists like to do science and not paper work. And *quis custodict*? The safest thing for them to do would still be to stamp everything *Secret*; they'll never get in trouble that way even if it does slow A.E.C. down to a crawl. I'll explore the idea and give you a report, but I think it's a policy matter."

The second commissioner said flatly: "We can't change the classifications policy, Dan. There hasn't been a spy scare worth mentioning in three years. The public's on our side. We've built up a favorable press and congressional attitude slowly and painfully and we're not going to wreck it now. Sure, we'd make a short-term gain if we published all data. But come the appropriations bill debate! Congress would cut our funds fifty per cent across the board—nail us to the cross to show us who's boss. You've got to do the best you can with what you've got, and never forget the political climate. What else did you have up your sleeve?"

Holland glanced at the chairman and looked away. Then he said slowly: "Third, something I don't understand at all has come up. A.D.M.P. was set up personnel-wise and equipment-wise to handle one ton of thorium metal a month." The chairman coughed nervously. "I learned yesterday," Holland went on, "that for two months they've been getting only .75 tons a month from Raw Materials. They thought the reduction came from me. I checked with R.M. and found that the office of the chairman ordered a monthly quota of .25 tons of thorium to the Air Force Experimental Station with a priority overriding A.D.M.P. So R.M. quite correctly diverted the A.F.E.S. quota from A.D.M.P.'s quota. I haven't checked so far on what the Air Force has been doing with our thorium." He didn't mention his anger at being by-passed, or his weary disgust at realizing that some fifteen hundred A.D.M.P. personnel had been idle as far as their primary mission was concerned for one sixth of a year because they lacked material to work with.

"Dan," said the chairman slowly, "I owe you an apology on that one. You recall how General McGovern came to bat for us at the last joint Committee hearings. Praised us to the skies for our grand co-operation, said we were all patriots, gentlemen, and scholars he was proud to work with? Half the Committee members at least are red-hot Air Force fans, so it did us a lot of good. Well, McGovern's price for that was the thorium allotment. His boys at A.F.E.S. think they can use thorium war heads in air-to-air guided missiles. The Weaponeering Advisory Committee tells me it's a lot of nonsense and furthermore A.F.E.S. hasn't got anybody who could do the work even if it were possible, so Air's not really fishing in our lake."

"Can we get their thorium quota back to A.D.M.P.?" Holland asked.

"No. I'd be afraid to try it. McGovern's been talking about a bigger quota, to serve notice on me that he's not going to be whittled down. And I live in fear that the Navy will find out about it and demand a thorium allotment of their own. That's why I was so damned secretive about it—the fewer people know about these deals, the better. Maybe we ought to have Raw Materials set up a new group to expedite thorium-ore procurement and refining—but my point was, no; the Air Force has got it and they won't let go. We've got to get along with the military, Dan. You know that. They can make us look awfully bad if they've a mind to."

"Well," said Holland, "that's that. I'll get you a report you can show Interior by tomorrow morning. Were there any other points for me?"

"Gentlemen?" asked the chairman, looking around the table. There were no other points, and the general manager left them.

The third commissioner said: "I'm a little worried about Holland. He seems to be going cynical on us."

The chairman said: "He's a little stale from overwork. He refuses to take a vacation."

"Like an embezzler," said the ex-banker, and they laughed.

"He doesn't see the big picture," said the second commissioner, and they nodded thoughtfully and got up to go their various ways:

The chairman to weigh the claims of two areas pleading to be the site of the next big A.E.C. plant;

The first commissioner to polish a magazine article on "Some Lessons of Aquinas for the Atomic Age";

The second commissioner to lobby three congressmen in connection with the appropriations bill coming up in eight months;

The third commissioner to confer with the Secretary of State on the line that State's overseas propaganda broadcasts should take concerning A.D.M.P. as proof of America's peace-loving nature.

Holland, in the privacy of his office, took four soda-mint tablets and burped luxuriously. He phoned his assistant Weiss, and passed him the job of drafting tomorrow morning's report for the Secretary of the Interior.

His "While You Were Out" pad said:

"12:15—Senator Hoyt's office called for an appointment 'as soon as possible.' Said I would call back.

"12:20—Mr. Wilson Stuart called from Los Angeles and asked you to call back today 'on the private number.'

"12:45—Senator Hoyt's office called again. Said I would call back.

"12:48—the Associated Press called asking for an interview at your convenience. I said you were occupied for the coming week and referred them to the P. & T.I. Office.

"1:15—Senator Hoyt's office called again. Said I would call back."

He sighed and knocked down an intercom button. "Charlie, tell Hoyt's people he can come right over. Get me Stuart on—no, I'll place it."

"Yes, Mr. Holland."

The general manager didn't have a phone on his desk,

but he did have one in a drawer. It had a curiously thickened base, the result of some wire-pulling in A.T. & T. The curiously thickened base housed a "scrambler" of the English type which matched one in Wilson Stuart's bedroom phone. It was a fairly effective measure against wire taps. He pulled out the phone and placed the call.

His old friend must have been waiting by his own phone in the big white Beverly Hills house. "Hello?" said the voice of Wilson Stuart.

"Hello, Wilson. How is everything?"

"Let's scramble."

"All right." Holland pushed a button on the phone. "Can you hear me all right?"

"I hear you." The quality of the transmission had taken an abrupt drop—the result of Wilson Stuart's voice being torn into shreds by his scrambler, hurled in that unintelligible form across the continent, and reassembled by Holland's device. "Dan, things are going sour out here. They're trying to take Western Air away from me—a nice little phony stockholders' revolt. One of my rats in the Oklahoma Oil crowd tipped me today. I don't know how far they've got in lining up their proxies, but it could be bad."

"What's the squawk?"

"I stand accused of running the board of directors like a railroad—which, God knows, I do, and a good thing for Western. Also, and this is the part that scares me, I'm supposed to be squandering the company's resources."

"Um. It isn't a real rank-and-file thing, is it?"

"Act your age, Dan! It's the old Bank of California program: kick Stuart out of Western Air and integrate it with their other holdings. This time they've met Oklahoma Oil's terms."

"Who's fronting?"

"That's the only cheerful part. They've got some squirt Air Force two-star general named Reeves. He commands Great Falls A.F.B. in Montana. They've sounded him out and he's supposed to be willing to take over as board chairman after I get the boot. Such patriotism."

"I can do something about that. Know Austin?"

"I was thinking of him—he'd put the screws on the fly-

237

boy. Will you get in touch with him?"

"Sure. Fast."

"Another thing . . . I'll be in a lot stronger position for the showdown if I can pull a big, big A.E.C. contract out of my hat. What have you got?"

Holland thought for a moment. "Well, Reactor Program's got some big orders coming up. Die-cast-one-inch rods, aluminum cans, and some complicated structural members. It might all come to twenty-five million dollars. You set up for die-casting?"

"Hell now, but what's the difference? We can subcontract it to anybody who *is* set up. All I want is the money to show those monkeys on the board."

"You'll get it. How's Amy?"

"No complaints. She brought Clifton's widow home. Too bad about that. You never knew the guy, but he used to work for me—a real character."

"That so? Tell Amy to drop in and say hello next time she's East. I haven't seen her for months."

"I sure will, Dan. Take care of yourself. *And* the flyboy. *And* the contract. Good-by."

Holland hung up and put the phone back in its drawer. He said over his intercom: "Tell Fallon from Reactor Program Procurement that I want to see him. And get me Undersecretary Austin on the phone—the Air Force Austin."

The Air Force Austin was only an acquaintance, but he had a low boiling point, and handles that stuck out a yard. There were many things that he hated, and one of them was military men who used their service careers as spring-boards to high-pay civilian jobs.

"Naturally I don't want to meddle in your area, Austin," Holland was telling him a minute later, "but we're all working for the same boss. Can you tell me anything about a Major General Reeves—Great Falls A.F.B.?"

Austin's suspicious New England voice said: "Supposed to be a brilliant young man. I don't know him personally. What about him?"

"I hear he's getting involved in a big-business crowd. If you want me to stop talking and forget about it, just say so."

Austin snapped: "Not at all. I'm glad you called me.

What exactly did you hear?"

"The people are supposed to be Oklahoma Oil and Bank of California. The way the story went, they want to hire him as a front for the reorganization of some aircraft company or other."

"Nothing illegal? No hint of cumshaw?"

"None whatsoever. Just the usual big-salary bait."

"Glad of *that*. Thanks, Holland. If Reeves thinks he can use the Air Force, he's got a great deal to learn. I'll have this investigated very thoroughly. If you're right, he'll be A.F. Liaison officer in Guam before he knows what hit him."

Holland grimaced at the thought. It was punishing a man for exercising his freedom of contract; as a lawyer he couldn't be happy about it. Unfortunately, Austin was right too. Industry cheerfully fished the armed-forces and civil-service pond for able and underpaid executives; it had to be discouraged. Carry the process far eough and industry would hire away the best military and Government brains, leaving the nation—and itself—defended by an army of knuckleheads and adminstered by a bureaucracy of nincompoops . . .

And of course there were other reasons for lowering the boom on Reeves.

"Mr. Fallon to see you," said his secretary.

"Send him in." Fallon was in his early thirties, but there was something about him that made him look younger to Holland. The general manager thought he could guess what it was. "Is this your public-service job, Fallon?"

"Yes, Mr. Holland."

"What did you do before this?"

"I was with General Motors. Up in Detroit Purchasing, assistant to the department head."

"That was a good job. Why'd you leave it for us?"

He knew why. The itch you can only scratch with service, the uncomfortable feeling that they needed you, the half-conscious guilt that you owed more than your taxes. He knew why. It had ridden him all his life. Fallon tried to put it into words, and didn't succeed. There were glib hacks who could talk your ear off about it, and there were sincere guys like this who couldn't make themselves a case. "I guess I just thought I'd be happier here, Mr. Holland."

"Well. I wanted to talk to you about the upcoming contracts for breeder cans, moderator rods, and retaining-wall members. Five-nineteen, twenty, and twenty-one, I believe. Are you going to invite Western Aircraft to bid?"

Fallon was puzzled. "I'd swear they haven't got die-casting facilities on that scale, Mr. Holland. I wasn't figuring on it, but of course I'll include them if they can swing it."

"They can handle part of it as prime contractor and subcontract the rest."

"But the procurement policy is——"

"This is a special case. I want you to understand that their bid may seem high, but that they deserve very serious consideration. It's essential that we have no buildup on these castings, and I've practically decided that Western Air can do a better job of seeing them through to delivery than any other outfit that's likely to bid. They're a very able, deadline-minded outfit, and the over-all picture at this time indicates that we need their talent."

Fallon was getting upset. "But we've never had any trouble with Inland Steel or G.E., to name just two fabricators who might bid, Mr. Holland. They come through like clock-work, they know our procedure, we know the people there, they know us—it greases the ways."

"Really, Fallon, I think my suggestion was clear enough. I can't be expected to fill you in on the reasons for it. Some of them are military secrets, others are policy matters, and none of them is any particular business of yours."

Fallon looked at him, no longer wide-eyed. "Sure," he said woodenly. "How is Mr. Stuart? I hear he's a good friend of yours."

Well, this was it. The cat was clawing at the bag; the beans were about to spill. Coldly Holland channeled the fear that was exploding through him into artificial rage. He was on his feet, and his chair crashed to the floor behind him. In one stride he was towering over Fallon in the desk-side chair. Holland thrust his face almost into the face of the man from Purchasing. His voice was a low, intense growl.

"*Watch your language, son.* I've been taking a beating for twenty-eight years in public service." *Talk.* Keep him off balance, make him feel young and raw, make him ashamed, make him unhappy. "They've called me a Communist and a fascist and a bureaucrat and a bungler but they've never called me a crook. My worst enemies admit that if I wanted money I've got the brains to get it honestly. If I wanted money, I could quit A.E.C. today, open a law office tomorrow and have half a million dollars in retainers by next month."

Fallon was beginning to squirm. "I didn't——"

"Shut up. If you think you've turned up evidence of dishonesty, I'll tell you what to do. Pick up your hat and run right over to the Senate Office Building. There's a crowd there that's been trying to nail my hide to the wall ever since you were in knee pants. Maybe you've succeeded where they failed."

"I meant——"

"Shut up, Fallon. You told me what you meant. You meant that I've got nothing to show for twenty-eight years of trying to help run the purest democracy left in the world. That was news to me. I've known for a long time that I wasn't going to get rich out of the Government service. I decided long ago that I couldn't marry, because either the marriage or the work would suffer. I know I haven't got any pride left; I stand ready at any hour of the day or night to get my teeth kicked in by those county-ring Solons up on the Hill. But I thought I had the loyalty of my own kind of people. It seems I was wrong."

"Mr. Holland——"

He didn't interrupt, but the youngster didn't go on. Holland stared him down and then straightened to sit on the edge of his desk. "Go on over to the Senate Office Building, Fallon," he said quietly. "Get your name in the paper. I can stand one more kicking-around and you can use the publicity. Maybe they'll ghostwrite a series of articles for you in the Bennet rags."

But Fallon was almost blubbering. "That's not fair!" he wailed. "I tried to tell you I was sorry. I can't help it if I have an Irish temper and a big mouth. I know what your record is, Mr. Holland. It's a—it's a wonderful record." He pulled himself together and got up. "Mr. Holland," he said formally and mournfully, "I feel I should submit my resignation."

Holland slugged him on the bicep and said gruffly: "Not accepted. I could use a hundred more like you. I've got a thick hide—usually. Just that crack . . . but don't let it worry you. Clear about that bid?"

"Clear at last, Mr. Holland," Fallon said with a melancholy smile. "I'll try not to make a damned fool of myself again. You have troubles enough."

When he was alone, the general manager set up the kicked-over chair, leaned back, and lit a cigarette with fingers that shook. It had been a very near thing. Lord, how long could a man be expected to keep this up? The perpetual sweat about wire tappers, loose talkers, shrewd newsmen who might put two and two together, the political opposition relentlessly stalking every hint of irregularity.

Once in T.V.A. he had turned in a friend and classmate for trying to recruit him into a footling little Communist industrial-espionage apparatus. The revelation had been shattering; his duty had seemed clear. But that had been a long time ago . . .

His intercom said: "Senator Hoyt is here, Mr. Holland."

"Send him in, Charlie." He sprang from behind his desk to shake the senator's hand. "Good to see you again, Bob," he burbled cheerfully.

The senator's meaty face broke into an actor's smile. "Mighty nice of you to find time for us, Dan," he said. It was a reminder that he'd had to wait on Holland's convenience to make the appointment and a threat that some day Holland would sweat for it. The senator did not forget slights, real or imaginary.

"How're you, Mary?" asked Holland, a little dampened.

"So—so," Mary Tyrrel, the senator's secretary, said vaguely. It was odd that she was Hoyt's five-thousand-per secretary, because until last year she had been a twenty-thousand-per Washington by-liner for the Bennet newspapers. But lots of odd things happen in Washington.

"Well, Bob, what can I do for you?"

"I'm collecting a little information, Dan. Normally my investigating staff would handle it. But out of respect for your high position I thought I ought to ask you straight out myself."

Cat and mouse, thought Holland. What's he got?

The senator lit a cigar deliberately. "I like to consider myself a member of the loyal opposition," he said. "Our democracy has kept its vigor because of constant, intransigeant criticism and pressure by reformers—realistic, practical reformers—against the abuses of an entrenched bureaucracy. I've been in some good scraps, Dan, and I've loved them. I fought the A.E.C. when it tried to give jobs to foreigners of doubtful loyalty. I've fought when you people tried to give moral lepers and degenerates control of our most precious military secrets. I've fought to root out loose-tongued drunkards from the A.E.C."

"It hasn't done you any harm, Bob," Holland said.

The senator wasn't thrown off his stride. "No," he said. "It hasn't. I've enjoyed the rewards of good citizenship. I have the respect of my constituents, and on a national scale have the backing of a great chain of patriotic newspapers. But Dan, I'm on the track of something that—God willing—will lead to the highest office in the land."

"Dewey didn't make it," Holland said.

The senator waved his cigar expansively. "He got to be governor at least. If he didn't have the imagination to make the jump to the presidency, it was his fault. Of course in his day the techniques weren't as developed as they are now. I know you take the old-fashioned, strict-construction view of politicking: work hard, improve yourself in knowledge and skill, one day you'll get the nomination on a silver platter. With all respect to you as a student of government, Dan, that theory is as dead as the Lincoln-Douglas debates.

"This is an era of high-level energy in science, industry—government. The nervous tensions under which we all live and work rules out leisurely reflection on the claims of this candidate or that. You've got to electrify people. Make them know who you are. Keep dinning your name at them so it drowns out any other candidate's name. Immerse them in your personality.

243

Have it drummed at them twenty-four hours a day, inescapably. The standing machinery of the press and broadcasting will do it for you if you just give them a news peg to hang it on."

The senator—and his secretary—were watching him narrowly.

Holland said: "You figure you've got a news peg?"

The senator tapped cigar ash to the floor. "I might come up with one," he said. "A scandal and an investigation—the biggest ever, Dan. A blowup that will be on every tongue for a solid month. Housewives, factory hands, professional people, children—there'll be something in it for everybody. Dan! What would you think of a public servant who ignored a great discovery instead of promulgating it for the use of the people of the United States? Wouldn't it be—treason?"

"I thought you used to be a lawyer, Bob," Holland said. "It sounds like malfeasance to me."

"What if every indication was that this public servant behaved in no way different from an enemy agent, Dan?"

"Look," said Holland. "If you're going to denounce any of my A.E.C. boys for incompetence or malfeasance or mopery with intent to gawk, go ahead and do it. We've screened and processed our people to the utmost limit of practicability. You're hinting that a spy got through in spite of it. So all I can say is, that's too bad. Tell me who he is and I'll have Security and Intelligence grab him. Is that what you came to see me about?"

"Oh," the senator said mildly, "we just wanted your general reaction to the situation. Thanks for hearing me out so patiently. If anything else turns up I'll let you know."

He smiled and gave Holland a manly handshake. The general manager saw them to the door of his office, closed the door and latched it. He leaned against the oak panels with sweat popping from his brow. Somebody at Hanford had been talking to a Bennet reporter.

They didn't seem to have anything yet on the fiscal or personnel angles.

Time was getting very short.

8

The story on page four of Novak's morning paper said:

SPACE SHIP ENGINEER
FOUND SHOT TO DEATH
AT ROCKET CLUB MEET

The soaring interplanetary dreams of 146 rocket-club members turned to nightmare at Slovak Sokol Hall last night when the body of engineer August Clifton, trusted employee of the American Society for Space Flight, was found in a washroom of the hall as a meeting of the society was in full swing on the same floor. Assistant medical examiner Harry Morales said death apparently was caused by a head wound from a single .25-caliber bullet. A Belgian automatic of that caliber was found lying near Clifton's right hand, with one shot fired according to Homicide Bureau Lieutenant C.F. Kahn.

The victim's attractive blond wife Lilly, 35, was taken in a state of collapse to the Beverly Hills home of aircraft manufacturer Wilson Stuart by his daughter Amelia Stuart, a friend of the Cliftons and a member of the rocket club.

"The club secretary, Joel Friml, 26, said Clifton had been authorized to spread "sizable" sums of club money in the course of his work, which was to build a pioneer space ship that club members hoped would go to the Moon. Friml said he did not know of any irregularities in Clifton's accounts but added that he will immediately audit club financial records for the past year with an eye to any bearing they may have on the death.

Other friends of Clifton said he was in good health but "moody" and "eccentric."

Lieutenant Kahn said he will not comment until police fingerprint and ballistics experts have analyzed the evidence. An inquest will be held Wednesday morning.

245

The body was discovered by Dr. Michael Novak, 30, an engineer also employed by the club, when he slipped out of the meeting room during the showing of a movie. Novak immediately called in the aid of A.E.C. security agent J.W. Anheier, who was attending the meeting as a visitor. Anheier stood guard in the washroom to prevent evidence from being disturbed until police arrived. He later told reporters: "There is no security angle involved. It was just a coincidence that I happened to be there and Dr. Novak called on me."

Two one-column photographs flanked the story. One was Amy Stuart, very society-page looking, captioned: "Socialite shelters stricken wife." The other was a view of *Prototype*: "Dead engineer's unfinished 'moon rocket.'" All tied up in a neat little package with a bow, Novak thought bitterly. Without saying it, the newspaper told you that Clifton had blown his brains out, probably after embezzling A.S.F.S.F. money. If you didn't know Clifton, you'd believe it of course. Why not? "They wouldn't print if it wasn't true."

He went from the lobby newsstand to the hotel coffee shop and ordered more breakfast than he thought he could eat. But he was a detective now; he'd have to act unconcerned and unsuspicious while he was slowly gathering evidence——

Oh, what the hell.

It wasn't real. None of it had been real, for months. Asignment to Neutron Path Prediction, when he didn't know whether neutrons should take paths or four-lane superhighways. Slugging his boss, quitting his job under a cloud-research and development men didn't *act* like that. Going to work for the A.S.F.S.F., an organization as screw-ball as Clifton himself.

He wanted to laugh incredulously at the whole fable, finish his coffee, get up and walk into the job he should be holding at N.E.P.A.: a tidy salary, a tidy lab, and tidy prospects for advancement. But the climax had eclipsed even the lunacy of the past months. Somehow he had talked himself into pretending he was a detective. Detectives were hard-eyed, snap-brimmed, trench-coated, heroic. On all counts he fell down badly, Novak thought.

But a man was dead, and he thought he knew why.

And he had been threatened cold-bloodedly with a smear backed up by all A.E.C.'s prestige, and perhaps with a perjury frame-up, if he tried to get help. Novak looked helplessly at his scrambled eggs, gulped his coffee, and got up to call the A.S.F.S.F. business office. There was a disagreeable, uncontrollable quiver in his knees.

Friml and MacIlheny were there. It was incredible that they might be spies or killers—until he remembered the bewildered, ashamed, ordinary faces of spies on the front pages of tabloid newspapers.

"Hello, Dr. Novak," the president of the A.S.F.S.F. said. "Friml and I were discussing the possibility of you taking over Clifton's job as engineer in charge."

There was no time to stop and think of what it might mean. Friml and MacIlheny might be innocent. Or they might be guilty but not suspicious of him. There was no time. He forced surprise: "Me? Oh, I don't think so; I'll be busy enough on my own. And I don't think I could handle it anyway."

"I see you had some years of aeronautical engineering."

"Well, yes—undergraduate stuff. Still, Clifton did say there wasn't a lot of work left."

"He did that much for us," MacIlheny said bitterly. "The damned fool."

"Mr. MacIlheny!" said Friml, with every appearance of outrage.

"*Yes*, Mr. Friml," said the insurance man sardonically. "*De mortuis nil nisi bonum*, as you B.B.A.s and C.P.A.s put it. If he was so nuts he had to kill himself why didn't he resign first? And if he didn't have time to resign, *why* did he have to do it at a meeting? Everything happens to the poor old A.S.F.S.F. Clifton's death is going to set us back in years in getting public recognition. And our industrial sponsors——" MacIlheny buried his head in his hands.

"I never thought he was a very stable person——" Friml began smugly.

"Oh, shut up!" MacIlheny snarled. "Just stick to your hitting. If I want your learned opinion I'll ask for it."

Novak was appalled at the naked enmity that had flared between the two men. Or the pretense of enmity? Nothing would hold still long enough to be examined. You had to keep talking, pretending. "Could I see," he asked conciliatingly, "just where we stand with respect to structural work on *Proto?"*

"Show him the cumulatives, Friml," said the president, not looking up. With his lips compressed, Friml pulled a folder from the files and handed it to Novak. It was lettered: "Engineering Cumulative Progress Reports."

Novak sat down and forced himself to concentrate on the drawings and text. After a few minutes he no longer had to force it. The papers told what was to a technical man the greatest story in the world: research and development; cool, accurate, thoughtful; bucking the cussedness inanimate nature, bucking the inertia of industrial firms; bucking the conservatism, ignorance, and stupidity of hired hands—and getting things done. It was the story of *Prototype*'s building told by the man who could tell it best, Clifton.

It started about one year ago. "Contacted Mr. Laughlin of the American Bridge Company. I don't think he believed a word I said until Friml took out the A.S.F.S.F. passbook and showed him our balance. After that, smooth sailing."

Sketches and text showed how the American Bridge Company, under Clifton's anxious, jealous eyes, executed ten-year-old A.S.F.S.F. blue prints for the skeleton of *Prototype*. The tower of steel girders rose in the desert to six times the height of a man, guyed down against the wind. There was a twelve-foot skeleton tetrahedron, base down, for its foot. From the apex of the tetrahedron rose the king post, a specially fabricated compound member exactly analogous to the backbone of a vertebrate animal. It bore the main stresses of *Proto's* dead weight; it was calculated to bear the strains of *Proto* in motion; and it was hollow: through its insulated core would run the cables of *Proto's* control systems. Structural members radiated laterally from the king post to carry the weight of *Proto's* skin, and from its top sprouted girders over which the nose would be built.

Reports from Detroit: "I been going the rounds for a solid week and still no dice. If a plant's got the forming presses, its toolroom stinks. If its toolroom is okay, the superintendent won't let me barge in to stand over their die-makers and tell them what to do. But that's the way it's going to be; those hull plates are too tricky to order on an inspect-or-reject basis."

Later: "I found a good little outfit named Allen Body Company that does custom-built jobs. They got one Swedish-built forming press 40×40 (very good), a great toolroom with a wonderful old kraut named Eichenberg heading it up who's willing to work closely with me, and a good reputation in the trade. Told them to submit bid to Friml fast and suggest he fires certified check without haggling. These guys are real craftsmen."

Later: "Oskar and me finished the forming and trimming dies for first tier of plates today. Twenty-four tiers of plates to go, plus actually stamping and machining them. I guess ninety days tops."

Eighty-five days later: "Mr. Gowan of the Union Pacific says he'll have a sealable freight car at the Allen siding tomorrow, but that it's out of the question for me to ride aboard with the plates. That's what he thinks. I bought my folding cot, Sterno stove and beans already."

Sketches showed what "the plates" were like: mirror-finished steel boxes, formed and machined to exact curvature. The basic size was 36″×36″×6″, with some larger or smaller to fit. The outer, convex wall of the box was of three-quarter-inch steel; the inner, concave wall was one-inch armor plate. Each box was open along one of its narrow 6″ × 36″ faces, and each was stuffed with compressed steel tool—the best shock absorber A.S.F.S.F. brains had devised to slow down and stop a pebble-sized meteorite if one should punch through the outer shell. There were six hundred and twenty-five of the plates, each numbered and wrapped in cotton wool like the jewel it was.

Three days later Clifton arrived aboard his freight car in the Barstow yards. When a twenty-four-hour guard of A.S.F.S.F. volunteers was mounted over the freight car, he located a trucking company that specialized in fine furniture removals. "Not a scratch and not a hitch. We got them stacked in order under the tarps at the field. I think it will be okay to use some volunteers on the welding. I checked with the Structural Ironworkers, the Shipbuilders, and the Regional C.I.O. people. It seems nobody has union jurisdiction on building space ships, so Regional said we could use unpaid helpers so long as they don't touch the welding torches while they're hot. Tomorrow I go down to the shipyards to get myself the best six damn master welders on the Coast. I figure on letting them practice two—three days at beadles welding on scrap before I let them start tacking *Proto's* hide on. Meanwhile I rent a gantry crane. It'll make a better platform for the welders than scaffolding and cut down your chance of spoilage. Also we'll need one later when we come to installing heavy equipment."

He got his master welders and his gantry crane. Two of the welders grinned behind their hands, refusing to follow his rigid specifications on the practice work; he fired them and got two more. The fired welders put in a beef with the union and the others had to down their torches. Clifton lost a day. "I went down to the hall and gave the pie cards hell. I brought some of the junk those two bums did and I threw it on their desks and they said they'd kill the beef and let them know if there's any more trouble, which I don't think there will be with the new boys."

There wasn't. The first tier of plates went on, and fitted to a thousandth of an inch. Volunteer kids working at the field were horrified to see the lattice-work skeleton of the *Prototype* sag under their weight, and Clifton told them it was all provided for down to the last hairsbreadth of sag.

As the shining skin of *Proto* rose from the ground in yard-high tiers, the designers of the A.S.F.S.F. passed through the acid test and came out pure gold. Nameless aero-engineers, some long gone from the Society and some still with the engineering professors and students at U.C.L.A., Cal Tech and Stanford, girl volunteers punching calculators in teries, had done their job. The great equation balanced. Length of materials, form of members, distributed stresses and strains, elasticities and compressibilities added and scaled one complete hull: a shiningly perfect bomb shape that could take escape velocity. Six plates equally spaced and the eleventh tier and one plate in the eighth tier were not welded in. The six were to be fitted with dead-bolts and the one with a manhole.

The welders crawled through the eighth-tier hole for their last job: two bulkheads which would cut the ship into three sections. The first cut off *Proto's* nose at the ninth tier. It was the floor of her combined living quarters and control room—a cramped, pointed dome some ten feet in diameter and twelve feet high at the peak. From this floor protruded the top of the king post, like a sawed-off tree stump sprouting girders that supported the nose. The second bulkhead cut *Proto* at the seventh tier. It made a cylindrical compartment aft of the control room that could store five hundred cubic feet of food, water, and oxygen. This compartment also doubled as the air lock. The outside manhole would open into it, and from it a second manhole would open into the control room above.

Aft of the bulkhead was two thirds of the ship—an empty shell except for structural members radiating from the king post. It was reserved territory: reserved for a power plant. The stiff paper rattled in Novak's hands for a moment before he could manage them. He had almost been lost in cool, adult satisfaction, as he followed the great engineering story, when fear struck through. This triumph—whose? MacIlheny and Friml glanced briefly at him, and he sank into the reports again.

"Sorry to say . . . repeated twelve times . . . seems conclusive . . . obviously a bonehead play . . . some of the new silicones may . . . deadlight gaskets . . ." Novak's heart beat slower and calmer, and the words began to arrange themselves into sense. Clifton's report on the six planned deadlights was negative. Vacuum-chamber tests of the proposed gasketing system showed that air leakage would be prohibitive. There simply wasn't a good enough glass-to-metal seal. The ring of deadlights was *out*, but a single deadlight in the nose was indispensable. Air leakage from the nose deadlight was cut to an almost bearable minimum by redesigning the assembly with great, ungainly silicone gaskets.

This meant blind uncertainty for any theoretical occupants of *Proto* during a theoretical ascent. The nose deadlight, an eighteen-inch optical flat at the very tip of the craft, was to be covered during the ascent by an "aero-dynamic nose" of sheet metal. In space the false nose would be jettisoned by a power charge.

The next series of reports showed Clifton in his glory—control devices, his specialty.

In one month, working sometimes within A.S.F.S.F. specifications and quite often cheerfully overstepping them, he installed: an electric generator, manhole motors, lighting and heating systems, oxygen control, aerodynamic nose jettison, jato igniters, jato jettison, throat vane servos (manual), throat vane servos (automatic, regulated by a battery of fluid-damped plumb bobs). Controls for these systems were sunk into the head of the king post that jutted from the control-room floor. There was nothing resembling a driver's seat with a console of instruments and controls.

And there were two other control systems indicated in the drawings. At the input end they had provisions for continuous variation of voltage from zero to six, the power plant's maximum. At the output end there was— nothing. The two systems came to dead ends in *Proto's* backbone, one at the third tier and one at the fifth.

Novak had a short struggle with himself. Play dumb, or ask about it? They say they think you're smart enough to take over . . . He asked.

"Fuel-metering systems," MacIlheny said. "We assumed of course that something of the sort would be needed eventually, so we had Clifton put in dead-end circuits."

"I see."

He was nearing the end of the sheets. The last report said acceleration-couch tests were proceeding satisfactorily with no modifications yet indicated. And then the folder came to an end.

"I think," Novak said slowly, "that I can handle it after all. He's just about finished the job—as far as any private outfit can take it."

MacIlheny looked up and said evenly: "There's some more construction work to be done—on the same basis as the dead-end control systems. Naturally there's got to be a fuel tank, so we're going to put one in. Here's the drawings——" He had them ready in a blue-print file.

It was another of the "J. MacI" jobs, with the same date as the too-specific drawings for the throat liner and chamber. Novak wondered crazily whether MacIlheny or Friml had a gun in his pocket, whether the wrong reaction meant he'd be shot down on the spot. He studied the sheet and decided on his role. The "fuel tank" was a fantastic thing. It filled almost the rear two thirds of the *Prototype* and made no sense whatever.

There was one section forward that consisted of stainless steel. A section aft, much smaller, was quartz-lined lead, with a concrete jacket. Atomic. There was a lead wall indicated between the stainless-steel tank and the *Proto's* aft bulkhead. Atomic. This was a tank for a fuel that burned with atomic fire.

He told them, businesslike: "It's going to cost a hell of a lot of money, but that's your business. I can install it. Just don't blame me if it has to be ripped out again when A.E.C. comes out with an atomic fuel that doesn't fit it."

MacIlheny said into the air, slowly and with burning emphasis: "*Can't* people understand that *Proto's* not a moon ship? Can't they get it through their heads that she's just a dummy to study construction problems? What the hell difference does it make if the fuel A.E.C. comes up with doesn't fit her system? All we're after is the experience we'll need to build a system that does fit."

Novak said hastily: "Of course you're right." Lord, but MacIlheny was convincing! "But it gets a grip on you. Half the kids think it's a moon ship——"

"All right for kids," said MacIlheny grimly. "But we're all adults here. I'm sick of being ribbed for doing something I'm not doing at all. Good—and—sick." He stared at the engineer challengingly, and then his grimness vanished as he added: "I wish it *was* a moon ship, Novak. I wish it very much. But——" He shrugged.

"Well," said Novak uncertainly, "maybe I'll feel that way about it after a year or so of the ribbing. By the way, can you tell me where Miss Stuart lives? I ought to go and see Mrs. Clifton if I can be spared today, and I suppose things are still in a state of flux."

"Thirty-seven twenty-four Rochedale," said Friml, and he jotted it down.

"I suppose it's all right," said MacIlheny. "God, what a

253

headache. Just when things were going smoothly. Suppose you check in tomorrow morning and we may have some plans made for you."

"Won't the membership have to——"

"The membership," said MacIlheny impatiently, "will do what it's told."

9

Novak thought he should phone the Wilson Stuart residence before he tried to pay a call. He couldn't find the number in the book and naively asked Information. Information sharply told him that the number was unlisted.

Well, he tried.

He got a downtown cab and enjoyed a long ride into the rolling country lying north of Los Angeles. "Pretty classy," he said.

"*I* should know?" asked the cabby blandly, and added in a mutter something that sounded like: "Stinking rich."

A mile farther on, the cab stopped. "Check point," the driver said. Novak saw a roadside booth, all chrome and class, with two cops in beautifully fitting uniforms. One of them came out to the car, the driver gave him the address, and they rolled on.

"What was that about?" Novak asked.

"A trifling violation of our civil liberties," the cabby said. "Nothing to get upset about. At night, now, they take your name, and phone on ahead if they don't know you."

"California!"

"All over," the cabby corrected him. "Grosse Pointe, Mobile, Sun Valley—all over. I guess that is it."

Thirty-seven twenty-four Rochedale was extreme California modern: a great white albatross of a house that spread its wings over a hilltop. "Well, go on up the driveway," Novak said.

"Nope. If you had any business with folks like that you'd have your own limousine. *You* go in and get arrested for trespassing. These people don't fool around." He turned down the meter flag and Novak paid him.

"I hope you're wrong," the engineer said, adding a half dollar. He started up the driveway.

It was a confusing house. He couldn't seem to find a place where it began, or a doorbell to ring. Before he knew it, he seemed to be inside the Stuart home, unannounced, after walking through a row of pylons into a patio—or was it a living room? They didn't build like that in Brooklyn or Urbana.

A shock-haired old man rolled into the living room— or patio—in a wheel chair pushed by a burly, Irish-looking fellow in a chauffeur's dark uniform. "I'm sorry," Novak exploded jumpily. "I couldn't find——"

"Who the devil are you?" demanded the old man, and the chauffeur took his hands from the chair, standing exactly like a boxer about to put up his fists.

"My name's Novak. I'm a friend of Mrs. Clifton's. I understand she's here—if this is the Wilson Stuart residence."

"I'm Wilson Stuart. Do you know my daughter?"

"We've met."

"I suppose that means she didn't invite you. Did she give you the address?"

"No—she's a member of the A.S.F.S.F., the space-flight society. I got it from the secretary."

The old man swore. "Keep it to yourself. A person has no damned privacy in one of these places and I can't build a wall because of the zoning laws or covenants or whatever they are. Grady, get Miss Amelia." The chauffeur gave Novak a no-funny-business look and left.

"Uh, how is Mrs. Clifton?" Novak asked.

"*I* don't know; I haven't seen her. I'm not surprised by any of this, though. I thought Clifton's mind was giving way when he took that job with the rocket cranks. Not that I'd keep him on my pay roll. He told my V.P. for Engineering that he didn't know enough to build an outhouse on wheels. That tore it." The old man chuckled. "He could really ram things through, though. Didn't give a damn whose floor space he muscled in on, whose men he gave orders to, whose material he swiped for his own projects. Where are they going to find another lunatic

255

like that to build their rocket?"

"I'm taking it over, Mr. Stuart." What a callous old beast he was!

"You are? Well, be sure you have nothing to lose, Novak. What are they paying you?"

"Rather not say."

It made Wilson Stuart angry. "Well, isn't that too bad! I can tell you one thing. Whatever it is, you're putting a blot on your record that no responsible firm can afford to ignore." He spun the chair to present his back to Novak and scowled through the pylons that formed one wall of the ambiguous room.

Novak was startled by the burst of rage, and resentful. But you didn't tell off a cardiac patient at will—or a multi-millionaire.

The chauffeur and Amy Stuart came in. "Hello, Dr. Novak," she said. The old man silently beckoned over his shoulder to the chauffeur and was wheeled out.

"How's Mrs. Clifton?" Novak asked.

"Father's doctor says she should rest for a day or two. He's given her some sedatives. After that—I don't know. She's talking about going back to her family in Denmark."

"May I see her?"

"I think so. Dr. Morris didn't say anything about it, but it should do her good. Come this way."

Crossing large, glass-walled rooms he said: "I don't think I should have come at all. Your father was upset by my knowing the address. Mr. Friml gave it to me."

"Mr. Friml should have known better," she said coolly. My father has no reserves of energy for anything beyond his business and necessary recreation. It's cruel discipline for him . . . he's held speed and altitude records, you know."

Novak uttered a respectful mumble.

The girl asked: "What are they going to do about a replacement for Cliff?"

"I think I get the job. I've done some aero-engineering and there's very little structural work left to be done. I suppose if there's anything I simply can't handle, they'll hire a consultant. But I can probably swing the load."

"You can if you're checked out by MacIlheny. The man's a——" She started to say "fanatic" and then interrupted herself. "That's the wrong word. I admire him, really. He's like—not Columbus. Prince Henry the Navigator of Portugal. Henry stuck close to his desk and never went to sea, but he raised the money and did the paper work."

"Um. Yes. Has Lilly—Mrs. Clifton—been asking for a biomathematicist, I wonder? She has such faith in them that it might do her good at a time like this, when it's a matter of psychological strain."

The girl looked startled. "That's very odd," she said. "As a matter of fact she hasn't. I suppose recreations like that show up in their true light when the pressure is on. Not that it would do her any good to ask for one. Dr. Morris would break the neck of any biomathematicist who showed up here."

She pushed open a flush door of blond wood and Novak saw Clifton's widow in the middle of a great modern bed with sickroom paraphernalia on a side table. "Visitor, Lilly," Amy Stuart said.

"Hallo, Mike. It was good of you to come. Amy, you mind if I speak alone vit' Mike?"

"Not at all."

"Sit down," she said with an unhappy smile as the girl closed the door. "Mike, what's gonna happen now? You don't think Cliff kill himself, do you?" She was fighting back tears with a heartbreaking effort. "He act cra-a-azy. But that was yust because he enjoy life and didn't give a damn for nobody. He wasn't no crazy man to kill himself, was he, Mike?"

"No, Lilly," Novak said. "I don't think he killed himself." And he bit his lip for saying it. The woman was under sedation, she might babble anything to anybody——"

"Mike," she said, "I'm glad you say so." She sniffed and dried her brimming eyes, as a child would do, on the hem of her bed sheet.

"How're you fixed for money, Lilly?" he asked. "I thought you might need a little ready cash for—expenses and things."

"T'anks, Mike, no need. We had a yoint bank account vit' couple t'ousand dollars in. Mike, honestly you don't believe Cliff kill himself?"

He thought it over. "Have you taken any medicine?"

"Last night the doc gave me couple pink pills and he tol' me to take couple more today—but I don't. You know I don't t'ink much of doctors."

"I don't want to tell you what I think about Cliff's death if you're full of medicine or if you're going to be. You might talk to somebody about what I tell you. It might mean my life too." It was her business, he told himself silently.

After a stupefied pause, Lilly slowly asked: "Please tell me all about it, Mike. Who'd kill Cliff? Who'd kill you? Those few crazy kids in the Society, they don' like Cliff ever, but they wouldn't kill him. You tell me what it's all about, Mike. Even if somebody tear the eyes out of my head I don' talk."

He pulled his chair to the bedside and lowered his voice. "Yesterday Cliff and I thought we found something fishy about one of the A.S.F.S.F. blue prints. I thought it meant that a foreign country was using the Society to build it a rocket ship. Maybe with Friml or MacIlheny or both fronting, and nobody else in on it. We went to the A.E.C. Security office downtown and saw that man Anheier. He brushed us off—didn't believe a word of it. Last night Cliff got killed and it looked like suicide. But it could have been murder by anybody who could have sneaked into the washroom when he was there—and that's anybody off the street and practically anybody who was at the meeting.

"I don't know how—whoever did it—got wise to his visit to Security or why nobody's taken a shot at me that I know of. Maybe spies keep a twenty-four-hour watch on the Security office to see who visits it. Maybe Cliff's visit was the signal for his death. Maybe I wasn't identified because I'm new in town.

"But none of that matters right now. What matters is that Anheier wouldn't let me tell the police about my idea. He tried to convince me that I was a paranoid. When that didn't work, he threatened to ruin me for life and jail me for perjury if I talk, now or ever."

"You not gonna tell the po-lice, Mike?"

"No. I'm afraid of the smear and—it probably wouldn't do any good. The A.E.C. would make counter-charges and any foreign agents would escape in the fuss. I told Anheier the hell with him, I'd nail them alone."

"No," she said, pale-faced. "Not alone, Mike. Vit' me."

"Thanks, Lilly," he said softly, and she was crying at last.

"Don' mind me," she said. "T'anks for coming to see me and now you please go. I cry better by myself . . ."

He left in silence. She was with him—it felt better. The morning with MacIlheny and Friml, every question a step on a tightrope over the abyss, had told on him.

Amy Stuart laid down a magazine and got up from a rocky chair. "How is she, Dr. Novak?"

"I'm afraid I made her cry."

"It's good for a woman to cry at a time like this. Have you a car?"

"No; I came in a taxi. If I could phone for one——"

"You're downtown, aren't you? I'll drive you; I have some shopping."

Her car was a two-seater English sports job. It looked like a toy in the garage between the big Lincoln and a suburban wagon.

As they went winding through the scrubbed-clean roads he broke the silence. "To me it's just an interesting job, you know. I'm not a Prince Henry like MacIlheny is and maybe Cliff was. Or—what was her name? The girl who raised her hand at the meeting. The one you stepped on."

"Gingrich?" Amy Stuart said dispassionately. "She's not particularly interested in space flight and she's a bloody fool besides. If Gingrich and her friends had their way, there'd be a full-dress membership vote by secret ballot on there to put each rivet in the *Prototype*."

The little two-seater rolled past the police sentry box and Amy Stuart waved pleasantly to the two policemen. They saluted with broad smiles and Novak abandoned himself to mutter thoughts for a moment.

"Jeffersonians, they think they are," the girl brooded. "But wouldn't Jefferson be the first man to admit that things have changed since his day? That there's a need for something beyond sheer self-regulating agrarian democracy?" The question was put with an intensity that startled him. It was overlaid with a portentous air that made him think of nothing so much as a doctor's oral where, literally, your career is made or unmade by a few score words spoken in a minute or two. What was

259

the girl driving at?

"People are always accusing engineers of not thinking about social problems," he said carefully. "In my case, I'm afraid they're right. I've been a busy man for a long time. But I wonder—are you by any chance flirting with fascism or Communism?"

"No," she said scornfully, and fell silent.

It was some minutes before she spoke again. "You were in A.E.C. Did you ever read anything by Daniel Holland? He's a friend of father's. And mine."

There was something he could talk about. "I didn't know he wrote, but your friend runs a hell of a silly organization. You know what my field is. Believe me or not, but I swear I was transferred out of it and into a highly specialized branch of mathematical physics. I was absolutely helpless, I was absolutely unable to get back to my own work. Finally I—I had to resign."

She said patiently: "That's exactly the sort of thing Holland fights. In his books he analyzed the warped growth of modern public administration under the influence of the Jeffersonian and Jacksonian mistrust of professionals. He calls it the 'cincinnatus complex.'"

He recognized the allusion and felt pleased about it. Cincinnatus was the Roman citizen who left his plowing to lead the army to victory and then returned to his plow, turning down glory and rewards. "Interesting concept," he said. "What does he suggest?"

The girl frowned. "If you'd thought about it, you'd know that's damn-all he could suggest. His books were only analytical and exploratory, and he nearly got booted out of public service for daring to raise the problem—challenging the whole structure of bureaucracy. He thought he could do more good in than out, so he stopped publishing. But he'd stepped on some toes. In *Red Tape Empires* he cited a case from the Nevada civil service. The Senator from Nevada on the joint A.E.C. Committee badgered him from then on. Wonderful irony. He was a master of all the parliamentary tricks that were originally supposed to carry out the majority will without infringing on minority rights."

He was worried about Lilly and getting shot and future long, precarious talks with MacIlheny. "I suppose," he said absently, "you're bound to have a rotten apple in every barrel."

Amy Stuart said flatly but emphatically, with her eyes on the road: "You scientists deserve exactly what you got." And she said nothing more until she dropped him off at his hotel and proceeded to her shopping. Novak had a queasy, unreal feeling that he'd just failed his doctor's oral.

10

The high-temperature lab was built, and its equipment installed by the able construction firm that had done the field layout. During this time Novak worked on the manhole problem, and licked it. Studebaker *had* ungreased its titanic boring mill and for a price had cheerfully put a super-finish on the manhole and its seating. In an agony of nervousness for the two priceless chunks of metal, Novak had clocked their slow progress by freight car across the country from South Bend to Barstow.

It was one of those moments when Lilly Clifton or Amy Stuart was helpfully by his side, and this time it happened to be Amy. They stood outside the machine-shop prefab, squinting into the glare of the *Prototype's* steel skin, and at an intenser, bluer glare that was being juggled by a hooded welder on the gantry-crane platform, twenty feet up. The manhole cover and seating assembly were being beadlessly welded into the gap in the ninth tier of plates. It was a moment of emotional importance. *Proto* externally was an unbroken whole.

Novak's pulse pounded at the thought, while the matter-of-fact welder up there drew his hell-hot point of flame like an artist's brush along the gleaming metal. The engineer couldn't be matter-of-fact about it any more. He had plunged into the top-boss job at the Barstow field determined to give a realistic imitation of a space hound, and had become one.

There was no reason not to. In theory, he told himself, he was waiting for a break but one never came. There were no further irregularities beyond the four on which he had committed himself: money, secrecy, the "J. MacI." drawings, and the death of Clifton.

MacIlheny never offered any surprises. He was an insurance man and a space-flight crank. He had cloudy industrial contributors in his pocket and he used them as a club to run the Society his way. His way was to get *Proto* built as a symbol and rallying point for those who demanded a frontal smash by the Government into the space-flight problem instead of the rudimentary, uncoordinated, and unimaginative efforts that were all the United States could show, for whatever reason.

Friml continued to be—Friml. Bloodless, righteous, dollar-honest, hired-hand, party-of-the-second-partish Friml. A reader of the fine print, a dweller in the Y.M.C.A., a martyr to constipation, a wearer of small-figured neckties which he tied in small, hard knots.

The engineer members of the A.S.F.S.F. continued to be hobbyists, hard to tell one from the other, showing up on weekends, often with the wife and kid, for an hour or so of good shoptalk and connoisseurs' appreciation of *Proto* as the big, handsome jigsaw puzzle that she was—to them.

The A.S.F.S.F. youngsters continued to be hagridden kids escaping from humdrum jobs, unhappy families, or simply the private hell of adolescence by actually helping to pay for and work on and dream over *Proto*. Some day it would carry them on wings of flame to adventurous stars where they'd all be broad-shouldered males six feet tall or slim but luscious girls with naturally curly hair. They worked like dogs for the new engineer in charge and didn't even ask for a dog's pat on the head; all they wanted was to be near enough to *Proto* to dream. They fought ferociously with words on occasion over this detail or that, and Novak eventually realized that their quarrels symbolized a fiercer squabble they hoped was coming over the passenger list of man's first moon ship.

Novak stood comfortably midway between the engineers and the kids—he hoped. *Proto* was big medicine. The dream of flight which has filled the night lives of countless neurotics since, probably, the Eolithic era, had been no dream since the balloons of Montgolfier. This new wish fulfillment of space flight had been for fifty years standard equipment on your brilliant but dreamy youngster. It soaked into you from earliest childhood that some day—not quite in your time, but some day—man would reach the planets and then the stars. Being around *Proto*, putting your hands on her, tinkering with her equipment, smelling her hot metal in the desert sun, hearing her plates sing as they contracted in the desert-night chill, did something to you, and to the "some day" reservation about space flight. Friml had become a true believer, and with each passing week wondered more feverishly what in hell's name he was doing: building a moon ship for China? Running up dummy? Or just honest engineering? Each week he told himself more feverishly: one week more; just get the manhole licked, or the silicone gaskets, or the boron carbides.

The blue, hard twinkle of the welding torch twenty feet up snapped off; the welder shoved back his hood and waved genially. The platform of the gantry crane descended.

"That does it," Novak said hazily to Amy. He lit a cigarette. "You want to push the button?"

"If it doesn't work, don't blame me," she said. There was a six-volt line run from the machine shop into *Proto's* sewer-pipe stern and up through the king post to feed the electric systems. She snapped the control for the manhole motor to open, and they stared up again. The dark disk against the shiny steel plate developed a mirror-bright streak of microfinish bearing surface along one edge. Noiselessly and very slowly the wire-fine streak grew to a new moon; the manhole slowly stood out in profile and halted, a grotesque ear protruding from the ship.

"Okay, Amy. Close it." She snapped the switch to *Shut*, and very slowly the disk swung back and made *Proto* an unbroken whole again. The welder stepped from the gantry platform and asked: "She all right, Mr. Novak?"

"Fine, Sam. Fine. Was there any trouble fitting the lug into the receptacle?"

"Nope. Only one way to do it, so I did it. It surely is a fine piece of machinery. I used to work at the Bullard Works in Hartford and they didn't make their custom-built machine tools any prettier than your—thing. Confidentially, Mr. Novak, is——"

He held up his hand protestingly. "It's a full-scale mock-up for structural study and publicity purposes. Does that answer the question, Sam?"

The welder grinned. "You people are really gonna try it, aren't you? Just don't count on me for a passenger is all I ask. It's pretty, but it won't work."

As they walked to Novak's refractory lab, Amy said: "I worry about everything Cliff installed, like the manhole motor, until it's tested. I know that verdict, 'while of unsound mind' and so on is just legal mumbo jumbo, but . . . why should the manhole have opened that slowly? It was like a movie, milking it for suspense."

He glanced at her. "Perfectly good reasons. It runs on a worm gear—low speed, power to spare. The motor has to open it against the molecular cohesion of the biggest gauge-block seal ever machined. In space or on the Moon the motor would get an assist from atmospheric pressure in the storeroom, pushing against zero pressure outside."

She laughed. "Of course. I suppose I was being jittery. And there's sometimes melodramatic suspense in real life, too, I suppose."

He cleared his throat. "I've got Lilly in there aging a new boron-carbide series. Want to watch? You can learn enough in a few hours to take some routine off my neck. The volunteer kids are fine and dandy, but they mostly have jobs and school hours. What I need is a few more people like you and Lilly that don't have to watch the clock."

"It must be very handy," she agreed abstractedly. "But you'll have to excuse me. I'm due back in town."

Novak stared after her, wondering what was biting the girl. And he went on into his lab.

It was the dream layout he had sketched not too long ago, turned real by the funds of the A.S.F.S.F. Lilly was in the cooling department clocking temperature drops on six crucibles that contained boron carbides in various proportions. She was looking flushed and happy as she sidled down the bench on which the crucibles were ranged, jotting down the time from the lab clock and temperatures from the thermocouple pyrometers plugged into each sampler. Her blond hair was loose on her creamy neck and shoulders; she wore shorts and a blouse that were appropriate to the heat of the refractories lab but intensely distracting. She turned and smiled, and Novak was distracted to the point of wondering whether she was wearing a brassiere. He rather doubted it.

"What are the temperatures now?" he asked.

She read off efficiently. "Seventy-two, seventy-four, seventy-eight, seventy-eight point five, seventy-eight point five, seventy-nine."

The leveling was unexpected good news. "Interesting. Are you afraid to handle hot stuff?"

"Naw!" she said with a grin. "Yust not vit' my bare hands."

"Okay; we'll let you use tongs. I want you to take the lid off each crucible as I indicate. I'll slap the ingot in the hydraulic press, crush it, and give you the dial reading. Then I'll put it in the furnace. After all the ingots are crushed and in the furnace I'll turn on the heat and watch through the peephole. When they melt I'll call out the number to you, and you note the temperature from the furnace thermocouple. Got it?"

"I t'ink so, Mike."

It went smoothly. The ingots were transferred safely, they crushed under satisfactorily high pressure, and the furnace flashed red and then white in less than five minutes. Staring through the blue glass peephole at the six piles of glowing dust, waiting for them to shimmer, coalesce, and run into liquid, with hypnotically soothing—except that he could sense Lilly at his side, with her eyes on the thermocouple pyrometer and her full hips near him, giving him thoughts that he found alarming.

He stared at the cones of glowing dust and thought bitterly: *I don't want to get any more mixed up in this than I am now.* One of the glowing piles shimmered and looked mirrorlike. Abruptly it shrank from a heap of dust into a cluster of little globes like an ornamental pile of Civil War cannon balls and an instant later slumped into a puddle.

"Number five!" he snapped.

"Got it, Mike," she said, and her thigh touched him. *This thing's been coming on for a couple of weeks. I'll be damned if I don't think she's giving me the business. She ought to be ashamed. But what a shape on her. Amy wouldn't pull a stunt like this.* He felt a little regretful and hastily clamped down on *that* train of thought. "Number three!"

"Got it."

Minutes later he was at his desk with the figures, and she was an interested spectator. He explained laboriously: "The trick is to reduce your unknowns to a manageable number. We have mixing point of the original solution, rate of cooling, final temperature, and melting point. You call them T1, dT/dt—that's derivative of temperature with respect to time—T2 and T3. Do you follow it so far?"

She leaned over his shoulder and began: "I don't see——"

He found out that she wasn't wearing a brassiere. "The hell with it," he said, and kissed her. She responded electrically, and in her candid way indicated that she meant business. The faint voice of Novak's conscience became inaudible at that point, and the business might have been transacted then and there if the lab door hadn't opened.

Hastily she pulled away from him and tucked in her blouse. "You go see what is, Mike," she ordered breathlessly.

"Fine thing," he growled, and slapped her almost viciously on the rump.

"I know how you feel, boy," she grinned.

"Oh—no—you—don't." He cleared his throat and stalked out from the small private office into the lab. One of the machine-shop kids was waiting. The boy wanted to know whether he should use hot-roll or cold-roll steel for the threaded studs of the acceleration couches; the drawings just said "mild steel." Novak said restrainedly that he didn't think it made any difference, and stood waiting for him to leave.

When he got back to the private office Lilly was putting her face on. She said hastily: "No, Mike. Keep the hands off me for a minute while I tell you. This is no place. You wanna come to my house, we do this t'ing right."

"I'll be there," he said a little thoughtfully. Conscience

was making a very slight comeback. He hadn't been to the Clifton house since the day of the murder. But the lady was willing, the husband was six feet under, and it concerned nobody else.

"Good boy. You go back to work now."

He watched her drive from the field in the big maroon Rolls and tried to buckle down. He got nothing done for the rest of the afternoon. He tried first to set up matrix equations to relate the characteristics of the six boron carbides and committed howler after howler. He decided he'd better lay off the math until he was feeling more placid. In the machine shop he took over from an uncertain volunteer who was having trouble threading the acceleration-couch studs. Novak, with a single twitch of the lathe's cross-feed wheel, made scrap out of the job.

It wasn't his day. Among the condolences of the machineshop gang he declared work over and bummed a ride back to Los Angeles in one of the kids' jalopies.

He bolted a meal in the hotel dining room and went upstairs to shower and shave. There was a minor crisis when he found out he didn't have a belt. Normally he was a suspenders man, but he had a dismal picture of himself struggling with the suspender loops at a tender moment, maybe getting his foot caught in them . . . he shuddered, and sent a bellboy down to the lobby haberdasher's shop to get him a belt. When he put it on he didn't like the feel of it around his middle, and his missed the feel of the suspenders over his shoulders. But first things first.

Not until he was dressed and down in the lobby did he realize that he didn't remember the Clifton address—if he had ever heard it. Cahunga, Cahuenga Canyon, something like that, and he could probably find the house from a taxi window. He went to the phone book to look up Clifton, and found nothing under August. There were three A. Cliftons with middle initials, but none of them lived on anything that sounded like Cahunga, Cahuenga, or whatever it was. He tried Information and got the standard Los Angeles answer—unlisted number. A girl waiting outside the half-opened door of the phone booth turned red and walked away after overhearing part of his comments on that.

Now what the devil did you do? He recalled suddenly that Friml was good on addresses, just the way you'd expect his card-file type to be. He looked up the Downtown Y.M.C.A. and was connected with Friml's room.

"This is Novak, Friml. I hate to bother you after hours, but I wonder if you can give me Clifton's address. I, um, need it for some reports and he isn't in the phone book."

The secretary-treasurer's precise voice said: "Just one moment, Mr. Novak. I have it in a memorandum book. Please hold the line."

Novak held on for some time and then Friml gave him the address and—unsolicited—the phone number. He jotted them down and said: "Thanks. Sorry to be such a nuisance."

Friml said with a martyred air: "Not at all. I'm not good at remembering numbers myself." There was a plain implication of: "Sor why the hell don't you keep a memorandum book like good little me?"

Mildly surprised at the admission, Novak thanked him again and hung up. Now for a taxi. Walking up the street to a stand where he could climb in without having to tip a doorman, he wondered how he'd got the notion that Friml kept his address book in his head. Probably just the type of guy he was made you think so. Probably he did nothing to discourage you from thinking so. Probably there was a lot of bluff behind any of these ice-water types . . .

And then he stopped still in the street, realizing what had made him think Friml was a walking address book. He'd asked once for the Wilson Stuart address, and the secretary-treasurer had rolled it out absently as if it were no great feat to recall offhand where a rank-and-filer of the Society lived. He started walking again, slower and slower.

There was something very wrong. Friml had memorized the Wilson Stuart address, presumably of negligible importance to him. All he could possibly have to do with the Wilson Stuart address was to send a bill for annual dues, meeting notices, the club bulletin—no not even that. All those items were addressographed. Friml had not memorized the August Clifton address or phone number, although presumably he'd be constantly dropping notes and making calls to him for engineering data. If he didn't know the Clifton number and address off-hand he was decidedly no good at numbers, as he admitted.

Novak walked slowly past the cab rank and crossed the street. Stepping up to the curb, his right heel caught in the unfamiliar sag of his trouser cuff, and he thought: damn that belt.

It was, clearly, the first break in the Clifton killing. Friml wasn't what he seemed to be. Clearly there was a link of some sort between the secretary-treasurer and Amelia Earheart Stuart—or her father. Now how did you exploit a thing like this? Raid Friml's Y.M.C.A. room looking for the Papers? Tell that fathead Anheier about it and have him laugh in your face? Confront Wilson Stuart with it and have him conk out with a heart attack—or throw you in jail for trespassing? Try to bluff the facts out of Amy?

Friml has even visited the Clifton bungalow—*feller who broke the big mirror and my Svedish glass pitcher and your cat'ode-ray tube. That was Friml, Mike. He gets pretty bad.* It had been a gag—maybe. Nothing strange about a Friml swilling his liquor like a pig and breaking things now and then. And talking . . .

He raised his arm for a passing taxi.

"Downtown Y.M.C.A.," he told the driver.

11

He called up from the lobby. "Friml? Novak again. I'm downstairs. I'm at a loose end and I wonder whether you'd care to join me for a drink or two some place. Maybe we can have a general bull session about the Society. I've been working like a dog and I need some un-stringing."

The voice said grudgingly: "Well . . . come on up, Dr. Novak. I had some work for this evening, but . . ."

Friml had a two-room suite, medium-sized and anti-septically clean. He seemed proud of his place. He showed Novak his desk: "Some people tell you it's a sign of inefficiency to take your work home with you. I don't believe that for a minute. You, for instance—I can tell that you don't leave your job behind when you leave the field."

"I don't think any really conscientious person would," Novak agreed with gravity, and Friml glowed dimly at the applied compliment.

"You're right about—unstringing," said the secretary-treasurer. "I'm not a *drinker*, of course. I'll be with you in a minute." He went into the bathroom and Novak heard the lock turn.

He stood undecided over the desk and then, feeling that it was a childish thing to do, tried its drawers. They opened. In the shallow center drawer where pencils, rulers, paper clips, and blotters were kept, Friml kept pencils, rulers, paper clips, and blotters. In the top left drawer were letterheads, carbon paper, second sheets, and onionskin in a rack. In the second left-hand drawer were card-file boxes and a corduroy-bound ledger with red leather corners and spine. In the bottom drawer were books with brown wrapping-paper covers on them, the kind school children use on textbooks.

Before he heard water roaring in the bathroom there was time to lift out three books and look at their title pages: *The Homosexual in America, History of Male Prostitution, Impotence in the Male.*

The poor bastard. What a way to be.

Friml appeared, looking almost cheerful. "There's a quiet little place on Figueroa Street," he said. "The pianist does request numbers. He's pretty good."

"Fine," said the engineer, depressed.

The place on Figueroa Street wasn't a fairy joint, as Novak had half expected it would be. They sat at a table and had a couple drinks apiece while the pianist played blues. Novak knew vaguely that it was a big blues-revival year. The engineer made conversation about his membership report for the next meeting. "I don't know just what the members expect, because Clifton spoke off the cuff and there aren't any transcripts."

Friml said relaxedly: "Just give 'em the high spots. About fifteen minutes. And don't go by what Clifton did. Sometimes he used to just get up and joke. Other times he used to be 'way over their heads with math and electronics."

"That sounds like him. I was wondering about visual aids. Do you think I ought to have some easel cards made up? I think the whole trouble is, I don't know whether the membership report is just a formality or whether they really pay attention. If it's just a noise I'm supposed to make so everybody will feel he's getting his money's worth from the Ph.D., then I won't bother with the cards. If they really listen and learn, I ought to have them."

"You ought to just suit yourself, Novak," Friml said rather expansively. "They like you and that's the main thing. How'd you like *my* job, with everybody calling you a son of a bitch?" He took a deep swallow from his drink. He was having blended rye and ginger ale, the drink of a man who doesn't like to taste his liquor.

Novak excused himself and went to the phone booth. He called Lilly Clifton.

"Mike?" she asked. "Ain't you gonna come 'round to-night like you said?"

"Later, I think," he told her. "Listen, Lilly. I think I've found out something about the death of—of your husband." That was an awkward thing to say.

"So? Tell me." Her voice was unexpectedly grim.

It didn't sound like much in the telling, but she was impressed. "You got somet'ing," she said. "See if you can bring him around here later. I t'ink he goes for me."

He told her about Friml's books. She said dryly: "I see. I guess maybe he was a liddle bit queer for Cliff. It drived him nuts the time he was out here, the way Cliff played around vit' me affectionate. Every time Cliff gimme a feel or somet'ing, Friml took a bigger drink. I guess I was flatt'ring myself. You bring him anyway if you can."

He said he'd try, and went back to the table. Friml was a drink ahead of him by then, and said: "No more for me, Mike," when Novak tried to order. He sounded as though he could be talked into it. The pianist, a little black man at a little black piano on a platform behind the bar, was playing a slow, rippling vamp between numbers. "Coffee Blues!" Friml yelled unexpectedly at him, and Novak started.

The vamp rippled into a dragging blues, and Friml listened bleakly with his chin propped in his hand. He signaled their waiter after a few bars and drank his shot of blended rye without mixing or chasing it. "Great number," he said. *"I like my coffee—sweet, black, and hot . . . I like my coffee—sweet, black, and hot . . . won't let no body fool . . . with my coffee pot . . .* I always liked that number, Mike. You like it?"

"Sure. Great number."

Friml beamed. *"Some folks like—their coffee tan and strong . . .* You ever know any colored girls, Mike?"

"There were a few from Chicago in my classes at Urbana."

"Good-looking?" Friml wouldn't meet his eye; he was turning over in his hands the pack of matches from the table ash tray.

"Some of them yes, some of them no."

Friml gulped his drink. "Could I borrow a cigarette?" he asked. Novak tapped one out of his pack and held the match for the accountant. Friml got his cigarette wet, but didn't cough. From behind a cloud of smoke he asked: "Did any of the white fellows at the university go around with the colored girls?"

"Maybe some in Liberal Arts College. None that I remember in Engineering."

"I bet," Friml said broodingly, "I bet a fellow could really let himself go with a colored girl. But if a fellow's trying to build up a good solid record and get some place it wouldn't look good if it got out, would it?"

Novak let him have it. "It wouldn't make much difference if a fellow was just fooling away his time on one bush-league job after another."

Friml quivered and stubbed out his cigarette, bursting the paper. "I really ought to be getting out of here," he said. "One more and then let's beat it, okay?"

"Okay." He signaled and told the waiter: "Double shots." And inquiringly to Friml: "All right, isn't it?"

The secretary-treasurer nodded glumly. "Guess so. 'scuse me." He got to his feet and headed for the men's room. He was weaving. Novak thoughtfully poured his own double shot into Friml's ginger ale.

A sad little man, he thought, who didn't have any fun. Maybe a sad little man who had slunk out of the auditorium of Slovak Sokol Hall during the movie and put a bullet through Clifton's head for an obscure reason that had to do with the Stuarts.

Friml came drifting back across the floor and plopped into his chair. "Don't do this often," he said clearly and gulped his double shot, chasing it with the ginger ale. He put a half dollar on the table with a click and said: "Let's go. Been a very pleasant evening. I like that piano man."

The cool night air did it. He sagged foolishly against Novak and a cruising taxi instantly drew up. The engineer loaded him into it. "You can't go to the Y in this shape," he said. "How about some coffee some place? I have an invitation to Mrs. Clifton's. You can get some coffee there and take a nap."

Friml nodded vaguely and then his head slumped on his chest. Novak gave the cabby the Clifton address and rolled down the windows to let a breeze through.

Friml muttered during the ride, but nothing intelligible.

Novak and the cabby got Friml to the small front porch of the Clifton bungalow, and Novak and Lilly got him inside and onto a couch. The engineer noticed uncomfortably that she was wearing the strapless, almost topless, black dinner dress she'd had on the night Cliff died. He wondered, with a faint and surprising touch of anger, if she thought it would excite him because of that. The bungalow inside had been cleared of its crazy welter of junk, and proved to be ordinary without it. One lingering touch: on spread newspapers stood a sketch box and an easel with a half-finished oil portrait of Lilly, full face and somber with green.

She caught his glance. "I make that. Somet'ing to do." She looked down at Friml and asked cheerfully: "How you feeling, boy? You want a drink?"

Incredibly, he sat up and blinked. "Yeah," he said. "Hell with the job."

"The yob will keep," she said, and poured him two fingers from a tall bottle of cognac that stood on a coffee table. He tossed it down in one gulp.

"Don't do this often," he said sardonically. "Not good for the c'reer. The ol' man wouldn't like it."

Wilson Stuart. It had to be. Fighting a tremor in his voice, Novak said: "It's a shame to see a trained man like you tied up with a crackpot outfit like the Society."

"That so?" asked Friml billigerently. " 'm doing a

better job than anybody thinks. And they all call me a son of a bitch for it. So do you. But *I'm* the guy that sees he gets dollar for dollar. I mean dollar's value for a dollar spent." Friml looked cunning. "I got a c'reer, all right. You may not think so, but I'm gonna be com'troller of a certain big aircraft company one of these days. Not at liberty to tell you which. How's *that* for a c'reer? I'm only twenny-six, but I'm *steady.* 'at's what counts." He fell back on the couch, his eyes still open and glassy, with a little smile on his lips. "Where's'at drink?" he muttered.

Lilly poured another and put it by his hand. "Here y'are, feller," she said. He didn't move or change expression. She jerked her head at Novak and he followed her to the bedroom.

"What you t'ink?" she asked in a whisper.

"Wilson Stuart and Western Air," he said flatly. "They are the famous 'industrial backers.' Friml is Stuart's man in the A.S.F.S.F. to watch Stuart's money. Stuart gives orders to MacIlheny and Friml's right there to see that they get carried out."

She raised her eyebrows. "Old Stuart don't hire such punks, Mike. Cliff told me."

"He seems to have been hired right out of his graduating class for the sake of secrecy," Novak said. "And he must look like a fireball on paper. Straight A's, no doubt. He's a screwed-up kid, but the pressure has to be right before you realize it." He told her about "Coffee Blues."

She snorted. "I guess once his mama catched him in the bat'room and beat his ears off."

"Maybe he should be factored by a biomat'ematicist," he said, straight-faced.

She flicked him on the jaw with her fingertips. "Don' tease me," she said crossly. "I'm t'rough vit' them. All they want is you' money. You so smart, tell me what old Stuart wants vit' a moon ship and where he got atomic fuel for it."

"There's no answer," he said. "It's got to be a government working through him. What countries does he sell big orders to? What small countries with atomic energy programs and dense populations? I guess that narrows the field down a little. And it makes the thing harder than ever to swallow. Wilson Stuart of Western Air a foreign agent." He thought of what Anheier would say to that, and almost laughed. The thing was not completely beyond the realm of credibility. And it was in their laps.

They went silently back into the living room. The brandy glass was empty again and Friml's eyes were closed at last. He was completely out.

"Mike," she said, "I guess you better leave him here."

"But what about——"

"You a sveet boy, but some other time. This yerk depresses me."

She gave him a cool good-night kiss, and he hiked down the road to a shopping street and taxi stand, reflecting that he might as well have worn suspenders after all.

12

Novak saw, with a pang, that Lilly was not on the field. He asked casually around whether she had phoned or left word with anybody. She hadn't. After last night's fiasco with the drunken secretary-treasurer, he supposed, she felt shy . . .

Amy Stuart was there, reporting for assignment, and he savored the mild irony of the situation. Her father, board chairman of Western Air, was funneling money into the A.S.F.S.F. and dictating its policies. And his daughter was reporting for assignment to a hired hand of the Stuart funds. He toyed for a moment with the notion of assigning her to make the lunch sandwiches and dismissed it as silly. She had training and keep intelligence that he needed for *Proto*, whatever *Proto's* destiny was to be.

"Help me in the refractories lab?" he asked.

She said a little woodenly: "I thought that was Lilly's job."

"She didn't show up today. You're not afraid of hot stuff, are you?"

"Hot-radioactive or hot-centigrade?"

He laughed with an effort. She was very boldly playing dumb. "Hot-centigrade. Two thousand degrees of it and up. Tongs, gauntlets, masks, and aprons are furnished. But some people get trembly anyway and drop things."

"I won't," she said. "Not if Lilly didn't."

He taught her routine for an hour and then set her to compounding six more boron carbides by rote. "Call me if there's any doubt at all about procedure," he said. "And I hope you have a conscience. If you make a mistake, start all over again. A cover-up of a mistake at this stage would introduce a hidden variable in my paper work and wreck everything I'm doing from now on."

"You don't have to impress me with a wild exaggeration like that, Mike. I know my way around a chemistry lab."

The arrogance of the amateur was suddenly too much for him. *"Get out,"* he said. "Right now. I'll get by somehow without you."

She stared at him, openmouthed, and her face became very red. And she left without a word.

Novak strode to the compounding area. His hands deftly did their work with the great precision balance while his mind raged at her insolent assurance. He was letting the beam of the balance down onto the agate knife-edge fulcrum for the sixteenth time when she spoke behind him: "Mike."

His hand, slowly turning a knurled bronze knob, did not twitch. "Minute," he growled, and continued to turn the knob until he felt the contact and the long pointer began to oscillate on the scale. He turned and asked her: "What is it?"

"What the devil do you think it is?" she flared. "I'm sorry I got you sore and in the future I'll keep my mouth shut. Is that satisfactory?"

He studied her indignant face. "Do you still think I was trying to impress you with a wild exaggeration?"

She set her mouth grimly and was silent for a long moment. Then she stubbornly said: "Yes."

Novak sighed. "Come with me," he said, and took her into the small private office. He pulled out yesterday's work sheets and asked: "Know any math?"

"Up to differential calculus," she said cautiously.

That was a little better than he had expected. If she could follow him all the way it would be better for her work—far better than her taking him on faith.

In a concentrated one-hour session he told her about the method of least squares and how it would predictably cut his research time in half, about matrix equations and how they would pin down the properties of the boron carbides, about n-dimensional geometry and how it would help him build a theory of boron carbides, about the virtues of convergent series and the vices of divergent series, and about the way sloppy work at this stage would riddle the theory end of it with divergent series.

"Also," he concluded, "you made me mad as hell."

Laughter broke suddenly through her solemn absorption. "I'm convinced," she said. "Will you trust me to carry on?"

"With all my heart," he grinned. "Call me when the batches are ready for solution."

Cheerfully he tackled yesterday's data and speedily set up the equations that had defied him yesterday.

Amy Stuart called him and he guided her through the rest of the program on the six new carbides. She was a neat, fast worker who inked her notes in engineer's lettering. She wasn't jittery about handling "hot-centigrade" material. A spy? A handy one to have around. Lilly didn't have her cool sureness of touch.

They worked through the morning, finishing the batch, had sandwiches, and ran another batch in the afternoon. She left at five with the machine-shop gang and Novak put a third batch through himself. He wrote his weekly cumulative report during the four hours it sat aging. The report included a request for Friml to reserve sufficient time with I.B.M.'s EBIC in New York to integrate 132 partial differential equations, sample enclosed, and to post bond on their estimate at $100 per hour, the commercial rate. With this out of the way he ran tests on the third batch and phoned Barstow for a cab. The gate guard's farewell was awed. Night hitches were unusual.

Novak had dinner in the desert town while waiting for the Los Angles bus. He asked at his hotel's desk whether there had been any calls. There had been no calls. Phone her? No, by God! He wanted to be alone tonight and think through his math.

In ten days of dawn-to-dusk labor, he had his 132 partial differential equations. The acceleration couches got finished and installed. He ordered the enigmatic "fuel tanks" and left the fabrication to the vendor, a big Buena Vista machine shop. He was no aero-engineer; all he felt competent to do was give them the drawings and specify that the tanks must arrive sufficiently disassembled to pass through *Proto's* open end for final assembly in place.

Amy Stuart continued to be his right bower; Lilly did not reappear at the field. She phoned him once and he phoned her. Astonishingly, they were on a we-must-get-together-some-time basis. He asked about Friml and Lilly said vaguely: "He's not such a bad kid, Mike. I t'ink you don't do him yustice." Novak wondered fleetingly whether Friml was wearing a belt or suspenders these days, and realized that he didn't care a great deal. Amy Stuart asked after Lilly regularly, and he never had anything to tell her.

On a Friday afternoon he zipped a leather brief case around twenty-two ledger sheets on which were lettered in Amy's best engineer style the 132 equations that EBIC would chew into.

"Drive me to town?" he said to her. "I'd like to get to the office before they close up."

"With—the Papers," she said melodramatically, and they laughed. It came to him with a faint shock that it should be no laughing matter, but for the moment he couldn't persuade himself that there was anything sinister about this pretty girl with the sure, cool hands. The shared research, a common drain on them in progress and a mutual triumph at its end, was too big a thing to be spoiled by suspicion—for the moment. But depression stole over him on the desert road to Los Angeles, as he rode by Amy's side in the little English sportster.

She dropped him in front of the run-down building at 4:30.

He hadn't seen Friml since the secretary-treasurer's brannigan had broken up his plans for an evening. Without a blush, Friml laced into him. He seemed to be trying out a new manner for size: bullying instead of nagging; Friml the Perfect Master instead of Friml the

Perfect Servant. "I'm *very* glad to see you again, Dr. Novak. I've tried several times to advise you that you should report regularly, at least once a week, in person, or by telephone if unavoidable."

Nuts. Let him have his fun. "Been pretty busy." He tossed the brief case on Friml's desk. "This is the stuff to send I.B.M. When's our reservation?"

"That's just what I wanted to see you about. Your request—it was fantastic. Who—*who*—is this Mr. Ebic whom you wish to call in as a consultant at *one hundred dollars an hour*?" His voice was a sort of low, horrified shriek.

Novak stared at him in amazement. "Didn't you check to see what it was if you had doubts?"

"Certainly not. It's insane on the face of it. Just what do you think you're up to?"

"Somebody's been feeding you raw meat, Friml. And I think I know who." Friml looked smug for a moment. "EBIC is I.B.M.'s Electron—Binary—Integrating—Calculator. Get it? It's the only major electronic calculator available to the private citizen or firm, thanks to I.B.M.'s generosity and sense of public relations."

The secretary-treasurer said petulantly: "You might have made your request clear, Novak."

"Doctor Novak to you," said the engineer, suddenly very sick of the new Friml. It was such a stinking, messy thing to run into after such a beautiful spell of research work. "Now just get me lined up for a crack at EBIC. It's I.B.M., New York. One hundred and thirty-two partial differential equations. Just get it done and stay out of my hair until then."

He walked out of the office, boiling, and picked up a pint of bourbon at a drugstore before he went to his hotel. Swear to God, he thought, this deal's as lousy as A.E.C. and you don't get a pension either.

There were several slips in his pigeonhole at the hotel mail desk. They all said to call Miss Wynekoop at such and such a number as soon as he could, please. He had never heard of Miss Wynekoop, and the phone number didn't ring any bells. He took off his shoes when he got to his room, had a drink of the bourbon, and called the number.

A woman's brightly noncommittal voice said: "Hello?"

"This is Michael Novak. Miss Wynekoop?"

"Oh, Dr. Novak. I wonder if I might see you this evening about employment?"

"I'm not hiring."

She laughed. "I meant employment for you. I represent a firm which is adding to its technical and executive staff."

"I have a job. And a one-year contract with options."

"The contract would be our legal department's worry," she said cheerfully. "And if you meet our firm's standards, I think you'd hesitate to turn down our offer. The pay is very, very good." Then she was crisp and businesslike. "Are you free this evening? I can be at your hotel in fifteen minutes."

"All right," he said. "Why not? I suppose from the way you're putting all this that you're not going to tell me the name of your firm?"

"Well, we do prefer to keep such things quiet," she apologized. "There's speculation and wasted time and broken hearts for the people who think they're going to get it and don't. I'm sure you understand. I'll see you very soon, Dr. Novak." She hung up and he stood for a moment at the phone, undecided. More funny business? Wait and see.

He put his shoes on again, grunting, and chain-smoked until Miss Wynekoop knocked on his door. She was tall, thirty-ish and engaging in a lantern-jawed way. "Dr. Novak. I could tell you were a scientist. They have a look—— It was very good of you to let me see you on a moment's notice like this. But I hesitated to contact you through the A.S.F.S.F. In a way I suppose we're trying to steal you from them. Of course our legal people would buy out your contract with them so they'd suffer no financial loss in retraining a man to take your place."

"Sit down, please," he said. "What are these standards your firm wants me to meet?"

She settled herself comfortably. "Personality, for one thing. Our technical people have looked over your record and decided that you're the man for the job if you're available—and if you'll fit in. Our department head—you'd recognize the name, but of course I can't tell you yet—our department head would like me to check on some phases of your career. We're interested, for example, in the events that led up to your separation from A.E.C."

"Oh, are you?" he asked grimly. "As far as anybody is concerned, I resigned without notice after a short, hot discussion with Dr. Hurlbut, the director of the Argonne National Lab."

She giggled. "I'll say. You socked him."

"Well, what about it? If you people thought that means I'm incurably bad-tempered you wouldn't be here interviewing me now. You'd be trying the next guy on the list."

Miss Wynekoop became serious again. "You're right. Naturally we don't want a man who's going to fly off the handle over a trivial difference of opinion. But we certainly wouldn't hold it against you if you had actually been pushed to the breaking point by intolerable conditions. It could happen to anybody. If you will, I'd like you to tell me what brought the disagreement about."

The thing was sounding more legitimate by the minute—and is there anybody who doesn't like to tell his grievance? "Fair question, Miss Wynekoop," he said. "What brought it about was several months of being assigned to a hopelessly wrong job and being stymied every time I tried to get back to my proper work. That's not just my subjective opinion; it's not a gripe but a fact. I'm a ceramics engineer. But they put me into nuclear physics theory and wouldn't let me out. Hurlbut apparently didn't bother to acquaint himself with the facts. He insulted me viciously in public. He accused me of logrolling and incompetence. So I let him have it."

She nodded. "What are the details?"

"Details. What details?"

"Things like, when were you transferred and by whose authority. Your relationship with your superiors generally."

"Well, last August, about mid-month, my transfer order came through without warning or explanation. It was signed by the director of the Office of Organization and Personnel—one of the Washington big shots. And don't ask me about my relationship with him; I didn't have any. He was too high up. My orders before that had always been cut by my working directors."

She looked understanding. "I see. And the working directors: did they ride you? Keep you short of supplies? Stick you on the night-side? That kind of thing?"

Night-side. He had known reporters, and that was newspaper talk. They said without thinking: day-side, night-side, city-side, sport-side. "*Smear us, Novak,*" Anheier had grimly said, "*and we'll smear you back.*" He tried not to panic. "No," he said evenly. "There never was anything like that."

"What was your relationship with, say, Daniel Holland?"

Novak didn't have to fake a bewildered look. "Why, I had nothing at all to do with anybody on his level," he said slowly. "Maybe there's been a mistake. Do you have it clear that I was just a Grade 18? I wasn't in the chain of command. I was just hired help; why should I have anything to do with the general manager?"

She pressed: "But we understand that your transfer order was put through by the director of the Office of Organization and Personnel on the direct suggestion of Mr. Holland."

He shook his head. "Couldn't be. You've been misinformed. Holland wouldn't have known me from Adam's off ox."

Miss Wynekoop smiled briefly and said: "We were pretty sure of our facts. There's another matter. Your AEC Personnel Form Medical 11305 was altered by some means or other last September. Were you retested by the psychologists before that happened?"

"What the deuce is my Personnel Form Medical whatever-it-was?"

" 'Personality card' is what they call it unofficially."

Oh. Personality cards he knew about; they were an A.E.C. joke. You took a battery of tests during employment processing and a psychologist evaluated the results and filled out the card with attention to such things as "attitudes," "anxieties," "responses," and other items supposed to give your working director an idea of how to handle you. Your personality card went everywhere with you and it was never, never altered. It was a very peculiar question and it was becoming a very peculiar interview. "Yes," Novak lied. "They ran me through the works again at N.E.P.A. It was some psychologist's brilliant idea of a controlled experiment."

That rocked Miss Wynekoop back on her heels. She smiled with an effort and said, rising: "Thanks very much for your co-operation, Dr. Novak. I'll call you early next week. Thanks *very* much."

When he saw the elevator door at the end of the corridor close on her, Novak called Information. He asked: "Do you have Directory Service in this city? What I mean is, I have a phone number and I want the name and address of the subscriber."

"Yes, sir," said Information. "Just dial the exchange of the number and then dial 4882." Same routine as Chicago.

Directory Service said Miss Wynekoop's phone was an unlisted number and that was that. He called Miss Wynekoop's number again and a man with a pleasant voice answered, saying: "Howard here."

"Let me talk to the editor, Howard," Novak said.

There was a long pause and then: "Who is this, please?"

Novak hung up. "Editor" had meant something to Howard—or maybe Howard just wasn't a quick thinker.

Novak had last seen Anheier, agent in charge for the Los Angeles Regional A.E.C. Security and Intelligence Office, at the inquest on Clifton. Novak had woodenly stood and recited his facts while Anheier's calm eyes were on him, with their threat of instant and total ruin if he voiced his suspicion that Clifton had been murdered in some shadowy atomic intrigue. The verdict had been suicide . . .

The engineer hesitated a long minute and called the Security Office in the Federal Building. "Mr. Anheier, please," he said. "This is Dr. Michael Novak."

A man said: "Mr. Anheier's gone home, sir. I'll give you his home phone if it's important, or take a message."

Novak said: "It's important," and got Anheier's home phone number.

The agent in charge was as placid as ever. "Good to hear from you, Dr. Novak. What can I——"

Novak cut him off. "Shut up. I just want to tell you something. You were afraid of my ideas getting into the papers. You said you'd smear me if I did anything to publicize them. I want you to know that the newspapers are coming to me." He proceeded to tell Anheier what had been said, as close to verbatim as he could. At the end of the recital he said: "Any questions?"

"Can you describe this woman?"

He did.

Anheier said: "It sounds like somebody who hit town today. I'm going into the Federal Building office now. Will you come down and look at some pictures? Maybe we can identify this Wynekoop."

"Why should I?"

Anheier said grimly: "I want your co-operation, Dr. Novak. I want to bè sure you aren't leaking your story to the papers and trying to avoid retaliation in kind. The more cooperation we get out of you, the less likely that theory will seem. I'll be waiting for you."

Novak hung up the phone and swore. He drank again from the bottle of bourbon and took a taxi to the Federal Building.

There was a long wait in the dimmed hall for the single after-hours elevator. When its door rolled open on the eighth floor, Novak saw that the Security office glass door was the only one on the floor still lit from inside. Twenty-four hours a day, he had heard, with the teletype net always up.

He gave his name to the lone teletype operator doubling at night as receptionist.

"Mr. Anheier's in his office," said the operator. "You see it there?"

Novak went in. The tall, calm man greeted him and handed him a single eight-by-ten glossy print.

"That's her," he said without hesitation. "A reporter?"

Anheier was rocking gently in his swivel chair. "An ex-reporter," he said. "She's Mary Tyrrel. Senator Bob Hoyt's secretary."

Novak blinked uncomprehendingly. "I don't see what I can do about it," he said, shrugging, and turned to leave.

"Novak," Anheier said. "I can't let you out of here."

There was a gun in his hand, pointed at the engineer.

"Don't you know who killed Clifton?" Anheier asked. "I killed Clifton."

13

Night of a bureaucrat.

The bachelor apartment of Daniel Holland was four rooms in an oldish Washington apartment house. After six years in residence, Holland barely knew his way around it. The place had been restrainedly decorated in Swedish modern by the wife of a friend in the days when he'd had time for friends. There had been no changes in it since. His nightly track led from the front door to the desk, and after some hours from the desk to the dressing closet and then the bed. His track in the morning was from the bed to the bathroom to the dressing closet to the front door.

Holland was there in his second hour of paper work at the desk when his telephone rang. It meant a wrong number or—trouble. His eyes slid to the packed traveling bag he always kept beside the door; he picked up the phone and gave its number in a monotone.

"This is Anheier in L.A., chief. Let's scramble."

Holland pushed the scrambler button on the phone's base and asked: "Do you hear me all right?"

"I hear you, chief. Are you ready for bad news?"

The general manager felt a curious relief at the words; the moment had arrived and would soon be past. No more night sweats . . . "Let me have it."

"Hoyt's got the personnel angle. Tyrrel's been grilling Novak. The questions showed that she had just about all of it on ice."

"What does Novak know?"

"Too much. I have him here." The Security man's voice became embarrassed. "I have a gun on him, chief. I've told him I shot Clifton to let him know I mean business. And we can't leave him wandering around. Hoyt would latch onto him, give him a sugar-tit, listen to all he knows and then—we're done."

"I don't doubt your judgement, Anheier," Holland said heavily. "Put him in storage somewhere. I'll fly out to the coast. I've got to talk to him myself."

"You can't fly, chief. It'd be noticed."

"Too much has been noticed. It's a question of time now. Now we must ram it through and hope we're not too late. Good-by." He hung up before Anheier could protest, and went to get his hat and coat.

Novak listened to the Los Angeles end of the conversation, watching the gun in Anheier's big, steady hand. It never wavered.

The Security man put his odd-looking telephone back into his desk drawer. "Get up," he said. "You won't be killed if you don't make any foolish moves." He draped a light raincoat over the gun hand. If you looked only casually it would strike you as nothing more than a somewhat odd way to carry a raincoat.

"Walk," Anheier told him.

In a fog, Novak walked. It couldn't be happening, and it was. Anheier guided him through the office. "Back late tomorrow, Charles." Yell for help? Break and run? Charles was an unknown, but the big black gun under the coat was a known quantity. Before the thing could be evaluated they were in the corridor. Anheier walked him down the lonesome stairs of the office building, sadly lit by night bulbs, one to a landing. Swell place for a murder. So was the parking lot back of the building.

"I know you drive," Anheier said. "Here." He handed him car keys. "That one."

Use your head, Novak told himself. He'll make you drive to a canyon and there you'll get it without a chance in the world of witnesses. Yell here, and at least somebody will know——

But the big gun robbed him of his reason. He got in and started the car. Anheier was beside him and the gun's muzzle was in his ribs, not painfully.

The Security man gave him laconic traffic directions. "Left. Left again. Right. Straight ahead." Aside from that, he would not talk.

After an hour the city had been left behind and they were among rolling, wooded hills. With dreamlike recognition he stopped on order at the police sentry box that guarded the wealthy from intrusion by kidnappers, peddlers, and thieves. The gun drilled into his ribs as he stopped the car, painfully now. Anheier rolled down his window and passed a card to the cop in the handsomely tailored uniform.

Respectfully: "Thank you, Mr. Anheier. Whom are you calling on?" The best was none too good for the rich. They even had cops who said "whom."

"Mr. Stuart's residence. They'll know my name." Of course. The gun drilled in.

"Yes, sir," said the flunky-cop. "If you'll wait just a moment, sir." The other man in the booth murmured respectfully into his wall phone; he had his hand casually on an elegant repeating shotgun as he listened. He threw them a nod and smile.

"Let's go, Novak," Anheier said.

The gun relaxed little when the booth was behind them. "You're all in it," Novak said at last, bitterly.

Anheier didn't answer. When they reached the Stuart place he guided Novak up the driveway and into the car port. Lights in the rangy house glowed, and somebody strode out to meet them. Grady, the Stuart chauffeur. "Get out, Novak." For the first time, the gun was down.

"Grady," Anheier said, "Keep an eye on Dr. Novak here. We don't want him to leave the grounds or use the phone or anything like that." He stowed the gun in a shoulder holster. "Well, let's get into the house, shall we?"

The old man was waiting for them in his wheel chair. "What the hell's going on, Anheier? You can't turn this place into an office."

"Sorry," said the Security man briefly. "It can't be helped. The chief's coming out to see Novak. He's found out too much. We can't leave him wandering around."

Wilson Stuart glared at Novak. "My daughter thinks you're intelligent," he said. "I told her she was crazy. Anheier, when's all this going to happen?"

"I don't know. Overnight. He said he'd fly. I tried to talk him out of it."

"Grady," the old man said, "put him in a bedroom and lock the door. I'll have Dr. Morris mix something to give him a good night's sleep."

Incongruously the chauffeur said: "This way, sir."

The bedroom was the same one Lilly had been put up in. Its solid door closed like the door of a tomb. Novak dashed to the long, low window and found it thoroughly sealed to the wall. The place was air-conditioned. Of

287

course he could smash it with a table lamp and jump. And be brought down by a flying tackle or a bullet.

Grady was back in five minutes with a yellow capsule in a pillbox. "Dr. Morris sent this for you, Dr. Novak," he said. "Dr. Morris said it would help you rest." Grady stood by expectantly as Novak studied the capsule. After a moment he said pointedly: "There's water and a glass in the bathroom, sir."

Put on a scene? Refuse to take this nassy ole medicine? He cringed at what would certainly happen. These terrifyingly competent people would stick him with a hypodermic or—worse—have their muscle man hold him while the capsule was put in his mouth and washed down. He went silently to the bathroom and Grady watched him swallow.

"Good night, Dr. Novak," the chauffeur said, closing the door solidly and softly.

The stuff worked fast. In five minutes Novak was sprawled in the bed. He had meant to lie down for a minute or two, but drifted off. His sleep was dreamless, except that once he fancied somebody had told him softly that she was sorry, and touched his lips.

A man was standing beside the bed when he awoke. The man, middle-aged and a little fleshy, was neither tall nor short. His face was a strange one, a palimpsest. A scholar, Novak fuzzily thought—definitely a pure-research man. And then over it, like a film, slipped a look so different that the first judgment became inexplicable. He was a boss-man—top boss-man.

"I'm Daniel Holland," he said to Novak. "I've brought you some coffee. They told me you shouldn't be hungry after the sleeping capsule. You aren't, are you?"

"No, I'm not. Daniel Holland. A.E.C.? You're——"

The top-boss face grinned a hard grin. "I'm in this too, Novak."

What was there to do? Novak took the coffee cup from the bedside table and sipped mechanically. "Are you people going to kill me?" he asked. The coffee was helping to pull him together.

"*No*," said Holland. He pulled up a chair and sat. "We're going to work you pretty hard, though."

Novak laughed contemptuously. "You will not," he

said. "You can make me or anybody do a lot of things, but not that. I guess just a few clouts in the jaw would make me say anything you wanted me to. Those Russian confessions. The American police third degree. If you started to really hurt me I suppose I'd implicate anybody you wanted. Friends, good friends, anybody. You can do a lot of things to a man, but you can't make him do sustained brainwork if he doesn't want to. And I don't want to. Not for Pakistan, Argentina, the Chinese, or whoever you represent."

"The United States of America?" asked Holland.

"You must tl   ⸱ I'm a fool," Novak told him.

"I'm workin〔 〕or the United States," said Holland. "God help me, but it's the only way left. I was hemmed in with this and that——" There was appeal in his voice. He was a man asking for absolution.

"I'll tell it from the beginning, Novak," he said, under control again.

"In 1951 a study was made by A.E.C. of fission products from the Hanford plutonium-producing reactors. Properties of one particular isotope were found to be remarkable. This isotope, dissolved in water and subjected to neutron flux of a certain intensity, decomposes with great release of energy. It is stable except under the proper degree of neutron bombardment. Its level of radioactivity is low. Its half-life is measured in scores of years. It is easy to isolate and is reasonably abundant. Since it is a by-product, its cost is exactly nothing."

"How much energy?" asked Novak, guardedly.

"Enough to flash the solvent water into hydrogen and oxygen by thermolysis," Holland said. "You've seen the drawings for *Prototype's* fuel tanks, as we called them . . ."

Anheier came into the room and Novak barely noticed him. His engineer's mind could see the blue print unrolled before him again. The upper tank containing the isotope-water solution . . . the lower tank containing a small heavy-water "fish-bowl" reactor for the neutron source . . . the dead-end control systems completed, installed, one metering the fuel solution past the neutron spray of the reactor, the other controlling flux level by damper rods run in and out on servomechanisms . . . the fuel solution droplets flashing into hell's own flame and roaring from the throat with exhaust velocity unobtainable by merely chemical reaction . . .

Holland was talking again, slowly. "It was just numbers on paper, among thousands of other numbers on paper. It lay for years in the files until one of the high-ranking A.E.C. technical people stumbled on it, understood its implications and came to me. His exact words were: 'Holland, this is space flight.' "

"It is," Novak breathed. His voice became hoarse. "And you sold it . . ."

"*I saved it*. I saved it from the red-tape empire builders, the obscurantists, the mystagogues, the spies. If I had set it up as an A.E.C. project, the following things would have happened. First, we would have lost security. Every nation in the world would shortly have known the space-flight problem had an answer, and then what the answer was. Second, we would have been beaten to the Moon by another nation. This is because our personnel policy forbids us to hire the best men we can find merely because they're the best. Ability ranks very low in the category of criteria by which we judge A.E.C. personnel. They must be conservative. They must be politically apathetic. They must have no living close-relatives abroad. And so on. As bad as the personnel situation, interacting with and reinforcing it, is the fact of A.E.C.'s bigness and the fact of its public ownership. They mean accounting, chains of command, personnel-flow charts—the jungle in which third-raters flourish. Get in the A.E.C., build yourself a powerful clique and don't worry about the work; you don't really have to do any."

The words were fierce; his tone was dispassionate. Throughout his denunciation he wore the pure-research man's face, lecturing coolly on phenomena which he had studied, isolated, linked, analyzed endlessly. If any emotion was betrayed it was, incongruously, the residual affection of a pure-research man for his subject. When the pathologist calls it a beautiful carcinoma he is being neither ironical nor callous.

"As you know," Holland lectured quietly, "the nation that gets to the Moon first has the Moon. The lawyers will be arguing about it for the next century, but the nation that plants the first moon base need not pay any attention to their arguments. I wanted that nation to be the United States, which I've served to the best of my ability for most of my life.

"I became a conspirator.

"I determined to have a moon ship built under non-Government auspices and, quite frankly, to rob the Government to pay for it. I have a long reputation as a dollar-honest, good-government man, which I counted on to help me get away with quite outrageous plundering of the Treasury.

"A study convinced me that complete assembly of a moon ship by a large, responsible corporation could not be kept secret. I found the idea of isolated parts manufactured by small, scattered outfits and then a rush assembly was impractical. A moon ship is a precision instrument of huge size. One subassembly under par would wreck the project. I admit I was toying with the idea of setting up a movie company and building the moon ship as, ostensibly, a set for a science-fiction film, when the A.S.F.S.F. came to my attention.

"Psychologically it seems to have been perfect. You deserve great credit, Dr. Novak, for stubbornly sticking to the evidence and logic that told you *Prototype* is a moon ship and not a dummy. You are the only one who has. Many people have seen the same things you did and refused to believe it because of the sheer implausibility of the situation.

"Hoping that this would be the case, I contacted my old friend Wilson Stuart. He and his company have been the pipeline for millions of Government dollars poured into the A.S.F.S.F. I've callously diverted thousands of A.E.C. man-hours into solving A.S.F.S.F. problems. I had you transferred within the A.E.C. and had your personality card altered so that Hurlbut would goad you into resigning—since the moon ship needed a full-time man with your skills."

"You dared——" choked Novak, stung with rage.

"I dared," Holland said matter-of-factly. "This country has its faults, but of all the nations in the world I judge it as least disqualified to operate a moon base. It's the power of life and death over every nation on the face of the earth, and some one nation has got to accept that power."

Suddenly his voice blazed with passion and the words came like a torrent. "What was I to do? Go ahead and do it the wrong way? Go to the commissioners, who'd go to the congressmen, who'd go to their good friends on the newspapers? Our secrecy would have been wiped out in twelve hours! Set up a Government project staffed with simon-pure but third-rate scientists? Watch the thing grow and grow until there were twenty desk men for every man who got his hands dirty on the real work—and all the desk men fighting like wild beasts for the glory of signing memos? Was I to spare your career and let those A-bomb racks on the Moon go by default to the Argentines or Chinese? Man, what do you think I am?"

"A killer," Novak said dully. "Your man Anheier murdered my friend Clifton."

Anheier's voice was cold. "Executed," he said. "You were there when I warned him, Novak. The penalty for espionage is death. I told him so and he smiled at me to tell me that I wouldn't dare. I told him: 'The penalty is death.' And he went to his home and telephoned his contact, Mr. Boris Chodorov of Amtorg, that he'd have something for him in a day or two. God almighty, Novak, be reasonable. Should I have written Clifton a letter? I told him: 'Import-export used to be a favorite, but it was too obvious.' So he smiled at me and went home to call his contact. He had something juicy, something out of the general run-of-the-mill industrial-preparedness information he collected for the Soviets.

"*He* may have thought he was just augmenting his income, that it wasn't *really* espionage, that the United States hasn't got the guts to hit back anyway——" His voice trailed off. "I killed him," he said.

"Clifton a spy," Novak said stupidly. He began to laugh. "And Lilly?"

"Just a stupid woman," Anheier said. "We monitored the Cliftons for a long time, and nothing ever emanated from her."

Novak couldn't stop laughing. "You're quite wrong," he said. A hundred little things slipped suddenly into place. "There is no doubt in my mind that Lilly was the brains of the outfit. I can see now that Lilly was leading me by the nose for weeks, getting every scrap of information I possessed. And when she got just one chance she landed Friml and is now milking him."

Anheier had gone white. "How much does Friml know?" asked Holland.

The Security man said: "Friml knows he's employed by Wilson Stuart. And he can guess at a lot of the rest. The way there's always enough material on hand when we order it for a jobber—even gray-market stuff like copper and steel. Our work. And he knows there are calls to and from Washington that have a connection. Between his brains and Mrs. Clifton's, I think we'd better assume that secrecy is gone." He looked and sounded sick.

"Novak," the general manager asked softly, "are you in this too?"

Novak knew what he meant. "Yes," he said. "It looks like the right side of the fence to me."

Holland said: "I'm glad . . . how close to finished is the moon ship?" He was the boss-man again.

"Is the fuel solution ready and waiting?"

"It is. Waiting for word from me. I've also oiled the ways for the diversion of a fish-bowl reactor for your neutron source. It's going to go astray on its way to Cal Tech from Los Alamos."

"EBIC's got to work out my math and I've got to fabricate the liner and vane. At the same time, the ship could be stocked with water, food, and the pressure dome. At the same time the dead-ended circuits can be completed. Do you have the food and water and air tanks and lockers?"

"Yes. Give me a figure!" Holland snapped.

Novak choked on it, terrifyingly aware that no man ever before had borne such tidings as he spoke in the bedroom of a rich man's house in Beverly Hills. "It could take off in two weeks," he said. Here we are at last, Novak thought. Time to close the old ledger on man. Add it up, credit and debit, and carry your balance forward to the first page of the next ledger . . .

"And now," said Holland grimly, "we ought to go and see some people. They'd both be at her house?"

Novak knew what he meant, and nodded. "I suppose so. It's Saturday."

He led the way to the garage. Amy Stuart's little

sports car was at home.

"Mr. Holland," Novak said, "there's going to be a hell of a smash when this comes out, isn't there?"

"We hope not," the general manager said shortly. "We have some plans of our own if they try to jail me for fraud and Anheier for murder and the rest of the crew for whatever they can think of."

"Why should Amy be mixed up in this?"

"We need her," Holland snapped. His manner ruled out further questions. They got into Anheier's car and the Security man drove them to the house in Cahuenga Canyon.

14

Lilly met them at the door in a housecoat. "Hallo, Mike," she said. "Who're these people? Oh, you' Anheier, ain't you?"

"My name is Daniel Holland, Mrs. Clifton," the general manager said. She didn't move a muscle. "Do you mind if I come in?"

"I t'ink I do," she said slowly. "Mike, what is all this?"

Novak looked at Holland, who nodded. "Espionage," he said.

She laughed tremulously and told him: "You cra-a-azy!"

"Lilly, you once asked me to find out who killed Cliff. I found out. It was Anheier. Cliff was a spy."

Her expression didn't change as she said: "Cliff was a damn bad spy. Come on in. I got somet'ing to tell you too."

They filed into the living room. "Where's Friml?" Novak asked. She jerked her thumb carelessly toward the bedroom door.

"He's a lot smarter than any of you t'ought," she said, making a business out of lighting a cigarette. "He told me what he saw and figgered out, and I did some figgering too. You' a very smart man, Mr. Holland. But what I got to tell you is I got this stuff to a friend of mine already. If he don't hear from me by a certain time, he sends it on to the newspapers. How you like that, killer?" She blew a plume of smoke at Anheier.

The large, calm man said: "That means you've got it to your employers by now."

"Does it?" she asked, grinning. "It don't matter. All I got to do is sic the papers on you, and you' democra-a-atic country does the rest for us like always. I don't know you' rocket fuel yet. Prob'ly wouldn't know what to do vit' it if Friml brought me a bottleful; I don't know science. But it don't matter; I don't worry. The papers and the Congress raise hell vit' you and lead us right to the rocket fuel so our people that do know science can move in and figger it out."

Stirred by a sudden, inappropriate curiosity, Novak coulldn't help asking: "Are you a Communist? Your husband reported to an Amtorg man."

She was disgusted. "Communist, hell! I'm a European."

"I don't see what that——"

"Listen, Mike," she said flatly. "Before you' friends kill me or t'row me in yail or whatever they gonna do. You fatbelly people over here don' begin to know we t'ink you all a bunch of monkeys vit' the atom bombs and movies and at'letes and radio comics and two-ton Sunday newspapers and fake schools where the kids don' work. Well, what you guys going to do vit' me? Shoot me? Prison? Drop an atom bomb? Solve everyt'ing? Go ahead. I been raped by Yerman soldiers and sedooced vit' Hershey bars by American soldiers. I had the typhus and lost my hair. I walked seventy-five kilometers on a loaf of sawdust bread for a yob that wasn't there after all. I speak t'ree languages and understand t'ree more a liddle and you people call me dumb because I got a accent. You people that don' even know how to stand quiet in line for a bus or kinema and t'ink you can run the world. I been lied at and promised to by the stupid Americans. Vote for me and end you' troubles. I been lied at and promised to by the crazy Russians. Nah, vote for *me* and end you' troubles.

"*Sheissdrek.* So I voted for me-myself and now go ahead and drop you' damn atom bomb on the dumb squarehead. Solve everyt'ing, hey boys? *Sheissdrek.*"

She sprawled in the chair, a tight grin on her face, and

deliberately hoisted the skirt of her housecoat to her thighs. "Any of you guys got a Hershey bar?" she demanded sardonically, and batted her eyes at them. "The condemned European's la-a-ast request is for a Hershey bar so she can die happy."

Friml was standing there with his thinnish hair tousled, glasses a little crooked on his face, wrapped in a maroon bathrobe. His skinny, hairy legs shook with a fine tremor.

"Hallo, sugar," she said to him with poisonous sweetness. "These yentleman and I was discussing life." She turned to them and lectured elaborately: "You know what happen in Europe when out came you' Kinsey report? This will kill you. All the dumb squareheads and the dumb dagoes and the dumb frogs and krauts said we knew it all the time. American men are half pa-a-ansy and the rest they learn out of a marriage book on how to *zigzag*." She looked at Friml and laughed.

"P-p-pull your skirt down, Lilly," Friml said in a weak, hoarse voice.

"Go find you'self a nice boy, sugar," she said carelessly. "Maybe you make him happy, because you sure as hell don'——" Friml's head bobbled as though he'd been slapped. Moving like an old man, not looking at anything, he went to the bathroom and then to the bedroom and closed the door.

"Like the yoke!" giggled Lilly half-hysterically. "He'll do it too; he's a manly liddle feller!"

"I think——" said Novak starting to his feet. He went to the bedroom door with hurried strides and knocked. "Friml! I want to—to talk to you for a minute!"

The answer was a horrible, low, roaring noise.

The door was locked; Novak lunged against it with his shoulder repeatedly, not feeling the pain and not loosening the door. Anheier pulled him back and yelled at him: "Cut that out! I'll get the window from outside." He rushed from the house, scooping up a light, toylike poker from the brass stand beside the fireplace.

Holland said at his side: "Steady. We'll be able to help him in a minute." They heard smashing glass and Novak wanted to run out and look through the window. "Steady," Holland said.

Anheier opened the door. "Get milk from the kitchen,"

he snapped at Novak. The engineer got a brief glimpse of dark red blood. He ran for the kitchen and brought a carton of milk.

While Holland phoned for a doctor, Novak and Anheier tried to pour the milk into Friml. It wouldn't go down. The thrashing thing on the floor, its bony frame and pallid skin pitifully exposed by the flapping, coarse robe, wasn't vomiting. They would get a mouthful of milk into it, and then the milk would dribble out again as it choked and roared. Friml had drunk almost two ounces of tincture of iodine. The sickening, roaring noises had a certain regularity. Novak thought he was trying to say he hadn't known it would hurt so much.

By the time the doctor arrived, they realized that Lilly was gone.

"God, Anheier," Novak said white-faced. "She planned it. A diversion while she made her getaway. She pushed the buttons on him and—is it possible?"

"Yes," the Security man said without emotion. "I fell down badly all around on that one."

"Damn it, be human!" Novak yelled at him.

"He's human," Holland said. "I've known him longer than you have, and I asure you he's human. Don't pester him; he feels very badly."

Novak subsided.

An ambulance with police pulled up to the house as the doctor was pumping morphine into Friml's arm. The frightful noises ebbed, and when Novak could look again Friml was spread laxly on the floor.

"I don't suppose——" Novak said, and trailed off.

"Relation?" the doctor asked. He shook his head. "He'll linger a few hours and then die. I can see you did everything you could, but there was nothing to be done. He seared his glottis almost shut."

"Joel Friml," Novak told the sergeant, and spelled it. It was good to be doing something—anything. "He lives at the Y in downtown L.A. This place is the home of Mrs. August Clifton—widow. He was spending the night here. My friends and I came to visit. Mrs. Clifton seems to have run out in a fit of nerves." He gave his name, and slowly recognition dawned on the sergeant's face.

"This is uh, kind of funny," the cop told him. "My brother-in-law's in that rocket club so I happen to re-

297

member—it was her husband, wasn't it? And wasn't there an Anslinger——"

"Anheier," said the Security man. "I'm Anheier."

"Funnier and funnier," said the sergeant. "Doc, could I see you for a——"

The doctor had been listening, and cut him off. "Not necessary," he said. "This is suicide. The man drank it like a shot of whisky—threw it right straight down. (Was he a drinker, by the way?" "Yes." "Thought so.") There aren't any smears on the lips or face and only a slight burning in the mouth, which means he didn't try to retain it. He drank it himself, in a synchronized toss and gulp."

The sergeant looked disappointed, but brightened up to ask: "And who's this gentleman?"

Holland took out a green card from his wallet and showed it to the sergeant. Novak craned a little and saw that it was a sealed, low-number White House pass. "Uh," said the sergeant, coming to something like attention, "I can't see your name, sir. Your finger——"

"My finger stays where it is, sergeant," said Holland. "Unless, of course, you *insist*——?" He was all boss.

"No, no, no, not at all, sir. That's quite all right. Thank you." The sergeant almost backed away as from royalty and began to snarl at his detail of two patrolmen for not having the meat loaded yet.

They rushed into action and the sergeant said to nobody in particular and very casually: "Think I'd better phone this in to headquarters." Novak wasn't surprised when he heard the sergeant say into the phone, louder than he had intended: "Gimme the city desk, please." Novak moved away. The thing had to come out sooner or later, and the tipster-cop was earning a little side money honestly.

After completing his call, the sergeant came up beaming. "That wraps it up except for Mrs. Clifton," he said. "She took her car? What kind?"

"Big maroon Rolls Royce," Novak said. "I'm not sure of the year—maybe early thirties."

"Well, that don't matter. A Rolls is a Rolls; we'll be seeing her very soon, I think."

Novak didn't say what he thought about that. He didn't think any of them would be seeing Lilly again. He thought she would vanish back into the underworld from which she had appeared as a momentary, frightening reminder that much of the world is not rich, self-satisfied, supremely fortunate America.

In Anheier's car on the road back to the Wilson Stuart place, the Security man asked tentatively: "What do you think, chief?"

"I think she's going to release everything she's got to the newspapers. First, as she said, it means we'll lose secrecy. Second, it would be the most effective form of sabotage she could practice on our efforts. The Bennet papers have been digging into my dirty work of the past year for circulation-building and for Hoyt, whom they hope to put in the presidency. The campaign should open in a couple of days, when they get Lilly's stuff as the final link.

"I've got to get to Washington and contract a diplomatic illness for the first time in my life. Something that'll keep me bedridden but able to run things through my deputy by phone. Something that'll win a little sympathy and make a few people say hold your horses until he's able to answer the charges. I can stall that way for a couple of weeks—no more. Then we've got to present Mr. and Mrs. America with a *fait accompli*. Novak!"

"Yessir!" snapped Novak, surprising himself greatly.

"Set up a *real* guard system at the moon ship. If you need any action out of Mr. MacIlheny, contact Mr. Stuart, who will give him your orders. MacIlheny—up to now—doesn't know anything about the moon beyond Stuart. Your directive is: *build us that moon ship. Fast.*"

"Yes, sir."

"And another thing. You're going to be busy, but I have some chores for you nevertheless. Your haircut is all wrong. Go to a really good barber who does theatrical people. Go to your dentist and have your teeth cleaned. Have yourself a couple of good suits made, and good shoes and good shirts. Put yourself in the hands of a first-rate tailor. It's on the expense account and I'm quite serious about it. I only wish there were time for . . ."

"How's that, sir?" Novak couldn't believe he had heard it right.

"Dancing lessons," snapped Holland. "You move across a room with all the grace of a steam thresher moving across a Montana wheatfield. And Novak."

"Yes?" said the engineer stiffly.

"It's going to be rough for a while and they may drag us down yet. Me in jail, you in jail, Anheier in the gas chamber, Stuart fired by his board—if I know the old boy he wouldn't last a month if they took Western away from him. You're going to be working for your own neck —and a lot of other necks. So work like hell. Hoyt and Bennet play for keeps. This a bus stop? Let Novak out, Anheier. You go on downtown and let's see production."

Novak stood on the corner, lonely, unhappy, and shaken, and waited for his downtown bus.

His appetite, numbed by last night's sedative, came on with a rush during the ride. After getting off, he briskly headed for a business-district cafeteria, and by reflex picked up a newspaper. He didn't get into the cafeteria. He stood in the street, reading.

DEATH STRIKES AT 2ND ROCKET-CLUB CHIEF:
POISONED ON VISIT TO 1ST VICTIM'S WIDOW
POST *Special Correspondent*

Violent death struck late today at a leader of the American Society for Space Flight, nationwide rocket club, for the second time in less than a month. The first victim was club engineer August Clifton, who committed suicide by shooting in a room next door to a meeting of the club going full blast. Today club secretary-treasurer Joel Friml, 26, was found writhing in pain on the floor of a Cahuenga Canyon bungalow owned by Clifton's attractive blond widow Lilly, 35. Both bodies were discovered by club engineer Michael Novak. A further bizarre note lies in the fact that on both occasions A.E.C. Security agent J.W. Anheier was on the scene within seconds of the discovery.

Police Sergeant Herman Alper said Novak and Anheier paid a morning visit to Mrs. Clifton's home and chatted with her and Friml, who had arrived earlier. Friml disappeared into the bedroom, alarming the other guests. They broke into the bed-

room by smashing a window and found Friml in convulsions, clutching a two-ounce bottle of a medicine meant for external use. They called a doctor and tried to give milk as an antidote, but according to the physician the victim's throat had been so damaged that it was a hopeless try.

Friml was taken by ambulance under sedation to Our Lady of Sonora hospital, where no hope was given for his recovery. In the confusion Mrs. Clifton fled the house, apparently in a state of shock, and had not returned by the time the ambulance left.

Friends could hazard no guess as to the reason for the tragedy. Friml himself, ironically, had just completed auditing the rocket club's books in a vain search for discrepancies that might have explained the Clifton suicide.

It was bad. Worse was coming.

15

Novak moved out to the field, bag and baggage, that night and worked himself into a pleasant state of exhaustion. He woke on his camp cot at nine to the put-put of an arriving jalopy. It was a kid named Nearing. He made a beeline for Novak, washing up in a lab sink.

"Hi, Dr. Novak." He was uncomfortable.

"Morning. Ready for business?"

"I guess so. There's something I wanted to ask you about. It's a lot of nonsense, of course. My brother's in the C.B.S. newsroom in L.A., and he was kidding me this morning. He just got in from the night shift and he said there was a rumor about *Proto*. It came in on some warm-up chatter on their teletype."

Already? "What did he have to say?"

"Well, the A.S.F.S.F. was—'linked' is the word, I guess—with some big-time Washington scandal that's going to break. Here." He poked a wad of paper at Novak. "I thought he was making it up. He doesn't believe in space flight and he's a real joker, but he showed me this. He tore it off their teletype."

Novak unfolded the wad into a long sheet of cheap paper, torn off at the top and bottom.

BLUE NOSE AND A PURPLE GOATEE.

HA HA THATS A GOOD ONE. U KNOW ONE ABT BISHOP OF BIR-MINGHAM???

SURE WHO DONT. OGOD THREE AM AND THREE HOURS TO GO

LOOK WHOS BITCHING. HERE ITS SIX AM AND SIX HOURS TO GO.

WISH ID LEARNED A TRADE OR STAYED IN THE NAVY.

WHAT U DO IN NAVY???

TELETYPE OPR. CANT GET AWAY FROM DAM PTRS SEEMS AS IF. MIN FONE

WHO WAS IT???

ELEANOR ROOSEVELT ASKING FOR A DATE U NOSY BASTRD

HA HA   OGOD WOTTA SLO NITE, ANY NUZ UR SIDE???

NOT YET. FIRST CAST HALF HOUR. NUZMAN CAME IN WITH RUMOR ABT SOME UR LOCAL SCREWBALLS TO WIT LOS ANGELES SPACE FLITE CLUB.

HEY HEY. NUZRITER HERE GOT KID BROTHER IN CLUB. WOT HE SAY???

SAID STRICTLY PHONY OUTFIT WITH WA TIEUP TOP ADMIN-INXXX ADMINISTRATION GOT IT FINALLY FIGURES.

GOVT MONEY GOES TO CLUB AND CLUB KIX BACK TO GOVT OFFICIALS. SWEET RACKET HUH.

MORE???

NO MORE. MIN I ASK. SAYS GOT IT FM BENNET NUZ SVC MAN. NO MORE.

TNX. COFFEE NOW.

WELCM. DONT SPILL IT.

HA HA U R A WIT OR MAYBE I AM ONLY HALF RITE.

Nearing said as Novak looked up from the paper: "Of course Charlie may have punched it out himself on a dead printer just to worry me." He laughed uncomfortably. "Oh, hell. It's just a rumor about a rumor. But I don't like them tossing *Proto's* name around. She's a good girl." His eye sought the moon ship, gleaming in the morning sun.

"Yes," Novak said. "Look, Nearing. I'm tightening up the guard schedule and I'm going to be very busy. I'd like to turn the job of handling the guard detail over to you. I'll put you on salary, say fifty a week, if you'll do it."

"Fifty? Why sure, Dr. Novak. That's about what I'm getting at the shoe store, but the hell with it. When do I start and what do I do?"

"Start now. I want two guards on duty at all times. Not under twenty-one, either. At night I want one guard at the gate and one patrolling the fence. I want strict identification of all strangers at the gate. I want newspapermen kept out. I want you to find out what kind of no-trespassing signs we're legally required to post and how many—and then post twice as many. I want you to get the huskiest youngsters you can for guards and give them night sticks." He hesitated. "And buy us two shotguns and some shells."

The boy looked at Novak and then at the *Prototype* and then at Novak again. "If you think it's necessary," he said quietly. "What kind of shells—bird shot?"

"Buckshot, Nearing. They're after her."

"Buckshot it is, Dr. Novak," the shoe clerk said grimly.

He worked all morning in the machine shop, turning wooden core patterns for the throat liner on the big lathe. Laminated together and rasped smooth, they would be the first step in the actual fabrication of the throat liner. Half a dozen youngsters showed up, and he put them to work routing out the jacket patterns. Some of the engineer-members showed up around noon on their Sunday visits and tried to shop-talk with him. He wouldn't shop-talk.

At three in the afternoon Amy Stuart was saying to him firmly: "Turn that machine off and have something to eat. Nearing told me you didn't even have breakfast. I've got coffee, bologna on white, cheese on rye—"

"Why, thanks," he said, surprised. He turned off the power and began to eat at a workbench.

"Sorry they pulled rough stuff on you," she said.

"Rough?" he snorted. "That wasn't rough. Rough is what's coming up." Between bites of sandwich he told her about the teletype chatter.

"It's starting," she said.

The next day the dam broke.

Reporters were storming the gate by mid-morning. In due course a television relay truck arrived and from outside the fence peered at them with telephoto lenses.

"Find out what it's all about, Nearing," Novak said, looking up from his pattern making.

Nearing came back with a sheaf of papers. "They talked me into saying I'd bring you written questions."

"Throw 'em away. Fill me in in twenty seconds or less so I can get back to work."

"Well, Senator Hoyt's going to make a speech in the Senate today and he's wired advance copies all over hell. And it's been distributed by the news agencies, of course. It's like the rumor. He's going to denounce Daniel Holland, the A.E.C. general manager. He says Holland is robbing the Treasury blind by payments to the A.S.F.S.F. and Western Air, and getting kickbacks. He says Holland's incompetence has left the U.S. in the rear of the atomic weapons parade. Is my time up?"

"Yes. Thanks. Try to get rid of them. If you can't, just make sure none of them get in here."

There were days when he had to go into town. Sometimes people pointed him out. Sometimes people jostled him and he gave them a weary stare and they either laughed nervously or scowled at him, enemy of his country that he was. He was too tired to care deeply. He was working simultaneously on the math, the controls, installation of the tanks, and the setup for forming the liner and vane.

One day he fainted while walking from the machine shop to the refractories lab. He came to in his cot and found Amy Stuart and her father's Dr. Morris in attendance.

"Where did you come from?" he asked dimly.

Dr. Morris growled: "Never mind where I came from. You ought to be ashamed of yourself, Novak. Playing the fool at your age! I'm telling you here and now that you are going to stay in bed for forty-eight hours and you are not going to use the time to catch up on your paper work either. You are going to sleep, eat, read magazines—*not* including the *Journal of Metallurgical Chemistry* and things on that order—and nothing else."

"Make it twenty-four hours, will you?" said Novak.

"All right," Dr. Morris agreed promptly and Novak saw Amy Stuart grin.

Novak went to sleep for twelve hours. He woke up at eleven P.M., and Amy Stuart brought him some soup.

"Thanks," he said. "I was thinking—would you get me just the top sheet from my desk? It won't be *work*. Just a little calculation on heat of forming. Really, I'd find it relaxing."

"*No*," she said.

"All right," he said testily. "Did the doctor say you had to keep a twenty-four-hour guard on me?"

"He did not," she told him, offended. "Please excuse me. There are some magazines and newspapers on the table." She swept out and he wanted to call after her, but . . .

He got out of the cot and prowled nervously around the room. One of the papers on the table was the Los Angeles paper of the Bennet chain.

HOYT DARES "ILL" HOLLAND TO SHOW M.D. PROOF!

shrieked it banner headline. Novak swore a little and climbed back into the cot to read the paper.

The front-page first-column story was all about Hoyt daring "ill" Holland to show M.D. proof. Phrases like "since Teapot Dome" and "under fire" were liberally used. Also on the front page a prominent officer of a veterans' organization was quoted as daring "ill" Holland to show M.D. proof. So were a strident and aging blond movie actress, a raven-haired, marble-browed touring revivalist, and a lady Novak had never heard of who was identified as Washington's number-one hostess. The rest of the front page was given over to stories from the wire services about children rescuing animals from peril and animals rescuing children from peril.

Novak swore again, a little more strongly, and leafed through the paper. He encountered several pages of department store ads and finally the editorial page and feature page.

The double-column, heavily-leaded editorial said that no reasonable person could any longer ignore the cold facts of the A.E.C.-Western Air-rocket-crackpot scandal.

Beyond any doubt the People's money and the People's fissionable material—irreplaceable fissionable material—was being siphoned into a phony front for the greed of one man.

For Bennet patrons who wanted just the gist of the news, or who didn't read very well, there was the cartoon. It showed a bloated, menacing figure, labeled "Dan Holland," grinning rapturously and ladling coins and bills from a shoe-box Treasury Building into his pockets. There was one ladle in each hand, one tagged "Western Aircraft" and the other "Rocket Crackpots." A tiny, rancid, wormy, wrinkled old man was scooting in a wheel chair in circles about the fat boy's ankles, picking up coins Holland carelessly let dribble from the overflowing ladles. That was Wilson Stuart, former test pilot, breaker of speed and altitude records, industrialist whose aircraft plants covered a major sector of America's industrial defense line. Other little figures were whizzing in circles astride July-fourth rockets. They also were grabbing coins. Wild-eyed and shaggy under mortarboard hats, they were the rocket crackpots.

On the opposite page there was something for everybody.

For the women there was a column that wept hot tears because all America's sons, without exception, were doomed to perish miserably on scorching desert sands, in the frozen hell of the Arctic, and in the steamy jungles of the Pacific, all because of Daniel Holland. "How long, O Lord, how long?" asked the lady who wrote the column.

For the economist there was a trenchant column headed: "This Is Not Capitalism." The business writer who conducted the column said it wasn't capitalism for Western Air's board of directors to shilly-shally and ask Wilson Stuart exactly where he stood vis-a-vis Daniel Holland and what had happened to certain million-dollar appropriations rammed through under the vague heading of "research." Capitalism, said the business writer, would be for Western Air's board to meet, consider the situation, fire Stuart, and maybe prosecute him. Said the business writer: "The day of the robber barons is past."

For the teen-ager there was a picture of a pretty girl, with enormous breasts and nipples clearly defined under her tight blouse, holding her nose at some wiggly lines emanating from a picture of the Capitol dome. Accompanying text:

"Joy-poppers and main-liners all, really glom onto what Mamaloi's dishing this 24. I don't too often get on the sermon kick because young's fun and you're a long time putrid. But things are happening in the 48 that ain't so great so listen, mate. You wolves know how to handle a geek who glooms a weenie-bake by yacking for a fat-and-40 blues when the devotees know it's tango this year. Light and polite you tell the shite, and if he doesn't dig you, then you settle it the good old American way: five-six of you jump him and send him on his meddy way with loose teeth for a soo-ven-war. That's Democracy. Joy-poppers and main-liners, there are grownups like that. We love and respect Mom and Dad even if they are fuddy-duddy geeks; they can't help it. But what's the deal and hoddya feel about a grownup like Danny-O Holland? And Wheel-chair Wilson Stuart? And the crackpot cranks with leaky tanks that play with their rockets on dough from your pockets? Are they ripe for a swipe? Yeah-man, Elder. Are their teeth too tight? Ain't that man right! Sound off in that yeah-man corner, brethren and cistern! You ain't cackin', McCracken! So let's give a think to this stink for we, the youths of America today, are the adults of America tomorrow."

For those who vicariously live among the great there was the Washington column. "Local jewelers report a sharp, unseasonal drop in sales. Insiders attribute it to panic among the ranks of Dan (Heads-I-Win-Tails-You-Loose) Holland and his Little Dutch Boys over the fearless exposé of his machinations by crusading Senator (Fighting Bob) Hoyt. Similar reports in the trade from the West Coast, where Wilson (Wheel-Chair) Stuart and the oh-so-vionsary-but-where's-the-dough pseudo-scientists of the A.S.F.S.F. hang out. Meanwhile Danny Boy remains holed up in his swank ten-room penthouse apartment claiming illness. Building employees say however that not one of his many callers during the past week has carried the little black bag that is the mark of the doctor! . . . What man-about-Washington has bought an airline ticket and has his passport visaed to Paraguay, a country where officials are notorious for their lack of co-operation in extradition proceedings—if their palms are properly greased?"

For lovers of verse there was a quatrain by one of the country's best-loved kindly humorists. His whimsical lines ran:

> They say Dan Holland will nevermore
> Go anywhere near a hardware store.
> He'll make a detour by train or boat
> Because he knows he should cut his throat.

Novak smiled sourly at that one, and heard a great tooting of horns. It went on, and on, and on, and on. Incredulously he clocked it for three solid minutes and then couldn't take any more. He pulled on his pants and strode from the pre-fab into a glare of headlights. There were jalopies, dozens of them, outside the fence, all mooing.

Nearing ran to him. "You ought to be in bed, Dr. Novak!" he shouted. "That doctor told us not to let you——"

"Never mind that! What the hell's going on?" yelled Novak, towing Nearing to the gate. The two guards were there—husky kids, blinking in the headlights. They'd been having trouble filling the guard roster, Novak knew. Members were dropping away faster every day.

"Kids from L.A.!" Nearing shouted in his ear. "Came to razz us!"

A rhythmical chant of "*O-pen up!*" began to be heard from the cars over the horns.

Novak bawled at them: "Beat it or we'll fire on you!" He was sure some of them heard it, because they laughed. One improbably blond boy in a jalopy took it personally and butted his car into the rocket field's strong and expensive peripheral fence. It held under one car's cautious assault, but began to give when another tanker joined the blond.

"All right, Eddie!" Novak shouted to the elder of the gate guards. "Take your shotgun and fire over their heads." Eddie nodded dumbly and reached into the sentry box for his gun. He took it out in slow motion and then froze.

Novak could understand, even if he couldn't sympathize. The glaring headlights, the bellowing horns, the methodical butting of the two mastodons, the numbers of them, and their ferocity. "Here," he said, "gimme the goddam thing." He was too sore to be scared; he didn't have time to fool around. The shotgun boomed twice and the youth of America shrieked and wheeled their cars around and fled.

He handed back the shotgun and told Eddie: "Don't be scared, son." He went to the phone in the machine shop and found it was working tonight. People had been cutting the ground line lately.

He got the Stuart home. "Grady? This is Dr. Novak. I want to talk to Mr. Stuart right away and please don't tell me it's late and he's not a well man. I know all that. Do what you can for me, will you?"

"I'll try, Dr. Novak."

It was a long, long wait and then the old man's querulous voice said: "God almighty, Novak. You gone crazy? What do you want at this time of night?"

Novak told him what had happened. "If I'm any judge," he said, "we're going to be knee-deep in process servers, sheriff's deputies, and God-knows-what-else by tomorrow morning because I fired over their heads. I want you to dig me up a real, high-class lawyer *and fly him out here tonight.*"

After a moment the old man said: "You were quite right to call me. I'll bully somebody into it. How're you doing?"

"I can't kick. And thanks." He hung up and stood irresolutely for a moment. The night was shot by now—he'd had a good, long rest anyway——

He headed for the refractories lab and worked on the heat of composition. He cracked it at six A.M. and immediately started to compound the big batch of materials that would fuse into the actual throat-liner parts and steering vane. It was a grateful change of pace after working in grams to get going on big stuff. He had it done by ten-thirty and got some coffee.

The lawyer had arrived: a hard-boiled, lantern-jawed San Francisco Italian named DiPietro. "Don't worry," he grimly told Novak. "If necessary, I'll lure them onto the property and plug 'em with my own gun for trespassing. Leave it in my hands."

Novak did, and put in an eighteen-hour stretch on fabricating pieces of the throat liner. Sometime during the day Amy Stuart brought him some boxes and he mumbled politely and put them somewhere.

With his joints cracking, he shambled across the field, not noticing that his first automatic gesture on stepping out of the shop into the floodlit area was to measure the *Prototype* with his eye in a kind of salute.

"How'd it go?" he asked DiPietro.

"One dozen assorted," said the lawyer. "They didn't know their law and even if they did I could have bluffed them. The prize was a little piece of jail-bait with her daddy and shyster. Your shotgun caused her to miscarry; they were willing to settle out of court for twenty thousand dollars. I told them our bookkeeper will send his bill for five thousand dollars' worth of medical service as soon as he can get around to it."

"More tomorrow?"

"I'll stick around. The word's spread by now, but there may be a couple of die-hards."

Novak said: "Use your judgment. Believe I can do some work on the servos before I hit the sack."

The lawyer looked at him speculatively, but didn't say anything.

16

A morning came that was like all the other mornings except that there was nothing left to do. Novak wandered disconsolately through the field, poking at this detail or that, and Amy came up to him.

"Mike, can I talk to you?"

"Sure," he said, surprised. Was he the kind of guy people asked that kind of question?

"How are the clothes?"

"Clothes?"

"Oh, you didn't even look. Those boxes. I've been shop-

ping for you. I could see you'd never have time for it
yourself. You don't mind?"

There it was again. "Look," he said, "have I been snap-
ping people's heads off?"

"Yes," she said in a small voice. "You didn't know
that, did you? Do you know you have a week-old beard
on you?"

He felt it in wonder.

"I've never seen anything like it," she said. "The
things you've accomplished. Maybe nobody ever saw
anything like it. It's finished now, isn't it?"

"So it is," he said. "I didn't think—just installing the
last liner segment and hooking on the vane. Mechanical
oper——

"*God, we've done it!*" He leaned against one of *Proto's*
delta fins, shaking uncontrollably.

"Come on, Mike," she said, taking his arm. She led
him to his camp cot and he plunged into sleep.

She was still there when he woke, and brought him
coffee and toast. He luxuriated in the little service and
then asked abashedly: "Was I pretty bad?"

"You were obsessed. You were a little more than
human for ten days."

"Holland!" he said suddenly, sitting full up. "Did anybody——"

"I've notified him. Everything's going according to
plan. Except—you won't be on the moon ship."

"What are you talking about, Amy?"

She smiled brightly. "The counter-campaign. The
battle for the public being waged by those cynical, mani-
pulating, wonderful old bastards, Holland and my
father. Didn't you guess what my part in it was? I'm a
pretty girl, Mike, and pretty girls can sell anything to
America. I'm going to be the pilot—hah! pilot!—of the
first moon ship. So gallant, so noble, and such a good
figure. I'm going to smile nicely and male America will
decide that as long as it can't go to bed with me, the least
it can do is cheer me on to the Moon."

She was crying. "And then I showed I was my father's
daughter. The cynical Miss Stuart said we have a fire-
works display in the takeoff, we have conflict and
heroism, we have glamor, what we need is some nice refined sex. Let's get the dumb engineer Novak to come

311

along. A loving young couple making the first trip to the Moon. Irresistible. Pretty girl, handsome man—you *are* handsome without that beard, Mike." She was crying too hard to go on. He mechanically patted her shoulder.

Her sobs abated. "Go on," he said.

"Nothing to go on about. I told 'em I wouldn't let you go. I love you too much."

His arm tightened around her. "That's all right," he said. "I love you too much to let you go without me."

She turned her tear-stained face to him. "You're not going to get noble with *me*——" she began. And then: "Ouch! Mike, the beard!"

"I'll shave," he said, getting up and striding to the lab sink.

"Don't cut yourself, Mike," she called after him. "But—please hurry!"

There was one crazy, explosive week.

There was something in it for everybody. It was a public relations man's dream of heaven.

Were you a businessman? "By God, you have to give the old boy credit! Slickest thing I ever heard of—right under the damn Reds' noses, stuck right out there in the desert and they didn't realize that a rocket ship was a rocket ship! And there's a lot of sense in what Holland had to say about red tape. Makes you stop and wonder—the armed services fooling around for twenty years and not getting to first base, but here this private club smacks out a four-bagger first time at bat. Illegal? Illegal? Now mister, be sensible. Don't get me wrong; I'm not any admirer of the late F.D.R., but he did get us the atom bomb even if he did practically hand it to the Reds right after. But my point is, F.D.R. didn't go to Congress with a presidential message that we were going to try to make an atomic bomb. He just quietly diverted the money and made one. Some things you have to do by the look; others you just plain can't. For my money, Dan Holland's a *statesman*."

Were you a girl? "Oh, that dreamy man Mike! It just chills me when I think of him flying all the way to the Moon, but it's kind of wonderful, too. Did you ever notice the way he's got kind of a dimple but not quite on the left when he smiles?"

Were you a man? "Amy's got real looks and class. Brains, too, they tell me, and God knows, she's got guts. The kind of girl you'd want to *marry*, if you know what I mean. He's a lucky guy."

Were you old folks? "Such a lovely couple. I don't know why more young people aren't like that nowadays. You can see how much they're in love, the way they look at each other. And the idea of them going to the Moon! I certainly never thought I'd see it in my time, though of course I knew that some day . . . Perhaps their rocket ship won't work. No, that's absurd. Of course it'll work. They look so nice when they smile at each other!"

Were you young folks? "I can't get over it. Just a pair of ordinary Americans like you and me, a couple of goodlooking kids that don't give a damn and they're going to shoot off to the Moon. I saw them in the parade and they aren't any different from you and me. I can't get over it."

Were you a newspaper publisher? "Baby, this is *it*! The perfect cure for that tired feeling in the circulation department. I want *Star-Banner-Bugle-and-Times-News* to get Mike-and-Amy conscious and stay that way. Pictures, pictures, pictures. Biographies, interviews with roommates, day-by-day coverage, our best woman for Amy and our best man for Mike. The hell with the cost; the country's on a Mike-and-Amy binge. And why shouldn't it be? A couple of nice young kids and they're going to do the biggest thing since the discovery of fire. A landmark in the history of the human race! And confidentially, this is what a lot of the boys have been waiting for with Bennet. Naturally only a dirty Red rag would attack a fellow-publisher, but I don't see any ethical duty to keep me from sawing off a limb Bennet crawled out on all by himself. He's mouse-trapped. To keep his hard core of moron readership he's got to keep pretending that *Proto's* still a fake and Holland's still a crook and only taper off slowly. I'm almost sorry for the dirty old man, but he made his bed."

Were you a congressman? "Hmmm. Very irregular. In a *strict* sense illegal. Congress holds the purse strings. Damn uppity agencies and commissions. Career men. Mike and Amy. Wonder if I could get photographed with them for my new campaign picture. Hmmm."

On the fourth day of the crazy week they were in Washington, in Holland's office.

"How's it going?" he demanded.

"I don't know how MacArthur stood it at his age," Amy muttered.

There was a new addition to Holland's collection of memorabilia on the wall behind his desk: a matted and framed front page from the New York *Times*.

HOLLAND BREAKS SILENCE, CALLS ASFSF NO FRONT

SAYS CLUB HAS MOON SHIP READY TO MAKE TRIP

WILSON STUART DAUGHTER, ENGINEER TO PILOT

The agitation of the *Times* was clearly betrayed in the awkwardly rhyming second line.

"The Air Force gentlemen are here, Mr. Holland," said the desk intercom.

"Send them in, Charlie."

Three standard-brand Air Force colonels, one general and an off-brand captain walked in. The captain looked lost among his senior officers, six-footers all. He was a shrimp.

"Ah, gentlemen. General McGovern, Colonels Ross, Goldthwaite, and Behring. And the man you've been waiting to meet, Captain Dilaccio. Gentlemen, you know Amy and Mike, of course. Please be seated."

They sat, and there was an ugly pause. The general exploded, almost with tears in his voice: "*Mister* Holland, for the last time. I will be perfectly frank with you. This is the damn'dest, most unreasonable thing I ever heard of. We have the pilots, we have the navigators, we have the experience, and we ought to have the moon ship!"

Holland said gravely: "No, General. There's no piloting involved. The landing operation simply consists of putting the throat-vane servo on automatic control of the plumb bobs and running in the moderator rods when you hit. The navigation is child's play. True, the target is in motion, but it's big and visible. And you have no experience in moon ships."

"*Mister* Holland——" said the general.

Holland interrupted blandly. "And even if there were

logic on your side, is the public deeply interested in logic? I think not. But the public is deeply interested in Amy and Mike. Why, if Amy and Mike were to complain that the Air Force had been less than fair with them——"

His tone was bantering, but McGovern broke in, horrified: "No, no, no, Mr. Holland! They aren't going to do anything like that, are they? Are you?"

Holland answered for them. "Of course not, General. They have no reason to do anything like that—do they?"

"Of course not," the general said glumly. "Captain Dilaccio, good luck." He and the colonels shook hands with the puny little captain and filed out.

"Welcome to the space hounds," Novak told Dilaccio, trying to be jovial.

The captain said indistinctly: "Pleasure'm sure."

On the flight back to Barstow he didn't say much else. They knew he had been chosen because he was (a) a guided-missile specialist, (b) single and with no close relations, (c) small and endowed with a singularly sluggish metabolism. He was slated for the grinding, heartbreaking, soul-chilling job of surviving in a one-man pressure dome until the next trip brought him company and equipment.

On the seventh day of the crazy week, Daniel Holland heard somebody behind him say irritably: "Illegal? Illegal? No more illegal than Roosevelt taking funds and developing the atomic bomb. Should he have gone to Congress with a presidential message about it? It was the only way to do it, that's all."

Holland smiled faintly. It had gone over. The old clichés in their mouths had been replaced by new clichés. The sun blazed into his eyes from the polished shell of the moon ship, but he didn't turn or squint. He was at least a sub-hero today.

He caught a glimpse of MacIlheny as the band struck up the sedate, eighteenth-century "President's March." MacIlheny was on the platform, as befitted the top man of the A.S.F.S.F., though rather far out on one of the wings. MacIlheny was crying helplessly. He had thought he might be the third man, but he was big-bodied and knew nothing about guided missiles. What good was an insurance man in the Moon?

The President spoke for only five minutes, limiting himself to one humorous literary allusion. ("This purloined letter—stainless steel, thirty-six-feet tall, plainly visible for sixty miles.") Well, *he* was safely assured of his place in history. No matter what miracles of statesmanship in war or peace he performed, as long as he was remembered he would be remembered as President during the first moon flight. The applause was polite for him, and then slowly swelled. Amy and Mike were walking arm in arm down a hollow column of M.P.s, Marines and A.F.P.s. Captain Dilaccio trailed a little behind them. The hollow column led from the shops to the gantry standing beside *Proto*.

Holland felt his old friend's hand grip his wrist. "Getting soft, Wilson?" he muttered out of the corner of his mouth.

The old man wouldn't be kidded. "I didn't know it would be like this," he said hoarsely. Amy's jacket was a bright red patch as the couple mounted the stand and shook hands with the President. Senile tears were running down Wilson Stuart's face. Great day for weeping, Holland thought sullenly. All I did was hand the U.S. the Moon on a silver platter and everybody's sobbing about it.

The old man choked: "Crazy kid. Daniel, what if she doesn't come back?"

There was nothing to say about that. But—— "She's waving at you, Wilson!" Holland said sharply. "Wave back!" The old man's hand fluttered feebly. Holland could see that Amy had already turned to speak to the President. God, he thought. They're *hard*.

"Did she see me, Dan?"

"Yes. She threw you a big grin. She's a wonderful kid, Wilson." Glad I never had any. *And* sorry, too, of course. It isn't that easy, ever, is it? Isn't this show ever going to get on the road?

The M.P.s, Marines, and A.F.P.s reformed their lines and began to press back the crowd. Jeeps roared into life and began to tow the big, wheeled reviewing stand slowly from the moon ship. With heartbreaking beauty of flowing line, Amy swung herself from the platform to the hoist of the gantry crane. Mike stepped lightly

316

across the widening gap and Captain Dilaccio—Good God, had the President even spoken to him?—jumped solidly. Mike waved at the crane-man and the hoist rose with its three passengers. It stopped twenty-five-feet up, and there was clearly a bit of high-spirited pantomime, Alphonse-and-Gaston stuff, at the manhole. Amy crawled through first and then she was gone. Then Dilaccio and then Novak, and they all were gone. The manhole cover began to close, theatrically slow.

"Why are we here?" Novak wondered dimly as the crescent of aperture became knifelike, razorlike, and then vanished. What road did I travel from Canarsie to here? Aloud he said: "Preflight check: positions, please." He noted that his voice sounded apologetic. They hunkered down under the gothic dome in the sickly light of a six-watt bulb. Like cave people around a magic tree stump they squatted around the king-post top that grew from the metal floor.

"Oxygen-CO_2 cycle," he said.

That was Dilaccio's. He opened the valve and said, "Check."

"Heater." He turned it on himself and muttered, "Check."

Novak took a deep breath. "Well, next comes fuel metering and damper rods—oh, I forgot. Amy, is the vane servo locked vertical?"

"Check," she said.

"Right. Now, the timers are set for thirty seconds, which is ample for us to get to the couches. But I'd feel easier if you two started now so there won't be any possibility of a tangle."

Amy and Dilaccio stood, cramped under the step-sloping roof. The captain swung into his couch. Amy touched Mike's hand and climbed to hers. There was a flapping noise of web belting.

"Check."

"All secure," said Dilaccio.

"Very good. *One*—and *two*." The clicks and the creak of cordage as he swung into his couch seemed very loud.

Time to think at last. Canarsie, Troy, Corning, Steubenville, Urbana, N.E.P.A., Chicago, Los Angeles, Barstow—and now the Moon. He was here because his parents had died, because he had inherited some skills and acquired others, because of the leggy tough sophomore from Troy Women's Day, because Holland had dared, because he and Amy were in love, because a Hanford fission product had certain properties, because MacIlheny was MacIlheny——

Acceleration struck noiselessly; they left their sound far behind.

After a spell of pain there was a spell of discomfort. Light brighter than the six-watt bulb suddenly flooded the steeple-shaped room. The aerodynamic nose had popped off, unmasking their single port. You still couldn't pick yourself up. It was like one of those drunks when you think you're clearheaded and are surprised to find that you can't move.

She should have spent more time with her father, he thought. Maybe she was afraid it would worry him. Well, he was back there now with the rest of them. Lilly, paying somehow, somewhere, for what she had done. Holland paying somehow for what he had done. MacIlheny paying. Wilson Stuart paying.

"Mike," said Amy's voice.

"All right, Amy. You?"

"I'm all right."

The captain said: "All right here."

A common shyness seemed to hold them all, as though each was afraid of opening the big new ledger with a false or trivial entry.

Postscript to *Takeoff* by Frederik Pohl

Takeoff is about an event that has already happened— the first human venture into space—and the event did not happen the way Cyril Kornbluth expected it to.

Nevertheless, I do not think that Cyril was wrong, and I'll tell you why.

If you go back and read the literature of space flight prior to the latter stages of World War II, you will find that very little of it envisioned the multi-stage Apollo-type craft that finally did make it. It doesn't much matter whether the literature you look at was sf or science "fact"—assuming you can use the term "fact" about something that looked as improbable on the face of it as sending a man out of the Earth's atmosphere into the void. A great many wise heads did not believe it could happen at all, and they included not only the British Astonomer Royal and most ballistics experts but even T. O'Conor Sloane, Ph.D., who was the editor of *Amazing Stories* in the late 1930s. Doc Smith had his spaceships operate on atomic power in *The Skylark of Space* et seq. H.G. Wells invented the anti-gravity stuff called Cavorite. It was not until Werner von Braun aimed at the stars and hit London with his V-2s that there was enough data, obtained from large scale use of operational rockets, to show that the thing was possible—barely possible—by sitting one rocket on top of another until you added up enough thrust to get some minute fraction of the total mass into orbit. Even Von Braun did not foresee exactly what would happen; in one of his few ventures into science fiction, published several years after the end of World War II, he explained that the first interplanetary travelers would have to reconcile themselves to protracted stays, a year or so at least, with only very infrequent radio contacts with Earth because of power demands, rather than the quick weekend lunar jaunts with 24-hour radio and TV coverage that actually came to pass.

I asked Von Braun about that once, around 1972. The circumstances were not conducive to prolonged conversation—he was sitting in my lap at the time*—and he didn't answer directly, but somebody next to us said, "Who knew that kind of money would be available?" and Braun grinned and nodded.

No sensible human being, I think, would have supposed before World War II that any person or nation would

---

*It wasn't what you think. There were six of us in a VW beetle, on the way to a Georgia fish-fry, and *everybody* was in somebody's lap but the driver.

invest billions of dollars in shooting one or two people into space for a quick trip. At the same time, most human beings who knew much about the subject, or had thought much about it, intuitively felt that *somehow* space travel would occur. Science-fiction writers invented their Cavorites and their copper thrust-bars, or their machines for "climbing the lines of the Earth's magnetic field of force" (Lester del Rey) or aligning the random Brownian movement of molecules so that they all pushed in the same direction at once (John W. Campbell)—whatever. Less imaginative writers simply supposed a highly concentrated fuel could be developed—until some spoilsports showed that from fundamental physical constraints there could not be any such chemical fuel. After Hahn and Meitner showed that nuclear energy could be released by neutron bombardment, and particularly after Hiroshima, the energy source looked clear. Atomic power! Obviously!

Well, we know a lot now that nobody knew for sure in 1952. For example, we know that nuclear power has its own limitations, the most depressing of which is its tendency to spray deadly radionuclides around. For electricity-generating purposes the spray can be contained (we hope); but there is no way of containing the exhaust of a nuclear rocket. Until one is found it is not likely that any such ship as the one Cyril Kornbluth describes will ever take off from the surface of the Earth.

But I still think he was not wrong. He rejected the multi-stage chemical rocket as preposterously inefficient, and that reasoning still stands as sound.

It is my personal belief—no, absolute conviction!— that at some point space travel, by which I mean getting into a spacecraft somewhere on Earth, getting off it on Mars or the Moon, and getting back onto it for another trip to, oh, say, Ganymede, is going to happen in almost as routine a fashion as I can now get onto a JAL 747 in New York to fly to Honolulu, get off it to stroll around Hawaiian soil for a while, and get back on to it for the next flight to Tokyo. I don't know what will drive this spacecraft. I don't know when it will occur. But I don't believe that it will be anything like as Rube-Goldbergishly clumsy as Apollo, either.

And in that sense I think Cyril was wholly right—and it is the world itself that went wrong.